# a PLACE BEYOND the MAP

Samuel Thews

A PLACE BEYOND THE MAP
All rights reserved.
Copyright © 2011 Samuel Thews
Cover Layout Copyright © 2011 by Larque

To my first readers – Mom, Heather and Eva

## Author Acknowledgements

I cannot possibly list everyone that has made this book possible in one way or another, either through their direct efforts or simply by their impact upon my life. So, I will only thank my loving wife for her patience in designing my cover and for continuing to indulge my many (sometimes fleeting) obsessions, one of which is writing.

# CONTENTS

# 1

## Phinnegan Qwyk

Phinnegan Qwyk drummed his fingertips on his desk, oblivious to the hair-raising screech of chalk grating across an old blackboard as Mr. Rowlands scribbled arithmetical figures. Phinnegan had always disliked the cold, unforgiving nature of numbers, even on an ordinary day - and today was anything but ordinary.

No, today was special – or at least it would be once the final grains of sand trickled from top-to-bottom in the large hourglass seated on Mr. Rowlands's desk. Phinnegan had never understood why it was called an hourglass. The ornate timepiece held three hours of sand, not a moment less or more. At home, Phinnegan's mother used a similar glass to time her baking, but it ran through in a neat half-hour. The term "hourglass" wasn't appropriate for either.

But whatever it was called, Mr. Rowlands began each morning with one "run of the sand" before allowing the children a break for lunch and recess. The afternoon likewise consisted of a single run of the sand, which, much to Phinnegan's pleasure, was at an end.

As the final grain slipped through the narrow waist of the glass, Phinnegan sat straighter, anticipating the dismissal of the class. Mr. Rowlands was always prompt in ending his classes, reasoning that he had once been young and knowing full well that such restless minds would ignore him once his time had run its course.

Today, however, Mr. Rowlands seemed not to notice.

Phinnegan waited a minute, then another, and then a third.

*Any moment now.*

But the screeching continued, as did the drone of Mr. Rowlands's mundane voice. On an ordinary day, Phinnegan would not have cared in the least. He did not mind school as much as many of the other pupils. But as the moments passed, not a single schoolmate sought to inform the teacher of the time. His impatience mounting, Phinnegan rustled his papers, packing away drawings he had created during the day's lesson. Still, Mr. Rowlands continued in his unrelenting monotone. At last impatience won out. Phinnegan raised his hand, and spoke without waiting to be noticed.

"Excuse me, sir?" he said, his voice just escaping his throat. Two boys in front of him turned toward him, but Mr. Rowlands seemed not to hear. On he went, scratching out a set of numbers while he prattled on about their significance.

Clearing his throat, Phinnegan tried once more.

"Sir?" he said more forcefully. This time, Mr. Rowlands heard him. Pausing, the chalk in his hand a mere inch from beginning a new string of figures, he turned to face his class.

"Yes?" he said as he surveyed his pupils. Spying Phinnegan's hand, the ghost of a smile touched his lips.

"Ah, Phinnegan. A question?"

"Yes, sir," Phinnegan said, lowering his hand. "Well, err, not really, sir. You see, it's the sand."

"The sand? What about it?" Mr. Rowlands said, his smile fading to confusion.

"Well, it's gone, sir."

"Gone?" Mr. Rowlands asked, using the back of his chalk-dusted hand to nudge a tattered pair of glasses back onto the bridge of his nose. Glancing around, he caught sight of the large hour-glass on his desk.

"Oh! I see." With a forlorn look to the figure-laden blackboard, he let his arm drop and waved a hand.

"Off you go, lads. But remember, tomorrow there will be-"

The ruckus that ensued overpowered Mr. Rowlands' thin voice so that none could discern his words, least of all Phinnegan, who sprung from his seat like a rabbit. He was out of the class and down the hall before most had gathered all of their materials.

Just as he reached the exit, Billy Fagin sauntered into his path.

*Not today...*

"In a bit of a hurry, Qwyk?"

"Yes," Phinnegan said with a grimace, dropping his eyes to the floor to avoid looking up into the older boy's eyes. He glanced quickly to the right and left, for wherever Billy Fagin was, Patrick Keene was as well.

"Shame, that. Thought you might fancy a game of cricket."

"Cricket?" Phinnegan questioned, his head snapping up, expecting to see the mocking face he knew would be there. But it wasn't.

"You want . . . *me* to play cricket?" Phinnegan asked, his eyes wide.

"Yeah, we're one short. Think of it as a peace offering," the larger boy said, a slanting smile showing two rows of crooked teeth.

Phinnegan stared. Were the older boys really asking him to play cricket? And of all people, Billy Fagin - the same Billy who had bullied him since he first came to school?

"Why?" Phinnegan managed to ask.

"Like I said, Qwyk," the older boy said while holding up a finger. "We're one short."

Phinnegan wondered for a moment if it were some sort of trick, but then a group of boys Billy's age sidled over.

"Game on or off then, Fagin?" one of the larger boys said with a smirk.

"Hang on a moment," Billy said. "I'm rounding up another. So how 'bout it, Qwyk? Grow up from your stories long enough to play with the big boys?"

While Billy had meant the remark as a taunt, Phinnegan remembered that he was in a hurry.

"Um, thanks, but I really should be getting home," he said, trying to push his way past.

"Why, got a girl waiting for you?" one of the boys mocked.

"Qwyk, a girl?" Billy snorted. "More like a leprechaun riding a unicorn. Come on, Qwyk, have a game will you. Half an hour."

Phinnegan stood, frozen as his mind evaluated each choice. But Billy's loud voice broke his thoughts.

"Oy! Doyle! Fancy a cricket match?"

Phinnegan turned in time to see a red-haired boy with freckles wave past him to Billy.

"Cricket? I'm in!"

Billy pushed past Phinnegan, jostling him with his shoulder.

"Maybe next time Qwyk. Run along and read your books."


More than an hour later, Phinnegan rounded the final corner before the small pond at the end of Mr. O'Toole's property and the beginning of his parents's. Once past the back edge of the pond and hidden from O'Toole's troublesome dog by the trees that divided the properties, Phinnegan broke into a slow trot and then into a run. He sped by his own dog, Bergin, pausing only long enough to tousle the dog's fur.

Crashing through the back door, he came to a screeching halt as he nearly barreled into his mother, who was bustling about the kitchen preparing the evening meal.

"Careful!" she said, raising a stone cookpot laden with a hearty roast over his head. Mrs. Qwyk was well acquainted with the enthusiasm of school-aged boys.

"Sorry, mum," Phinnegan mumbled as he scurried from the kitchen.

"Your father's in his study," she called after him.

She needn't have told him. Where else would his father be? Now that he was home, that is. He had been away on one of his trips to the north and had only just returned.

Phinnegan came to a stop just outside the slightly open door to his father's study. The scent of burning pipe tobacco wafted through the crack, and he could hear the familiar rustling of a newspaper. Phinnegan inclined his chin and stood tall. He smoothed his hair and straightened his shirt before rapping three times on the door.

"Enter," his father's voice called. Phinnegan obeyed and found his father much as he had expected, relaxed in his favorite chair, a pipe in his mouth and a newspaper in his lap. On his left, three cork-stopped glass bottles, each filled with a different tobacco, stood on the polished wood table. On his right, a half glass of whiskey. His feet were propped on the shaggy old ottoman his mother had tried to add to the rubbish collection on more than one occasion.

"Phinnegan," his father said, removing the pipe from his mouth as he smiled. "Come, you simply must smell this blend," he added, tossing his paper aside and gesturing for Phinnegan to come forward. Clenching his pipe between his teeth, its bowl bobbing up and down as he spoke, Phinnegan's father removed the cork from one glass jar that held a dark tobacco that looked like ribbons of black velvet.

"Here," his father said, handing him the open jar. "William McDowell in Dublin blended it at my request. It's a luxurious blend of Cavendish and Turkish latakia, cured slowly with molasses." Leaning back in his chair, his father took a long, slow draw on his pipe. When his lips parted, the expelled smoke was thick and almost white, so dense that it sank in the air, falling like a marshy fog around Phinnegan's feet.

"Heavenly," his father sighed, closing his eyes and crossing his arms behind his head. The smoke indeed smelled delightful as it sifted through the air past Phinnegan's nose. Bringing the jar up, he inhaled the aroma of the dark ribbons. The tobacco itself had much the same luscious smell as the smoke, though more earthy than the smoke's biting, yet not unpleasant, spiciness.

"It's wonderful," Phinnegan breathed as he corked the jar, ensuring it was snug to prevent the precious contents from drying, just as his father had taught him. He placed the reassembled jar alongside its companions, each of which contained its own precious cargo, one a light brown and the other a reddish color with yellow flecks throughout.

"Phinnegan, my boy, you do not know what you are missing," his father said, his lips curling in an impish grin while his teeth maintained a hold on the pipe. Phinnegan smiled at the jest.

"Yes, Papa," he said, watching as his father winked open one eye.

"Ah, but you are too young for that just yet. And besides, I'd wager other things are more important to you today. And, I might add, I expected you home much earlier, given the circumstances."

"Yes, Papa," Phinnegan said. "I...umm...I was held up at school."

"Caught up in a game, then?" his father asked, a hopeful tone to his voice.

"Not exactly," Phinnegan replied, his eyes slipping away from his father's.

"Oh, I see." His father pushed himself to his feet and rested a strong hand on Phinnegan's shoulder.

"I wonder if I am doing the right thing with you. These books...really you are too *old* for fairy tales."

"But...I like them," Phinnegan said, a slight shrug in his shoulders as they sagged.

"I know, lad, but some day you'll have to put down the fancies of your childhood and become a man. And a man needs good friends; he needs responsibility, respect."

Phinnegan was silent, his eyes downcast. But the hand on his shoulder gave a reassuring squeeze.

"One day, lad..."

"Yes, sir."

His father's smile widened.

"Your mother will not be finished with supper for awhile yet. If you hurry, maybe you can read a new story or two."

Phinnegan's face brightened and he grabbed his father's arm.

"You brought it? Where is it?" he questioned, bouncing in his excitement.

"Settle down, settle down," his father said with a laugh. "I left it on your bed. Run along, you've time to open it."

Beaming, Phinnegan gave his father a quick hug before flying from the room. As he rounded the corner to climb the stairs, he heard his mother call out to him.

"No running in the house, Phinnegan," she scolded.

"Yes, mum," he called back, slowing until he was out of sight and then bounding the last few steps.

In his room, he found a small package wrapped in brown paper and tied with twine lying on his bed. He had the paper off in a flash and his hands grasped a bright yellow book, its binding fresh and unblemished beneath his fingers.

The front of the book was embossed with a detailed scene of a winged woman floating high in the sky, the rays of sunshine warming her slim figure. On the spine, the silhouette of a cat stood out in gold filigree, along with the book's author and title.

"The Yellow Fairy Book," Phinnegan whispered, running his finger over the etched words. The book was the fourth in a collection of fairy tales from around the world. It had only just been published, and Phinnegan's father had promised he would obtain one for his son.

With the care that comes with an appreciation for books, Phinnegan opened the book slowly and, as was his habit, let it fall open to where it chose.

"Story of the Emperor's New Clothes," he read softly to himself. And then he was lost in the tale.

# 2

## A Late Night Visitor

Phinnegan awoke suddenly, the bite of a late November night's breeze upon his face. After gobbling his dinner, Phinnegan had rushed straight to his room to again immerse himself in the new tales contained in the Yellow Fairy Book until sleep overcame him. This sudden chill was odd, though it did not really bother him. Harrumphing, he pulled his blankets tighter about him.

It was then that he heard it.

The sound was faint and not one that could be called unordinary. It seemed to be a muffled gasp or squeak, like the sound you would make if startled by a cat you knew was in the house but were surprised to find rubbing against your leg. It was not the sound itself that startled him so, his large brown eyes round and wide in the darkness, but that he should hear this sound now, in his bedroom, in the middle of the night.

It could have been his mother or father, of course, checking on their son in the middle of the night as mothers and fathers are wont to do. But as Phinnegan lay on his side, the blankets up to his ears and just his eyes peeking out, he saw that his window was open.

*That window was closed when I went to bed.*

Pricking his ears for the slightest sound, Phinnegan heard only the rain at first, the footsteps of each droplet pitter-pattering in the shallow puddles that formed upon the ground just outside his bedroom window. The melodic rhythm of the rain soothed his mind and he wondered if he had heard any sound at all. Glancing to his left, he saw the yellow book just where he had left it after reading for a few hours after dinner. Perhaps these stories were playing tricks with his mind.

But then he spied something else.

On the floor beneath his window, he saw the wet imprints of two smooth-soled shoes.

His breath caught in his throat. Phinnegan lay still as the dead, straining his ears against the pressing silence. When he heard the faint familiar creak of the loose floorboard just in front of his door, he shut his eyes and prayed for this to all be a dream.

Just then a second strange sound reached his ears. Even with his ears strained, it was barely audible: a timorous little melody, a lullaby so light, so airy and so fragile that to speak of its existence would be its destruction. If a sound could be from far away, but at the same time be close at hand, it could not have been more so than this melody. He felt it tug at his thoughts, pulling his fears away and rendering him light-headed. His mind felt fuzzy and warm, and as the melody assuaged away the last of his fear, he felt himself at peace. And then the sound was gone.

Phinnegan bolted upright in his bed. His heart hammering in his chest, he shook his head to rid himself of the soft, blurred feeling that the melody had left him. With the melody now gone, his mind felt sluggish. But his fear was gone, and in its place remained a wild courage, apparent even in his large brown eyes, which no longer were doe-eyed and naïve, but touched with feral twinkle.

His eyes searching, Phinnegan spied that the door to his room was ajar and beckoning. Feeling rather adventurous, he tossed the covers from his bed and crept to his door, avoiding the creaky board with unconscious effort.

The hallway beyond Phinnegan's door was thick with darkness against the scant bit of light that entered through his open bedroom. At first his eyes could not penetrate more than a few feet before him as he peered around the edge of his door. But as his eyes adjusted, familiar shapes began to materialize as if from a fog.

Seeing that the hallway appeared clear of any intruders, Phinnegan tiptoed through his doorway and crept to the bend in the hallway, his footsteps softened by the hall's well-trodden runner.

Looking around the corner Phinnegan saw that the landing above the stairs was empty. Summoning his courage, he straightened and rounded the corner.

As he stood facing the stairs, the melody came to him once again. The sound wafted up the stairs like a gentle breeze, and he felt it drawing him evermore towards it.

The feral twinkle once again flashing in his eyes, he made one last glance back towards his now empty room before slinking down the stairs. He skipped the third step from the bottom - a step known to creak. Reaching the bottom, he turned his head this way and that, listening for the elusive melody.

When he turned his head to the right, in the direction of the two sitting rooms and his father's study, the melody grew louder.

Careful to avoid the veritable minefield of creaky boards, potted plants, end tables, and other scattered furniture, he snuck through the larger of the two sitting rooms, more by the guidance of his memories than by his eyes. The music grew louder.

Phinnegan's eyes were now well adjusted to the darkness and he could see into the shadowed corners of each room, finding them all empty. If the melody came from within the house, there was only one room left that could be its source. Just ahead of him the door to his father's study was open. For the second time that night, a door ajar beckoned to him.

Even the music's tonic of courage could not suppress the chill that ran up his spine. A soft glow emanated from his father's study. It did not flicker like a candle, nor dance like the flame of a lamp. It did not waver nor falter, but was steady and haunted the doorway with an unearthly cast.

He took two small steps forward and to the left, positioning himself so as to have a glimpse through the slight opening in the doorway. At first he saw nothing save the same eerie glow. But then the intensity of the glow changed, as though it moved closer to one wall than another. The glow changed again, and then the shadow of a figure appeared on the far wall.

Phinnegan stood frozen, not daring to breath.

*Someone* was in there.

The shadow moved now, and Phinnegan's mind had cleared just enough for him to hear sounds other than the melody. First, there was a scraping sound, as if someone were dragging a heavy object across the floor. Then the scraping ceased and all was quiet once again, with the exception of the melody that continued to drift across Phinnegan's mind.

Phinnegan shuffled forward the last few feet and stood behind the door, his face an inch from the opening. His breathing quickened and he felt his heart pound against his ribcage. More sounds came from the study, rustling of papers and the quiet "tink" of glass upon glass. He heard a soft "pop" sound and then a sound he never expected to hear.

Sniffing.

More soft pops were followed by still more sniffing. After about the sixth or seventh pop and sniff, there was a pause. A deeper sniff followed and then a quiet sigh of pleasure.

At last, the curious sounds getting the better of him, Phinnegan peeked around the door.

He never expected the sight that greeted him.

The room was bright compared to the rest of the house, and sitting on his father's desk was the source of that light. A small sphere, which Phinnegan assumed had to be some kind of miniature oil lamp, rested there amongst the strewn papers and bathed the entire room in a white-blue light. Phinnegan had never seen a lamp like this: a solid glass orb, with no discernable light source. No flame flickered within, and even if there was, no air could have reached it.

But the light was not the half of it.

Standing atop his father's heavy oaken chair was a man. Or at least Phinnegan thought it was a man, at first. But as Phinnegan watched, he noticed that he was not large enough to be a man at all, though he did not appear to be a child.

The man, or person, or whatever he was, had not yet noticed Phinnegan. He did not look in Phinnegan's direction at all, but had his attention fixed on an object in his hands. Leaning his head further into the room to get a better look, Phinnegan momentarily lost his balance, brushing against the door and causing a loud creak. Startled, he snapped his head back, hoping he had been quick enough to escape the small person's attention.

Phinnegan stood in silence for what felt like several minutes - though surely was only a half of one - holding his breath and daring not to make a sound lest he give himself away. After he began to breathe again, he crept back the few steps that he had just retreated and stood once again next to the door. Careful not to touch the door and create yet another squeak, Phinnegain ventured another peek.

The intruder gave no outward sign indicating that he had paid the creak any mind, for he stood just as he had before, still observing the item he held in his hands. He was hunched over, turning the object of his attention over and over in his hands.

Even with the light, Phinnegan could not see the intruder very well, but there was something odd about him. His hair appeared light, but Phinnegan could not discern its color, for the glowing orb upon the desk was nearer his feet than his head and cast little light up towards his face. His manner of dress was also very peculiar. Phinnegan expected that the roguish types who would break and enter into a person's home would be dressed in common clothes, rough-spun wool or coarse linen. But this man wore trousers of a lush ivy-green, tight-fitting through the thigh and looser near the ankle. His arms were bare, but his torso bore a vest of the same shade of green, an indiscernible pattern worked upon it in silver.

Minding the door, Phinnegan slipped his entire head and his shoulders through the doorway to get a better view of this strange man. As his ears cleared the opening, the melody grew louder. He glanced this way and that for some source of the music, but nothing was out of place.

Except the shortish person standing on his father's chair, of course.

Phinnegan came to the only conclusion that he could, given the circumstances. Somehow the melody was coming *from* this person. To an adult, such a notion would have been impossible. But Phinnegan's mind was still young, as of yet still clear of the barriers that sometimes prevent grown-ups from believing things to be as they really are. Phinnegan, his mind populated over the years with story after story, accepted that which his senses told him was true.

As he listened to the melody, his mind again became warm and fuzzy. Any trace of fear dissipated and his eyes twinkled. His senses seemed to come alive. The melody became clearer and his eyes began to adjust to the light coming from the glowing orb atop the desk.

He slipped further into the room. With the man's back to him, Phinnegan was safe from the reach of his vision. Phinnegan flattened himself against the wall, looking up at this strange figure and trying to decide what to do. But when the figure turned slightly, his profile became visible, and his hands came into view. Phinnegan saw what had held this strange man's interest: his father's pipe.

Seeing his father's pipe in the stranger's hands brought the earlier sounds into perspective. Phinnegan knew his father kept his pipe, matches and other tobacco paraphernalia on a shelf above his desk. When he looked up at the shelf, which was certainly far too high up for this little stranger to reach (thus explaining the chair), Phinnegan saw the shelf was empty save for the matches. On the desk below sat several glass jars, each filled with a different kind of pipe tobacco as well as the jars's cork stoppers. The tinkling of glass, the soft pops and the sniffing sounds all made sense to him now.

When he looked back to the stranger, Phinnegan saw that he was no longer holding the pipe but instead was just moving his hands away from one of the front pockets in his trousers. Phinnegan saw the silhouette of his father's pipe beneath the ivy-green fabric. Phinnegan's eyes widened at the sight. His father loved that pipe. It had belonged to his father, and his father's father before that, passed down through the family for at least three generations. One day, when he was old enough and man enough to own a pipe, Phinnegan's father would pass it to him.

His courage soared.

"Here, now! What are you doing with my father's pipe?"

Before Phinnegan had even finished his question the man started violently and lost his balance on the chair. A short cry escaped his lips as he tumbled to the floor. When he hit the floor, the light from the glowing orb snuffed out and the two were plunged into darkness.

# 3

## Periwinkle Lark

"Just what are you playing at?"

The voice came from just behind Phinnegan's right ear, lilting and musical, but with a sharp tone to the question. He wanted to jump right out of his skin. But when he tried to lift his arm, he found that it was pinned to his side. Phinnegan did not feel the intruder's hands upon him, nor could he see how this stranger could have otherwise restrained him in those short moments since he fell from the chair and the light went out. It was if the air itself held him in place.

"What's the matter? Cat got your, err, tongue? That's the phrase isn't it? Cat got your tongue?"

"Yes, I mean no. I mean...I can't move!"

"Well *of course* you can't move. You bloody well nearly made me snuff it there, with your little tricks. Sneaking up on somebody like that in the dark, and on a Tuesday! Quite rude, that is. Why do you suppose I would let a rude person, such as yourself, go puttering about after what you did? You might bloody well do it again, mightn't' you? Hmm?"

"But...how can you...you're not *holding* me. Why can't I move?"

Phinnegan received no answer. He opened his mouth to speak again, but just as he did the space around him filled with a white-blue light. He squinted his eyes against the sudden light and tried to turn his head from the source.

Phinnegan could sense movement in front of him. As his eyes adjusted to the light he saw this small man, who was even more peculiar than Phinnegan had first thought.

The ivy-green trousers and vest were a lush fabric that had the texture of velvet but moved like a much lighter fabric. The silver workings upon the vest were of a five-petal flower - artfully done and not unlike a purple flower that Phinnegan had seen growing in some of the gardens outside people's homes. A dark purple belt encircled the man's waist, a sliver buckle clasped at the center. Phinnegan thought that this was quite a strange outfit, particularly for a thief.

In addition to his clothing, Phinnegan noticed how small the man was: no taller than himself. Examining the man's face, Phinnegan could not guess at his age. His eyes twinkled with a fiery wisdom only acquired through many years, while his face displayed a smoothness and youth of someone not a day over twenty. His was an ageless face.

But perhaps the most startling thing about this person was his eyes. They were *purple*. Not the dark purple of the belt with the silver buckle, but a light purple. Phinnegan had never seen someone with such a shade of eye color, and he did not know what to make of it. His confusion increased when he saw the man's hair was of a matching hue.

For his part, this oddly dressed man with the purple hair and purple eyes, scrutinized his captive just as his captive scrutinized him. Holding the light before him, he peered at Phinnegan, first from the right then from the left. After studying him for a few moments, he leaned forward, his brow knitted in thought.

"Hmmm. So what are you? A Finch? A Thrush?" He peered closer, arching an eyebrow as he peered at Phinnegan.

"You're not a Crow, are you?"

Phinnegan was confused. It was quite obvious that he was in fact not a bird, nor any other animal.

"No...I'm not a finch, a thrush, nor a crow. I'm a boy."

The strange man rolled his eyes and scowled at Phinnegan, wagging a slender finger in front of his face.

"Oh, don't be daft. *Of course* you are a boy, anyone can see that, just as I am a boy. I mean who do you belong to? What clan?"

"Clan?"

"Don't play coy with me. Yes, what clan? Sparrow? Robin? Grosbeaks? Doves?" He peered closer. "Titmouse?"

Phinnegan thought that this man was indeed quite mad. And mad men often did strange things, and Phinnegan had no desire to have strange things done to him.

"I don't know what you're talking about. I don't belong to any clan." He added after a pause, "I come from the family Qwyk though, if that's what you mean."

The man straightened, putting his hands on his hips and looking straight into Phinnegan's eyes. Although he expected to see madness, Phinnegan only saw annoyance written on the man's face.

"Qwyk? I've never heard of any clan Qwyk. You take me for a fool, do you? Trying to tell me you come from some clan that doesn't exist when everyone knows that all Faë belong to *some* clan, all of which are well documented. You might as well come clean on it." The man reached forward, fingering Phinnegan's hair. Phinnegan recoiled from the touch, his head no longer restrained by the unseen force that bound his arms and legs. The man frowned in thought.

"You aren't a Mud are you? Someone's bastard? You have the color but that could just be a disguise."

Phinnegan felt his blood rising.

"Here, now! That's uncalled for, that is. I've had enough of this rubbish. All these silly questions about what kind of bird I am and what *clan* I belong to. I am no one's bastard. Me mum and dad are upstairs sleeping right now!"

A puzzled look passed over the man's face at Phinnegan's retort. Tilting his head to one side he regarded his captive.

"Your mum and dad?" He paused a moment and then his eyes flashed with recognition.

"Oh!" He eyed Phinnegan with a smirk. "I guess you really don't have a clan do you?"

Suddenly, whatever was restraining Phinnegan vanished. Without the support from these invisible bonds, he stumbled, falling back and landing on his bottom. When the man offered a hand to help him to his feet, Phinnegan scowled and swatted the hand away.

"Easy now, I've set you free haven't I?" offered the stranger.

Phinnegan continued to scowl at the man.

"So? I don't even know how you were holding me there." Phinnegan took two steps away from the man as he asked, even though he doubted it would make little difference if the man sought to restrain him again.

"Who are you?"

The man only smiled, showing exquisite, white teeth.

"Well, I am sorry about that. But you can't be too careful these days, not with the clans at each others's throats as they are, all jostling for recognition." He paused, tilting his head at Phinnegan. "But I guess none of that makes any sense to you, now does it?" The blank stare he received in return was answer enough.

"Perhaps we should start over, yes? Allow me to introduce myself," the man said, sweeping his arm wide as he bowed low, his head dipping below the level of his waist.

"I am called Periwinkle Lark, artist extraordinaire and purveyor of fine English tobaccos. At your service, of course."

Phinnegan could only stare. The man's name was the strangest he had ever heard and his assertion that he was a purveyor of English tobaccos seemed to be a bit off the mark.

"You mean you *steal* English tobaccos, as well as pipes!"

Periwinkle shrugged, a smirk on his face.

"What's a young Faë to do in these times, eh? Vermillion has his claws into everything nowadays it seems. It's not like it used to be. If he gets the throne we're all in for it, I tell you. And the worst part is seeing all the other clans scrapping with one another for favor with that red-headed lout." He shrugged again, gesturing to the jars of tobacco on the table. "Besides, all the best smokes come from the finest leaf in *your* world, everybody knows that."

Phinnegan by now was so perplexed that he didn't know which question to start with. So he just asked them all.

"Who is Vermillion? What throne? And what do you mean *my* world? And what is this Faë business you keep talking about?"

"Ah, easy there, friend. So many questions." Periwinkle stroked his chin as he regarded Phinnegan standing before him. "To one of those questions I am sure you already know the answer. *I* am a Faë. Surely you have heard of us?"

Phinnegan shook his head, but just as Periwinkle was about to speak, he blurted out what he *did* know.

"Well, I've heard of faeries, of course. And leprechauns, elves, and dwarves. Are they similar?"

Periwinkle shook his head and waved his hand.

"In a way. They scratch at the truth, but they're all perversions, really. Some poor soul from your world saw some Faë mucking about in his garden or in the woods and probably came out the worse for it, as we Faës can be a tricky lot when we have a mind to, and so by the time the story's told a hundred times, you've got a whole new race of little people to tell your kiddies about. But it's all as empty as the last glass of blackberry ale that was set in front of me."

"Well, what about the leprechauns and their pot o' gold at the end of the rainbow, then?"

The Faë laughed and then shook his head.

"That old one? It's one of the worst! What Faë would hide his gold in such a place, eh? I ask you, who would be that stupid? Rainbows are always in such a state of flux that you'd never be able to guess where it would go next. One minute your life's work is right there at your back door sitting at the bottom of a rainbow and the next, poof, gone. No, no. No Faë values his money so little that he would be so careless."

"But...you mean there *is* an end to the rainbow?"

Periwinkle gave him a quizzical look.

"Well *of course* it has an end. Where else would we get all our......ahem. You're not a very smart boy, are you?"

Phinnegan suppressed a scowl.

"So you're saying that you, that is, the Faë, are the source of the stories about faeries, brownies, and the like?"

"More or less," the Faë said with a nod and a shrug. "We're all that's really important anyway. The Pixies are pesky little buggers, but other than that they are hardly worth mentioning, really."

Phinnegan regarded the smallish figure in front of him, trying to make sense of all that he was hearing. The next question on his lips was the one he most wanted answered, but was the most afraid to ask. But ask it he did.

"If you're a Faë, and all of these other stories come from your people, does that mean that you can do magic?"

A lilting trill burst from the Faë's lips, which Phinnegan took to be laughter.

The very next moment, the Faë vanished.

"Do you mean like this?"

The voice made Phinnegan jump, for it came from right behind him, where a moment before the Faë had quite obviously not been. He whirled around and perceived the Faë, who now leaned against the wall behind.

"For your people here in this world, I suppose that would be a bit of magic, eh? Then there's always the binding charm I used on you earlier. It's quite a tricky charm to pull off. Nearly impossible for the target to break, but it leaves the Faë performing the charm susceptible to all manner of counters. I should have guessed when you threw up no defenses that you were not a Faë. But as I said before, you could have been being tricky." He shrugged. "My mistake."

Phinnegan felt only excitement. Here before him was a living Faë, a creature he had never before heard of, but that was just as exciting as seeing a leprechaun, faerie, or any other magical creature. The fact that this Faë was in his home was quite miraculous. The Faë's intended theft no longer even crossed his mind.

"What else can you do? Can you fly? Can you turn people into frogs? Can you move things with your magic? Throw fire? Please tell me!"

"Well, turning people into frogs is just plain silly. But as for the others..." As his voice trailed off, he tossed the glowing orb up into the air in front of him. Just before it returned to his outstretched palm, it stopped in midair. Following the motions of his fingers, it spun slowly on its axis. Phinnegan stared in wonder, his eyes following the path of the sphere as it twirled in midair. He looked to the Faë, who was smiling back.

"That's amazing! How do you do it?"

"It's quite easy really," Periwinkle said, letting the sphere fall into his palm. "Levitation of objects is one of the first things we learn. It's a bit difficult here of course, what with the Passes being mostly blocked and all."

Phinnegan could see that the Faë blushed as he said the last, perhaps because he had let something slip that he should not have.

"What are the Passes?" Phinnegan asked. A few moments passed as Periwinkle chewed his cheek before he finally answered.

"The Passes are what connect our two worlds." The Faë paused for a moment, considering before he continued. "In the past, they were open and our people came here often, thus the fodder for all of your myths and legends. But recently they have become narrower and many are blocked entirely." His eyes fell to the floor and he stood in silence for a moment before he added, "It's very dangerous to come here now, and our abilities sometimes fail us when we are here."

"Well what has happened? Why are the Passes blocked?"

"We dare not speak of it, not here," Periwinkle whispered. Phinnegan saw that the Faë was quite distraught over whatever was happening with these passes. He questioned no further and the two stood in silence, the Faë rolling the glowing orb between his fingers.

"Who's down here?!?" a voice bellowed from somewhere outside the study. Phinnegan recognized his father's voice, but to Periwinkle, the shout was cause for alarm.

"Who's that?" he asked, whirling to face the door.

"It's just my father. He won't hurt you."

Periwinkle glanced at Phinnegan.

"You've got that right, mate."

And then he was gone.

Phinnegan blinked at the empty space in front of him where the Faë had stood a moment before. He wondered if the Faë had truly gone, or if he had only performed the same trick as before, making himself appear invisible. He did not have long to ponder this, however, for his father burst through the door, lantern in one hand and a poker in the other.

"All right you devils, show yourselves!" his father bellowed as he entered the study. With his arm out in front of him, holding the lantern aloft, he whirled this way and that, swinging the light in all directions.

"Phinnegan? Why are you out of bed, lad? Who else is here? I heard voices, I am sure of it. Are you all right?" Not waiting for any answers, his father continued his vigilance, searching around the study, walking to each corner and pausing with his lantern. After checking every corner and examining even the walls, Mr. Qwyk stopped at his desk. He saw the open tobacco jars out of place atop the desk and the empty shelf above that now held only a box of matches.

His pipe was nowhere to be seen.

Mr. Qwyk motioned for Phinnegan, who skulked over to stand by his father.

"Yes, Papa?"

"Phinnegan, where is my pipe?"

Phinnegan shuffled his feet, recalling the silhouette of his father's pipe against the ivy-green pants of the Faë and desperately hoping a believable explanation would come to his mind.

"I...I'm sure I don't know, sir."

His father looked down at him and gestured to the open jars of tobacco atop the desk.

"And do you know why these jars are down here on the desk, and why they are open?"

Phinnegan, who had never been a very good liar, broke his father's gaze and looked at the floor.

"No, Papa."

Phinnegan ventured a glance up towards his father. He saw the strong jaw clench as Mr. Qwyk glared at the chair, which was perfectly positioned to boost a short person within reach of the shelf. Mr. Qwyk's glare shifted from the chair back to Phinnegan, who averted his eyes. Even in that brief moment, he knew his father was pondering the lie. Phinnegan had no idea what he could say to prove his innocence. Mr.

Qwyk would never believe the truth. Phinnegan himself scarcely did.

"Are you lying to me, lad?"

Phinnegan winced at the tone in his father's voice. Rather than tell another lie, Phinnegan told the truth – not the *whole* truth, but the truth nonetheless.

"It wasn't me, Papa. I didn't do it. I don't have your pipe."

Anyone could see that Phinnegan was hiding something. His feet shuffled, his face reddened, and his eyes darted.

Mr. Qwyk looked at the opened jars, the missing pipe, and the chair positioned just so.

Hands on his hips, he faced Phinnegan, towering over the boy by at least a foot and a half.

"Let us go and have a talk, lad."

Phinnegan swallowed hard, but this time no melody came to arrest his fear.

# 4

## A Second Visit

That night and the following morning, Phinnegan tried to explain his innocence to Mr. Qwyk, insisting that someone had broken into their home and disturbed the tobacco jars and pipe. Phinnegan had even shown his father the open window in his room, although when he went to point out the wet footprints, they had already dried and disappeared. His father did not believe him; he could tell Phinnegan was not telling him the truth – or at least not the whole truth.

Phinnegan was punished with more chores around the Qwyk household than he could have ever imagined possible. Mr. Qwyk traveled to the cities in the north for work, leaving Phinnegan, his brother Quinn, and his mother to care for the house. This week, in addition to his normal chores of sweeping the house and the porch and tending the garden, Phinnegan had been tasked to split a cord of wood to feed the home's three fireplaces for the next several weeks. Normally a chore for Quinn, his older – and stronger - brother, the task had taken him the better part of two days, and he still wasn't finished. Phinnegan stood by the remainder of the un-split cord, his arms aching, certain they were only one log away from falling off, when Quinn approached him at a trot.

"Phin! There you are," Quinn panted. "Been looking all over for you. Have you got a moment?"

Phinnegan stared at the remainder of the cord briefly before turning to face his brother.

"Yeah, I guess so."

"Good. Got a bit of homework, I have. A bit of reading called 'Gulliver's Travels'," Quinn said, presenting a rather tattered book to Phinnegan. "Ever heard of it?"

Despite his exhaustion, Phinnegan's eyes brightened when he saw the book.

"Of course. "I've read it at least a half-dozen times."

"Thought you might of," Quinn said. "Look, a bunch of us are planning a party tonight and –"

"Haven't read it have you?" Phinnegan interjected.

"Not a word," Quinn said flatly. "Got to hand in a report about it on Monday. Spare a few minutes to help your brother out?"

Phinnegan always jumped at a chance to delve into the world of fairy tales, but glancing at the remaining cord of wood beside him, he knew he could not this time.

"You know I'd like to Quinn," Phinnegan began before pausing to gesture at the pile of wood beside him. "But there is my punishment. I'm still not finished."

Quinn's eyes flicked between the wood, the book and his brother.

"I'll chop, you talk," he said, grabbing the axe that leaned against the stump the Qwyks used as the base for splitting wood. Phinnegan took the book from his brother's outstretched hand and ran his fingers over its worn cover.

"So, what's it about?" Quinn asked as he positioned a squat log on top of the stump.

"It's about a man, a traveler," Phinnegan said simply.

"And I guess he was called Gulliver, eh?" Quinn quipped as he raised the axe for a mighty chop.

"Why yes, he was. First, he visited the Lilliputians, a race of –"

"Lilly-what?" Quinn asked harshly.

"Lilliputians. They were a race of little people from the land of Lilliput."

"Honestly Phin, I don't know how you read this stuff."

Phinnegan could only smile.

Phinnegan provided a rather detailed summary of Gulliver's adventures to his brother Quinn, who split log after log as Phinnegan answered his questions about the book. When he reached the end of Gulliver's travels, Quinn had reached the end of the wood pile. Every log was now split into halves and quarters, as its thickness demanded, the resulting pieces stacked alongside the Qwyks' house. While Quinn was exhausted, his skin covered in bits of wood and sweat, Phinnegan felt rejuvenated.

The day was bright, sunny, and warm, all uncharacteristic for a November day, and Phinnegan decided to take a long walk to the edge of a nearby forest. As he walked, his mind began to wander.

It had been four days since the ivy-green clad Periwinkle Lark had broken into the Qwyk home, and Phinnegan began to wonder if he would ever see the little person again, or if he even wanted to. He had taken a mysterious glimpse into another world, one filled with magic and creatures of legend.

The Faë's short visit had left so many questions unanswered. Who was this Vermillion who Periwinkle seemed to revile? And what was wrong in his world that it was now so dangerous? Phinnegan wondered if it would be possible to travel to this world himself. His heart skipped a beat with the thought, yet he knew that such a thing was improbable. He doubted he would ever see the Faë again.

Shaking his head to clear these thoughts from his mind, he sat down with his back against the base of a wych elm, its once smooth grey bark now brown and cracked. In his hands he still held his brother's tattered copy of 'Gulliver's Travels'.

Phinnegan closed his eyes and let the book fall open, then began to read. He had not been reading long when he felt a tickle upon his left ear. He swatted at the insect he assumed caused the tickle and continued to read. Again he felt the tickle, and again he swatted, turning his head and looking for the little winged perpetrator, yet he saw nothing.

The third disturbance was more than a tickle. It was a voice.

"Sorry about all that punishment business, mate. Fancy a smoke?"

Phinnegan jumped up from his spot beneath the tree, his book flying from his lap. He whirled around to see Periwinkle Lark leaning against the trunk of the wych elm, his arms crossed over his chest.

His clothes were different than before, but they were still outlandish. His shirt was a metallic silver, and his trousers were black, once again snugly fit and made of velvet-like fabric. He wore high black boots up to his knee, the bottoms of his trousers tucked into them. A light purple cloak, the color of the Faë's hair, draped across his shoulders. On his head, a black tricorn hat hid much of his strangely colored hair, which hung long, down past his shoulders. And, as a final touch, Periwinkle's lips clenched Mr. Qwyk's pipe.

Phinnegan scowled at Periwinkle and before he knew what he was doing, lunged forward.

"Give that back!"

The Faë, far more agile than a twelve year old boy, dodged the lunge and laughed.

"Is that the best you can do? It will take a wee bit more than that if you want to catch me."

Again Phinnegan watched with dismay as Periwinkle vanished. He spun around, looking frantically for any sign of the elusive Faë.

A tap on his shoulder startled him, and he turned around to see the grinning face of Periwinkle.

"I'm only having a joke. Here, take it. I've got plenty anyway."

Phinnegan snatched the offered pipe from Periwinkle's outstretched hand. He inspected it for any damage before tucking it into a front pocket of his trousers.

"There now, see? You have your father's pipe back and you can run home to give it to him. No harm done."

Phinnegan shook his head.

"How can I give it back to him when I have told him a dozen times that it wasn't me that took it?"

The Faë smirked.

"Ah, that is a sharp little mind you have there, mate," remarked Periwinkle, his voice lilting. "Very sharp. Well, I suppose you can be giving it back to me then, eh? Seeing as how you can't be restoring it to its rightful owner and all, can't waste a good pipe now can we?"

The Faë held out his hand, waving the fingers and gesturing for Phinnegan to return the pipe. Phinnegan took a step back.

"I think I will keep it, thank you very much."

"Suit yourself then," the Faë said with a shrug. He walked over to the wych elm where Phinnegan had been reading only minutes earlier and plopped down with a huff. He removed his hat and sat it on the bare ground beside him. Turning around, he rapped his knuckles on the trunk of the tree.

"So, what's your story, eh?"

Phinnegan opened his mouth to answer, but the Faë rapped harder on the elm's trunk.

"Hallooo, anyone in there?" the Faë called, leaning closer to the tree.

Phinnegan furrowed his brow, seeing that the Faë was talking to the tree and not to him.

"What are you doing?"

"Well, I was trying to be cordial to our friend here, seeing as I'll be planting me bum on his roots, but he's not being very friendly."

Phinnegan eyed the Faë warily and took a step towards him.

"Why would it be friendly? It's a tree."

Periwinkle turned toward him, his head cocked sideways, a question upon his face. Then his mouth cracked with a broad grin and he laughed, slapping his thigh with an open hand.

"Pah! I always forget your trees can't talk. Sorry, mate." Periwinkle patted the tree, while Phinnegan looked on, wide-eyed.

"And yours can?"

Periwinkle shrugged and flashed a smile up at young Phinnegan.

"Of course they can, mate. As long as you're friendly and respectful-like. Awfully good stories they can tell. Seen a lot, they have." The Faë reached into his trouser pocket and pulled out a short black strand of some kind. Biting the end and pulling, he tore a piece off into his mouth. Phinnegan felt his stomach rumble at the site of what looked like a piece of black licorice. He had not eaten in several hours. Periwinkle saw the look on Phinnegan's face and offered the black strand to him.

"Here you go, mate, have a bite. Quite satisfying, it is."

Phinnegan took the licorice-like substance cautiously and sniffed it. His nose wrinkled and he moved the strand away from his face. Definitely not licorice.

"What is it? Is it candy?"

The Faë only shrugged.

"You ask too many questions, mate. Just take a bite. You've got to learn somehow."

With more than a hint of reservation, Phinnegan bit into the tough black strand and tore off a piece. As he chewed, the tough black piece became gummy and stuck to his teeth. The taste was not foul, but neither was it very good. He tried to spit it out, but it was stuck to his teeth. He could only chew and swallow every now and then, gradually working the tacky candy from his mouth. The Faë laughed as he reclaimed his snack.

"Not quite to your liking, eh?"

Phinnegan could only shake his head, for his mouth was still quite engaged in chewing. As the Faë tore off another piece and gulped it down, Phinnegan realized that he did not chew - he only swallowed.

"I forgot to tell you that you aren't supposed to chew it, like. Just bite and swallow. Gets quite messy, it does." He bit off another piece and swallowed. "It's called sticky root."

Phinnegan tried to open his mouth, but the more he chewed the tougher and more glue-like it became. The Faë saw his struggles and offered another piece of advice.

"It's a lot like...oh what do you call it?" He thought for a moment, a finger on his dimpled chin. "Oh yes, quicksand! The more you struggle, the faster it pulls you under. Just stop chewing. It will settle down and then just swallow it. You'll be careful with the next bite."

Phinnegan glared at the Faë, but followed his advice and stopped his ferocious chewing. Periwinkle sat in silence, eyes twinkling as he finished off the remainder of the sticky root and watched Phinnegan's jaw begin to slacken. Finally he swallowed noisily, twice, and then opened and closed his mouth a few times, working the muscles.

"You could have warned me."

Periwinkle only laughed, brushing his hands on his trousers as he stood.

"Warn you? On the contrary, mate, no warning was needed as I was giving you a bit of a lesson. Be wary of a Faë bearing gifts. We're no Pixies but we are the tricksters now and then."

As the Faë stood smiling in front of Phinnegan, he wondered just how this Faë had stumbled upon him so far from his home, and on the edge of the forest.

"Just what are you doing out here anyway? Are you following me?"

Periwinkle withdrew, his hand on his chest and a pained look across his face.

"Following you? You suggest that I have some ulterior motive and wish you harm?"

"No, I didn't mean that. It's just what with the pipe and now this mucky root thing-"

"Sticky root," the Faë corrected.

"Aye, sticky root. What with that and all, well, it just seems like you may be up to no good. You did after all say you Faë are a tricky lot."

"So I did!" the Faë exclaimed. His eyes appraising Phinnegan, a knowing smile spread across his lips.

"I may have spotted you now and then these past few days. Perhaps I even spied you earlier, with your brother. A veritable Scheherazade, you were."

Phinnegan's cheeks colored at the comparison, but a small smile touched the corners of his lips. *One Thousand and One Nights* was one of his favorite books.

"Don't be bashful," Periwinkle chided. "It was really rather clever, that. And I do so like clever – it has so many uses. Why do you think I've troubled myself to return to this world not once, but twice? And in one week? Unheard of!"

Still uncertain, Phinnegan remained silent.

"I've given you back your father's pipe as well, haven't I?," the Faë announced. "Besides," he said while digging in his pocket. "I wanted to show you something."

With a flourish of his wrist, Periwinkle produced a small white stone. It looked like a marble, only the substance of which it was made appeared more akin to true stone rather than glass.

"What is it? It looks like a marble."

The Faë's face suddenly became solemn, and Phinnegan could not tell if he was really serious or if it was again some sort of mockery. But Periwinkle seemed very serious indeed when he spoke.

"A marble? A *marble*? Have you never heard of a wishing stone?"

When Phinnegan shook his head, the Faë looked dismayed.

"Honestly, with all the reading you do, you've never heard of a wishing stone? What nonsense are you filling that little head of yours with?"

Phinnegan, who may not have ever heard of a wishing stone, was still sharp of wit and caught something the Faë might not have meant for him to catch. His eyes narrowed.

"How do you know I do a lot of reading?"

A look of fear flashed over the Faë's face. Phinnegan saw he had indeed said more than he intended, but he recovered quickly.

"How do I know? Because I use logic, mate. Here you are on a beautiful sunny afternoon, and what are you doing? You're out here alone, at the edge of the forest, where no one could find you, reading. Tells a pretty grim tale of your social life."

Phinnegan's heart sank a little. He did not have any real friends. Perhaps that was why, even though the Faë had been nothing but trouble, Phinnegan was drawn to him. What better way to make up for not having any friends than to have one who was magical? This thought drew his eyes back to the stone.

What was a wishing stone?

"What does it do?" Phinnegan breathed as he took the stone from the Faë's outstretched hand. "Does it give me three wishes?"

The Faë regarded him with a flat stare.

"You *definitely* read too much. This three wish nonsense is another one of your human concoctions. What good are only three wishes? No, no. Wishing stones are *unlimited!*"

"So I can make a wish for whatever I want, and this stone will give it to me?" Phinnegan inquired, his face brightening. He looked eagerly at the Faë, a smile creeping across his face.

"Well, not exactly. You see, this one is rather small. It has a limited capacity for what it can do. Got a spot of school work you don't want to do? It can take care of it. Need to sweep up a bit? No problem. But it can't give you a pile of gold or anything like that, if that's what you're after."

The smile on Phinnegan's face faded.

"That's disappointing, isn't it? It can do my chores and my homework? I can do that myself. Not much of a wishing stone."

"Well, it does have other uses," the Faë remarked with a sly smile.

"Like what?"

Periwinkle reached into Phinnegan's hand and took the stone back. Waving a hand to silence Phinnegan's protest, the Faë took the stone and rolled it between his two palms. A few moments passed.

And then Phinnegan heard the melody. His eyes widened and he stared at the Faë's palms.

"You hear it I see," the Faë whispered as he continued to roll the marble in his hands.

"Yes," Phinnegan whispered in return. "I've heard it before. The night you stole into my house. When I followed you down the stairs and through the house, the sound grew louder. And then when you fell-"

"You mean when you nearly made me snuff it," the Faë interjected in a sharp whisper.

"When you fell," Phinnegan continued, "the melody stopped. And I haven't heard it since. It was coming from that little marble?"

The Faë nodded and opened his hands wider, letting more sound escape.

"It's beautiful," Phinnegan breathed. "What is it?"

"It's –" the Faë began, but never finished, for the sound coming from the stone became a shriek. Phinnegan pressed his hands to his ears to try and muffle the sound, but to little effect. The look on Periwinkle's face was one of pure dismay.

"Oh, bloody hell," he exclaimed. "Now I've done it."

"Done what? What's happening?"

The Faë looked him in the eye and was for once completely serious.

"They found me."

Phinnegan was at a loss.

"Who found you? What is going on?"

The Faë never answered. Instead a booming voice shook the very earth beneath their feet.

*PERIWINKLE LARK, YOU ARE HEREBY ORDERED TO APPEAR BEFORE THE HIGH COURT.*

Phinnegan watched in horror and listened to the booming voice declare Periwinkle a criminal. The stone was growing in size and becoming more translucent and fluid. Phinnegan could not understand what was happening, but he saw that

Periwinkle appeared to be fading before his eyes. Without thinking, he reached out to grab the Faë's hand.

"No! Don't!" Periwinkle shouted. But the warning came too late. Phinnegan had already reached across the shimmering orb of fluid translucence.

Just as Phinnegan touched the Faë's hand, he saw a bright flash and heard a crash like thunder.

And then everything went black.

# 5

## Under the Mountain

When Phinnegan opened his eyes, a black darkness surrounded him. Not the black of his bedroom on a moonless night, but a total and complete darkness of impenetrable depth. He held his hand up in front up his face, or at least he tried to, but as he saw nothing, he really couldn't be sure that he had.

*The flash of light.*

Could he be blind? The flash had seemed bright and sudden enough to damage his eyes. Or could it be that the invisible force that grabbed him by the core and pulled him with some unnatural strength that damaged his eyes? Or worse, was he dead? People who had transcended the veil of death and returned to tell their tales did describe seeing a bright, white light.

Just then, he heard a faint cough from his left.

*I can't be dead. People don't cough after they die.*

Still unable to see through the dense darkness, the strange cough unsettled him. The hair on his arms stood on end and he scrambled backwards across the rough floor until his back bumped against a wall. He heard the cough again, fainter than before.

"Who...who's there?" Phinnegan called out into the darkness.

The only answer was another faint cough. He pushed himself up onto his hands and knees and felt his way forward.

"Hello? Is anyone there?" he called out again.

A familiar lilting voice replied, though weakened from coughing.

"It's only me, mate. Your favorite Faë."

Periwinkle's voice was now closer. Phinnegan assumed that Periwinkle, too, was feeling his way through the darkness.

"Where are we? What happened?" Phinnegan queried the darkness. "You were rubbing that stone and then there was a flash of light and a crash...are we dead?"

"Not dead, mate. But close enough."

"And the voice..." Phinnegan whispered, his words trialing off as he recalled what the voice had said about the Faë. Could those things really all be true?

"We are in a very dark place, mate. Figuratively and literally. So dark I can't see my own bloody hand in front of my face. I know of only once place that would be this dark. Féradoon. A black place in more ways than one, I'll promise you that."

"Féradoon?" Phinnegan asked. "What's that?" He paused, remembering the booming voice. "That voice said it, right? Doesn't sound like any place I've ever heard of."

"You wouldn't have heard of it, mate," the Faë answered, his voice becoming stronger. It sounded like he was only a few feet away from Phinnegan now. "It's not in your world. Even in mine it's not a topic for polite conversation."

Phinnegan's heart lurched at Periwinkle's words, which he spoke so nonchalantly.

"Do you mean we're not in Ireland anymore?"

The Faë barked a short laugh.

"Ireland? Uh, no. No, we definitely are not in Ireland anymore. Nor England nor France nor the Americas. We've left your world all together. Welcome to the land of the Faë. Though this isn't really a proper spot for a visit."

Phinnegan's breath caught and his limbs quavered beneath him. He heard Periwinkle's words, but his mind could not comprehend them. He struggled with the innate impossibility of somehow traversing into another world. But behind the fear that now gripped him, anger trickled forth. Phinnegan began to suspect the Faë was playing some cruel joke on him.

"Are you having a joke on me? You've said yourself that you Faë are a tricky lot. How do I know this isn't some...some, illusion?"

"Illusion? Look around you, mate, if you can that is. For me, it's blacker than pitch. I don't deny that I've had some fun at your expense with the sticky root and the like, but this is not my doing. We're in a tight spot."

Phinnegan remained unconvinced.

"But how do I know that this isn't some magic trick? Maybe I'm blind-folded and you're just standing there smirking at me while I look the fool. And another thing – "

"Oh, stop your bleating," Periwinkle interrupted, his tone exasperated. "I know more about magic than you can imagine and I can promise you this is *no* magic trick. Do you think I just shone a pretty light in your face and then pulled the wool over your eyes, is that it? No, mate. This is bad and this is real, or I'm Morgan le Fay."

"Well, if all you say is true," Phinnegan whispered after several silent moments, "this does sound bad."

"Believe me now, do you," the Faë sneered. "And oh yes, it is bad. Quite. The devil take me for being so careless." Periwinkle continued speaking, but his voice dropped so and he assumed the Faë was talking to himself.

"How could you be so stupid? Did you really think they wouldn't notice?"

"Notice what?" The question escaped Phinnegan's lips before he could hold it back. Raised with manners as he had been, he thought it rude to listen in on another's conversation, even when that conversation was with one's self. But he couldn't deny he wanted to know the answer to that question.

The Faë became silent. As the moments passed, Phinnegan's anger and frustration rose once again and they betrayed him in his voice when he spoke.

"Would you just tell me what the bloody hell is going on?"

Phinnegan's demand was greeted with further silence. He could almost feel the harsh glare Periwinkle was undoubtedly casting in his direction.

"What's going on is we've been captured," Periwinkle stated after a few moments.

"*Captured?* By whom?"

"Well if the stories are true, and I have no reason to believe they are not, then Féradoon is now sort of the unofficial headquarters for that favorite son of the Faë, Vermillion. He and his lot are our most likely captors. I told you, they've got a vice grip on this world now. And they're squeezing her for all that they can. I never should've activated that stone."

"Activated the stone?" Phinnegan recalled the smooth, spherical wishing stone. "Is that what you were doing then, when you were making it sing?"

Although he could not see Periwinkle, Phinnegan assumed the Faë must have been nodding his response out of habit, forgetting that they conversed in total darkness.

"Err, yes. "When the wishing stones are activated, they open a sort of window between our worlds. Not anything you can travel through, not one that size anyway, but you can see and hear things. The stones are linked to the Faë that saved them."

He paused for a moment, then continued, his voice quiet.

"They've been watching mine, no doubt, so I thought to trick them by using the stone of another. I was going to give it to you, if you remember. Evidently their tracking methods are better than I gave them credit for."

The Faë's admission that he was likely being watched reminded Phinnegan of the deep, booming voice they had heard back in Ireland beneath the wych elm.

"If they were watching you...does that mean that you did those things that the voice said? That you are a thief? A traitor?"

"Well, mate, I don't need to tell you that I am a bit of a thief. Your father's pipe, if you recall. As to the traitor bit, if standing up to that lout labels me a traitor, then I wear it proudly."

Phinnegan pondered this answer. In his short life, he had heard of courageous rebels who resisted some unfair authority, even peacefully, and were labeled criminals and traitors. Of course, these people had all been written about in books, whether fictitious or historical, but the principle was the same.

"What did you do?" Phinnegan swallowed the lump in his throat.

"Did you kill someone?"

Periwinkle chuckled in the darkness.

"I may be a thief and a 'traitor,' if they want to call me that. But I assure you I am no murderer. I've only...well, shall we say disrupted...some of his plans. That's all. I'm a bit of an instigator, you could say."

"What sorts of things have you done then?" Phinnegan asked, his curiosity piqued by this admission.

"Most of it mostly boils down to a bit of thieving. But with a Faë like that, stealing some trophy ruins the whole conquest for him. But I've done a bit of vandalism as well. Once, a few years back at the beginning of this mess, when Vermillion first proclaimed himself as some sort of prince-in-waiting, he commissioned a statute to be made in our capital city of himself." The Faë chuckled. "When it is was all finished, I made a few improvements."

"Well? What did you do?"

"I'm getting to it. Let's just say that Vermillion didn't like the looks of himself in a dress."

Phinnegan smiled to himself in the darkness and a small giggle escaped his lips.

"You painted a dress on the statue?" Phinnegan tried to imagine the statue of a tyrant, painted over with a dress

"Oh, I did more than paint, mate. It was a real dress. Bit of an evening gown, really, some shimmer and some sheer. Quite lovely, actually, on the right person. Of course Vermillion didn't quite see it that way, as you might expect."

While Phinnegan found the story quite funny, he thought it was a stretch to call such an act of defiance, while humiliating for Vermillion, treason. He sensed there was more to the Faë's "criminal" activities than Periwinkle let on.

"But are you sure that's all you have done, then? Stealing a few treasures and dressing up a statue is enough to be labeled a traitor? I don't know if I like the sound of your world. Sounds a bit...mean."

Though Periwinkle did not speak, Phinnegan could feel him shuffling in the darkness. He assumed that the Faë did not want to speak about anything else that may have happened. When he did speak, his voice was hollow and empty.

"There is one other thing that Vermillion holds against me." He sighed. "And I hold it against him as well, rotten oaf that he is. Emerald Wren."

"Emerald Wren? What – er, who's that? Is that another Faë? A girl?"

"A girl yes, but not just another Faë. The most beautiful Faë that I've ever seen. We loved each other."

*Loved?*

"Is she all right?"

"All right?" Periwinkle repeated. "Yes, she's all right. At least I think she is. She's Vermillion's daughter, and I don't know what he has done with her. He doesn't approve of us, never has. Not even when we were young and just innocent friends catching starflies together." The Faë again became silent. Before Phinnegan could prod further, Periwinkle continued.

"He forbade us to be together or even see one another. I ignored him, of course. And now she is gone and I am a traitor."

Phinnegan, who understood little about love - other than what he read about in his books - could not comprehend the Faë's situation, but he could hear the sadness in Periwinkle's voice.

"I'm...uh... I'm sorry. Do you know where she is now? Surely Vermillion would not have harmed his own daughter, right?"

"Well there's a bit of the difficulty, mate. I have no way to know what he has done with her. I haven't a clue. After I took her away-"

"Wait," Phinnegan interjected. "You took her away? You mean you kidnapped her?"

"You could say that. She was willing, of course. As I said, we loved each other."

"Well, I guess that's all right then," Phinnegan mused. "If she went with you willingly I guess it wasn't really kidnapping." But one thing still puzzled him. "Why do you keep saying 'loved'? Don't you still love her?"

"Of course I do!" Periwinkle cried, his voice filling with emotion for a moment. When he continued though, he again sounded flat and hollow.

"I just figure it's easier to think of her as in the past. Makes the loss easier to swallow, you know?"

"You mean you are giving up on her? Just like that?"

"I'm not giving up on anything," Periwinkle retorted. "I'm just being realistic."

"Maybe if you just talked to him –"

"Have you not been listening?" the Faë interrupted. "He bloody well owns this world and he has no fond feelings towards me."

"Well, if a way existed that you could be with her, would you do it?"

"Of course!"

"Well then, we just have to find out what that way is," Phinnegan replied with a tone of finality.

"We?"

Phinnegan nodded, although the Faë could not see him in the darkness, of course.

"Yes, we. I'll do all I can to help." Phinnegan turned around in the darkness. "If you can get us out of here, that is."

"Well that's very kind of you, mate, though there is nothing that you can do to change his mind, that I know." He sighed. "As for getting out of here, there's only one way that I know."

"And what's that? Do you know a secret way out?" Phinnegan's hopes rose as he contemplated escaping this stifling darkness.

"Not really a secret. This isn't some kind of jail where you can pop of the barred window and flee to freedom. It's a cavern at the bottom of a mountain. The only way out is up."

"Well how do we go 'up,' exactly?"

"We wait."

Phinnegan was confused.

"Wait for what? It's dark and I am hungry. It's well past supper time."

The Faë only chuckled.

"I'm hungry as well, mate. But there's nothing for it. When they're ready, they'll bring us up."

"But how?"

He heard Periwinkle shuffling in the darkness and wondered what he was doing.

"I guess we will just have to wait and see. I've heard my fair share of tales, but there is no telling which one is true."

"Well what are we supposed to do now?" Phinnegan groaned in frustration.

"Sleep."

"Sleep? Now? How?" Phinnegan prodded. "Periwinkle?"

Periwinkle ignored him, and before long he heard Periwinkle's slow breathing.

Phinnegan sat in the darkness, contemplating his situation. He missed his family, his home. He had no idea how long they had already been gone, but his stomach told him it was indeed well past supper time.

Having nothing to eat, he decided to follow the Faë's advice. He sank to his side and put his arm under his head for a pillow, laying in darkness and waiting for sleep to come.

# 6

## Féradoon

Phinnegan had just fallen asleep when he awakened to the sensation of movement. He couldn't see in the darkness but the faint grating of stone on stone proved that they were moving. Not left and right or back and forth, but *up*, just as the Faë had predicted.

"Periwinkle, do you feel that?" Phinnegan called out into the darkness.

"Aye, mate. We're on the move."

"Should we...*do* anything?" Phinnegan queried.

"Nothing to do," Periwinkle said with a sigh. "Just wait, like."

After what seemed like half an hour Phinnegan noticed above them a ragged outline of faint light. As the light grew brighter, Phinnegan wondered what would greet them at the top.

The movement shuddered to a stop and the chamber filled with light. Phinnegan shielded his eyes as the floor beneath him lurched upwards again.

Again the movement halted. Phinnegan sat motionless, his eyes shut against the light and his ears straining for any sounds. He heard a faint trickle of water and the echo of footsteps on stone.

Phinnegan opened his eyes. The light was blinding after the complete darkness of their prison below the mountain.

When his eyes adjusted, Phinnegan saw that he was in a large chamber, lit by glowing torches mounted on hundreds of smooth, stone columns. Goosebumps spread over his arms, and he rubbed them unconsciously. Phinnegan even saw his warm breath as it met the cold air. He tilted his head, taking in the stone walls that stretched upward into impenetrable heights.

He pushed himself to his knees and peered around the expansive chamber. It was enormous. Looking left and then right, Phinnegan could not even discern the walls. The room seemed to extend forever on both sides. He tried to count the columns that surrounded him, but there were just too many.

Phinnegan spun around to the sound of echoing footsteps. He saw no one but Periwinkle, who sat a few feet away, gaping at the expanse of the chamber.

"Not one for grand things is he?" the Faë quipped.

"This is amazing," Phinnegan whispered. "How did they build all this?"

"Well he didn't do it himself, I can tell you that. Likely some poor Turnstones."

"What are Turnstones? Some type of creature?"

The Faë shook his head.

"No mate, another clan. Quite reclusive group they are too. They prefer to work with their hands." He gestured to the massive columns. "Grand things like this are not their normal fare; they're more humble, like. But I know of no one else that has the ability to build something like this."

Phinnegan stood and took a few steps toward one of the columns. He reached his hand out to touch the surface. "Smooth as glass," he muttered to himself. A wide spiral wound its way up the column, and Phinnegan marveled at the perfection of the curve.

"It's so smooth. How did they do it?"

"Don't know, mate. Like I said, they're a reclusive bunch and they guard their secrets. But before you go on admiring that, remember they likely only did it because they were forced to. No Turnstone would make something so...haughty...of his own accord."

Phinnegan understood Periwinkle's point, that these Turnstone Faës were forced by Vermillion to craft these stone columns like slaves. Still, he could not help but admire their beauty.

"Where are we? Is this still Féradoon?" Phinnegan asked.

"Aye, but now we're somewhere closer to the top, I reckon," the Faë responded, rising to his feet. Periwinkle turned in a circle with his head tilted back looking upwards into the depths. "It's a huge mountain in the south of our lands. The stories speak of multiple prisons deep within the heart of the mountain and expansive halls and courts in the higher elevations. Vermillion himself has a palace upon the mountain's peak. Castle Black. Fitting name for a Wren."

"Wren? So that's his...clan?" Phinnegan asked, finally feeling as though he was grasping something of Faë culture.

"Yes, and what a rotten clan it is. Only ones worse are the Crows."

"You asked if I was a Crow," Phinnegan remarked.

"That I did. Sorry, but you never can be too careful. The Crows are trickier than most and you could have been one in disguise."

"PERIWINKLE LARK!"

Both prisoners jumped at this sudden declaration. Phinnegan recognized the loud booming voice that now reverberated off the far flung walls of the cavern. It was the same one that had emanated from the wishing stone just before it had banished them to this mountain prison. The voice echoed many times over and bombarded his ears from all sides. Out of the corner of his eye, he saw the Faë cringe.

"This, my young friend, is going to be an adventure," Periwinkle muttered out of the corner of his mouth, as he stared straight ahead. When Phinnegan followed the path of the Fae's eyes, he saw only the same darkness beyond the light of the torches that he saw in every direction.

"Why are you staring like that?" Phinnegan whispered out of the corner of his own mouth, following Periwinkle's example for a lack of a better alternative. "I don't see anything out there."

"Are you sure? To the right of that furthest, visible column, hidden within its shadow. Do you see it?"

Phinnegan leaned forward and squinted his eyes, trying to focus on the area surrounding the indicated column. At first he saw nothing, but when he shifted a bit to the right, he saw a flicker of movement. It looked more like a disturbance, a haze, than an actual figure.

"It looks like some sort of blur; like it's there, but then it isn't. What is it?"

"It's a gholem. They're very rare; I've only seen one meself. And they are *very* dangerous. Chances are, most things you meet in or around Féradoon will be dangerous, but a gholem is particularly so. It can melt into the darkest shadows and you would never see it, especially with your human eyes."

"What's wrong with my eyes?" Phinnegan asked, glancing at the Faë.

"They just aren't as used to spotting magical creatures as those of a Faë," Periwinkle answered with a slight shrug. Sure enough, Phinnegan found it very difficult to keep track of the gholem that waited in the shadow of the far away column. Each time he blinked, he had to refocus on the blur. He thought it was important to keep this creature within his sight if it was as dangerous as Periwinkle said, and he had no reason to doubt that it was.

"What is it doing here? Is it the source of the voice?" Phinnegan gasped as he saw the blur emerge from the shadow of the column momentarily, only to step into the shadow of a second, closer column. Even at this distance, Phinnegan could see the grotesque nature of the gholem's proportions.

"He's only a guard, most likely; meant to keep us from making a break for it, not that we could make it out of here anyway. It's just a bit of psychological games. And no, he is not the source of the voice, of that I am sure."

"How can you be sure," Phinnegan demanded in a whisper.

"That's easy, mate. Gholems have no tongues, at least not in this form. Quite difficult to speak without a tongue, it is. Tried it, I have, and it was no fun at all. They're more a grunting lot, really. I've heard that they can communicate amongst themselves, but I don't really believe it."

"So as long as we don't run, he won't harm us?"

"Probably not, although I wouldn't turn my back on him if he gets much closer," Periwinkle replied, his eyes locked on the gholem.

"And what did you mean about its form?"

"Well, they're shape-shifters now aren't they? Can look like our shadowy friend there, a rock, or maybe even someone you know. Quite spooky, really."

"I see. Well if he is not the source of the voice, then where is it coming from? I don't see anyone else," Phinnegan mused, casting his eyes around the chamber.

"Don't know, mate, but I reckon we will find out soon enough. And when we do, let me do all the talking, like. I'm in a spot of trouble here, but I can handle myself. I'm a bit of a troublemaker, as I've said. You just keep quiet. You never should have touched that stone."

"I didn't know I would end up here! I was trying to help you," Phinnegan responded, a hint of anger in his voice.

"I warned you not to touch it, now didn't I?"

"YOU SHOULD HAVE DONE MORE THAN WARN HIM, PERIWINKLE LARK!"

The voice roared, louder than before. The torches flared on each column with a hissing sound. The chamber now blazed with light. Phinnegan could see much further in each direction, just making out each wall of the chamber. The chamber was at least one-hundred meters long on each side, with large, sinuously curved columns positioned every ten meters or so.

"Oh, bloody hell," the Faë swore. Phinnegan, who had been peering into the depths when the chamber brightened, started as he spun around and saw that a massive desk had appeared.

The desk was more a bench, like you might find in a grand courtroom. The top of the bench stood taller than a man and spread a full seven or eight meters from end to end. It was carved from a dark, rich wood and looked heavy. The wood was a dark, red-tinged brown.

Carvings of dense, leafy vines covered the front of the bench, like those that grow on the side of a building or a tree trunk. When Phinnegan looked more closely, he realized that the vines were not carved at all, but were indeed real vines. Even as he watched, they writhed and crept along the front of the desk, reaching towards each corner and wrapping around the edges before disappearing from his sight.

Phinnegan had been so absorbed in the magnificence of the bench in front of him that he had not even noticed the peculiar person sitting behind it. Phinnegan was certain that this man was some sort of judge. Though he did not look like the judges of England or Ireland - no white wig adorned the crown of his head - he did wear a black robe, which covered from his neck and down his torso out of sight behind the bench, as well as down the length of his arms, which were crossed in front of his chest.

His features also hinted at his position as an arbiter of the law. His eyes were tired and beady, set deep beneath a heavy brow. A large hooked nose and the thin lips set in a grim line of annoyance completed the picture. Phinnegan thought the judges always looked annoyed. He couldn't blame them; what could be more boring than sitting day after day listening to people argue about the law? The man's silvery-hair was long and thick and fell far past his shoulders, standing out quite starkly against the black of his robes.

Periwinkle cleared his throat and then spoke in a mocking tone.

"Well, well, fancy you being a judge. Where's Vermillion? Sent you down here to do his dirty work for him, eh? The silver suits you, mate. You were always too boring to be a Cerulean anyway."

Even though they stood a few meters away from the judge, Phinnegan could see the muscles of his jaw flex in consternation as Periwinkle spoke. Phinnegan wondered if this tired looking man was also a Faë. He assumed he must be, for he could not imagine that he was a human, like himself. His bright blue eyes, even though surrounded by wrinkled and sagging skin, burned wild and fierce. They held the same vibrancy of Periwinkle's purple eyes.

"I see your insolence has yet to be checked," the man responded, his bright eyes fixed upon Periwinkle. Phinnegan recognized that the voice was the same that had heralded his banishment to this other world.

"Insolent? Me?" A melodious laugh burst from Periwinkle's lips, drawing further ire from the man behind the bench. He slammed his fist upon the dark wood of the bench.

"Silence!" he roared, his voice, echoing around the chamber many times as Phinnegan stood, rooted to the spot. The laugh died upon Periwinkle's lips, and he stood still as a stone, hands clasped behind his back. But still he could not - or would not - control his tongue.

"I'll be silent, but not until after I've said my piece. You owe me that much."

The judge leaned back, and Phinnegan took this as a signal that he would listen to Periwinkle's plea. Phinnegan was quite confused about what was transpiring before him, but he was certain that these two Faë knew each other. Beside him, he heard Periwinkle draw a deep breath.

"I should kill you where you sit, you know," Periwinkle growled through gritted teeth.

The judge raised a silvery eyebrow.

"Now, that would not be a wise move, given the circumstances. I assume you have seen the gholem?" the judge said, motioning toward the blurry figure that floated nearby. But Phinnegan thought he detected something in his voice that betrayed understanding of Periwinkle's sentiments.

"Of course I've seen the gholem. Do you take me for a fool? Even he has seen it," Periwinkle said, jerking his thumb in Phinnegan's direction. The judge flicked his gaze toward Phinnegan's. His face darkened and his thin lips curled into a frown.

"Ah, yes. The *human*," the judge spat with noticeable disdain. "We will deal with him soon enough. Now make haste boy, and speak your piece."

Periwinkle again laughed at the stoic judge.

"Boy? Now *that* is a good one. You know my age, *Jay*: three-hundred and eleven, a good half-century older than your silvery, crusty old self."

Phinnegan's mouth fell open in shock. This purple-haired Faë, who moved with the grace of a cat and had the youthful face of a boy not yet twenty, was more than *three-hundred* years old? It was not possible. Yet the judge seemed to confirm this.

"Older you may be, but it has been *your* choice to remain in this preposterous form for all these years. You should have Changed decades ago. A Faë of your years still bearing the colors of youth? It's an abomination!"

"Better an abomination than an Aged. You lot sicken me," Periwinkle sneered, and his face contorted as if a heavy stench assaulted his nose.

"We must all become Aged, Periwinkle," the man sighed, his voice cooled from its earlier heat. "You only do further damage to yourself by waiting this long. You pollute the minds of the Young with your rebellious deeds and speeches."

"I've made my choice. Being an Aged is not for me, nor do I think it is something that any Faë should aspire to be."

The judge smiled wolfishly, baring his yellowing teeth.

"Ah, but this choice will no longer be yours to make, not when Vermillion has assumed the throne. He shall make it law that *all* Faë must Change no later than the end of their second century." The man's smile broadened. "This is only the beginning, of course. He intends to mandate that any Faë over the age of ninety-nine who has not Changed will be imprisoned. Perhaps even put to death. His Majesty has not decided."

Periwinkle's face contorted with disgust.

"He would dare *force* a Faë to Change? And before his one-hundredth birthday? Has Vermillion gone mad?"

"Hardly," the judge replied with a sly grin. "He is merely performing his duties to protect the Faë." The smile faded as the judge raised a pale hand and pointed at Periwinkle.

"He is doing it to keep the peace. He is doing it to keep rebellious criminals like you from disrupting our way of life."

"Peace? Open your eyes, man. Vermillion doesn't want peace. He wants dominion! He wants control, not just over Faë like me but those like you as well. But he's already got that, hasn't he? Tell me, *Jay*, what price did you pay to gain that seat?"

Phinnegan noticed the judge shift in his seat.

"You know the price well, *Lark*," the judge sneered. Something in Periwinkle's question had struck home with the Faë who perched behind the bench.

"Aye, and it is a price I'll never pay. I'd rather I were a Mud."

The judge's eyes widened so quickly that Phinnegan would not have been surprised in the slightest had they jumped forth from his face.

"You go too far! You will show this court proper respect," he sneered. He stood, rapping his gavel three times upon the bench. A jury box materialized out of thin air to Phinnegan's right, accompanied by a tall dark-haired Faë. Stepping forward, this Fae unfurled a scroll and began to read.

"The High Court of Féradoon is now in session. The Honorable Julius Jay now presiding."

"You named yourself after a dead Caesar?" Periwinkle scoffed.

Although he had heard the expression, Phinnegan had never actually seen a man's face turn purple with rage - until now.

"Enough!" The judge bellowed, rising to his full height and leaning forward over the edge of the bench.

"This court will suffer no more of your useless banter. You will answer for your crimes before the Jury of Fédaroon."

Before he could comprehend what was happening, a hard wooden chair scraped across the floor, of its own volition. It slammed into the backs of Phinnegan's knees, forcing him to sit. Thick metal chains swung up from beneath the chair and clamped around his wrists.    Looking left, he saw that Periwinkle was now perched atop a small wooden platform, his hands likewise chained together in front of him, and his feet chained to a post that had arisen in the center of the platform.

With an air of satisfaction, the judge threw himself back into his chair.

"Proceed with the Reading of the charges."

# 1

## Judge and Jury

The tall, thin Faë with the dark-hair read the litany of charges with a nasal voice. He droned on for several minutes leveling charge after charge at the recalcitrant purple-haired Faë. When he finished speaking, Periwinkle glanced up at the Honorable Julius Jay, perched high above the dark bench.

"Is that all?"

The judge ignored Periwinkle's remark, and nodded to the Faë that had been reading the scroll.

"That will be all, thank you."

The dark-haired Faë bowed deeply in the direction of Julius Jay. When he rose he sneered at Periwinkle before vanishing right before Phinnegan's eyes. He wondered if he would ever get used to people appearing and disappearing right out of and into thin air.

High above, Julius Jay cleared his throat.

"You have heard the charges brought against you, Periwinkle Lark. You can save us all a lot of time by being honest from the beginning." He leaned forward, his hands gripping the edge of the bench as he peered down at Periwinkle.

"How do you plead?" Jay asked, his voice grim. Periwinkle met the Aged's bright blue eyes with the purple of his own and smiled a roguish smile.

"What evidence do you have of these crimes? If I am to enter a plea, I should know the particulars of what it is I am accused, don't you think?"

"The charges against you have been read for all present to hear. To what further evidence do you suppose yourself to be entitled?"

"Pfah! These charges are bogus, Jay, and you well know it."

The judge's face reddened and he spoke through tight lips.

"I will not remind you again to show this court due deference. One more slip and you will spend a week in the salt mines. Do I make myself clear?"

Periwinkle's smile vanished and he nodded his understanding.

"Is that a yes?" the judge asked, peering down at Periwinkle.

"That is a yes." He paused and seeing that the judge awaited his honorific, clenched his teeth and hurried the words forth.

"Yes, your Honor."

Julius Jay smiled. He leaned back in his chair, his hands folded across his chest and his fingers intertwined.

"Now. Again I ask you, how do you plead?"

"And again I respond, your Honor, that I wish to know more of the particulars of these crimes of which I am accused. Do you have evidence of these crimes? This treason of which I am accused, for example. Who dares to stand before this court and say that I, Periwinkle Lark, am a traitor to the Faë?"

"You wish to hear the evidence against yourself?" Julius Jay said with a smile. "Very well then." The judge ruffled through a stack of papers atop his bench and, pulling one out, he read a name aloud in a booming voice.

"This court calls Sextus Sparrow of the Aged, formerly known as Burgundy Sparrow, to appear before this court and offer his testimony."

Before Phinnegan could blink, a short, round little Faë with salt-and-pepper hair appeared before them, perched upon a small stage that now stood just beneath the judge's bench. Phinnegan, by this point discerning the pattern that all Faë belonged to a clan and that each clan bore the name of a particular bird, thought if any person looked to be a sparrow, it surely was Sextus Sparrow.

The small, round Faë was quite nervous. Whether this was his normal demeanor or a result of the sudden summoning that had brought him to this immense courtroom, one could not be sure. Beneath the shaggy salt-and-pepper hair was a round face to match the round body. He was dressed in a way that could only be described as foppish; a wrinkled drab brown jacket was buttoned askew across generous girth and the matching colored trousers were a few inches too short. He wrung his hands as he looked anxiously around the courtroom.

"Someone summoned me?" His squeaky voice matched his countenance in every way. High above, Julius Jay leaned over the front of his desk to get a good view of Sextus Sparrow.

"It was I, High Justice Julius Jay of the Court of Féradoon. You have been summoned here to give testimony against this Faë." He gestured to Periwinkle Lark, drawing Sparrow's attention to the defendant before him.

"Oh, my," he squeaked. "P-P-Periwinkle Lark?" He reached into the inside breast pocket of his jacket and removed a small pair of eyeglasses. Placing them atop the bridge of his nose, he leaned forward to get a better look. Recognizing his old friend, Sparrow jumped from the raised platform, landing awkwardly on the ground, yet keeping his feet beneath him. Before anyone knew what had happened, he had leapt to the wooden platform that held Periwinkle Lark. The round Faë threw his arms around the more lithe body of Periwinkle, chains and all.

"Oh it *is* good to see you, dear, dear Periwinkle! How long has it been, eh? Four decades? Five? Too long, I dare say!"

Even with the chains on his wrists and feet, Periwinkle was still able to smile and laugh.

"Too long indeed, mate. But, Burgundy, what has happened to the trim young Faë that scaled the cliffs of Hadek with me all those decades ago? You're a veritable boulder now!"

The brown-haired Faë laughed jollily as he hugged his old friend.

"I've put on quite a bit of weight, it is true. But being an Aged does that to you. Did you know that-"

"What is the meaning of this?" the judge interrupted, his voice incredulous and his beady blue eyes bulging wide and ready to pop. "Mr. Sparrow, you have been called before this court to provide testimony *against* the defendant, not make this sickening display of emotion and fraternization. Return to your place *at once*! And you, Accused, will refer to Mr. Sparrow by his proper name of Sextus Sparrow. He is no longer one of the Young and it is an insult to his person and to this court for you to address him as such!"

Sparrow reluctantly released his friend and turned to walk away, mumbling under his breath.

"I liked being called Burgundy."

Unfortunately for him, the judge had excellent hearing.

"Now, Mr. Sparrow. And if I hear language like that again I will find you in contempt of this court!"

Sparrow shuffled to the platform where he had appeared only moments before. Phinnegan felt sorry for him, for he seemed a genuinely nice person and clearly had a liking for

Periwinkle. As well, of the three Aged Faë he had seen thus far, Sparrow was the only one that still seemed to retain the friendliness displayed by Periwinkle.

Once Sparrow was settled in position, the judge resumed.

"Ahem. Mr. Sparrow, you have been brought before this court to testify on behalf of our Prince, and King-in-waiting, Vermillion Wren, who has seen fit to charge this court to bring the Accused, Periwinkle Lark, to justice for his high crime of treason against the Faë. You are hereby ordered to provide the exact details of the events which transpired on the eve of April 24 in the 57th year of the 72nd Neptune Cycle. Please proceed."

"Er, April 24th in the 57th year of the...what was it? 17th Neptune Cycle? April 24th...57th year...17th...I...I don't believe I was even alive during that cycle. Not even a glimmer in my mother's eye, I wasn't." The judge rolled his eyes and leaned forward over the bench railing, fixing his beady eyes on Mr. Sparrow.

"It's the 72nd cycle, Mr. Sparrow, not the 17th. I am quite certain that you were alive then, as were we all. Now, please proceed." But Mr. Sparrow was still confused.

"72nd Neptune Cycle, 72nd Neptune Cycle...umm, err."

With a heavy sigh, the judge pressed the fingers of his left hand to his temple.

"Mr. Sparrow, am I to surmise that you do not recall what transpired on the date in question?"

The round little Faë wrung his hands but shook his head.

"Not at all, Juliu- err, Your Honor."

"Then what seems to be the problem?" the judge asked, squeezing his temples.

"Well, I must admit that I don't often pay attention to exactly what year it is, so I, uh, well it makes it difficult for me to describe what happened on a particular date, seeing as I don't know when that was. Err, Your Honor."

The judge let his hand fall and once again raised himself to peer over the edge of his bench at the round, salt-and-pepper haired Faë. Phinnegan thought that as many times as he needed to peer over the edge of the bench, that perhaps he needed a smaller bench.

"Am I to understand then, Mr. Sparrow, that you do not know what year we are in?"

The round Faë laughed, not at all embarrassed.

"I'm afraid not. I never was one for numbers. Hard to keep track of the years and all, seeing as I have lived so many of them. I suppose that I cannot testify. Sorry old cha- err, Your Honor."

Periwinkle smirked and chuckled to himself, but the judge was not dissuaded.

"On the contrary, Mr. Sparrow. I am sure that we can in some way jog that memory of yours. I assume that even if you cannot remember exact dates, you can at least remember things that occurred in the last, say year or two?" Sparrow bobbed his head.

"But, of course!"

"Then would you please tell this court what events transpired on April 24th of last year."

"Err, my apologies, Your Honor," Sparrow said, raising a finger and shrugging his shoulders apologetically. "But I won't be able to do that."

"You mean you do not remember?" the judged asked, sharpness to his tone.

"It's hard to say really. It's the dates and all again." Sparrow shrugged his shoulders. "I'm no good with dates."

"Ah, to the devil with you! You cannot remember what happened on April 24th of last year?"

Sparrow rubbed his chin in thought for a moment before shrugging once more and dropping his arms to his sides in a heavy sigh.

"'fraid not."

"But this is preposterous! I have here in my very hand," and as the judge said this, he held up a cream-coloured parchment, "a sworn statement by you that you possess knowledge of what transpired between the Accused and a certain young Emerald Wren on April 24th, during the 57th year of the 72nd Neptune Cycle. Are you committing perjury?!?"

"Oh, no, I can tell you that. Why didn't you say so?" Sparrow regarded the judge with a look of curious innocence, the wide pupils of his eyes rimmed with only a thin trim of dark red iris. The judge's hand shook, and Phinnegan grimaced against the coming torrent he expected. But it never came. Instead the judge placed the paper back on top of his bench and motioned for Sparrow to speak, perhaps too upset to trust his ability to speak calmly.

"Shall I recount then?" Sparrow asked. The judge only nodded.

"Always happy to oblige the court, Your Honor. Now, where was I? Oh yes, the evening that young Master Periwinkle Lark and that beautiful young Faë Emerald Wren met for a drink at the Droopy Mushroom. I remember it like it was yesterday. When I heard from Janus Robin that he had heard from Brutus Magpie that he had seen Periwinkle and Emerald at the-"

"Wait," the judge interrupted. "Am I to understand that you did not actually *see* the Accused meet with Her Highness?"

"That's right, Your Honor. Shall I continue?"

The judge's face turned a deep shade of red and even from this distance Phinnegan could see his bottom-lip begin to quiver.

"Not exactly admissible evidence is it, Your Honor?" Periwinkle asked with a thin smile. The judge's lip trembled more violently until finally he slammed an open hand upon the table.

"Bailiff!" he yelled, prompting the thin, dark-haired Faë to reappear. "Please remove the charge of treason from the Accused's record, citing lack of evidence." The dark-haired man scowled at Periwinkle.

"Your Honor?"

"You heard me! Remove it. And take this *witness* with you when you remove yourself. The dark-haired man frowned and glared darkly at Periwinkle.

"Very well, Your Honor," the bailiff said, sneering once more in Periwinkle's direction. And then he vanished, as did Mr. Sparrow.

"Strike one, Your Honor," Periwinkle murmured.

# 8

# A Lack of Evidence

The next half-hour or so passed with further frustrations for the judge and Phinnegan began to have hope that the purple-haired Faë was indeed right that these charges were little but nonsense. Two more witnesses were summoned before the court to testify on two separate charges. But again, the judge was foiled.

Periwinkle remained in his chains for the duration of these questionings, a smirk on his face and only speaking now and then to taunt the judge whenever a snag in the judge's case became apparent. Phinnegan thought that in spite of his mounting anger, the judge showed remarkable restraint in the face of Periwinkle's jabs.

As the judge shuffled through his papers yet a fourth time, a member of the jury rose and cleared his throat.

"Ahem, err, Julius. I trust that somewhere in that stack of documents you do have at least *one* legitimate charge against the Accused?"

The Aged who had spoken was of middling-height with graying, brown hair cropped short. He spoke politely, but Phinnegan thought his voice betrayed a lack of sincerity and respect. "It would be gravely disappointing if you have succeeded only in wasting the time of myself and the remainder of this esteemed jury. Would you not agree?"

The Honorable Julius Jay clenched his teeth at the use of his familiar name by a member of the jury. He leveled a cold stare at the Faë who had questioned him.

"This court has sufficient evidence, *juror*, I assure you." The judge cleared his throat and looked back to his papers. Nonplussed, the juror spoke yet again.

"This evidence may be sufficient for you, perhaps, but it is whether this same evidence would be considered sufficient to we, the jury, that matters with regards to the predicament of the Accused. I am of course certain that a Faë and judge of your honor would have no need to be reminded that while it is the judge who presides and charges the Accused, it is the jury who casts the vote on his guilt or innocence, and when warranted, his punishment. I assure you that the jury would be quite happy to punish the Accused," he waved his hand in the direction of Periwinkle, "but only if the evidence so permits. I trust that this court at least has the appropriate evidence to have arrested the Accused thus and brought him here before the jury to pass judgment?"

The judge stared blankly at the juror. When at length he spoke, his voice was incredulous.

"Of course this court has evidence and the proper authority to arrest the Accused! Do you dare to question the motives and workings of this court?!?"

The juror only shrugged, a thin, tight smile upon his lips.

"The jury has no desire to delve into the motivations of the court. But the law is the law, and I, that is, *we*, the jury, would feel better if we were to see this evidence."

Phinnegan watched as the judge's face turned first to red and then to white as the color drained completely. His bottom lip began to quiver and when he spoke, his voice was tight and strained.

"Very well. The court will provide the evidence of the Accused's most recent crime, the reason for his arrest and incarceration, and the fomenter of this trial. Bailiff!"

Once again, the tall, dark-haired Faë appeared, and once again he held before him an unfurled scroll. He stared first at Periwinkle and then looked to Phinnegan, who had watched the tall Faë since he had first appeared. When their eyes met Phinnegan felt a chill run down his spine. He looked away and after a brief pause, the tall Faë began to read from his scroll.

"The Accused is hereby charged with the illegal use and activation of a wishing stone beyond the Boundary. The use occurred at approximately four-thirty in the afternoon, yesterday, near the forest outside Ballyknockan, County Wicklow, Ireland, being a part of the realm of Man, and therefore outside the Boundary. At the time of the Accused's illegal activity, he was in the presence of one human boy," and here the Faë paused and glanced at Phinnegan, who at this moment, felt quite small, "one Phinnegan Lonán Qwyk, who witnessed the activity of this stone. It is this court's position that the Accused activated said wishing stone with the knowledge that the human boy was present and indeed, with the express purpose of exposing him to the existence and capabilities of said stone. Therefore, this court has brought the Accused before a jury of Aged to determine the punishment to be handed down for his intentional actions, which, of course, endanger the whole of the Faë race and community, and run in direct opposition to the edicts agreed upon in the Counsel of Eagles, approved in the 32nd year of the 69th Venus Cycle. Thereby and therefore, the court asks that the jury impose the maximum possible sentence upon the Accused, up to and including," he paused, fixing a glare upon Periwinkle.

"Changing."

A hushed whisper spread through the jury, themselves veterans of the court of Féradoon, yet surprised by the severity of the requested sentence. Phinnegan had yelped when the bailiff had spoken, having already gathered that the Change these Faë spoke of was an important and personal manner. Yet, he saw that Periwinkle was little phased by this threat.

The judge smiled coldly, his gaze passing between the jury and Periwinkle, triumph written across his face.

"Is the jury satisfied with the reading of these charges and the evidence that this court has provided against the Accused? As you have now heard, not only did the Accused cause the activation of a wishing stone to occur beyond the Boundary, he allowed it to be seen by one not of our race, nor even our world. Further to this, he did so intentionally, baring the ways of the Faë to a human!" The judge slammed his fist upon the bench, fixing his bright blue eyes on each member of the jury one by one.

"I trust that we can now move forward without further questions, yes?" The judge smiled as he spoke thus, his yellowing teeth shining in the torch-lit chamber. The juror who questioned the authority if the court now stood and again bowed deeply in the direction of the bench.

"I beg the court's pardon, Your Honor. The jury is of course satisfied with this charge." So saying, the juror reclaimed his seat, casting a troubled glance in the direction of Periwinkle. The judge nodded in the direction of the jury.

"The court is pleased that the jury is satisfied with the evidence as presented. The court will now consider the charge – "

"Half a moment, if I may," Periwinkle interrupted, raising his hand with a clatter of chain.

The glowering face of the judge darkened as he regarded the purple-haired Faë.

"You wish to confess your guilt, perhaps, or beg for the mercy of the court?" he asked, although with little conviction in his tone. Phinnegan sensed that Periwinkle had one card left to play.

"Hardly," Periwinkle scoffed. "But I do have a question regarding the evidence that has been presented against me; a question which it is my right to ask."

"Oh, is that it then? What could you possible question? Do you deny the charges? Impossible. I am afraid that the dictations of time mandate that your request be denied. The jury has been patient enough through the...difficulties already experienced here today, and I will not further extend their duty by entertaining your lies. Your words would serve only to delay this court from performing –"

"Impossible? On the contrary, it is *very* possible. I do believe that my right to question the evidence presented is solidified in the case of Robin v. Cardinal, is it not? Need I go through the court's holding and reasoning in that case?"

Periwinkle smiled mischeviously and Phinnegan thought that he was quite calm for one who had, in his opinion, done exactly as the bailiff had recounted, which appeared to be a very high crime amongst the Faë. Phinnegan was sure that the Faë was doomed and had begun to wonder at his own fate. But it appeared as though Periwinkle was right, for though he grumbled and harrumphed, the judge pushed himself back in his chair and signaled for Periwinkle to continue.

"Thank you, Your Honor." Periwinkle turned to face the jury, a finger pressed into the dimple on his chin.

"I must confess that I am rather confused about one aspect of this court's case against me, and that aspect reflects on the question asked just earlier by you, good sir." He pointed to the juror who had stood to challenge the evidence.

"I am quite perplexed as to how it is that this court knew
I had activated the wishing stone."

The judge barked a laugh, clearly relieved by the
question.

"How we knew? Why, Periwinkle, I am surprised at you!
Could you not guess that given your record of rebellion and
crimes against his Highness that we would not be monitoring
your stone and other means of communication?"

Members of the jury snorted as they regarded the purple-
haired Faë, snagged by such a simple surveillance tool of the
court.

"You had all of the proper warrants to watch me thus, I
presume?" Periwinkle asked the judge.

"Of course," the judge replied, holding up a yellowed
document with a large wax stamp in the lower right corner.

"May I see it?"

The judge's eyes narrowed and he considered Periwinkle's
request for a brief moment before finally sighing heavily.

"I suppose it can do no harm. Perhaps it will convince you
to hasten the end of this nonsense." He leaned over the edge
of the bench, holding the parchment out to the bailiff who
reached up to accept it. He carried the paper to Periwinkle
who took it and studied it for a few moments before nodding
his head.

"Everything looks to be in order, for this stone at least.
However, where is the warrant for the other stone?"

"What do you mean the other stone?" a female member of
the jury questioned.

"Well, the warrant is for the stone owned by one
Periwinkle Lark, that would be me of course, but if the jury
would permit me a moment," he paused and dug his hand
deep into the pocket of his black trousers, which was no easy
task given the shackle upon his wrist. At length he produced
a round, white stone, which Phinnegan recognized as the

wishing stone he had seen in the clearing beside the wych elm; the very stone that had brought him to this strange place. Periwinkle held the stone up for all to see.

"If the court will indulge me but a moment?"

"Get on with it then!" the judge snapped.

Periwinkle held the stone before him in an open hand. He spoke clearly and loudly enough for everyone in the chamber to hear him.

"Spirit, who is your master?"

To Phinnegan's surprise, the stone spoke. A feminine voice, lazy and humming.

*My mistress is Emerald Wren.*

Gasps and murmurs spread through the jury and the judge banged his gavel on the bench.

"Quiet, I say! What devilry is this?"

"No devilry, Your Honor. You must know that a stone cannot be tricked to speak that which is not true. You have heard from this Spirit just as clearly as I have that it is not *my* stone."

The judge's mouth worked silently, opening and closing as his mind raced to find the words he sought.

"But...but, but this is preposterous! Do you expect this court to believe that –"

"I expect this court to believe nothing that is not true," Periwinkle replied. Turning to the jury he gestured with the stone in his hands

"You have all heard this stone speak the truth. The stone I carry is not my stone."

The male Faë in the jury who had questioned the court's authority earlier, stood and directed a question to the stone.

"Spirit, where were you last activated?"

The stone was quiet for a moment, a delay just the length one would need to ponder the answer to a rather simple question.

*Ballyknockan, Ireland.*

A second series of whispers passed through the jury, but the juror who stood waved for them to hold their tongues.

"Spirit, who activated you?"

Again a brief pause, and then the answer came.

*Periwinkle Lark.*

"There, you see!" the judge cried, rising from his chair and pointing a shaky finger at Periwinkle. "The stone has confirmed the truth of the charges. Jury, I order you to –"

"Not so fast," the juror said, raising a hand to forestall the judge.

"Silence! This nonsense is at an end," the judge bellowed. But again the juror interrupted.

"I am afraid that is all too true." He turned to face Periwinkle and with a heavy sigh and snap of his fingers, the chains on Periwinkle's wrists and ankles vanished.

"Periwinkle Lark, this court begs your pardon. You are free to leave. You will not be hindered."

The judge, his face purple with rage and his beady eyes now large and wide, yelled at the juror.

"What is the meaning of this! You hold no power to release the Accused. I command you to sentence this man as his crime befits!"

"We cannot punish him, Julius. It is over," the juror said. The judge laughed.

"The devil I can't! Bailiff, arrest that Faë!"

The members of the jury gasped at the judge's order to arrest one of their own. But the juror held his ground, fixing a cold stare upon the bailiff.

"Hold your place, bailiff. You know the law, even if *His Honor*, does not." He spoke the honorific with a sneer and then glared at the judge.

"The law?! He has broken the law! He has said nearly so much and the stone has confirmed what he hasn't."

"That may be true, but your warrant is invalid. The warrant was to survey the stone of Periwinkle Lark. This stone belongs to Emerald Wren. Unless you have a second warrant, you had no authority to arrest him, regardless of the fact that he *did* break the law, because your surveillance of that stone was illegal. I wonder, too, what His Majesty would think about this."

The judge's right eyelid twitched and his lips flubbed and blubbered as he sputtered.

"Th-that's preposterous! He is guilty, anyone can see that. For the last time, I order you to-"

The juror held up a hand.

"Do you have a warrant for the stone of Emerald Wren?"

Now completely flustered, the judge tore through the papers on his desk. Finding nothing he looked to the bailiff, who shrugged and cast his eyes to the floor. The judge looked back and forth between the bailiff and the juror.

"But..."

The juror sighed and gestured for his comrades to rise. He turned to face Periwinkle Lark, whose face now bore the wide grin of which Phinnegan had grown so fond.

"Free?" he asked, looking to the juror who confirmed with a grimace.

"Unfortunately."

Periwinkle wasted no time and as quick as a flash, had leapt from the wooden dais that had served as his prison during this short and ill-fated trial. He landed only a foot from Phinnegan, whose arm he grasped in his left hand.

Flashing one last grin in the direction of the judge, who stared in bewilderment at the events unfolding in the court of Féradoon.

"Until we meet again, Jay."

And then for the second time in only a few hours, Phinnegan and the purple-haired Faë vanished.

# 9

## A Place Beyond the Map

Phinnegan landed with a soft thud on a bed of bright-green grass, more lush than any he had ever seen, even in the rolling hillsides of Ireland. The air was thick with a sweet scent that he could not place, but that triggered a host of happy memories in his mind. He saw his grandfather on his 80th birthday. And then, the day when he first learned to ride a horse.

Memory after memory assaulted his mind, each more real and tangible than the last. His mind felt fuzzy and slow, but he did not care. He was happy, the tense hours spent in the mountain of Féradoon were far from his thoughts. Closing his eyes, he embraced the memories that filled his mind with happy pictures. His breathing slowed, and then slowed again. He felt very sleepy and felt himself longing for a nap, a promise of happy dreams awaiting him.

A hand grasped his arm, tugging. He resisted, but the arm pulled harder. The arm dragged him for a few inches on his back before he brought himself to his feet. A distant voice called to him, speaking his name and telling him to follow it, but his eyes were closed and he was lost to his dreams. But the hand would not relent and soon he felt himself being pulled forward, stumbling along in blindness.

After wobbling along for a few minutes guided by the unseen hand, his mind began to clear and he opened his eyes. The hand that held his arm was that of Periwinkle Lark. Phinnegan blinked several times, clearing the sleepiness from his eyes.

"What happened?" he asked with a yawn.

"Papavers."

Phinnegan withdrew his arm from Periwinkle's grasp and rubbed his eyes.

"Papavers? Is that a person?"

"Not at all, mate. It's a flower. They are mostly called dream flowers. Poppies, you would call them in your world, although poppies don't have the strength of these flowers. Papavers are quite dangerous if you haven't built up immunity to them, which most Faë have, before they Change, anyway. That's why I brought us here, in case any of those buggers thought they would try and follow. The Aged are very susceptible to the Papaver dream-sleep and it would have knocked them right on their arses before you could say your aunt was a boggart."

Phinnegan looked back over his shoulder, but he saw no sign of any flowers.

"I don't see any flowers."

Periwinkle turned and winked a bright-purple eye.

"That's because they are invisible. To you anyway; and to Aged. That makes them all the more dangerous. Faë never come here after they Change, it's too perilous. Only the Young venture here."

"What's this Change and Aged business? And why did those other Faë look so...*human*? And are you really over three-hundred years old?"

"Settle down, mate, settle down." The Faë's laugh was a beautiful sound, but it died on his lips as he surveyed the southern sky. Phinnegan followed his gaze to see a great red sun low in the sky and drawing closer to the horizon.

"Come on then, let's go. We'll be pushing sunset as it is."

"What happens at sunset?" Phinnegan asked, returning his attention to the direction of their travel. Periwinkle glanced back over his shoulder.

"Best you never have to find out, mate. Flowers aren't the worst of what's to be found out there. Crimson's place is a mile or so beyond the woods." He slowed to fix his gaze on Phinnegan over his shoulder. "And we *definitely* don't want to be in the woods at night."

"Is Crimson a friend of yours? And what's in the woods?"

But Periwinkle did not answer at first and the two trekked through the steadily heightening grass for several minutes before he responded.

"He's an acquaintance, shall we say. Friend may be a bit strong, but he owes me a favor, he does. And as for the woods, again, hope you don't have to find out."

They walked on for half an hour or more and Phinnegan nearly asked the Faë to answer the questions he had posed earlier. But something in the Faë's demeanor told him it was best to hold his tongue. He did not like Periwinkle being this silent. He had so many questions.

And he wanted to go home.

"When can I go home?"

The Faë missed a step, but recovered quickly and answered.

"All in good time, mate. That's one of the reasons we need to get to Crimson's."

After another hundred yards, they cleared the top of a small hill and there before them was the densest, blackest forest Phinnegan had ever seen. It was not green and beautiful like the forests of Ireland. The trees bore few leaves and the trunks were thick and gnarled. Remembering the Faë's warning, Phinnegan checked the height of the sun and saw that it had dipped nearly to the edge of the horizon. He spoke his concern to the Faë.

"Do you think we should go in there? It looks terribly...scary. And it's almost sunset."

"Well we don't want to be caught out here either. I think we can make it." He turned to look at Phinnegan, appraising him from head to toe.

"Can you run fast?"

Phinnegan, not the most athletic of boys, could, in fact, run quite fast. However, he did not like the fact that the Faë thought it important to ask that question.

"I can run," he said, pointing to the forest. "But can we even see in there? It looks almost black."

"Darkwater Forest. Nasty place, that. But as long as we stick to the path we'll be fine. No more than half an hour to the other side." Periwinkle checked the sun once more. "We should just make it. Come on."

Phinnegan strode forward to catch up with the Faë, who had sprung off with a gait that was quite fast but looked effortless as he moved towards the forest. In a minute or two they reached the forest's edge. Phinnegan tilted his head back, looking up to the tops of the trees, out of sight in a thick fog that was quickly forming high in the forest.

"That fog will be down here soon enough. Best be moving quick, like."

The Faë moved swiftly into the woods and Phinnegan took long, awkward strides to keep pace. The Faë's movements were nimble and he seemed to bound with each step. Phinnegan marveled at his grace, so much so that less than twenty yards into the woods, he caught his foot on an exposed root and went crashing to the forest floor. Periwinkle appeared at his side in a moment to offer him a hand.

"Watch your step, mate. And stay on the path. Whatever you do, *stay on* the path." Phinnegan opened his mouth to ask a question, but the Faë raised his hand to forestall him.

"Just do it. *Stay on the path.*"

Phinnegan nodded his understanding and then they were off again.

The forest was even darker than Phinnegan had expected from the foreboding presence it held from a distance. Looking up, he could only catch glimpses of the sky now and then. The setting sun provided just enough light for him to follow the Faë out in front and to mind the path.

They walked for some ten minutes or so, nearly half the time that Periwinkle had suggested it would take to cross the forest, before they heard the first howl. Phinnegan yelped when he heard it, a ghostly presence that seemed at once far away and right off the path. A second howl answered from the opposite side, sounding the same eerie, confused distance.

"I don't suppose that those are friendly, are they?" Phinnegan asked, the slightest bit of hope in his voice.

But the Faë shook his head.

"Faolchú are not exactly what you might call friendly. More like deadly."

"Faolchú? Wild hounds?" Phinnegan recognized the word as one his grandfather had taught him, his attempt to keep his country's native tongue from heading toward extinction.

"That's right. Their kind has infested Darkwater for centuries. Vicious, foul creatures; they hunt and kill anything that enters their forest. Exceedingly difficult to kill, they are, and impossible to escape amongst these trees. Though we Faë have a few tricks that will do in a pinch."

"Where did they come from?"

"The Devil himself if you ask me," Periwinkle said under his breath. He stepped lightly over a felled tree before turning to smile over his shoulder at Phinnegan.

"But not to worry. We'll be all right if we don't step off the path. They know we are here, but they cannot see us."

"Why not?"

"The path. An old Faë charm protects those that stay on it, at least while the sun's still out. It's sort of a camouflage. But their eyesight is much stronger in the night and they can make out movement even with the charm in effect." Pausing, Periwinkle checked the intensity of the light filtering through the gnarled treetops. "We should make it to the other side before nightfall."

Periwinkle continued on at a swift pace and Phinnegan thought that he did not seem very concerned about these Faolchú. Either they were not as bad as he made them sound, or the path really was protected. He would prefer to be out of the woods and not have to worry about it one way or the other.

Several more minutes passed in silence, and the forest became darker and darker still until Phinnegan could barely make out the path beneath his feet. He kept his gaze fixed on the Faë's silhouette, following in his footsteps. But Phinnegan began to feel nervous about the sun. He was sure that if it had not already set, it would do so at any moment. He looked up and what little glimpses of the sky he could see were nearly black. Looking back the way they had come, he saw the same darkness that lay ahead.

Then, out of the corner of his eye, he saw a lighter area in the distance. He turned and not one-hundred yards distant he could see the edge of the forest.

"Look," he reached forward and tapped Periwinkle. "We're almost through." Without a second thought, he took a step towards the light.

The first sound he heard was the sharp crack of a twig beneath his foot.

"What the hell are you doing?" Periwinkle hissed.

The second sound followed swiftly: the baying of hounds.

"Daggers! Did I not tell you to stay on the path!?"

"I...I was just heading for the forest's edge-" Phinnegan broke off as Periwinkle darted ahead of him, also off the path, in the direction of the faint light ahead.

"Don't just stand there. Run!"

Phinnegan didn't need to be told twice.

Branches tore at his skin and clothes as he ran, almost as if they had come alive to arrest his progress, delaying him just enough for the hounds to catch him. He paid them no mind, but felt the trickle of blood down his cheek where one branch had rent the skin.

He saw the Faë leap up ahead, and though he could not see why, Phinnegan gauged his distance behind the Faë and lept as well. His back foot just grazed something hard, a large rock or felled tree. He sprinted on, the Faë was still several strides ahead but Phinnegan maintained his distance.

The forest floor was softer here, soggy and like the beginnings of a bog beneath a thick covering of leaves. His feet made a sucking sound as he pulled them and placed them ahead one after the other. The terrain was slowing him down, as it was the Faë. The baying seemed closer, or was it just the pounding of his own heart in his ears?

Suddenly the Faë was struck by a moving shadow. He cried out as he hit the ground. Phinnegan was on him in a moment, nearly tripping over the Faë's body.

"It's no use now," Periwinkle said, his voice coming in a wheeze. "They've caught us."

Phinnegan, who now knelt beside the fallen Faë, raised his head to look around them. At least three sets of eyes shimmered in the darkness, their shadowy owners merely dark bulks moving in the fog that had now descended nearly to the forest floor. The baying had ceased some few moments ago, but was now replaced by the low rumbling growl of the wild hounds.

One hound, whose shadowy hulk appeared larger than the rest, inched forward. Phinnegan's heart raced and his breathing came in ragged gasps. He crouched down lower, but to no avail. There was nowhere to hide and hounds were behind him just as they were in front.

"What do we do?" he asked in a whisper, hoping the Faë had some trick up his sleeve that could save them from certain death. But his hopes were not to be answered.

"Nothing." The Faë pushed himself up onto his elbows, but did not try to escape.

"Welcome to a Place Beyond the Map."

# 10

## Nightmares

With the growl of the beast ever nearer, Periwinkle flicked his wrist and the same glowing orb that Phinnegan had seen on the first night when the Faë had broken into his home appeared in the Faë's hand. Phinnegan wished it hadn't.

"Faolchú," Periwinkle whispered, the fear apparent in his voice.

The light from the orb fell on the hound that was moving towards them, showing its fur to be short and red. Not the reddish-brown of a tame hound but darker, a rich red the color of blood and rust. The fur was missing in spots, revealing a white, translucent skin that glistened like the underbelly of a snake. Veins and arteries wove like blue and purple spider webs beneath the skin.

The leg muscles of the hound were long and sinewy, and they rippled with constrained strength as the hound crept nearer. The paws bore five toes, each with a short, but sharp, white claw. The hound had no tail and its ears were short and pointed and bore no fur. The snout was long and the jaw was strongly muscled. The hound's lips curled back in a snarl, displaying teeth that were stained yellow from either age or diet, and with gums bearing the same translucent skin as the body, blood vessels bulging beneath. The eyes were solid white, no pupil or iris, but Phinnegan could feel the gaze of the Faolchú appraising him.

Phinnegan held his breath as the hound leaned forward and sniffed at the boots of the Faë. Periwinkle pulled his foot back in surprise, drawing a low growl from the throat of the Faolchú. Phinnegan had never seen the Faë scared before, even when he stood before the court in Féradoon, but now he saw the light waver on the face of the hound as Periwinkle's hand shook with fright.

Around him, Phinnegan could hear the remainder of the pack inching closer. When one let out a short bark behind him, he felt the warm breath on his neck, and the fetid smell filled his nostrils. He swallowed hard, praying for a miracle.

"Can't you do some magic?" Phinnegan asked the Faë in a whisper. He was answered by a shake of the head.

"No, mate, not in here." The Faë sighed and sank lower against the ground.

"What about those tricks you mentioned?" Phinnegan hissed.

"Probably should have mentioned I didn't actually have any of those tricks about my person, like." Periwinkle swallowed hard. "We're as good as done."

Staring into the pupil-less eyes of the Faolchú, Phinnegan believed that the Faë was right.

"Haaalllooooooooooooooo," the voice called, an eerie crowing sound that drew the attention of the Faolchú. The ears of the largest hound in front of them perked as it turned its head in the direction of the sound.

"Haaaallllllooooooooooo," the call came again, and this time the hounds renewed their growl, but it was directed outwards toward the darkness of the forest. Phinnegan wondered if the pupil-less eyes could see far in night.

The growls turned to painful yelps as a bright searing light filled the forest. Phinnegan covered his face with his arm, shielding his eyes from the blinding light.

"Bíodh misneach agat, bráthair!" the voice cried in the distance. Bráthair? Phinnegan knew the word to be "brother" in Irish and he dared to hope that this was a friend. But he had little time to think on it, for Periwinkle was yelling at him.

"Take a deep breath, mate, and hold it!"

"What?" Phinnegan asked, confused by such a strange request.

"Just do it!" the Faë shouted, and by the deep gasp that followed Phinnegan knew he had held his own breath. He filled his lungs with air and held his breath. Not a moment later, the whistling sound of arrows pierced the night. He heard two thuds as the arrows struck the leaf covered forest floor around him, one each side of he and the Faë.

For a brief moment, the forest was quiet. And then a sharp hiss came from the directions of the two arrows. The hounds growled, but the growls were swiftly replaced by whimpers. He heard their feet on the ground as they stumbled away from the hissing arrows, but they did not make it far. Their bulky bodies crashed to the ground not more than a few yards from where Phinnegan lay.

He felt that more than a minute had passed, and his lungs burned for new air. But he guessed from the Faë's command to hold his breath, the hiss of the arrows, and the subsequent collapse of the Faolchú that whatever hissed forth from the arrows was poisonous.

He held his breath for far longer than he would have guessed that he could. When he opened his eyes, he found the forest once again only dimly lit by the scant sliver of moonlight that escaped the blotting net of the tree branches. He pushed himself up to his elbows and took in the scene around him.

Large shadowed bulks in the distance must have been the collapsed Faolchú. As he watched, he could see each body twitch.

As he listened, he still heard the hissing of the arrows, although very faint. He looked to the right and saw an arrow as long as his arm protruding from the earth. A wisp of smoke escaped from the earth where the arrow was embedded.

The sight of this smoke, which he imagined must be a very powerful poison, frightened him. He told himself that he must not breathe, but the burning in his lungs increased and at last, he gasped, expelling the spent air and refilling his lungs.

The burning in his lungs from the lack of oxygen was pale in light of what he now experienced. His eyes bulged and his throat tightened. He clawed at the ground with his hands and whirled his head to face the Faë. Periwinkle looked at him as if to say *I told you to hold your breath.*

And then he blacked out.

Phinnegan dreamed a dream like none he had ever experienced. He was not sure how he knew that it was a dream, but he did just the same. The eyes in his dream saw nothing but blackness, a cold blackness that chilled him to the core and made him shiver. He wondered if it was truly black or if his eyes were not open, but then when he exhaled, he could see the fog of his breath against the blackness.

For some few moments he lay in this cold, dark dream, longing for respite. But when the respite came, his dream became a nightmare.

His skin began to itch, just a little at first. But as he scratched, the itching worsened until he felt what were bugs of all types creeping across his skin. He swatted at his arms and legs, trying to brush the insects from him. But the itching only worsened.

When pale blue light appeared all around him, he looked down at his arms in horror. The crawling was not on his skin, it *was* his skin. He watched as the skin on his arms rippled and bubbled, as though a thousand insects were trapped just beneath, searching for the surface. He sprang to his feet, clawing at his arms to dispel the crawling insects.

*Please don't let it be spiders.*

A sharp laugh drew his attention, and he looked up to find the judge from Féradoon, Julius Jay, high atop his bench, cackling and pointing.

"What's the matter, boy? Something making your skin crawl?" The judge threw his head back, laughing maniacally. When the judge made a wave with his hand, Phinnegan felt a tug at his wrists. He looked down to see that a small hole had opened at each wrist. Out of each poured thousands of small spiders.

Knowing nothing else that he could do, Phinnegan screamed and tore at the skin on his arms. But for every handful of spiders he threw from his arms that many and more poured forth from his wrists. All the while, he heard the judge high above, cackling like a madman.

The itching worsened, and as he turned this way and that looking for something, anything, that could help him, he saw that the jury had now appeared. The Faë who had spoken out against the judge and had ultimately been responsible for Periwinkle's release stood staring at him, a long thin arm outstretched, a gnarled finger pointing directly at him.

Phinnegan froze, and for the moment, the itching ceased. He blinked and the scene around him had changed to replicate the High Court of Féradoon in every detail. When he noticed that his arms felt heavy, Phinnegan looked down to find the chains that had earlier been on Periwinkle's wrists, now on his own. But at least the spiders were gone.

The juror stood with a malevolent smile upon his face. As he stared, the Faë's face changed, the skin drawing tighter about the bones. The smile widened as the skin pulled the lips apart, revealing rotted, black teeth. When he opened his mouth to speak, the voice was guttural rasp.

"For your crimes against our race, I hereby sentence you to...death!"

A cry of jubilation erupted around him and Phinnegan whirled to see that the previously empty hall was filled with hundreds if not thousands of the Aged Faë, each with the same crackled skin that had overtaken the juror's face only moments before. They pressed in on him as they mumbled and crowed their approval of the ruling. High above, the judge's voice rang out, and it too was now a guttural growl.

"So be it!" The judge rose to stand and lean over the edge of his bench. Phinnegan kept his eyes fixed on the judge, even as the masses of decaying Faë closed in around him.

"Phinnegan Lonán Qwyk, you are hereby sentenced to Death by the High Court of Féradoon."

"By what manner shall we dispose of this criminal?" he continued, calling upon the masses to choose the form of execution for their prisoner. "Shall we take his head?"

Around him Phinnegan heard cries of yes as well as a few boos.

"To the axe!" one shouted.

"To the guillotine!" came the suggestion of another.

"Nay, neither is sufficient for this scum!"

"Hang him!"

The judge raised his hands to quiet the crowed, roaring in his guttural tone loudly to be heard above the fray.

"Some of you are not satisfied with beheading?"

Those in favor were now silent, as the naysayers called forth all manner of reasons that they preferred another form of execution. Phinnegan squeezed his eyes shut and did his best to ignore the screams around him. For a time, it had no effect. But then the voices began to recede and he felt his wrists lighten. He opened his eyes to see that his wrists were free. Looking around, he saw that he was no longer in the courtroom but was instead back in the middle of Darkwater Forest.

The forest was deathly quiet. No birds chirped, no rodents rustled in the underbrush and no breeze stirred the twisted branches of the tall, dark trees.

Phinnegan took a moment to scrutinize his arms for the wounds and blood that he knew must be there from his clawing, but he saw nothing. His arms were as smooth as any other day, and no spiders bubbled forth from his wrists. He reminded himself that he was in a dream, or at least he had been. Now he was back in the forest and the fantasy of the dream mixed with the last reality that he remembered.

Suddenly, the chill air returned and Phinnegan's breath turned to an icy fog. A branch snapped somewhere behind him and to the left. His heart skipped a beat and he feared to turn towards the source. Then came the sound of heavy breathing, forceful snorts and a low growl. Faolchú. Turning his head, he saw a Faolchú larger by half than those he had seen earlier. He could not possibly survive a fight with such a creature. So he ran.

The Faolchú stood transfixed for a few seconds, allowing Phinnegan to introduce some space betwixt himself and the beast. But then with a loud bark and a howl, the Faolchú hurled himself into the chase.

Phinnegan ran faster than he had ever run before in his life. He leapt over felled trees and rocks. Once he stumbled over an unseen branch buried beneath the leaves, but he kept his balance and ran on. In his peripheral vision, he caught sight of other Faolchú that had joined the chase, now running even with him some twenty yards away on either side. They snarled and barked at one another, communicating like no animals Phinnegan had ever seen.

Although he sprinted, the chase was soon over. The Faolchú were too fast by a large margin and they closed the distance to their prey in a matter of moments. The hound that came from the left hurled its bulk into Phinnegan, knocking him to the forest floor with a grunt. Pain seared through his leg and he thought that a Faolchú had bitten him. But looking down, he saw that his calf had landed on a sharp branch that projected from the underbrush, and that it had pierced through his pants and into his flesh.

The Faolchú crept closer and the scent of his blood on the air sent them into frenzy. They hurled themselves at one another with feral snarls and a great gnashing of teeth. But the large Faolchú who had been right behind Phinnegan was not to be denied. He proved his might to the other hounds, which now slinked to their place behind him, the leader of the pack.

His eyes were the same pupil-less white as the others, but he bore a long scar across his left and around his snout. Phinnegan's eyes raced over the hound's body and he saw more old wounds, so many that the red fur was practically hidden beneath the thick, white scars. This one had fought, and won, many battles.

The beast came forward and Phinnegan pushed himself backwards on his hands. The Faolchú bared his teeth, his lips curling upward in what would have been a smile, had the face been human and not that of a wild hound.

When the hound pushed back on his haunches, Phinnegan braced himself for the attack that was to come. The Faolchú's rear legs pushed hard against the earth and the hound leapt, jaws open.

Phinnegan heard himself scream.

When his eyes fluttered open, the world was washed out and bright. He squeezed his eyes shut to block out the light, and then slowly opened them so that only a sliver crept through. He felt himself bouncing, up and down, a natural rhythm to the motion. He rolled his eyes right and left and saw that he was no longer in the forest. The sky above was a dark purple, the hour just beyond sunset.

He felt support beneath him and after a few moments of clouded thinking, he knew them to be arms. He was being carried. His head rolled in the direction of the body that owned the arms which bore him. Looking up, he saw a pale face, the countenance one of youth juxtaposed against wisdom; the face of a Faë.

Atop the head a thick, tangled mass of dark red hair spilled forth. Sensing his stirring, the face looked down. Two bright red eyes shone from deep sockets. Even in his muddled state, Phinnegan could read worry plain on the Faë's face.

"Brostaigh," the Faë said, and Phinnegan felt the bouncing become more jostled. He felt himself slipping, and as his head rolled left against his shoulder, his last glimpse was the back of Periwinkle Lark, who jogged ahead into the darkness.

# 11

## A Friendly House

The next few days were an unrecognizable blur to
Phinnegan Qwyk, for his mind was not at all present in them.
He passed in and out of a restless sleep through morning and
night. His eyes opened only rarely, sightless and glassy.
Phinnegan heard a familiar voice speak to him now and then,
repeating the same phrase over, and over, and over, though
he knew not what it meant.

*"Tarraing anáil...Tarraing anáil."*

The two pairs of colorful eyes that watched over him grew
more distressed when their patient's lips moved, only to
repeat these same words. They watched over him, two vigilant
guards, knowing that behind the pale face the mind of their
charge wrestled with invisible demons. Had they been able to
see into his mind, as he lay in restless fits of sleep, they
would have seen that his mind was in angst, yet he dreamt
not. The nightmares that had assaulted him in the woods
after he inhaled the poisonous gas did not return.

On the fourth morning after their harrowing night in
Darkwater Forest, Phinnegan awakened, weak and
disoriented. A heavy scent of sweet, musky flowers filled the
air. The room was sparsely lit, and so his eyes accustomed
quickly. The ceiling was covered in wispy, intricate patterns
like none he had ever seen. Where was he? What had
happened? His mind panicked and he bolted up in bed, but

he was overcome with dizziness and crashed back onto the bed.

"Well, well. He returns from the dead after all. Gave us quite a scare you did; had a devil of a time just reminding you to breathe. "

Phinnegan recognized the voice as that of Periwinkle Lark, the purple-haired Faë who had broken into his home. The events of the previous day, at least to him it seemed like the previous day, came flooding back. The stone; Féradoon; the forest. The Faolchú. He tried again to push himself up.

"Take it easy, mate. Your mind is still recovering from the darkness brought on by the Fog."

Phinnegan lay still, turning only his head in the direction of the voice. There, of course, sat the purple-haired Faë, lounging in a large armchair, his legs thrown over one arm while his back rested against the other.

"Fog?" Phinnegan asked, rubbing the sleep and grit from his eyes. "What does the fog in the forest have to do with anything?

"Not fog, Fog, with a capital F. The gas that you saw coming from the arrow; it's called the Fog. It's a damn good thing you held your breath as long as you did. A few moments earlier and," the Faë made a strangled sound and drew a finger across his neck.

"I waited as long as I could...my lungs were burning."

"I know, I know." Periwinkle said. "Crimson never would have done that if he had known."

"Known what?"

"That you were human, like," Periwinkle said, stroking his chin as he mused. "Although I don't know how he would have gotten us out of there without the Fog."

"Did it kill them? The Faolchú, I mean." Phinnegan pushed himself slowly to a sitting position.

"Hardly," the Faë said with a laugh. "It would take a lot more than a lungful of Fog to kill a Faolchú. They were only knocked out, and just barely at that. Up and about in a matter of minutes would be my guess. Not the same can be said for you, of course. We thought we'd lost you. If Crimson hadn't lived so close..."

Phinnegan sat in silence as the Faë's voice trailed off. He had been only moments from meeting his death. That was a disturbing thought for a twelve year old. A fit of coughing snared him and only ended when Periwinkle brought him a glass of water.

The water tasted sweet and smelled of cinnamon. He drank the glass quickly, wiping his mouth with the back of his sleeve. The Faë laughed as Phinnegan put down the empty glass.

"Taking a liking to the pixie water, are you? Well be careful, it's a powerful healing elixir, but it is also mildly hallucinogenic. We don't want a relapse."

Phinnegan grasped the empty glass and peered into it, his stomach queasy as he was reminded of the nightmares that came to him in the forest.

"Is that what those...nightmares were then? In the forest? Hallucinations?" The Faë nodded.

"Aye, Fog is a very powerful hallucinogen. The mind can only take so much; particularly when the mind is unaccustomed, as yours would be. Like I said, if we hadn't gotten you back here so quickly it may have been too late."

Phinnegan felt his fear turn to anger within him and he lashed out at the Faë.

"Well why did you give me this pixie water? Haven't I had enough hallucinogens?"

The Faë only shrugged his shoulders, walking back to his chair near the foot of the bed.

"Like I said, pixie water has strong healing qualities. It's a calculated risk. Besides, it's just like a good night of drinking. On the morrow, sometimes the best thing for you is another drink."

Phinnegan remembered more than one occasion when his father had awakened on a Sunday morning after a long night at the pub only to head straight to the cupboard for a dram of whisky.

Thinking of his father reminded Phinnegan of his home. And recalling home only reminded him of how much he missed it. He wondered if his parents were worried about him. How could they not be? Their son had disappeared with no warning and without as much as a trace. He imagined his mother sitting by the fire, her head in her hands as she sobbed. His father stood behind her, his strong hand resting upon her shoulder. They would be devastated. How long had it been?

The sudden realization was that he did not know.

"How long was I...asleep?" he asked, his head lowered as he continued to long for his home and his family. The Faë mumbled to himself as he counted the days.

"Let's see, one...two...three. Yes, this is the fourth morning after the night that we arrived at Crimson's. That would be the same night that we were attacked by the Faolchú in the forest."

Phinnegan felt a knot tighten in his stomach.

"And before that? How long were we in Féradoon? How long since that stone snatched us from Ireland and brought us to...well wherever it is that you are from."

"We were barely in Féradoon for a night," the Faë responded. "So I would say four days at the most. And this," the Faë spread his arm out towards the walls of the room, and Phinnegan assumed he meant to gesture to the world as a whole. "This place has many names. By some it has been called Hy Breasail, by others Tir-nan-ōg. It has been called the Plain of Happiness, the Land of the Living and the Isle of the Wee Folk." The Faë paused and his brows drew down in annoyance.

"I'm not too fond of that last one. But never mind that. To us Faë, it is simply Home. We need no name to describe our world, for any Faë has only to say that they wish to go Home, and all others know what he means. But to your kind, for those lucky enough to set forth in our world, it is best known as a Place Beyond the Map, for it exists completely outside of your world. So if anyone ever tells you they've been to a Place Beyond the Map, you know they really have."

"How would I know they actually came here?"

"Simple. This is the only place where they would have heard it."

"Well what if I went back and told someone that name? Wouldn't they know?"

"Not so fast," the Faë said. "Did I forget to mention that a person such as yourself cannot utter those words to another person who has not yet been here himself?"

"You did fail to mention that, yes."

"Ah well, there you have it then. Bit of a security measure, like."

"Oh."

Such a short response seemed to perplex Periwinkle.

"What's the matter, mate? No questions? Not like you, that."

Phinnegan raised his head briefly to meet the purple eyes of the Faë.

"I want to go home."

"Ah. That's it then, isn't it," the Faë said, dropping his head and staring at his own lap. He sighed and then spoke quietly.

"About that..."

Phinnegan's head snapped up, which made him dizzy for a moment, but it passed quickly. Had he heard the Faë's tone correctly? It sounded...apologetic. He fixed his eyes on the purple-haired crown of the Faë's head.

"What do you mean 'about that'? I can go home, can't I?"

The Faë remained silent for several moments, all the while Phinnegan continued to stare at the top of his head. Phinnegan opened his mouth to speak again, but closed it when he heard the Faë's quiet voice.

"Yes, of course you can go home....in theory."

Phinnegan could not restrain himself.

"In theory?!" he exclaimed, his heart racing. "What do you mean 'in theory'? I want to go home!" His voice had risen to a yell as he spoke, making the silence before the Faë spoke again all the more deafening.

"Well, it's...err...it's complicated." The Faë looked to Phinnegan, spreading his hands apologetically. Phinnegan didn't know what to say. He wanted more than anything to just go home and now he was being told that *in theory* he could go home, but that it was *complicated*. He felt trapped, stuck in this fairy tale land and the only person who he knew at all was apparently useless.

"We should talk to Crimson," the Faë said at length, standing up and smoothing the wrinkles from his cream-colored trousers. As always, they were trim and snugly fit, while his purple-colored shirt swished with his movement. The cream colored buttons that ran up the center of the shirt were large and smooth.

"Will he know how to get me home?" Phinnegan asked, hopeful that the other Faë had more ideas than this one.

"He may," Periwinkle replied, pausing for a moment before continuing. "But like I said, it's complicated."

Phinnegan made a move to get himself out of bed but the Faë cautioned him against it.

"No, mate. You stay here. I will bring him to you. No sense in you running all about and weakening yourself even further," Periwinkle said as he left the room.

Despite the nagging tug in the pit of his stomach as he longed for home, Phinnegan was able to distance himself from that feeling long enough to take in his surroundings. The sweet, musky smell remained heavy in the room. He noticed several large bouquets of red flowers in various places around the room. The room itself was a simple square with a large window on both the left and right side. The bed in which Phinnegan rested was against one wall, and the only door in and out of the room was directly across on the far wall. The ceiling was high and was plastered a cream color like the walls. Thick, darkly colored exposed wood beams crossed each other on the ceiling. From what he could see, the floor was a similar dark colored wood. With the exception of the strange, sweet smell, the room looked like any that he would have seen back home. But of course, he wasn't at home.

Several more minutes passed before the door across from Phinnegan's bed opened and swung inward. Periwinkle entered first, his light purple eyes meeting Phinnegan's for a brief moment before he looked away. He was followed by a second Faë, who Phinnegan surmised must be Crimson. He had a pale face, much like Periwinkle, but it appeared even more so because he was dressed in all black. His hair was a rich red and this Phinnegan recognized from the forest, the Faë who had carried him from near death in the woods to the home and bed where he now rested.

A flicker of movement behind Crimson drew Phinnegan's attention, and he was startled to see a short, squat creature with dark skin, large ears and a large nose. Phinnegan thought that it was one of the ugliest things he had ever seen. The small creature carried a large book, several inches thick and obviously very heavy. The creature swayed to and from beneath the weight of the book, trying its best to follow in the footsteps of the Faë. When the Faë stopped in front of the bed, the creature also stopped, but Phinnegan saw it grimace beneath the weight of the book.

"Crimson," the purple-haired Faë said as he stopped at the foot of Phinnegan's bed, turning back to speak to the red-haired Faë. "Allow me to properly introduce our guest, Phinnegan Qwyk, of Ireland.

The red-haired Faë stepped forward and bowed in Phinnegan's direction.

"Pleasure to meet you. I am called Crimson Grouse, renowned scholar, sage and entertainer extraordinaire. My home and my person at your service, of course."

"Sage?" Periwinkle scoffed with a laugh. "Pulled that one right out of your arse didn't you?"

"Too much? I've been playing with that one. Trying to find a title that suits me and my, er, talents."

"Well keep looking."

The two Faë shared a laugh. Phinnegan cleared his throat and the two turned their attention back to him.

"Pleased to meet you as well," Phinnegan said, pushing himself up and forward on the bed. "Are you his brother then?"

"What?" Crimson said, a puzzled look on his face.

"When you rescued us, you called him brother. You said 'bráthair'."

"Ah, know a bit of Gaelic, do we?" Crimson said with a smirk. "But I am afraid you have confused bráthair, fraternal, with deartháir, a brother of blood."

"Oh," Phinnegan said. "I never knew there were two words for 'brother'. What was the rest then?"

"The rest? Bíodh misneach agat? It means 'take heart'; and so you would have had you known such a cunning Faë was your rescuer!"

"I see. Well, can you get me home?" The red-haired Faë smiled, displaying perfect, white teeth.

"You don't waste any time, do you? Right to the point. I like it. Far too much time is wasted on silly pleasantries and talking about the weather. Speaking of which, you have missed three beautiful days while you have been in your Fog-induced state. Clear blue skies and warm sunshine."

Crimson paused and cleared his throat.

"But I suppose none of that matters. You just want to go home. Although, I cannot fathom why anyone would want to leave such a place as this," he paused waving his arms around the room, gesturing to their surroundings, assumedly meaning the outside world and not this plain room. "But I understand that your circumstances are not such that you can bring yourself to enjoy our world. You want to go home. Yes, definitely understandable.

"Yes, I would. Can you send me home?" Phinnegan asked, the fact that his hopes all rested on what Crimson would tell him was plain in his voice.

"Well, it's a tricky thing, sending you home that is. I trust that Periwinkle has warned you thus?"

"He said it was complicated."

"Truly," Crimson responded with a grimace.

"Why?"

"That's easy enough. You – as in a human – are not meant to come to our world. Thus, the way to get back is not so easy."

Phinnegan thought about the words of the Faë for a few moments before responding.

"Why can't I go back the way I came? Through the wishing stone. Can't we just do that?"

"Not that simple I'm afraid." Crimson reached into his pocket and pulled out the smooth, white stone that had started Phinnegan's abduction to this world.

"This stone," he flipped the stone to Phinnegan who caught it reflexively, "isn't what brought you here. Vermillion's thugs brought you here, albeit while using the stone as a sort of locator. But on its own, it does not have the power to take you back to your world. It probably cannot even take you anywhere within our own after what Periwinkle did with it."

"You mean by bringing us here to, umm, wherever it is that we are now?" Phinnegan asked. He suspected that whatever Periwinkle had done to get them out of Féradoon had been very difficult.

"Yes, quite," Crimson said with a nod. "Féradoon is a powerful place and the power that the wishing stone would have had to hold to drive the Gate likely burned it out. We can't know for sure until a few more days yet. It takes up to a week for the stone to recover from that kind of power outlay, if it will even recover at all."

Phinnegan turned the stone over and over in his fingers while he listened to the red-haired Faë destroy every avenue of which he was aware that could lead to his escape from this world.

"Can't one of you just do a bit of magic, then? Send me home, like?"

The two Faë shared a glance and then it was Periwinkle that spoke.

"Possibly...but it would take the combined abilities of the two of us and even then there would be great personal risk to both of us. Not to mention you. Opening a Gate for travel to your world is hard enough to do for ourselves, if you recall me telling you how the Passes are narrowing and all. But to open one for another, and for a human at that..."

"Nearly impossible," the red-haired Faë finished his kinsman's thought.

Phinnegan lowered his head and stared at the blanket that covered his legs. Tears welled in his eyes but he refused to cry.

"I guess I must stay here forever..."

"You say it like it's a prison sentence!" Crimson exclaimed with a smile. "But do you not realize the opportunity before you? Humans in our world are few and far between. You can see wonders that you have never dreamed of..." Crimson's voice trailed off and the only sound in the room was the muffled sniffle as Phinnegan pulled the back of his sleeve across his face.

"I just want to go home..."

Crimson's face fell at the sound of the young boy's voice. He bit his lip and turned to Periwinkle. The two Faë put their heads together and spoke in hushed whispers for a few moments. And then they bent down and whispered with the ugly little creature that carried the big book. With a nod, the creature lumbered across the room to a stool, the right height for a table to a person of his stature, and sat the book on top. He wiped his brow before using both hands to lift the cover of the book. Running a knobby-knuckled finger down the page, he appeared to be searching for something. At length, he stopped and then flipped furiously through the book until he was very near the center. Here he stopped and beckoned to the two Faë.

Phinnegan had not been paying attention to the activity around him, but the extended silence began to weigh on him. He lifted his head and was perplexed to see the two Faë bending over the large book, the creature pointing and gesticulating wildly, speaking to them in a gravely whisper. Phinnegan could not make out the words, and was not sure if they would have been in a language that he could recognize had he been able to.

The three stood over the book for some time before Crimson finally straightened and began to pace back and forth in the middle of the room.

"It just might work," he said to no one in particular, yet Periwinkle either assumed the comment was directed at him or felt the need to respond in some way.

"It's not without its risks, but aye, it could work at that."

The creature interjected now, and Phinnegan was right that the words were nonsensical to him. But Crimson nodded furiously.

"Good point, Daga, good point. But we still have to get in. We can't just walk right up and say 'how do you do, might I explore your castle?' Not going to work."

The creature grumbled and crossed his arms, his suggestion evidently a good one, but not without its difficulties.

"Well hold on, mate," Periwinkle said, pulling a roll of parchment from an unseen pocket. "We might be able to just walk in at that." He handed the parchment to Crimson who cast a wary look before taking the parchment and unrolling it. As he read, a smile spread across his face.

"Brilliant! What luck!"

The red-haired Faë read the parchment a second time and then again for a third. When he finished, he handed it to the creature who read through it quickly. He too, smiled, or something like it. He cackled and uttered a few words which drew a laugh from Periwinkle.

"You're right at that. And we've just enough time to make it." He glanced at Phinnegan, who looked in wonder back and forth between the Faë and the creature. "Can he make it, you think?" Periwinkle asked, directing the question to Crimson.

"I'd wager that he can. Phinnegan, dear friend, we have quite possibly come across a way to get you home. But we've no time to lose and we have a long way to go. Can you handle it, you think?"

Phinnegan pushed the blanket back, which made him only slightly dizzy. He sputtered as he rushed his words.

"Ye...yes, I can." He paused to let the dizziness subside. "I...uh, I can't run but I can walk. I think...Where are we going? What have you found out?"

"Don't worry about running. We can't run there even if we wanted to. We've about a mile to the bridge. Can you walk that far?

"I...I think so."

"Good. Periwinkle and I can help you along if need be. Once we're to the bridge, it will be easy enough. Any good at riddles?" Crimson asked, casting an amused glance in Phinnegan's direction.

"What do riddles have to do with anything?"

"The troll, of course. I'm not about to pay if I don't have to."

"Troll?! But trolls are mean and...don't they eat people?"

The creature made a horrible gurgling sound just as Phinnegan asked this question. When he looked at it closely, he saw that it was laughing.

"You've heard too many stories, mate," Periwinkle said in between chuckles. "We'll be fine. But we must hurry."

"I don't understand! Why are we going to see a troll?"

"You'll see soon enough," Periwinkle called over his shoulder as he rushed from the room.

"But...!" Phinnegan shouted as he stumbled from his bed. "What is going on?"

"I'll explain on the way. We must hurry!" Crimson placed a hand firmly on Phinnegan's arm and steadied him as the two of them scurried from the room.

"Where are we going?"

"We, my friend, are going to Castle Heronhawk."

# 12

# The Troll Under the Bridge

They were quite a curious bunch, this group of four that set out at a brisk pace from the quaint cottage of one Crimson Grouse. The ruby-red-haired Faë led the way, a fine gray cloak now draped across his shoulders, billowing in the breeze. Behind him walked the flashy Periwinkle Lark, resplendent in a cloak of shimmering silver and a great black hat with a large purple feather tucked beneath the band. Leaning against him stumbled Phinnegan Qwyk, whose common cream shirt and worn brown trousers looked out of place beside the finery of the purple-haired Faë. In the rear waddled the stout little creature, naked save for a ruddy brown cloth that was draped over his body, resembling a brown sack with holes cut for his head and arms as much as a piece of real clothing.

Phinnegan, despite asking many questions as they made their way along the wide dirt road, had learned little about where they were going and why. Crimson had only deigned to say that they were going to the bridge and that this road led just there.

Periwinkle mumbled under his breath as they moved along, apparently searching his tricky mind for a riddle. Phinnegan wondered if Crimson was doing the same.

Sighing, Phinnegan let his mind follow his eyes, and wander across the countryside. He focused on the sweeping meadow that spread out from the road to their right. It covered the landscape as far as the eye could see with only a tree here and there to break the continuity.

He tried his best to ignore the left side of the road, for it was here that the edge of Darkwater Forest crept dangerously close to their path. But try as he might, the woods drew his eyes. When his gaze wandered to the dark tree line, he thought he saw more than one pair of eyes gazing back. Whether they were real or more hallucinations, he neither knew nor cared. But either way, he did not look upon the forest again.

As they walked, Phinnegan grew tired. This was the longest mile that he could ever remember walking, and he had walked a great many. But just when he thought to open his mouth and ask how much further it would be, the sound of rushing water reached his ears. Water likely meant a river, and where there was a river, there was bound to be a bridge.

"Almost there," Crimson called back over his shoulder. Phinnegan looked around but saw no evidence of any water, yet the sound grew louder and louder. When he and the others caught up to where Crimson had halted some moments before, he saw why no river had been visible.

They stood at the top of a small hill, or what had seemed a small hill when they had begun to climb it. But it was no hill at all. When Phinnegan reached the top he saw that it was instead a cliff. A narrow staircase began just at its edge, a few steps beyond where Crimson had stopped. The steps descended back and forth down the side of the cliff. Looking up and out, he saw perhaps a hundred yards away another cliff.

"Where's the bridge?" Phinnegan asked.

"Down there," Crimson said, pointing over the edge of the cliff.

"You mean we have to go down those stairs?" Phinnegan asked as he crept to the edge of the cliff and peered down. His knees wobbled. The bridge was indeed down there. *Very* far down there. He guessed the river must be at the very bottom of the chasm, and that the bridge was somewhere in between.

"It's not as bad as it looks. Just don't look down," Crimson said with a wry smile. "Come on then," he scolded as he led the way down. Periwinkle followed quickly behind him, looking back over his shoulder to catch Phinnegan's eye.

"Careful, mate. Stay close to the wall and you'll be fine. It's not as bad as it looks, honestly."

The four began their descent with Crimson and Periwinkle almost bounding as they swooped down the old and crumbled staircase. Phinnegan was more cautious, both because he still felt weak and also because he was scared he would fall to his death. There were no railings to protect a careless traveler from falling into the great abyss, nor was he as surefooted as the two Faë. He kept a hand on the wall to steady himself as he made his way down. The two Faë stopped now and then giving Phinnegan and the creature a chance to catch up. The creature was also slow because his short legs demanded it.

Despite Crimson's earlier assurance that they were not that far from the bridge, the descent took a half an hour. Phinnegan had maintained his balance for the most part, slipping only twice on his way down, but both times the creature had snickered behind him.

Phinnegan did not care for this little creature, not one bit.

When the final two reached the bottom they found the two Faë waiting for them.

"All right, all in one piece?" Crimson asked as he checked them all for any signs of trouble on the way down.

"Well enough it seems. You All right there, mate?" Periwinkle asked.

"Yes. I'm just tired."

"I'm sure you are. You should probably still be in bed, but that can't be helped. The physical part is over now. Although the hard part lies ahead."

"And what's that?" Phinnegan asked, still a bit short of breath from the climb down.

"We've got to make our way past the troll, of course. Used to be that you could just buy your way with some pretty thing, but now they practically want half your fortune – or your firstborn. Riddles are the only way to go now." Crimson cast a glance at Periwinkle. "Have you got a good one, then?"

"Fantastic. Just you wait."

Phinnegan, who had never before seen a troll, was frightened by the prospect. Trolls were large and ugly. They were strong, stupid and they ate people, particularly those that tried to cross their bridge. He voiced as much to the two Faë, as he had done before they left Crimson's cottage, but again he was met with laughter.

"You really *have* read too many stories," Crimson said, a hand over his mouth to stifle the dying giggles.

"Well what's a troll like then?"

"They aren't snarling huge beasts with tusks and cyclopean eyes!" Periwinkle joked, raising his arms over his head and pretending to be a monster, much to the delight of Crimson.

"Or would you prefer them to have big hairy bellies and fingernails like talons, as long as knives!"

"I've even heard the stories of little goblin trolls who work black magic," Periwinkle said in a quiet voice.

"That's not funny. Everything I've read says they are…"

"Ah, to the devil with your books," Crimson said. "You are about to meet a real troll. And I wager it will be nothing like you expect."

Phinnegan by now was growing angry at the jokes the two Faë shared at his expense. He frowned and crossed his arms over his chest.

"All right then, where is it?"

"Just over there," Periwinkle pointed down a slight embankment to where the bridge began. "Just under the bridge." He turned and walked toward the bridge. Crimson followed, as did the waddling little creature. Phinnegan had no choice but to bring up the rear, that or be left behind.

When they reached the edge of the bridge, Crimson headed for a rough hewn set of stairs that led down beside the bridge and then curved underneath. Phinnegan did not like the idea of going underneath the bridge, where he was still certain a monster would lurk.

"Must we go down there? Can't it come up here?"

"Well there is one very good reason why *it* cannot, and I am certain in all of your reading you have come across it. Probably the one truth in the bunch. Now what could that be eh?"

Periwinkle stood and stroked his chin while Phinnegan struggled to come up with an answer.

"Oh, of course. Sunlight! So that bit's true, then? They can't come out in the sunlight or they turn to stone?"

"Yes, that bit is. And likely the only thing in that rubbish you humans thought up that was." Periwinkle waved for Phinnegan to follow.

"Come on then, let's get started. This could take awhile."

Still afraid, although comforted by the fact that the troll could not chase him into the sunlight, Phinnegan shuffled behind Periwinkle, who was behind Crimson, the red-haired Faë already having gone under the bridge.

When Phinnegan reached the bottom of the stairs and looked around, he saw no troll. At least, he didn't think that he did. What he *did* see was a most beautiful woman. He was young and not overly taken with the prettiness of girls. Yet still, he knew beauty when he saw it, and this woman was perfection in every detail.

"Where's the troll?" Phinnegan asked.

Periwinkle smiled and nodded his head in the direction of the woman.

"She's right there."

Phinnegan's eyes grew wide and he looked from the smiling face of Periwinkle to the face of the beautiful woman. He looked at Crimson, who was stifling a giggle, and then returned his gaze to the woman. And then he just stared.

Her long, straight hair was a more natural red than the ruby color of the Faë. She was tall and slender, more than a foot taller than either Faë. She wore a white dress with long sleeves that were cut tight about her arms, and then flared at the wrists. Her skin was pale, with a flush in her cheeks that offset the blue brilliance of her eyes.

Phinnegan shook with a start when she tilted her head and looked at him. Her eyes swallowed him whole and he felt that she was peering into his soul. It made him rather uncomfortable. At length she spoke, directing her statement to Crimson, who stood just beside her.

"He's human. You know they will never let you in the castle with a human. Too dangerous." Her lips curled in a wicked smile, her eyes still fixed on Phinnegan.

"Why don't you just give him to me? What could two Faë and a bogle need with a human at Castle Heronhawk?" She grinned slyly in Periwinkle's direction. "Unless you were planning to steal something."

Phinnegan expected Periwinkle to laugh at the jest, but he remained quiet and looked to Crimson. Phinnegan found it odd that Periwinkle behaved in this manner, given that they possibly couldn't be going to steal anything. Although, he had no idea why they were going to the castle. He wondered if the woman, no, the *troll*, could be right. Crimson's voice distracted him from his thoughts.

"Now, now. What a horrible thing to say about two upstanding Faë such as us! Here we are just trying to show our young friend here a good time and you-"

"Well, why is he here then?" The troll strode over to Phinnegan, walking around him and putting her hand atop his head. Her touch was light and soothing.

*I can't believe that this is a troll.*

"He's here so that we can take him to the castle."

"No. Why is he *here*, in this world? It is against the laws of your people to bring a human into this world. Have you forgotten? What's to keep me from capturing the lot of you and handing you over for a nice reward, hmmm?" She gave Phinnegan's hair a playful tousle. "Except for this one of course."

Phinnegan felt a shiver run down his spine.

"He's here and that's all that matters. And he is not for sale."

She grumbled and removed her hand from Phinnegan's head, a bit more roughly than he felt was needed.

"Well what have you brought me then?" She snarled, her sweet voice taking on a sinister tone. "Gold? Jewels? I live in a land of treasure. Your paltry riches do not interest me."

"Nay, none of that. We come to offer you a riddle."

"Oh! A riddle is it? Well, that's an entirely different thing then." The troll's pleasant voice had returned and she looked upon the two Faë with a smile.

"I love riddles. Name your terms." She seated herself on a large boulder just under the edge of the bridge and folded her hands across her lap, looking up expectantly at Periwinkle and Crimson.

"If we win, you agree to send us up. No strings attached."

"Done. And for me?"

Crimson hesitated.

"For you...name your terms."

Smiling, the troll turned to face Phinnegan.

"I want him."

Phinnegan backpedaled away from the troll and bumped into Periwinkle who had moved around behind him.

"I should say not!" he said in the strongest voice he could muster. But he felt Periwinkle's hands upon his shoulders, light and delicate but with unseen strength. He flashed a grin to the troll.

"Half a moment, if you please." When she nodded, Periwinkle spun Phinnegan around to face him and looked him in the eyes.

"Listen, mate," he spoke in a whisper. "It's either this or you are stuck here. There's only one way out for you and that way lies past this troll. She's taken a liking to you and she's dead-set on having you if she can get her way."

"Well I'm not game. Tell her to pick another *prize*." Periwinkle's grip tightened on his shoulders and he could tell that the Faë was biting back his anger when he spoke.

"Look here, now, we've put ourselves in a bad spot. She knows you are here and she is right: you are not supposed to be. I got us out of Féradoon on a technicality, but if we are caught out here, all bets are off. She'll turn us in if we back out now."

"Well stop her then. We can just make a run for it across the bridge."

Periwinkle shook his head.

"Nothing for it, mate. She's got more magic in her little finger than me and Crimson put together. Besides, we don't need to go across the bridge anyway."

"Well where do we want to go then?"

Periwinkle turned Phinnegan back around and pointed to a small door that was at the base of the bridge amongst the rocks.

"That's where we want to go. And she'll never let us pass and we don't have the power to muscle our way through. It's this way or no way. Back to Féradoon, likely."

Phinnegan didn't like the feeling that he had been brought here without any explanation and now had no chance of turning back. He felt that they had tricked him, and now he had no choice but to submit and be the prize in some game with a troll, albeit a beautiful troll.

"I suppose I have no choice then," he said coldly.

The purple-haired Faë shrugged as he often did, but Phinnegan saw in his eyes that he did feel some bit of guilt.

"I'm afraid not, mate."

Phinnegan sighed and turned, pulling his shoulders from Periwinkle's grip. He faced the troll, who sat waiting patiently, running a pearl-colored comb through her hair.

"All right," Phinnegan said with a heavy sigh. The troll stopped combing her hair and looked at him with eager eyes, a wolfish grin upon her lips.

"So you agree, then?"

Phinnegan could only nod. Though she was indeed beautiful, he cringed at the thought of being the captive of a troll. Who knew if the men were as normal as she. He would have to remember to ask that question. If he made it away from this predicament, anyway.

"Excellent," she cooed, clapping her hands together in her excitement. "You will be such an adorable little pet. Shall we begin?

"Yes, of course. Shall we go first or will you?"

"The honor goes to my guests, of course," she said with a sly smile. "And I do expect you to invoke all of the formalities, of course."

"Of...of, course. Yes, the formalities." Crimson looked to Periwinkle, obviously oblivious to what this fair troll was talking about.

"Dear chap don't tell me you don't know the formalities?" Periwinkle asked with a hint of mockery. "All of your years in this world?"

"I don't know that I've ever been asked," Crimson replied, his tone betraying that he felt hurt by his lack of knowledge.

"Very well then," Periwinkle said, stepping forward to place himself in front of the troll. "I shall begin."

He stood for a moment in thought, either recalling a riddle or reminding himself of the formalities. At length he smiled broadly and bowed to the troll atop the rock. When he spoke at length, it was in verse.

"Riddle me this, riddle me that
I've a riddle for you, my fine trollish lass
Under this bridge and through yonder door
This game I propose; will you let me pass?"

The troll clapped her hands as he finished the rhyme. She wasted not a moment in response.

"Riddle me this, riddle me that
To such a request I cannot say nay
That human I demand as my winning price
Should you win this game, then pass, you may."

Just as she finished her rhyme, Phinnegan felt a chill in the air that he had not noticed before. The others must have felt it as well for the two Faë exchanged worried looks and the bogle glared at the troll.

"Why do I suddenly feel cold?" Crimson asked, looking from Periwinkle to the troll. She smiled.

"This area has been marked. No one can leave until the game is finished. You never can be too careful these days. It's why I always insist on the formalities."

*So much for running into the sunlight.*

# 13

## Riddles

"Of course, of course," Periwinkle stammered, but he recovered quickly and bowed once more to the troll.

"We understand completely. Now if I may?"

"Yes, please, do begin."

Periwinkle cleared his throat once more and shared one last look with Crimson before launching into his riddle.

"What's in a forest, but not in the trees?
What's part of an elbow, but not of a knee?
What comes in a month, but not in a week?
What's found in a mountain, but not in its peak?"

The brief pause that followed Periwinkle's riddle was shattered by the laughter of the troll. Her right hand rested on her breast, which heaved as she laughed. Phinnegan frowned. He had figured it out before Periwinkle had finished, and he assumed that she had as well.

"Silly Faë! Such a simple riddle that this young human already knows the answer. Did you truly think to fool me with something so juvenile?" She grinned as she waited for Periwinkle to answer, but he stood in silence, his cheeks flushing. At length she shrugged.

"Very well, then. The answer to your riddle is the letter 'o'. Correct?"

Periwinkle nodded slowly. The troll chuckled to herself as she shook her head.

"Will they all be this easy? It seems almost unfair. Almost." She flashed a wicked grin in Phinnegan's direction that made him squirm. He did not know the rules of this game, but guessed that the troll would now pose a riddle to Periwinkle. He hoped that riddle would be as simple.

"Your riddle?" Periwinkle asked, his voice quiet. She waved dismissively with one hand while the other stroked her neck as she thought.

"Half a moment." After another half a minute or so, she snapped her fingers and Phinnegan saw the same beautiful smile return to her lips. He was beginning to hate that smile.

"I have one for you my purple-haired friend. Are you ready?" Periwinkle nodded that he indeed was. The troll did not waste a moment.

"Move I do not, but yet turn everything around;
A thing you have left behind, in me it can be found;
Some ordinary things, with me are made absurd;
I always speak the truth, but never say a word.
What am I?"

Much to his dismay, Phinnegan found this riddle to be much more difficult. He did not know how he had known the first riddle posed by Periwinkle so easily, but he was quite confused by this second riddle. He looked to Periwinkle and saw that he, too, was quite perplexed. His eyes darted this way and that and Phinnegan thought that he looked quite scared.

*What does he have to be scared about? I'm the one that will have to go stay with the troll!*

More than a few minutes passed, and still Periwinkle made no answer. He paced to and fro in front of the troll, who sat with hands clasped in her lap, and a smile that would have been sweet, if one did not know her to be a troll. Phinnegan's stomach became uneasy as the moments passed. He wondered how much longer Periwinkle would be given to guess.

A sudden gasp from Crimson signaled that he had guessed the answer. Phinnegan sighed, thankful that someone knew the answer. When Crimson opened his mouth to speak, Phinnegan was certain that they were saved.

But Crimson said nothing, for his mouth worked silently and no sound came forth.

When he realized he could not speak, Crimson began gesturing wildly, pointing at his throat. Periwinkle thought it was a poor joke.

"Come on, then. What is it?"

But still Crimson moved his lips but made not a sound.

It was then that Phinnegan noticed the troll and saw that her smile had deepened. She stood from her perch atop the rock and walked over to Crimson. When she spoke, her voice was full of mock sympathy.

"What's the matter my dear Faë? What's that? Ah, I see. You have the answer to my riddle, is that it?" Crimson only glared.

Then, to Phinnegan's surprise he noticed a thin, leathery tail caressing Crimson's cheek. His eyes grew wide and he followed the curve of the tail just far enough to see it disappear under the hem of the troll's dress. Perhaps she was not as attractive as he had originally thought.

"I see that you have indeed guessed the answer. But of course, as you know, the proper forms do not allow for anyone but the person who was asked the riddle to answer. Thus, I am afraid, you'll just have to hold your tongue."

"Well that's hardly fair!" Phinnegan shouted, before he could stop himself with a hand clamping over his mouth. The troll turned, her now revealed tail thrashing about slowly as if in amusement.

"Fair? My child, you will soon see that much is not fair here. Nor I doubt is much fair in *your* world either. Rules are rules, after-all." She turned her attention back to Periwinkle, whose earlier apparent relief had now vanished as he realized that he was quite on the spot. He resumed his pacing, intentionally ignoring the eyes of the troll. When they had remained thus for what seemed like several minutes, the troll spoke.

"I do believe your time is up. Have you an answer?" Phinnegan felt her gaze as she flicked her eyes between him and Periwinkle.

"One moment, one moment," Periwinkle said, exasperation plain in his voice. He strode to the edge of the river bank and stared across to the other side. When he shook his head and looked down, Phinnegan felt his heart sink.

But just then the Faë's shoulders straightened and he took a keen interest in the water before him. He crouched down and stared. When he jumped up and spun around, a mirthful grin streaked across his face.

"My lady! Such a difficult riddle. But I have spied the answer to it only just here, in the river's edge."

She cocked an eyebrow and her smiled faded.

"Have you now?"

"Indeed I have," the purple-haired Faë said with a laugh and a wink in the direction of the relieved Crimson. "The answer, of course, is a mirror."

The answer now spoken, Phinnegan went over the words of the riddle in his mind and saw just how they fit. And now of course, the riddle seemed entirely obvious.

"Brilliant," he said, which drew a laugh from each of the Faë.

"Glad to see that you can speak again, brother!" Periwinkle said as he joined the red-haired Faë in front of the troll. While she was not angry, Phinnegan could read the disappointment clearly upon her face. Her nose in the air, she dipped her chin precipitously towards Periwinkle.

"The answer, as you have correctly guessed, is indeed a mirror. All even after the first pass, we are." Recovering her forgotten grace, she returned to the rock and sat down again.

"Who is next? How about the human?"

Phinnegan had not realized that he, too, would have to come up with a riddle that would challenge this troll. In a glance, Crimson must have seen this fact for he quickly stepped forward and bowed to the troll.

"Certainly the lady would do me the honor of hearing my riddle next?"

Her smile threatened to fade, but stood its ground.

"I suppose that would be fine, yes."

"Shall I observe the forms?"

"There is no need," the troll said, waving her hand dismissively. She pointed in the direction of Periwinkle. "His invocation of the forms was all that was needed to seal this place. One riddle is all that is required of you."

Crimson bowed slightly at the waist before proceeding on with his riddle.

"A house without windows, one door but no lock,
A thousand rooms there are, but no room for a clock.
Many visitors come and go, but with no mat to wipe their feet;
Inside they hoard a golden treasure, for you and I, a treat."

This time, the beautiful troll did not laugh dismissively and shake her head. Instead her brows furrowed and her eyes narrowed. She scrunched her nose and stroked her lithe neck with a slender hand. At least this time, she had to think.

Phinnegan too turned the riddle over and over in his head, trying to think of what house had so many rooms but so few doors. A golden treasure inside? He wondered if it could be a bank vault. He had never seen one, but had heard about them and read about them. It made some sense to him. A golden treasure; a thousand rooms could be individual boxes for each customer's money. No windows, one door...but no. It could not be a bank vault. Phinnegan was quite sure that most bank customers would want the vault where their money was kept to have at least one lock.

Phinnegan glanced to Periwinkle, who smiled a small smile. When he winked, Phinnegan knew that he already knew the answer. Still, the troll did not stir. Now with her chin cupped in her hand, she stared listlessly ahead. Phinnegan thought she looked weary, but guessed that she was probably only thinking. Several minutes passed in silence before Crimson cleared his throat.

"Ahem, dear lady, have you guessed the answer to my riddle?" Crimson could barely conceal the note of excitement in his voice. The troll flicked her gaze to his and regarded him coolly.

"A few more moments, I beg."

Phinnegan saw in the slight clenching of Crimson's jaw that more time was the last thing that he wanted to give, but in all fairness, Periwinkle had been given more than ample time to answer her riddle. He nodded his acquiescence.

Phinnegan thought further, going through things in his mind that fit each of the different limitations of the riddle. He came up with no answer that matched all of them, nor usually even more than one. He did think of egg for the last, but obviously an egg has no windows, doors, rooms, or anything of the sort. But none could deny the golden treasure inside.

He looked to the troll, who had not moved in the moments that had passed since she asked for more time. As he regarded her face, he thought for a moment that it might not be *too* terrible to be stranded with her in this strange place. But he could not guess where she would take him and what his fate would be. He was thankful that for the moment it seemed he wouldn't find out. She must be out of time by now.

But when a smile cracked her lips, Phinnegan felt his stomach flip.

"Quite an ingenious riddle, friend Faë. Perhaps a bit unfair in that I have certainly seen a beehive with more than one 'door'. Have you not?" Crimson swallowed slowly and the hope that had been upon his face vanished in an instant. When he spoke, his voice was quiet and more than a bit scratchy.

"Indeed, I probably have."

The troll laughed and her beautiful smile returned. Behind, her tail flicked quickly, almost like the wagging of a dog.

"Still it was *quite* a good riddle. I thought it rather worthy of our little game; much unlike that of your friend there," she said, nodding in the direction of Periwinkle, who barely suppressed a scowl. Crimson mumbled a word of thanks.

"Now then," she said, clapping her hands together. "It is my turn to ask a riddle again, I believe?" Crimson nodded and answered that it was indeed. Instead of breaking immediately into her riddle, she thought for a few moments.

"Aha! Try your tricky little mind at this, Faë."

"Screaming, soaring
Seeking sky;

Flowers of fire, flying high.
Thunder from powder,
Color from salt,
An ancient art doth their masters exalt."

Crimson frowned for a moment before stepping out from beneath the edge of the bridge just enough to cast his eyes to the heavens. He stood this way some time, and young Phinnegan could guess no reason why, save that perhaps he was trying to imagine what could seek the sky. A bird, a cloud? But they weren't made of fire, of course. He wondered if it could be the sun or the stars, but they could hardly be said to scream.

Phinnegan, too, crept to where he could look up into the darkening sky. How long had they been here? They had left no later than late morning, and now it appeared as if dusk approached. The air was cool as it blew across the river that coursed along beside them, and it reminded Phinnegan of late spring nights by the lake near his home. He thought back to the last time he had been there. It had been a birthday party for the city's mayor. There had been all manner of foods, dancing, desserts, games and to top it all off, a miraculous show of fireworks.

*Fireworks.*

Phinnegan could not believe it had taken him so long to guess. Flowers of fire? How simple. He smirked and a small laugh escaped his lips.

"It seems our little friend has the answer. Tell me that you do as well, brother," Periwinkle said with a slight smile as he spoke to his fellow Faë.

"I believe that I do," Crimson murmured as he turned back to face the troll.

"Fairly simple, really. The answer is fireworks."

This time the troll did not seem as taken aback. Whether it was that lengthy time taken by Periwinkle had served to raise her hopes or something else, Phinnegan could not be sure. But as her eyes left the red-haired Faë and moved to meet his, he couldn't help but feel that she did not mind because now it was down to him. And he felt keenly at a disadvantage.

"Well, it was not that difficult after all I suppose. What else could 'flowers of fire' in the sky be, anyway, right?" She smiled and beckoned for Phinnegan to approach her.

"I'll just have to make sure I can come up with a more difficult one for our little friend here. I am sure that he has a tough one for me, don't you sweetie?"

Phinnegan looked to Periwinkle for help, but he only spread his hands in front of him and shrugged. Phinnegan got the message. He was on his own, one on one with this beautiful woman, who was in fact, a troll. He rose slowly from his place near the riverbank and shuffled closer to the troll. When he passed Periwinkle, the Faë whispered into his ear.

"Chin up, mate. At least your fate is in your own hands, eh? Just come up with a good one and all will be fine."

Crimson nodded slightly as Phinnegan passed him by, and then he stood alone in front of the troll. She smiled broadly and rose from her place atop the rock to step forward until only a foot or two separated the two. She lifted her hands and put them on his shoulders.

"My dear little boy," she said, her voice full of concern. "You are trembling! Certainly it is not as bad as that? Have you not come up with a riddle to ask me?"

Phinnegan struggled to meet her gaze and instead let his head fall, his chin sinking to his chest. What could he do? He had thought of no riddle that he could ask that would have any chance of stumping this troll. He could only shake his head.

"There, there," she tut-tutted. "I suppose I can bend the rules this once and go out of turn. How would that be?"

Her voice was calm and soothing, and Phinnegan thought that this was a reasonable idea. What did he have to lose? The worst that could happen is that nothing would come to his mind, and as nothing was where he stood now, there would be little change. He nodded in agreement and the troll cooed with delight.

"Splendid! Of course, it might put a bit more pressure on you were you to guess incorrectly. But I am sure you will manage."

Phinnegan had not given that aspect much thought, but she was, of course, right. But he had little time to dwell on this possible mistake for the troll stepped back to seat herself on the rock and began to rattle off yet another riddle.

"My home is not silent, but I am not loud;
Together we move, though I in his shroud.
I owe him my life, in he I was spawned;
At times I must rest, yet he travels beyond.
Yes, I can be faster, and sometimes much stronger;
But he stretches further, his course, much longer.
Down mountains and through valleys, we travel together;
With him I remain, or else, I would smother."

If there is one thing that is bad for thinking, it is being frightened; and Phinnegan was certainly frightened. He considered anything and everything that had a home: snails, hermit crabs, turtles. Yet none of these even mildly matched the rhymes of the riddle.

He felt the eyes of the troll upon him, sitting there only a few feet away. He glanced up quickly, only to see her smile widening at each passing moment as he struggled with this riddle. Something about the words of the riddle tugged at his brain, like they had a certain meaning, almost as if she had given him a hint.

But Phinnegan Qwyk did not catch this hint, for his mind hit wall after wall and tears filled his big brown eyes. He had not the slightest idea what the answer to this riddle could be. Turning his back to the troll, he looked to Periwinkle and Crimson, not knowing how they could help him given the rules of this game. From the look on each of their faces, he knew that they both had solved the riddle.

Instead of giving him hope, this only gave him despair. He *should* know the answer! As he looked at Periwinkle, the purple-haired Faë shook his head slowly, and Phinnegan thought it was in disgust at how stupid he was, but something in his manner caught his attention.

No, he wasn't disgusted at all; the Faë was trying to help him!

What Phinnegan had at first mistaken for a shake, was more of a nod, in a particular direction. Phinnegan peeked over his shoulder to see if the troll was watching, but her eyes searched the skies while she swayed back and forth on her rock. He returned his gaze to Periwinkle. The nod became more insistent, and then his eyes rolled in the same direction. Phinnegan followed the signs with his own eyes and saw that the Faë was pointing him in the direction of the river.

Phinnegan's frown deepened. Did the Faë want him to escape? To swim? He mouthed the words, but Periwinkle grimaced and shook his head forcefully. No, definitely not escape.

And then Phinnegan remembered that the Faë had found the answer to his own riddle in the river, when he looked down and saw his reflection and the idea of a mirror struck him. Perhaps he thought the river could help Phinnegan as well, although the answer was most certainly not a mirror.

But, perhaps, the Faë knew what he was doing. He did, after all, seem to know the answer.

Phinnegan walked towards the edge of the river. His movement must have drawn the eyes of the troll, for her voice rang out and sent a shiver down his spine.

"Don't wander too far, little one. Time is running out and I want my prize to be close at hand."

He had no response that he could make, so Phinnegan ignored the troll and knelt at the water's edge. He looked down into the river and there saw his reflection. What a mess he was, his hair tousled and his cheeks pale. He looked as ill as he felt. He dipped his hand into the water, which was not too cool and not too warm. He splashed the water on his face, washing away the grime and dust that had built-up during his travels. The water was remarkably clear and Phinnegan could see that the bank sloped steeply so that the bottom was out of sight in mere feet.

He looked out to the middle of the river, which was not too far for it was no more than twenty-five yards wide. Something swam along in the middle of the river, and Phinnegan squinted to find that it was a great black snake. Probably harmless, but he was glad that it was in the river and not on the bank.

A flash of movement caught his eye and he looked down to the water just in front of him. He saw nothing at first, but then another flash and another. Soon his eyes focused on a spry little fish, darting this way and that, his silver scales glinting in the sunlight that penetrated the surface of the water. So happy this little fish must be, Phinnegan thought. Safe in the water, away from the troll and this stupid game. If only he could be a fish, swimming with current down the river, away from this place.

*Fish. River.*

He spun his head to look at Periwinkle, who offered a sly smile and a wink. Phinnegan leapt from his place beside the river, making himself more than a bit dizzy in the process, not that he cared.

"I know the answer!" he shouted, running past the two Faë and stopping in front of the troll, who regarded him warily.

"Oh? Are you sure? One guess is all you get." But Phinnegan was not cowed by her attempt to unnerve him.

"One is all I need. It's a fish! A fish and his home is the water, the river." He crossed his arms in front of his chest and beamed a smile.

The troll, however, did not smile.

"Came up with that answer on your own, did you?"

Phinnegan's smile began to falter, but Periwinkle quickly came to his rescue.

"Of course he did. How else was he supposed to come up with it?" Periwinkle said. The troll regarded him coolly.

"I asked the boy the question, and as to how else, *you* could have helped him."

Periwinkle only smiled.

"But, my dear, how could I when by the rules you have put into play I, and my friend here," and he pointed to Crimson, "are as mute as a mouse. I could not have told him had I tried to bellow and scream. Which I didn't, of course."

The troll remained unconvinced.

"Speaking isn't the only way that one can help." She sighed, running her hands through her lustrous red hair. "But I suppose it does not matter greatly. I only have to answer his riddle correctly and we can move on."

"But...but then we would be tied. What happens if we tie?" Phinnegan asked, his curiosity emboldened by answering the riddle correctly, even if he had been helped a little.

"Why, we fight to the death, of course."

Phinnegan's eyes widened and his mouth fell agape.

"To...to the death?" He looked to Periwinkle who shrugged before patting Phinnegan on the back.

"Make sure it's a good one, eh?"

Phinnegan swallowed. All eyes were on him and he had no way out this time. Neither Periwinkle nor Crimson could help him, and the troll had finished her turn, so it was left to him. He was too young to have heard many riddles, and too young still to craft them all on his own. He racked his brain for anything he had heard in his twelve short years and he found little. Stupid jokes and nursery rhymes were all that came to him.

There was, however, one exception. A little rhyme he had learned as a child that his mother had taught him. He had always found the story quite strange and thought that the rhyme would be easy for this troll. Still, he had no other option.

"There was a man of Adam's race;
He had a certain dwelling-place;
He wasn't in earth, heaven or hell,
Tell me where that man did dwell."

Phinnegan expected the troll to give the answer right away. But she did not. Nor did Periwinkle or Crimson appear to know the answer right away for they looked at each other and then at Phinnegan, both with a blank look.

The moments passed in silence and Phinnegan first chewed his fingernails, only to stop and then find himself chewing his lip. His mother always made him stop that, saying it was uncomely in a boy about to become a young man to display such nervousness. But he could not help it, for it was not a stretch to say that his life hung in the balance.

Phinnegan was content to let the troll have as long as she needed to try and answer the question. But Periwinkle was not.

"My lady, have you an answer to Phinnegan's question?"

The troll scowled and flung her hair over her shoulder. She glared at the two Faë and then at Phinnegan before speaking.

"More time, please."

"I believe the lady has already had enough time, wouldn't you say Crimson?" Periwinkle saw the advantage that they now held, and Crimson played right along.

"Just so, dear lady, for Phinnegan took no more time than you have already taken before he answered your riddle. It is only fair, after all.

"I said I need more TIME!"

With the last word, the troll's voice changed from sweet and lilting to a vicious growl. Phinnegan was not about to push her, and neither, it seemed, was Periwinkle.

"As the lady wishes," he said, bowing slightly and doffing his great black hat.

But the extra time did the troll no good, for many more minutes passed and she finally threw up her hands.

"Do you give up, then?" Periwinkle asked, his voice carrying a tinge of awe that the young boy could have stumped the aged and wise troll. To angry to speak, she could only nod. Periwinkle and Crimson each yelped for joy and both clapped Phinnegan on the back.

"Well done!"

"Well done? It was bloody brilliant!"

Phinnegan's broad smile returned as his two friends complemented his riddle. But their celebration was interrupted by the troll.

"Well? What was the answer?"

"It's uh, well he lived in a whale?" Phinnegan stammered. The troll's eyes widened with shock.

"A whale?!? Who has ever dwelled in a whale? What trickery is this?" She bolted to her feet and the air seemed to tingle as she spoke.

"J-J-Jonah dwelt in a whale."

"Who?!?

"Jonah. It's in the Bible?"

"The – Oh this rubbish! You can't ask riddles about things in your world. That's not fair! CHEATER!"

Before Phinnegan or the two Faë knew what had happened, the troll had swung out her arm and they were all thrown back by an unseen force that knocked the breath from their lungs. Phinnegan struggled to regain his breath, even as he heard the troll screaming above him.

"You dare to cheat ME of what is rightly mine by asking an unfair riddle? I will have your heads for this, all of them!"

Above them, Phinnegan could sense the sky getting darker and a howling wind that had not been there only moments before. *She's going to kill me.*

*She's going to cast some terrible spell and kill us all.*

But just as he braced for the awful to happen, silence broke in upon the raging wind. And then that silence was quickly broken by the screams of the troll.

"Unbind me! This is not FAIR!"

She continued to shriek and Phinnegan pushed himself up to find her standing not five feet away, frozen. Behind her, the bogle stood at the door beneath the bridge, his hand on the latch.

"Well brother," Periwinkle said, as he pulled Crimson to his feet. "It looks as though your bogle has claimed our prize. Come on, mate." The purple-haired Faë grabbed Phinnegan's arm and pulled him quickly to his feet.

Together, the two Faë and Phinnegan ran past the screaming troll, who remained bound by unseen hands. Her threats rang out even as they disappeared into the door beneath the bridge, like rabbits down a hole.

# 14

## The Plan Revealed

When the door slammed shut behind them, Phinnegan and his party were greeted by a profound silence. The screaming of the trollish woman, which had continued to crescendo, was now gone.

It was also dark, but some unknown source gave off enough light that Phinnegan could make out a low ceiling only a hand or so above the top of his head, and craggy rock walls not far to either side. The floor, too, was uneven and rocky. Now that he thought about it, it looked exactly like what you would expect to find on the other side of a door cut into the wall beneath a bridge: like a tunnel.

His eyes involuntarily squinted when each of the two Faë produced their glow globes with a flurry of wrists, bathing the rocky walls in bright, white light.

"Where are we?" Phinnegan asked, his eyes adjusting to the new light source. The bogle grumbled, but Crimson spoke up in answer.

"We," he said as he doused his own globe in favor of Periwinkle's, "are in the caverns. They're a pathway of tunnels and shafts that run beneath the ground and serve as a quick means of transportation."

"But I thought you Faë could just snap your fingers or cast a spell, what have you, and be where you want? Or use the wishing stone?"

"Well," Crimson said, furrowing his brow as he sought to explain. "We can use the stones to travel, yes this is true, but it is not always the best way. And there are some places, like where we are going now, that you cannot reach by using a stone. Ironically."

"What's ironic?" Phinnegan asked.

"Oh, you'll see when we get there."

"Which is where again?"

"Castle Heronhawk," the two Faë replied in unison.

"And we get to this castle through these tunnels, the caverns?"

"Yes, the only other ways to get there are not accessible to us. It's not a place we are often welcome."

"Why not?" Phinnegan saw the quick glance between the two Faë before Periwinkle deigned to answer.

"Giants don't normally like Faë."

"Giants?! We're going to a castle full of giants?" Phinnegan blurted, quite incredulous at the idea.

"Walk and talk, brothers, walk and talk," Crimson said as he started along the rocky path down the hall. Periwinkle followed, but spoke over his shoulder to address Phinnegan's question.

"Hardly full, only a few live there year round. Wouldn't you say Crimson?" The red-haired Faë nodded in ascent before Periwinkle continued. "Very selective bunch they are, sticking to themselves and not socializing with the 'wee folk' as we and any other creature that is not as tall as a tree is called. But they do open their doors once or twice a year for a festival. It is then that we are welcome there, for we have many crafts that they cannot replicate. They're not particularly good with clocks, for one."

"So is there a festival going on now, then?"

"Yes, a rather large one. Bigger than normal even." Periwinkle jerked his thumb in the direction of the bogle.

"That's what he was showing us in the book. Only happens every half century or so, which really isn't that long for us longevity speaking, but it is quite awhile to wait!

"And why are we going there again? This doesn't seem like a good time to celebrate. I thought you said you had a way to get me home?"

"We do, mate, we do. And it just so happens that this way lies in yonder castle, and that the only way we could ever have access to said way is by getting into the castle, which can only happen during a festival, which just so happens to be going on right this very minute. Follow?"

Phinnegan's brow crinkled as he listened, but he nodded that he had indeed followed.

"Good then," Periwinkle said." I'm glad we're umm, what is it you say? On the same page? Right, on the same page." He nodded to himself in satisfaction at remembering the saying.

Up ahead, Crimson disappeared from view and it was not until they had gone a few more steps that Phinnegan realized that he had turned down a hallway that led off the main tunnel to the right. He followed Periwinkle down this same hallway and noticed that while the ceiling height was the same, it was much narrower than the main hall. The two Faë and Phinnegan could barely walk the path without their shoulders scraping the walls.

Phinnegan went over the Faë's explanation for their journey in his mind. Something did not sit right. These giants, who evidently did not like the Faë very much at all, would suddenly be willing to help them send a boy, who was a human and Phinnegan guessed perhaps liked even less, home?

He was so deep in thought that he almost missed the left turn the two Faë ahead had made, and likely would have if the bogle hadn't grunted and intruded upon his thoughts. He slipped into a wide hallway, more like the first. Another quick right and the hallway became narrower again.

"So wait a minute. I'm to believe that these giants will help me? Why would they do that? What can they do?" This time it was Crimson who responded.

"It's not so much what they can *do*, but what they *have* that is of interest to us."

"What do they have?"

"Blimey! You ask a lot of questions don't you?" Crimson remarked as he led them on down the hallway.

"That he does." Periwinkle looked over his shoulder and gave Phinnegan a quick wink. "An inquisitive fellow he is."

"Well can you explain it to him? I'm trying to remember which way to go." Crimson took a long look at an opening to the right before continuing forward.

"No problem, mate. Well you see Phinnegan, the giants have quite a bit of…items, that they have amassed over their centuries in existence, and it just so happens that one of those items is particularly valuable, and, we believe, is an item that can get you home."

"What is it?"

"Well I haven't seen it myself, but the stories are that it is a wishing stone of immense size, as big as a fist, with a similar boost to all of its properties. Meaning, that it is our guess that such a stone would have enough power to send you home."

"And you think that they would let you use it so send me home?"

"Hang on a minute," Crimson said as he halted the progress of the group. "This is not right. I knew we should have taken that right back there."

The bogle interjected with some harsh utterances in his outlandish dialect which Phinnegan could not understand, but seemed to ruffle the ego of Crimson.

"Well I'm not a bloody guide, am I? I'd like to see one of you lot get us there."

The bogle responded with another short utterance and a gurgling sound that Phinnegan took for a chuckle.

"Oh, bugger off." Crimson turned around and marched back down the hallway in the direction that they had just come. "This way, I know where we are now."

The group turned and followed Crimson back to the opening in the wall that he had considered before, this time taking it and after a few moments entering a more cavern like environment, with walls further apart and a ceiling several times their height.

"This stone, then? They will let us use it?" Phinnegan asked, breaking the silence.

"Well, not willingly of course. As I said, very secretive lot. Very protective of their ill-gotten goodies. They wouldn't let us near it."

"Then why are we going there if they won't let us use it?"

Suddenly, Phinnegan remembered the troll's words.

*What could two Faë and a bogle need with a human at Castle Heronhawk? Unless you were planning to steal something.*

"Here we are, at last," Crimson said, as they came to a high, arching doorway that was filled from top to bottom with a fog as dense as the clouds. Phinnegan hardly noticed as he was still focusing on the troll's words.

"We're going to *steal* it?!" He asked, his voice high and strained.

"Not exactly, mate," Periwinkle answered as he followed Crimson into the dense mist. Poking his head back out so that it appeared to float bodiless on the mist he gave Phinnegan a quick wink.

"You are."

# 15

## An Unwilling Thief

When Periwinkle had uttered his plan for Phinnegan to steal the larger wishing stone from the giants, Phinnegan had been given little choice but to follow him into the cloudy fog and demand an explanation. It was either that or be left behind in the caverns, and even with the feelings he now had about the Faë, he thought that this would not be the best of ideas.

The fog was cool and damp against his skin, but when he emerged from it he was greeted by a warm, blinding sunlight.

His eyes were slow to adjust to the level of light, so he focused on the ground in front of him. Yet, there was no *ground*. He saw only the same thick, cloud-like fog that had demarcated the doorway to this strange place. His feet were invisible to him, as they were beneath the fog, which rose to the middle of his calf. He leaned over and stretched his hand out to test the substance that was beneath his feet, but his hand touched nothing. He felt only the cold of the fog, and his hand kept going, and going, much past where his foot seemed to have stopped.

"Don't worry, it will hold you." Periwinkle said from just ahead. "The clouds are penetrable if you move slowly and deliberately through them like that, but just walking on them is fine. Even for a heavy-footed human. Just don't think about it."

Phinnegan ignored the Faë's words when he looked up.

"I'm not stealing *anything*!" he said with a glare. But the Faë only smiled.

"I'm afraid you have little choice in the matter. That is, if you truly want to go home. This stone is your only option."

"Then we'll ask them if we can use it."

"That's not going to work, mate," Periwinkle said, with a shake of his head. He pointed to the silhouette of a massive castle in the distance. Multiple spires rose from the clouds reaching upwards, their multi-color tiled roofs shimmering in the sunlight.

"See the castle?" Phinnegan chewed his lip in anger, but nodded that he did indeed see the castle. "Good. Now, do you see those two towers just before the gate?" Phinnegan again nodded that he did. "Well those towers are for the guards. Big, angry guards, who would just as soon eat you as talk to you. And do you know what they are guarding against more than anything in this world?"

"Thieves like you?" Phinnegan quipped.

"Hardly. Thieves like *you*."

"I've already told you," Phinnegan said, his voice loud and defiant. "I'm not stealing it!"

"Well if you want to use it, you're going to have to." Periwinkle held up a hand to forestall Phinnegan from speaking. "And you can't ask them either, because the one thing they will not under any circumstances let into the castle is a human."

"Why not? You said they let everyone in during these festivals."

"Everyone from this world," Crimson interjected. "But not humans"

"Why not?"

"Because you're the only ones that can actually steal the stone. It's locked behind all manner of magic and spells that we can't ever hope to penetrate. But to a human, why, you can slip right through."

Phinnegan stared in silence at the two Faë, trying to process what they had just told him. He felt as though he were being used, even if the thing they wanted him to steal would allow him to go home.

"I'm not a thief," he said quietly. "I won't do it." Phinnegan's gaze dropped, too early to see the worried glance that passed between the two Faë.

"Don't be so hasty," Periwinkle said, walking over and resting a hand on Phinnegan's shoulder. "I'm telling you, honestly, that if you want to go home, this is the only way that I know of for you to do it. And I can tell you right now they won't let you use it, even if you could ask them." He gave Phinnegan's shoulder a light squeeze. "I'm sure you miss your mum."

The mentioning of his mother first brought rage, and Phinnegan shrugged off the Faë's hand, but this rage soon passed and left him weak. He thought of his mother, and how he missed her, and how he was certain she was beside herself with grief. The tears stung his eyes and he gladly took the light-purple handkerchief that Periwinkle offered him.

He stood for a few moments, his head hung, drying his eyes on the handkerchief, which smelled distinctly of lavender. He *did* miss his mother, and his father; and Quinn too, he supposed. And while he was not a thief, he thought that becoming one was a small price to pay to go home.

"Fine."

"That's the way!" Periwinkle said, perhaps a bit too cheerfully. He quickly tamed his tone and again patted Phinnegan on the back.

"It's the best way; the only way."

Phinnegan raised his head to look into the eyes of the Faë.

"But how do I get in there to...to steal it, if they won't even let me near the castle?"

"Aha," Crimson said, his finger raised in the air. "I'm glad that you asked that. We will use a Mask."

"A mask?" Phinnegan asked between sniffles. "Won't they still see that I am human?"

"Hopefully not, and if I am as good at my craft as I think, they most certainly won't. This is not a mask like you would wear at a fancy party, it's more of an illusion. It will cover you from head to toe."

"And I will look just like a Faë?"

"Spectacularly so," Crimson said with a smile. "Of course, it does have its limits."

"Like what?"

"Well, for one, you can't talk. It really is an illusion and you speaking might muck it up. Plus, you can't move too fast or it may not be able to keep up with you. And, if you go through certain spells it could strip the illusion right from you."

Periwinkle raised an eyebrow as he regarded Crimson coolly.

"You mean like the ones that will be guarding the stone?"

When Crimson nodded, Periwinkle frowned and voiced the question that was in Phinnegan's own mind.

"This doesn't sound like as good of a plan as you first made it out to be, mate. How is he supposed to steal the stone if the Mask will come off as soon as he goes near it?" He peered closely at Crimson. "Are you sure this will work?

"When is one ever really certain that a thing will work?" the red-haired Faë responded with a shrug.

"You know what I mean. Do you *think* it will work?"

"Absolutely, as long as everybody keeps their wits about them and does exactly what I say. Which, for starters," Crimson said, leveling his gaze on Phinnegan, "that means mum's the word for you, right? Let Periwinkle and I do all the talking. Understood?"

Phinnegan nodded his agreement. Not that he liked the plan, not at all. He had no desire to become a thief, and was worried about remaining silent when he would in all likelihood be scared out of his wits. But, he yearned for home and this seemed to be the only plan that the two Faë could come up with.

"I'll stay quiet." He paused to bite his lip for a moment, apprehensive about having magic done *to* him. "How do you put the mask on me? Will it hurt?"

"Not at all, not at all! Why, you wouldn't even know it was happening if I didn't tell you."

"I think I'd know it if you were changing the way I looked!"

Crimson responded with a sly smirk.

"Would you now?" He reached into his pocket and tossed something in Phinnegan's direction, who threw up his hands in just enough time to catch whatever it was. Phinnegan held the object up and saw that it was a small mirror. Looking into it he saw his reflection.

The Faë was right. Phinnegan had *not* noticed. The face that stared back at him from the mirror *was* his face, yet it wasn't. His cheek bones were slightly higher, his nose narrower and pointed and his complexion a brighter, livelier flesh-tone. But it was the hair that startled him the most. His thick mop of brown hair was gone, replaced by hair that was straight, and a lustrous blue, hanging down to his shoulders.

"That's incredible!" Phinnegan exclaimed as he continued to regard himself in the mirror.

"Now run your fingers through your hair," Periwinkle said with a wink. Phinnegan obeyed, and was even more startled to find that his hair did not feel straight and smooth, but short and tangled, as it normally would.

"Brilliant," he whispered.

"All an illusion. Which is why you have to be *very* careful. Just as that hair doesn't feel like Faë hair, nor will your voice have the lilting quality of ours. It will be same flat voice that you humans always have. Honestly, I don't know how you can bear it." Periwinkle said the last with a shake of his head.

"No need to be insulting," Phinnegan responded with a frown as he continued to gaze at himself in the mirror.

"All right then, enough of that," Crimson said suddenly, breaking Phinnegan from his trance. "Let's get on with it or else those guards are going to wonder why three figures are just standing out here instead of coming on. They're a very suspicious lot, these giants."

Phinnegan closed the distance between himself and Crimson to return the mirror. The Faë quickly pocketed it and then clapped his hands together.

"Shall we?"

"Let's," Periwinkle said with a smile, taking Crimson by one arm and Phinnegan by the other. Together the three proceeded arm in arm towards the castle in the distance. Phinnegan suddenly recalled the bogle, who apparently was not coming with them.

"What about him?" he asked, nodding over his shoulder in the direction of the bogle.

"He'll wait here. Getting you in and out will be trouble enough. No sense complicating matters any further, eh bogle?" Periwinkle shot the little creature a grin over his shoulder. Phinnegan was surprised to see the bogle make a most human gesture, sticking his tongue out at the purple-haired Faë.

"Completely uncalled for," Periwinkle said, adding under his breath, "ugly little goblin."

"Let it go, brother. Keep your mind on the task at hand," Crimson scolded amiably. "Now Phinnegan, as I said, you must not speak. Periwinkle and I will do all the talking. Just stick to one of us and we'll cover for you. Not that you should be roaming around in that place by yourself anyway. Not that any of us should for that matter."

"What shall we call him? Supposing someone asks, I mean."

"Azure Robin," Crimson responded quickly. Periwinkle nodded.

"Right, right. Good choice. Not likely to be any of that clan up here.

"Why not?" Phinnegan asked.

"Not the partying type for starters, and a bit on the poor side. They're loners really, which makes it all the more convincing that you don't talk much."

"Well if they aren't likely to be at a festival, then why am I here?"

"Easy," Crimson said. "We'll just say you're a friend of ours that was visiting and we dragged you up here, against your better thinking of course. That should be convincing enough should anyone ask."

"Look sharp, mates," Periwinkle said, jerking his head in the direction of the castle. Phinnegan looked up and was startled to see that the castle was very close now. The gate was only some several dozen yards away. He felt a queasiness begin in his stomach, which soon spread to a slight warming over his body as the fear began to creep through his veins.

"All will be well," Periwinkle said reassuringly. "Just stay quiet and follow our lead."

"But I don't even know what I am supposed to do. How I am supposed to...steal...this stone."

"All in good time, mate. Just relax."

Relax. *Easy for him to say.*

The trio stopped before two massive wooden doors that spanned the immense distance between two exceedingly massive stone towers. From a distance as the group approached, the stone of the towers looked a dull grey, but now being so close, it was apparent that the grey was only an illusion brought about by the distance. The stones themselves were colored in all manner of shades from a dirty white to a charcoal grey, yet never quite black. Each stone was easily eight or nine feet to a side and mostly square. The wood of the doors was a robust brown that was at the same time dark and lively. Thick bands of a dark metal served to bind the pieces of lumber together and provide strength and stability to the gates. Whoever built these gates was quite large, indeed.

The soft sound of a light breeze rustling the fabrics of the trio's clothing was the only one that reached their ears. The silence pressed in upon them, driving Phinnegan to speak.

"Should we say something, you think?" he whispered.

"I told you *not* to speak," Crimson hissed quietly. "Just wait half a moment. The guard will speak first, it is their custom."

Several more moments passed in this eerie silence. Phinnegan strained to hear any sound, but even those that would normally be only background noise were not to be heard. No birds chirped, no bugs creaked; only the fabric of their clothing whispered in the breeze. That and his heart pounding in his ears.

When a voice called down from the ramparts, Phinnegan started, but the two Faë held him fast by the arms.

"State your business, *Faë*," the voice rumbled from the top of the tower, spitting the final word as though it left a bad taste in the mouth.

"Why, to drink and be extraordinarily merry, of course!" Periwinkle shouted back.

"Sorry, we're full," the voice replied. Periwinkle shared a quick glance with Crimson. This was obviously not the response that they had expected. Periwinkle did his best to appear jubilant, calling back up with a laugh.

"Full? How can a party be full? Surely I have come to the right place. Is this not the castle of Horace the Great, whose generosity and excellence as a host on this special day is renowned from here to the land of the pixies?"

A silence followed, and then the short reply.

"It is."

"Splendid!" Periwinkle cried, a broad smile upon his face. "Then surely you cannot turn away three jubilant Faë such as us, so ready for revelry?"

Again, a silence. They exchanged looks, each of these three as puzzled as the others. Phinnegan, however, did relax, if only slightly. Perhaps he would not become a thief after all.

But then the voice answered.

"Enter."

No other words were spoken or heard by the three at the foot of the tower, but some orders seemingly passed amongst the guards, for now the massive wooden gates grated inward, their hinges moaning beneath the load.

Once the gates were open only a few feet, sounds of celebration and gaiety flooded through. The doors were quite thick and had shielded the trio from these sounds as they stood outside. The laughter and voices that reached their ears now lifted even Phinnegan's spirits. When the doors opened further, and he could get a good look at the courtyard of this immense castle, Phinnegan beheld a sight such as he had never seen.

Hundreds, no *thousands*, of Faë danced jollily in pairs, in trios, in fours and fives, and onwards into groups too large to count. The variety and vibrancy of their colors assailed him. Never had he seen so many different shades of purples and greens, blues and reds. There an orange like a sunset, there another like a sunrise. Yellows from canary to gold and back again. Before his eyes, this rainbow of Faë bounced and hopped, leapt and spun, and everything in between.

But even with this vision of splendor, something was quite amiss.

There was no music.

Not a note, not an air, not a waltz nor a jig. No sound other than the delighted voices of the Faë could be heard.

"Why are they dancing?" Phinnegan asked, keeping his voice in as low of a whisper as possible, though it was doubtful that anyone could hear him over this din. "I don't hear any music."

A wry smile spread across Periwinkle's face.

"That, mate," he said, deftly snatching three small cordial glasses from a tray just to their right, "is because you have yet to imbibe."

Periwinkle handed one glass each to Phinnegan and Crimson, the latter greedily downing the contents in one gulp. Phinnegan was more skeptical. He eyed the caramel brown liquid warily. He brought the glass to his nose and inhaled.

"Smells like grapes. Is it wine?"

"From the host's very own vineyards, I'd suspect," Periwinkle answered. "But this isn't like any wine in your world."

"What does it do?" No sooner than Phinnegan had asked the question, Crimson let out a raucous yelp and jumped into the nearest group of dancing Faë and disappeared into their numbers.

"It just makes everything a little more...vibrant," Periwinkle said, just before downing his own glass. He closed his eyes and sighed.

"Just stay close, mate. The effects wear off after a time and you must keep drinking. But we don't want to continue. We just need to blend in for a spell; then we'll make our move. Be looking for me, mate. I'll come for you when the time is right. Now blend in and be quiet."

The Faë has said all of this with his eyes closed, and now, having finished, he opened them and Phinnegan saw that Periwinkle's light-purple irises had deepened in color while his pupil's had dilated considerably. A broad grin split the Faë's face and he leapt forward to latch onto a female Faë with bright yellow hair, who accepted him as though she had known him forever.

To say that Phinnegan felt uneasy about the cordial glass in his hand would only be telling the half of it. His fingers tightened on the stem of the glass as he watched Periwinkle disappear into a dizzying whirl of Faë as they danced to an unheard song. His eyes flicked to the glass and a debate raged inside him about whether he should drink it.

It was then that the feeling of being watched began to creep up his spine. Turning, he saw one of the giants that inhabited this castle, large and brutish, but with an intelligent eye pondering him warily, a grim frown upon its face.

Phinnegan feared the worst from the start, as anyone would who had just had their head filled with the dislike the giants have for humans, and Faë, and the somewhat questionable nature of his disguise. Could the giant have heard him whispering to Periwinkle and somehow discovered that he was not what he appeared?

When their eyes met, Phinnegan forcefully swallowed the lump in his throat. The giant gestured clumsily in Phinnegan's direction, pretending to drink from an invisible glass. Phinnegan made no move, and the giant gestured again, more urgently emphasizing the entire motion with a throaty grunt.

Taking the giant's meaning, Phinnegan raised the glass shakily to his lips and tilted his head back. The liquid trickled across his tongue to the back of his mouth and ran down his throat. It was thicker than he expected, not quite a syrup, but almost. It was sweet to the tongue, but bit sharply and left a lingering warmness in the back of his throat.

Phinnegan lowered his glass and looked to the giant, who nodded curtly and then simply walked away.

In the first moments after drinking the liquid, nothing appeared to happen to Phinnegan. The warm sensation in his throat lessened slightly and the sweet aftertaste lingered precipitously on his tongue. Around him the Faë still danced and hooted, but he heard no music. He blinked once, then twice, but his eyes opened each time upon the same scene. Peering into the empty glass, he assured himself that he had indeed drunk every last drop. Out of frustration, he sighed and released the glass, letting it fall towards the ground.

As he sighed, he noticed that his tongue was thick and heavy. His other senses soon followed suit; his eyes could not focus and the sounds of the Faë came to his ears as if through a thin wall. He stepped back in a moment of dizziness and nearly lost his balance.

Phinnegan tried to catch the eye of Periwinkle or Crimson, but to no avail. For one, he could not focus on any face well enough to recognize either Faë. But making the task even more difficult was the swimming room about him, where everything moved as if in slow motion. Fighting a nauseous feeling, he closed his eyes and breathed deeply.

The sounds remained muffled, growing fainter until all at once the world was quiet around him. He felt no breeze, but he was suddenly cold. A shiver raced up his spine and his teeth threatened to chatter.

Just as the voices of the Faë faded completely, he heard a new sound. Faintly at first, but growing in strength, a single fiddle sang a bewitching melody, beckoning him to follow. *Follow where?*

He opened his eyes to total darkness save for a spot of warm, orange-tinted light, just visible in the distance. The sound of the fiddle was faint, but he guessed that it shared the same source as this small speck of light. The melody quickened its pace, belying the urgency with which it beckoned. The melody was not unlike the one he had heard in his bedroom some few nights past.

One step and then two, Phinnegan moved towards the source of the light. Yet, the light did not seem any closer. Several steps more, but the light still seemed just as distant. He looked down at his feet and took two more steps forward.

But his feet did not move.

Phinnegan felt that he should be afraid, but the melody calmed him. But how to get himself to the light was a tricky problem indeed. He felt drawn to it, as though the fiddle whispered his name, again and again. In a moment of inspiration, he thought to do a thing that would have made no sense a few days ago, but the strange ways of this world required a different perspective.

He called back. Not vocally, but with his mind, focusing on the melody of the fiddle, desiring that he should come nearer to it.

Suddenly, his eyes sensed that he had lurched forward, though he did not feel himself move. Peering at the light, he saw that it was indeed closer and the fiddle was louder. He kept his mind focused on the sound of the fiddle and watched as the spot of light grew and grew until he was almost to it – but something blocked his path.

A thick wall of nearly opaque glass stretched as far as the eye could see in any direction. Phinnegan noticed that he no longer felt chilled, and was in fact quite warm here in front of this glass wall. The light he had followed was bright and the sound of the fiddle filled the air around him, giving the impression that both were just on the other side.

Phinnegan stepped closer to the glass, placing his cheek against it. The glass was warm, almost hot. He looked for a door or any opening that would allow him to pass through, but he found none. When he rapped the glass with his knuckle, the resulting sound was high-pitched, indicating the solid thickness of the glass.

"Hello?" he said quietly, reaching out to touch the wall with the tips of his fingers.

And then, so suddenly that the silence seemed to thunder like a cannon, the violin stopped, just as the light vanished from behind the glass. The cold returned and Phinnegan drew a sharp breath. He was once again plunged into darkness.

"Hello?" he whispered. He moved his hand closer in the direction of the glass, but stopped just before touching it. He had heard something. It was there and then gone, a high-pitched tink like a pebble hitting a window. Then there it was again, this time high above his head. Several more followed, to his right and his left, racing towards him and away, and spreading everywhere in between.

The glass was cracking.

Not an instant too late, Phinnegan flung his arms in front of his face as a shield, for the glass shattered, exploding into a myriad of tiny fragments. He squeezed his eyes shut and waited for the fragments of shattered glass to come crashing down around him. But they never did.

When the fiddle began to play again it was loud and clear. The song was now lively and jovial, and just as the first was finished, a second fiddle joined in accompaniment. When the first pair of hands clapped in time with the beat of the song, Phinnegan barely recognized it for what it was. A second pair joined, then a third and a fourth, and so on until Phinnegan was surrounded by clapping hands.

But once again, everything stopped. However, only for a moment for the fiddle sprung into wild and frenzied song, joined by a flute, tom-toms and an uproarious yell.

Phinnegan dropped his arms and opened his eyes. He was back in the courtyard with dancing Faë as far as the eye could see. But above this marvelous din, Phinnegan heard the sound of breaking glass.

He looked down to see the glass which had held the strange, caramel brown liquid shattering on the ground.

A glass he would have sworn he dropped some time ago.

# 16

## A Door Within a Door

Phinnegan stared at the broken glass at his feet and tried to make sense of the last half hour or so. Or at least, what felt like half an hour. He remembered dropping the glass, but in his memory he had dropped it some time ago, before his strange journey through the darkness chasing a spot of light and a lone fiddle

*The fiddle. The music.* His head snapped up and he took in the courtyard once again. Yes, it was the same, but then it was altogether different.

The music was the most noticeable change. He could hear it now, and in spite of his confusion, Phinnegan smiled and filled with a sense of happiness as the music washed over him. He loved the fiddle, the airs and the chords. Those being played now were like none he had ever heard. But the music was only the beginning.

The brightly colored Faë he had seen before were now a whirling harmony of shades and hues that was beyond his comprehension only yesterday. Even now, though he could discern their differences, he had no names for these colors. There were greens and reds and blues and yellows, just as there had been before, but now there were others, combinations and mixtures of colors, but not themselves a color like any he could have put a name to.

Beyond just the Faë themselves, everything around him was vibrant and surreal; even the air defied description, being at the same time crisp like an autumn morning and fragrant as a summer's eve. No wonder the Faë loved this festival.

Quick as a cat, a hand grasped his forearm. The grip was gentle but with a strength that could not be ignored. Phinnegan was pulled into a ring of dancing Faë, each of his hands clasped to those of a beautiful female Faë, her bright-green hair long and straight.

"You looked quite alone, standing there," she said, with a small smile and a wink. "I thought surely you would like to dance."

Phinnegan was dumbfounded, but had no choice but to dance along. She was an inch or two shorter than him, and looked up at him with equally bright-green eyes.

"I am called Emerald."

Phinnegan started to offer his own name in reply, but caught himself, remembering the warnings of Periwinkle and Crimson. She laughed at his caution and leaned close so that only he could hear.

"A bit shy, are we? Or just cautious?" Her eyes narrowed slightly, a playful wariness crinkling her brow. "Very well. I've always found the mysterious to be attractive anyway."

Phinnegan liked her. Perhaps it was the small pursed lips of her mouth or the long eyelashes that fluttered and veiled her green eyes, he could not tell which. He was not accustomed to prolonged eye contact, his books normally occupying his gaze. But he found it easy to stare into those twin pools of emerald-green. So easy in fact that he forgot about the music, continuing to dance once the song had ended.

"Another, another!" she cried, dropping Phinnegan's hands to join the Faë around them in applauding the musicians, who Phinnegan spied now on a raised platform some distance to his left. When they picked up their instruments and the music began again, she turned to him and took his hands eagerly.

"Oh! This is one of my favorites." And just like that, Phinnegan was dancing once again among the Faë.

Phinnegan did not know how to truly dance. But to the Faë, dancing was nothing so formal and was more akin to the spinning and frolicking of young children. As far as Phinnegan was concerned, this was as it should be. He had soon forgotten his troubles, and even laughed when one over-exuberant Faë spun himself until so dizzy he could no longer stand, dragging his partner down with him.

"Your laugh is quite strange," Emerald said abruptly, eyeing him again with that same playful wariness. "I've never heard anything quite like it...Ah, don't look so sad! I think it's cute."

Phinnegan's heart beat in alarm. He feared that he had destroyed the Mask with a simple laugh. The fact that she thought his laugh cute did not even register with him; his mind had already given in to panic. He looked around nervously, but could not find a single eye upon him. But just as his face relaxed, a hand clapped him on the shoulder.

"Is this one causing you any trouble?"

Phinnegan's shoulder sagged with relief. The voice was Periwinkle's. There was a pause as her smile faltered when her eyes fell upon Periwinkle.

"No trouble at all," she said finally, her smallish smile returning. "On the contrary, he's been the perfect gentleman, though a bit quiet."

"Ah well, he is a bit shy, you see. Not too many Faë as fair as yourself where he comes from," Periwinkle said, bowing slightly to the green-haired Faë, who returned the gesture with her own bow.

"And I am quite sure given some time he'd be very happy to know you better, but alas, I must borrow him for the moment." Emerald nodded and then to Phinnegan's surprise, abruptly leaned forward, her hand brushing his chest just above the pocket on his shirt, and kissed him warmly upon the cheek.

"It has been a pleasure," she said before turning and disappearing into the ever-moving crowd of Faë. Phinnegan tried to catch a glimpse of her once again, and thought he saw a flash of her distinct color of green, but he was jerked roughly by Phinnegan.

"Come on, come on. No time to lose, mate. You would waste your time dancing, wouldn't you? We must hurry."

"What are you talking about?" Phinnegan managed to whisper as Periwinkle pulled him through the throng. "I've only been dancing for a few minutes."

"A few minutes? Check the sun, mate. We got here mid-day if not a bit earlier and it's late afternoon. You've been at it for hours." Phinnegan caught a glimpse of the sun's position in the sky just before Periwinkle pulled him into the castle, shutting a large wooden door behind him. As the Faë had said, the sun was just visible over the rampart, but was almost out of sight.

"Well, it felt like only a few minutes," Phinnegan mumbled.

"Time is slippery here, especially when on the drink. Which is why we must hurry. They'll lock the doors at sunset, and we want to be mingling out there and not trapped in here when that time comes."

The two scurried along through the hallways, their footsteps echoing throughout the cavernous castle. Periwinkle pulled Phinnegan along pausing now and then at an intersection before darting in one direction or the other.

"Do you know where you're going?"

"Certainly I do," Periwinkle said, without so much as looking in Phinnegan's direction. "Crimson and I already scouted the castle while you were fraternizing with the ladies. He's waiting up ahead, outside the chamber."

"What chamber?"

"The chamber that holds the stone."

Phinnegan mumbled that he was sorry and that he had most certainly *not* been fraternizing at all, but the Faë either did not hear him or did not care. His brow was furrowed and he chewed his lip, contemplating a particular intersection in the hallways. It was quite a change to see him so serious.

Several minutes and two turns later, they found themselves in a hallway wider than the others, with floors covered by luxurious carpets. Torches longer than Phinnegan was tall dotted the walls on either side, bathing the hallway in orange light. In the spans between the torches, paintings as large as the side of a house stretched from floor to ceiling. At the far end of the hall, Phinnegan could make out two large wooden doors. As they came closer, the wood was shown to be gnarled vines woven into a single piece.

"The doors are made of vines?" he questioned more than stated as they approached the doors.

"Aye. Indestructible by any magic that I possess, and resistant to fire as well." Phinnegan's hand stretched out towards the doors as the Faë spoke.

"Don't touch them!," Crimson snapped appearing from the shadows and causing Phinnegan to jerk his hand back just before his fingertips touched the doors. "Their skin is poisonous to Faë and I would wager humans as well. I doubt you want to test it."

Phinnegan could only stare at his fingers. How close they had been.

"If we can't touch the doors, then how are we to get in there?" Phinnegan looked to see the knobs of the two great doors some two or three feet out of his reach. "And even if we could touch them without being burned-"

"Poisoned," Periwinkle interjected.

"Right," Phinnegan said. "Poisoned. Either way, we can't even reach the handles to open them."

"First off, mate, *we* won't be doing anything. Door or not, if Crimson or myself were to step across that threshold," he paused, drawing a finger across his neck and making a choking sound. "So let's be clear. *You* wouldn't be able to reach the knobs of the door."

"Me, you, we," Phinnegan shot back. "None of us can reach it to get in there."

The two Faë were silent for a few moments, and Phinnegan felt a twinge of sadness that he may not be able to go home, at least not how they had planned. But a sly smile crept across Crimson's face as he stepped back and pointed to a section of the right-hand door that was the same, yet, somehow different than the rest.

"How about through here?"

Phinnegan glanced warily at the red-haired Faë, but stepped closer, peering at this same but different section of the door. His hand moved to touch it, but he halted, instead leaning closer, casting his eyes about the section until he discerned that its shape was rectangular, not unlike that of a door. A small door. His eyes flicked to the right-most edge where, sure enough, an edge was just discernable.

"Another door," he whispered.

"That it is," Periwinkle replied with a satisfied grin upon his face. "A door-within-a-door."

"But how are we, I mean, how am *I* to open it? I still cannot touch the door." The two Faë were silent but Phinnegan caught the wink and nod from Periwinkle to Crimson. "Can I?"

"Look just there," Crimson said, pointing to a specific leaf on the vines that ran through the center of the door-within-the-door. Phinnegan stared for several moments before he began to notice the differences between this leaf and those around it. While the other leaves were brown, this one maintained a slight hue of green. The veins of this leaf ran diagonally to the left, while those on the surrounding leaves ran diagonally to the right. The more that Phinnegan observed the leaves, the more this one leaf began to look nothing like the others.

"Do you see?" asked Crimson.

"It's...different," he said, still comparing this one leaf to the others.

"Indeed," Periwinkle said, joining the other two just in front of the door-within-the-door. "It's the one leaf, the one spot, on this whole death trap of a door that is not covered by a spell or the vine's own poison. That," he finished dramatically, "is how you will get in. You need only to give it a little push.

Without thinking, Phinnegan lifted his hand and was just about to press the leaf when it occurred to him that this all seemed rather odd. And quite convenient.

"What's the hold-up, mate? You must hurry. Press the leaf," Periwinkle urged, turning his head this way and that, checking the three hallways that led to the spot where they stood.

"I was only wondering how it is that this door is here, in a castle of giants. Why would they need such a small door?"

"Ah, a very good question, that," Periwinkle said, gesturing to the door before he continued. "It comes to mind that the giants had a servant once, long ago. Some three or four hundred years ago I guess it was. Little guy, Jack was his name I believe. Waited on them hand and foot too."

"Jack?" Phinnegan asked, the name drawing his interest. "Was he a Faë?"

"No, no, of course not. No Faë would allow himself to be caught by these stupid brutes. No, he was a human, like you. He's the reason you're even going to be able to do this. Jack was here when they placed all of the spells and other things that guard this castle, which is why none of them will harm humans. Couldn't allow their little servant to be blown to bits while he was cleaning the floors, now could they? That's why they never allow a human to enter, not that many try."

"What happened to him? Phinnegan asked quietly.

"Oh, he died some time back. Pretty old for your kind, but the magic in this world will only stretch your short lives so much."

"How did they catch him?"

"Ah, now there's a story. Silly boy couldn't keep his hands off Penny. She was the reason he was caught."

"Penny. It was a girl, then?"

"Not at all," Periwinkle said with a laugh. "A goose! The devil! Do you believe it? Enslaved for a lifetime over a bloody goose! We Faë have had a laugh or two over that for the past few hundred years."

"You can't be serious…" Phinnegan whispered. "Jack, of Jack and the Beanstalk?"

"What? No, nothing like that. Smith was the name I believe."

"Smythe," Crimson interjected.

"Ah! Quite," Periwinkle said with a nod. "Jack Smythe. The damndest thing was he supposedly kept mumbling about cows and beans and his poor old mum." Periwinkle shook his head. "A bit addled in the head I'd say. Here now, what's the matter? You look as though you've seen a ghost."

"Not quite," Phinnegan mumbled. *Unbelievable.*

"Ah, well. You couldn't have known him, long dead before you were born I would guess. Anyway, stop stalling and get on with it. Sunset cannot be that far off. You best hurry or this is all for naught!"

*Sunset. The castle will be locked. We'll be trapped.* Phinnegan had nearly forgotten. He licked his lips and reached towards the leaf that was the same yet different, pausing with his fingertip poised a mere inch away. He swallowed the lump in his throat.

"All I must do is push this leaf?"

"Aye," Periwinkle said with a nod that Phinnegan could barely glimpse from the corner of his eye. "Once you do, you'll be on the inside."

"Just like that?"

"Yes," Crimson chimed in.

"Then what?"

"Then, why, then you go in there and take the bloody stone!" Periwinkle snapped. "We've been over it enough."

Phinnegan turned to look at the purple-haired Faë.

"So it's that easy, is it?"

"More or less," Periwinkle said, shrugging his shoulders, indifferent yet apologetic. "There *could* be an obstacle or two, but nothing you can't handle."

"Obstacles?" Phinnegan said with a sharp look at Crimson. "What sorts of obstacles?"

The red-haired Faë, to his credit, had the conscience to at least look embarrassed as he spoke.

"Well, we don't even know that there will be an obstacle. Not for sure anyway. But-"

"But *what?*"

"Calm down, calm down," Periwinkle interjected. "Don't let him frighten you. There *may*, and I stress *may*, be some type of guardian in the chamber. But I can't imagine that he is still active."

"A guardian?" Phinnegan hissed, a bit too loudly. He glared at Crimson who sought to shush him with his own hiss, but nonetheless lowered his voice to a whisper.

"What kind of guardian? Neither of you said anything about a guardian. A giant? A troll? This is a terrible plan. I'm not doing it."

"Hey now, let's be reasonable," Periwinkle chided. "We've done quite a job to get you in here and-"

"Quick!" Crimson whispered sharply. "Someone's coming!" Behind the three, a large shadow crept along the wall, growing longer by the second.

"No time to waste, mate." Before Phinnegan could step away, Periwinkle had grasped his arm, shoving it so that his outstretched hand moved towards the leaf.

"No! Wait! What about the-"

But he never finished, for it was too late. His voice failed him and his finger impressed the leaf that was the same yet different. There was a sound like the gears of a giant clock working furiously. Phinnegan felt a familiar tug just behind his navel and then, without ever seeing the door open, he was standing on the other side, the door closed behind him.

# 17

## Jack

The chamber on the other side was round, the ceiling rising away from the walls toward the center of a hollow semi-sphere. There were no windows, save for a circle of glass at the apex of the dome. The air smelled faintly of sulfur. Phinnegan spotted several iron stands spaced around the perimeter of the chamber, each bearing a bronze disc filled with a burning substance, and he guessed the source of the sulfur smell.

The floor of the chamber was a white marble, something Phinnegan had never seen before in his entire life. Pillars of solid marble, trimmed in gold, were spaced throughout the chamber; not for support for they did not reach the ceiling, but for decoration, a display of opulence. Just a few steps from the door where he had entered, a two-inch band of slate stained black formed a ring around the entire chamber. Inside this ring lay the white marble, while outside a common stone spanned the few feet between the band and the walls.

Phinnegan, however, ignored the opulence around him. In the center of this room there was something that drew his attention. A single object, a flat-white sphere, rested upon a shortened stump of a pillar in the center of the room.

The stone had the look of a pearl, but without the common iridescent luster, flat where it should be glossy, and white all over with no hints of pink or green. From where he stood, the stone appeared to be only a hair smaller than his own fist, but it was larger in his mind, for it was more than just a stone - it was home.

The thought of being a thief did not cross his mind, nor did his hesitancies about magic, obstacles and guardians. Just so, he hesitated only a moment before running toward the stone.

"Hello? Who's there?" The voice was loud, forceful, almost as if it came from inside Phinnegan's own head.

"Speak!" the voice commanded, booming in Phinnegan's mind. He covered his ears, but to little avail. The voice truly was *inside* his head. "The price for intrusion is death! Speak!"

"Please," Phinnegan cried out. "Please," he said again, this time more softly. His hands remained tight about his ears and he slid to his knees.

"I...I-," he began, but the voice interrupted.

"Jack? Is that you? Where are you? Did you come in through the main door? That wasn't very smart of you, Jack. You know that door is forbidden now, even to you. Why didn't you come in the side? It is you, isn't it Jack? Why, of course it must be. I can sense that you are human and what other human would be here? None at all. Come now, Jack, speak up. Where are you? You know I cannot see."

As the questions sprang from the voice in his mind, Phinnegan's eyes grew wide. Was this the guardian that Periwinkle and Crimson had alluded may still be here? It obviously knew this room, speaking of front and side doors. And this Jack the voice referred to, could it be the same Jack that Periwinkle said had been caught by the giants all those years ago? *The* Jack, that Phinnegan reasoned could only be the same Jack spoken of in the story his mother had told him more than a time or two when he was but a small lad. These presented interesting possibilities, for the guardian could sense he was human, but could not see.

"Y-yes," Phinnegan began, clearing his throat and pushing himself to his feet. "It's me, Jack."

"Ah, Jack! How good it is for you to come and visit me. I get so few visitors." A pause ensued and Phinnegan began to respond, but the voice continued.

"It has been quite some time you know, or at least, it has seemed that way to me. But I do have a dreadful time with, well, *time*. It seems as though it was only yesterday that you were here, but I can sense that this chamber has been void of the living for a long time. How long has it been, Jack?"

"Ummm...months? A few years, perhaps?" Phinnegan could only guess at a believable answer. He was not yet sure what abilities this voice had. It could not see him, yet it seemed to have quite the knack for sensing the truth.

"Years it must be," the voice said in a sad, yet satisfied tone. "But years?" it questioned more sharply, and Phinnegan thought the voice sounded hurt. "Why so long, Jack? Do you no longer consider poor Howard your friend?"

"No, I mean, yes of course you are my friend D-Howard. I've only been...umm...sick. Yes, sick."

"Why, Jack," the voice said in alarm. "Someone should have told me you had taken ill. It must have been terrible, being sick for years. You humans are so fragile, I sometimes forget. Here, let me have a look at you."

In an instant, a bright orb of light suddenly appeared in front of Phinnegan. At least, it began as a single orb, then it was two, then three, then four, six, ten and then hundreds, all tumbling and swirling as one cloud of magnificent lights, now connected by wisps of hazy multi-colored smoke, and then lines of lightning. The cloud was eerily silent, for it appeared as though it should pop, crackle and hiss like a ball of fire or boom like lightning across the sky. The cloud transformed itself before Phinnegan's eyes into all manner of spheres, both lighted and dark, with no apparent pattern to their movement, save that perhaps they danced to an unheard tune. Just as the cloud drew near, it reformed itself into a single orb, not unlike an eye, a sphere of three or four layers floating lazily in front of him in a cloud of swirling tendrils.

"Hmmm. Yes, I do sense that there are some disturbances within you. If I did not know better, and I believe I do, I would say that you seem...afraid. Surely you are not afraid of Howard?"

"N-no, of course not...Howard. I'm still a bit under the weather, that's all. From being sick."

"Harumph. You humans are very odd. Very odd indeed."

The cloud of now seven orbs floated in front of Phinnegan for several moments, giving him the distinct impression that the cloud was weighing his words, gauging their veracity. He wondered if the cloud could sense his own overwhelming feelings of dishonesty. The cloud turned from green to blue and then back again before settling back into a single orb.

"It is so lonely here," the guardian said, its voice still the same in Phinnegan's head despite it now being visible and so close. "Perhaps this solitude is beginning to play with my mind, but you seem...odd."

Phinnegan pushed down the instinct to suck in a breath. Still, he flinched, and he perceived a slight flicker in the cloud that told him it had noticed.

"Tell me, Jack," the guardian spoke into his mind. "What is that tale you are always going on about? How you came to be here at Castle Heronhawk? Wasn't it about a goat? Do tell me the story, I do so love to hear it."

Phinnegan's breathing quickened. The guardian was testing him, trying to catch him in a lie.

"It was a, a cow actually," Phinnegan offered, racking his brain for every last detail of the story he had not heard in four or five years.

"Ah, yes. A cow. I had almost forgotten." The guardian's voice seemed somewhat relieved but maintained an edge of wariness. Phinnegan would have to tell the full story, from beginning to end, if he was to gain the guardian's trust.

"Well, it began one morning when our cow gave no milk-"

"And what was her name? The cow, I mean. I have nearly forgotten." But the tone of the guardian's voice betrayed the lie.

"She was called...Milky-White."

"Oh, yes! Quite. Now I remember," the guardian said, more of the wariness leaving its voice. "I have always thought it a strange name for a cow, or anybody really."

And so, after surviving this first test unscathed, Phinnegan continued the story from his memory, embellishing at times with wild gestures regarding the height of the beanstalk and the terrifying voice of the giant as it chanted its dreadful tune, continuing so until he came near to the very end.

"But just as I was making my escape, the harp cried out 'Master! Master!' and the giant awoke."

"Oh do stop, Jack! I cannot bear to hear the rest. How you were caught just at the bottom of the beanstalk. It is so terribly tragic." The guardian paused, it's singular orb duplicating before the whole cloud turned pink and its brightness dimmed.

"I'm sorry, Jack," the guardian spoke into his mind. "I thought that you were possibly an imposter, some type of thief. You were reeking of dishonesty after all. But that does not excuse my behavior. Will you accept my apology, Jack?"

"Uh, yes. Don't mention it," Phinnegan said sheepishly, for he was of course, just that. An imposter.

"Splendid!" the guardian exclaimed as the orbs brightened and swirled faster. "I knew you weren't the sort of chap to hold a grudge."

The guardian, relieved of its suspicions, danced in space like a giddy vortex of fire and glass, while Phinnegan looked on at the stone in the center of the chamber. He had succeeded in gaining the guardian's trust, at least. Now, how to use that trust to escape this chamber with the wishing stone. Chewing his lip as he thought, Phinnegan perhaps allowed too much time to pass, for the guardian roused him with a question, a hint of worry just detectable in its voice.

"Are you certain that you are not angry, Jack?"

"What? Oh, no, sorry. I was just thinking. I'm not mad. I promise."

"Thinking? What about, Jack?"

The affection that this strange orb had for "Jack" was undeniable, and Phinnegan pondered whether there was a way to use this affection for his own gain. The guardian obviously did not realize that the real Jack had died centuries ago. The idea of tricking the guardian any more than he already had was a sour one to Phinnegan, but so was the idea of staying in this world with no means of escape. Perhaps it would not be stealing if he told the truth, in the guise of Jack, of course.

"I was...I was thinking about my family. My mother. I miss her."

If a cloud of lighted orbs could be said to nod sadly, then this cloud did so. It's swirling slowed and its brightness dimmed.

"Ah, I knew there was an aura about you. Yes, you have lamented to me about your mother in the past. It is such a tragic story, shame on me for having you re live it again just now! I would help, of course, if I knew how. But alas, I am afraid you are trapped here."

The guardian was either a gifted liar or truly felt sorry for "Jack" and would have done whatever it could to help. Phinnegan saw no other path but to test this affection.

"What if there is a way...?" he whispered.

"What!" the guardian replied sharply, perhaps more so than it intended for it corrected itself in a softened tone.

"I mean, what did you say, Jack?"

"I said," Phinnegan began before pausing to clear his throat. "I said what if there is a way?"

Now the cloud sputtered and crackled like so many fireworks on the eve of the summer solstice, and Phinnegan at first feared he had angered it. But then he realized that it was actually *laughing*. Laughing at him.

"What's so funny?" Phinnegan snapped with a scowl.

"Oh," the guardian said amidst more crackling. "I don't mean to offend, dear Jack. I thought perhaps it was a joke; we've been over this so many times you know. No more magic beans, no way for you to get home."

Phinnegan was silent for a moment, considering whether to drop this charade, but he pressed onward.

"I've learned that there may just be a way."

"Truly?" the guardian questioned, its interest clearly piqued. "And how did you learn of this way?"

"Well, a Faë told me that-"

"FAË!" the guardian's voice boomed loudly in Phinnegan's head, driving him to his knees.

"Dirty, rotten SCOUNDRELS!" The guardian's color changed to a bright red, burning like a flame, and the cloud of orbs exploded into a thousand little specks of light, madly swarming like a hive of displaced bees.

"Please. Howard-"

"NEVER trust a Faë, Jack. Have I not warned you of this before? They should not even be near the castle, it's the worst kind of violation. Why was I not alerted? I must contact my masters and –"

"No, wait," Phinnegan managed to interrupt with a shout that he could barely hear above the din in his own head. "The Faë are here because of the festival."

"What? Festival?"

"Yes, yes, the festival," Phinnegan pleaded, his voice still loud. "You must know of it. Once each year they allow the Faë onto the grounds, to trade and celebrate." Phinnegan raised his head and watched the guardian spin and pulse just as madly as before, but then ever so slightly, the bright red faded to dull and the spinning slowed.

"Festival," the guardian's voice mumbled in his mind. "Hmmm...yes, I do suppose I recall something about a festival. I am so cut off from the goings-on around here, you know." The guardian was beginning to calm, but suddenly the cloud flashed a bright red and the voice snarled in his mind.

"But that does not change the fact that you must *never* trust a Faë!"

"Why not?" Are they so bad?"

"Why not? So bad?" the guardian's voice teased. "They are *worse* than bad. Why do you think that my masters never allow them within the castle? They're thieves, tricksters. They would just as soon rob you as speak to you. No, no. Faë simply cannot be trusted."

Phinnegan stood in silence. He chewed his lip as he thought. *What do I do now?* Part of him wondered if the guardian was right, if he truly should not trust the two Faë. They did often seem to keep vital details to themselves, not sharing them with him unless they must. And then there were those looks that passed between the two. But what choice did he have? Howard had no idea how to get him home and at least the two Faë had a theory.

"But what if they are right?" Phinnegan ventured quietly. "What if what they say is true and there is a way for me to go home?"

"Highly unlikely," the guardian said quickly and matter-of-factly. "I know of no way to get you home, nor have I ever known a Faë to look out for anyone's interests but their own. Ever."

"But that doesn't mean that they can't be right."

"Possibly," the guardian said, the heat draining slightly from its voice. "Well, what did they say? We'll consider it together, you and I, Jack."

"Well, they spoke of the Passes between our worlds having narrowed. They said it is not easy to travel between the two and that it was beyond their power to send me back –
"

"Well *that* is definitely a truth," the guardian scoffed.

"But, they said they really wanted to help me," Phinnegan continued, ignoring the interruption. "They think that they can send me home, just –"

"Why," the guardian interrupted once again. "Why do you suppose these Faë are so eager to help you? Quite unlike a Faë in my experience, and I have known a few of them in my time, which is not a short period, I trust you know."

The lie came so quickly to Phinnegan's lips that perhaps he had stumbled upon some hidden truth.

"It was one of them that sold me the magic beans."

"What?" the guardian said sharply. "Remorse from a Faë? This *is* very strange. Very strange indeed. Do you believe him?"

"Yes, I recognized him." Again the lie slipped from his tongue quickly, so quickly that he thought to embellish it. "I was quite angry at first, as you can imagine, but he...he umm, apologized. He wants to help."

"Ah, yes, well you would recognize him, wouldn't you?" The guardian grew silent, appearing to think as its colors flashed from green to red to yellow to purple." "It still seems strange to me. Tell me, Jack, what did these Faë suggest?

Phinnegan swallowed and licked his lips.

"They said they need the stone."

The guardian, for the first time since Phinnegan had laid eyes upon it, stopped swirling.

"The...the stone," the guardian stammered, its tone feeble and questioning. "M-my stone?" Phinnegan remained silent.

The guardian swam slowly in the air, first right and then left, then back to the right, like a man would pace in his study. Phinnegan continued to hold his tongue, his eyes following the floating cloud that now bore the weight of his hopes of going home. When the guardian slowed and stopped, Phinnegan had pushed himself on his toes and leaned forward. When the voice came, it spoke only one word.

"Impossible," the tone flat and dispassionate.

"But –"

"No. It is impossible. I would not trust a Faë even under normal circumstances, but to allow them control of MY stone? It is unthinkable." The guardian began to float to and fro again as it continued. "Besides, in all the centuries that I have guarded the stone, no one, not even one of my masters, has touched it. I am not certain of what would happen were it removed from its resting place. It is too dangerous."

"Dangerous? What do you mean?"

"Well, as guardian, it is my job to protect the stone. Who's to say what reactions are within me. For instance, earlier my alarms were set-off merely because you came in through the front door and not the side. No, no, even if I were to agree to this...this preposterous suggestion, I would not be held responsible for my own actions."

"But what if they are right? What if the stone can send me home?"

"I'm sorry, Jack," the guardian's voice spoke flatly in his mind. "I cannot allow you to take the stone."

Phinnegan had no reply to what seemed to be the guardian's final word. He walked over to the nearest iron stand bearing the bronze disk and gazed into the fire. The dancing flames of a fire tend to have a calming effect on those who gaze into their depths. Even a cat will sit and stare at a dancing flame, mesmerized by its beauty.

The solitary tear falling on Phinnegan's cheek made him squint his eyes.

*I am too old to cry.*

The guardian seemed to sense Phinnegan's sadness, and it must have been sense as it could not see the tear on his cheek or the sag in his shoulders. It approached and stopped just behind Phinnegan's shoulder.

"You miss her don't you, Jack?" the voice asked quietly. "Your mother, I mean. " Phinnegan only nodded.

Then, in that round chamber with domed ceiling, there could be heard the strangest sound, like the wind whistling down the chimney just before a storm. It seemed as though the guardian had *sighed*. Phinnegan found this rather human gesture somewhat comforting.

"Do you truly want to leave poor Howard?" the guardian asked, the voice quavering as the words fluttered through Phinnegan's mind.

"No...it's not that," Phinnegan mumbled. "I just want to go home, to my mother. To *my* home."

The guardian floated behind Phinnegan, unmoving, but a circus of light as the cloud changed from a few orbs to many. Phinnegan continued to stare at the fire, and the guardian appeared to *stare* at Phinnegan. When the second tear fell onto Phinnegan's cheek, the guardian moved closer, now hovering only a foot from Phinnegan's back.

"I'm sorry," the guardian said. "But it is simply too dangerous. Besides, what makes these Faë so certain they can use the stone?"

"Why couldn't they?" Phinnegan managed to say. "Is it broken?"

"Broken? Why, no, I do not believe so. Honestly, I am not quite sure what it does..."

Phinnegan lifted his head and turned to glance at the guardian.

"You mean you have been guarding this thing for all this time and you don't even know what it is?"

"Yes, I suppose that's true. My masters never thought to tell me." Phinnegan faced the guardian.

"Well I do. It's a wishing stone, the largest I have ever seen. I've seen their magic with my own eyes. And this one is twenty times the size of the ones I have seen before. I know it can send me home."

The guardian floated back a few feet, creating some distance between itself and Phinnegan.

"A wishing stone? Never heard of such a thing. Are you quite sure that is what it is?"

Phinnegan ran past the guardian to the center of the chamber and placed his hand on the stone.

"Now wait just –" the guardian began, but Phinnegan cut him off.

"Spirit, who is your master?" Just as in the court at Féradoon, the stone spoke. Again, a feminine voice, slow and melodic.

*My master is the Lord of Heronhawk.*

"The stone speaks?" the guardian's voice asked incredulously. The guardian sped to Phinnegan's side and hovered just above the stone.

"Yes. They can speak, the wishing stones I mean."

"I see. Tell me wishing stone, if that is what you are, what powers have you?"

Silence.

"I don't think it works that way," Phinnegan said. "I believe you must be touching it like I am, and address it as 'Spirit'."

"Hmmm. Well, ask it if it has the power to send you back to your world."

"I don't know if it can answer such a specific question."

"Well if it can't then it is probably not as powerful as these Faë told you that it was. Ask."

Phinnegan licked his lips and stared at the stone.

"Spirit...can you...*would* you send me home?" The stone was silent for a moment, and then spoke.

*Yes, if the proper words are spoken.*

Phinnegan, his eyes wide, placed a second hand on the stone.

"Spirit, send me home!"

Nothing happened. Phinnegan tried again.

"Spirit, please send me home."

But again, nothing happened. Phinnegan's shoulders sagged and his hands withdrew from the stone.

"The proper words," the guardian said softly in Phinnegan's mind. And then again, the sound of wind whistling down the chimney.

"Take it."

"What?" Phinnegan asked, his eyes fixed on the guardian.

"Take it, I say," the voice said quietly, but quickly sharpened. "But I warn you, I do not know what will happen if you try to take it. I can take no responsibility for my actions, for I fear they will be beyond my control." The cloud reduced itself to a single orb and ceased its swirling, standing stark and still before Phinnegan.

"Be careful, Jack. And don't trust these Faë any more than you must. They seem to have told you *a* truth, but I wonder if it was the whole."

Phinnegan couldn't speak, but the guardian seemed to recognize his silence for gratitude, the orb dipping slightly as though it nodded.

Phinnegan reached his hands back up to the stone. At least he knew that touching it would not set off any alarms. He touched it gingerly with one hand and then the other. The stone was as smooth as glass, and cool to the touch. After a moment, he scooped the stone from its place on the pedestal. He took one slow step backwards, then a second and a third.

"Anything?" he asked over his shoulder. A moment passed before the guardian answered.

"No."

Phinnegan turned and walked roughly half the distance between the pedestal and the door that he had entered some time earlier. Here he stopped.

"I guess we're safe," he said softly, marveling at the feel of the stone in his hands. It was not as heavy as he had expected.

"It would seem so." The guardian drifted away from where Phinnegan stood, its colors dimming slightly.

"Visit me if you can, Jack?"

"I promise," Phinnegan said without hesitation. "Goodbye, Howard."

"Goodbye, Jack."

Phinnegan, a twinge of guilt tugging at his mind, continued his march towards the door. His soft-soled shoes made muffled thuds as he walked across the marble. He told himself that he had not quite stolen the stone. Humans are wont to rationalize. All in all, it went as well as he could have hoped.

And then he crossed the black slate arc just before the door.

A crash like thunder shook the room around him and he felt each reverberation rocking his very bones. When the guardian's voice came, his mind screamed and he nearly fumbled the stone.

"STOP! THIEF!"

Phinnegan turned to see that the guardian had grown to a cloud twice the size of any it had been since he entered the room. Its color was a bright, violent red and the multitude of orbs pulsed with a fiery light while arcs of lightning jumped between them.

"THIEF! RELEASE THE STONE!"

Phinnegan wasted no time. The guardian had been right, there was some sort of alarm set within him and it had been tripped. He stumbled the final steps to the door and searched for the same leaf that had allowed him to enter.

But there was none.

Frantic, Phinnegan turned to see the guardian swelling again in size and pulsing rapidly. Again he searched the door, but found no leaf. Whether the door was poisoned on this side just as it had been on the other, he had no time to ponder. He thrust a hand at the door, and no sooner had his finger touched it than the door vanished. There, just across the threshold stood the two Faë, wide-eyed and pale.

"What did you *do?*" Periwinkle asked hoarsely, his face blanching further.

"Nothing, I took the stone and –"

"There is no time!" Crimson snapped. "We must hurry! This noise will have warned the dead, not to mention this whole bloody castle!"

Phinnegan needed no second warning. He lunged forward to join the Faë, but he was stopped short at the threshold. Something was holding him back.

"What are you waiting for?" Periwinkle yelled. *"Come on!"*

"I can't," Phinnegan said, his face panicked. "I can't pass through the doorway."

"It's the stone," Crimson said. "You can't pass out while holding it. Toss it out."

Without hesitation, Phinnegan tossed the stone into Crimson's waiting hands. Crimson cradled the stone, staring at the treasure in his hands.

"Come on then!" Periwinkle insisted. But when Phinnegan moved again to pass the threshold, he could not pass.

"It won't let me out! Help!" Phinnegan glanced back and saw that the guardian was moving in his direction.

"Periwinkle, do something!" Phinnegan pleaded, shouting over the crackling sound of the guardian's approach.

Periwinkle hesitated and then moved towards the doorway. But Crimson's hand upon his shoulder stopped him. The two Faë shared a look. Crimson's hand fell away and Periwinkle turned, his eyes meeting Phinnegan's. One look at Periwinkle's face and Phinnegan turned white.

"No," Phinnegan whispered.

"Sorry, mate."

"Wait!" Phinnegan cried out. "Wait..."

But, they were gone, and Phinnegan was alone. He turned just in time to see the guardian closing the final distance between them.

"THIEF!" the voice bellowed once more.

When the guardian's cloud of light touched Phinnegan, there was a brilliant flash followed by thunder without sound.

When the first giant lumbered into the chamber a few moments later, he found it empty.

The stone, the guardian and Phinnegan Qwyk were nowhere to be found.

# 18

## Pixy Led

An adventure in a book and an adventure in person are altogether a different sort of thing. Phinnegan found that he preferred the former.

He had felt no pain when the guardian's cloud of light touched him. Nor did he meet his death, which was certainly something that flashed before his mind as a possibility. Instead, there was little for him to feel at all; nothing in fact. But he was afraid.

Everything was gone. The Faë, of course, were gone, as was the stone. So, too, were the great domed chamber and the guardian, Howard. Everything that had been around him only moments before was now, simply not. There was a disturbing pattern in this world in that quite often things, and people, simply up and disappeared. Including oneself. The question now was, where exactly had Phinnegan disappeared to.

Looking around, nothing was familiar to him. He was outside and it was dark. The ground was soft and cool to the touch, though there was little grass, most of the ground being dirt and a scant few rocks. Although a thick, dark cloud approached from one direction, the sky directly above him was dotted with a billion stars, the Milky Way arcing across the nighttime sky. It comforted him to see something so familiar. Even here in this strange world, the same eyes looked down upon him from the heavens. It was as close to home as he had been these past few days.

The sight was so comforting, in fact, that Phinnegan sat on the ground for some time gazing upwards. For once, he was completely alone, with no one to tell him where to go, but neither was anything chasing him or trying to kill him. At least not at this very moment.

As he gazed at the stars, the dark cloud moved closer to him, slowly at first, but with increasing speed. When the cloud was nearly on top of him, Phinnegan rose to his feet and began to trek in the direction that the cloud was moving, trying to stay ahead. He had no idea where he was going, but perhaps he would find some kind of shelter.

After walking for some time, Phinnegan noticed that the area around him began to slowly fill with trees, first one then two and then ten. The open expanse of land was giving way to a forest, and in short order, Phinnegan was indeed within the borders of a dark and brooding wood. The trees became closer together and began to crowd around him. There was a path, but it was narrow and overgrown, and weaved amongst large trees such that a group would have needed to walk single-file to stay on the path.

When the first drop of rain fell on his head, Phinnegan shivered, both from the sudden chill of the rain and the wind that rustled the leaves about, as well as the memories of Darkwater forest and the Faolchú.

He walked on for perhaps half an hour more, always following the winding way of the path deeper into the wood. The trees were of varying types, elm and oak, ash and birch. One oak that he passed was darker and larger than any other tree around. Its branches were thick and gnarled, and hung gravely over the path. But Phinnegan paid it little mind.

Until he passed it a second time.

Even in the dim light of a cloudy night, the tree looked familiar. The same dark trunk, the same gnarled branches hanging over the path. Phinnegan stopped and looked long and hard at the tree, but the rain continued to pound and so he continued on.

Phinnegan shivered uncontrollably now; the rain was dreadfully cold and he had little to keep himself warm. The ice like rain and the increasing wind was draining his strength quickly. Phinnegan continued to search for a shelter: a bough that could shield him, a hollow, rotting tree in which to hide. But there was nothing. He continued to trudge through the forest, but his steps began to slow.

A flicker of motion caused him to raise his head. A speck of light like a firefly on a mid-summer's eve blinked not more than ten paces in front of him. It blinked a second time and then was gone, only to re-appear a few moments later more than twenty paces ahead.

*It must be nice to be your own light.*

He continued on, stumbling occasionally over the sinewy roots that ran from the trees and broke free of the ground. He moved as though within a daze, and more than once his feet seemed to know something that his mind did not, for now and then he would turn right, and then left, but could not remember deciding to do so. More than once, another speck of light, another little firefly, blinked somewhere in front of him. It could, of course, have been the same speck of light, but that thought never crossed his mind.

When the trees finally parted, Phinnegan stood in a small clearing, barely able to see more than a few paces in front of him. The rain had increased and the night was dark. But just ahead lay something even darker, like the great gaping jaw of a beast, black and ominous even in a black world. Just in front, to the right of this darkness, a firefly flickered.

Phinnegan stumbled forward several feet, coming ever closer to the gaping mouth in the darkness. When his steps finally brought him to the edge, and he crossed into this darkness, the rain stopped. The air here was warm, and an odor assailed him, though it was neither pleasant nor foul, only the heavy scent of fertile earth.

Wiping the water from his face and pushing his hair back, Phinnegan turned around. Only just behind him, the rain continued to fall and splash in newborn puddles. He could just make out the rough, rocky outline of the great gaping mouth that had been visible in the darkness. He was in a cave.

It was not a large cave, but the ceiling was tall enough for him to stand. The entry way was narrow so that his outstretched arms allowed his fingertips to graze both walls, but this throat widened into the belly of the cave, which was large enough for several people.

Though he was now out of the rain, Phinnegan was still cold and wet, not to mention hungry. He was also exhausted, which dampened his hunger. One glance into the downpour outside of the cave was enough to resign him to bed without supper.

He moved towards one corner of the cave, but just at the edge of his vision, he spied a small speck of light blinking furiously in the opposite corner. Something pulled him to this speck, but when he reached the corner, the speck was gone. The corner itself was extremely warm. The rock was almost too hot to touch.

Phinnegan pressed his back against the wall and began to lower himself down to the ground. When he placed his hand on the ground to brace himself, his fingers touched a pile of small, round objects. At first, he took them to be rocks, but a handful and a quick trip to the mouth of the cave showed them to be nuts. Nuts! Pecans and walnuts, chestnuts and acorns, as well as others he did not recognize. Upon his return to the corner, he found more than several pockets would hold.

A nearby rock serving as a nutcracker, Phinnegan ate nut after nut, smiling to himself that he should have such luck to find this cave with so warm a corner and such a lovely dinner.

When the last nut had been cracked, and Phinnegan's stomach was full to bursting, he lay down and curled himself tightly into a ball amongst the scatterings of shells. Within moments, he was fast asleep.


Phinnegan awoke with a jolt. He rolled his head from side to side, checking the area around him, but no one was there. From where he lay, the morning light was just visible, creeping in through the mouth of the cave.

He pushed himself to a seated position and stretched his arms high overhead with a yawn. His stomach rumbled but when he searched the floor around him, there was nothing but shells.

As he pushed himself to his feet, Phinnegan leaned close to one wall of the corner. On this wall there was a cleft in the rock, a little ledge, no bigger than would hold an apple. While there was something on this ledge, it was no apple, nor anything of the sort. There was, instead, a woman. No taller than a man's finger is long and as slender and lithe as a willow branch, she had been sitting with her knees pulled to her chest, but now bounded to her feet when Phinnegan's eyes fell upon her.

"Good morning!" she chirped in a voice that was small without being meek.

Phinnegan, his eyes wide, was speechless. The little woman cocked her head to one side, staring back into his wide eyes. Her skin was fair and her hair hung long and straight just past her waist, its auburn color the most natural that Phinnegan had seen in this world. But she was more than just a tiny woman. There, folded upon themselves, and sticking up just behind each shoulder, were wings. As translucent as the wings of a bee, but with a tint of orange, they seemed to sprout from her back.

But as odd as these wings were, Phinnegan did not look at them, nor did he look at her beautiful face. He stared at her feet, the red in his cheeks deepening.

She was, of course, as pixies tend to be, almost entirely naked.

"Hello?" she chirped again. "I said 'Good Morning'." Had Phinnegan looked at her face, he would have seen that delicate brow furrow as she placed her hands upon her hips. "It is very rude not to return a greeting. Didn't your mother teach you manners?"

"Ummm...good morning," he said, keeping his eyes on her feet. The pixie nodded satisfactorily.

"That will have to do, although you could speak more clearly. It is very hard for my tiny ears to understand you." Phinnegan only nodded, continuing to stare at her feet.

"Why are you looking at my feet?" she cried, her voice rising in alarm. "Are they dirty? Do I have mud on them?" Pixies are of course very particular about cleanliness, and this one was no different. She turned each foot around, and bent it back and forth, scrutinizing every spot until she was satisfied. But she remained puzzled, for Phinnegan continued to stare at her feet.

"What *are* you looking at?"

"Nothing...it's just that...well..."

"Well what? And I told you about speaking clearly," she scolded.

"Well..." he began, his cheeks darkening further. "You're naked."

The little creature's lips parted in confusion as she cocked her head to one side.

"So?"

"Umm...well I've never, you know..." he stammered at first, but then found his voice. "Shouldn't you be wearing clothes?" She shook her head.

"I don't have any."

"Oh."

Anyone could see that Phinnegan was quite uncomfortable, including the pixie. She looked around the ledge for a moment before finding what she needed. After a few quick movements, she stood proudly before Phinnegan.

"There, all better."

Phinnegan slowly raised his head. She had indeed covered herself, although just barely. Here long hair now draped in front of her shoulders, concealing her breasts. About her waist, a small ivy leaf hung precariously.

He looked to her face and found that the pixie smiled at him sweetly.

"Did you sleep well?" she asked.

"Yes...actually," he replied, his voice bearing an edge of surprise.

"Good. I could have led you elsewhere to something more comfortable than stone, but this cave was so near I thought it would do.

"What? You led me here? I don't remember that."

"Well what do you remember?"

"I remember," he began, squinting as he tried to remember the previous night. "I remember walking through the rain, though my memory is kind of foggy..."

"Quite natural, really. What else do you remember?"

"Well...not much else about the walk. Just that it was dreadfully long and cold. Then I came here, and it was dry and warm and I found a pile of nuts just there," he said, pointing to the ground around him. "And then I fell asleep."

"Nothing else?" she asked, leaning forward on her toes. Phinnegan appeared to think for a moment, but then shook his head.

"No, sorry."

The pixie frowned, and her shoulders sagged. She sat down on the ledge, her legs dangling off the end.

"I thought you might have seen me," she said with a heavy sigh. "No one ever notices me."

"Oh, well, I think I would have remembered if I had seen you."

"Really? Why?"

"Ummm...well you're very pretty. I think I would have remembered that." She laughed lightly like the song of a bird.

"Thank you." But her smile faded and she swung her legs restlessly.

"But I was there. No one ever notices poor Mariella."

"Mariella? Is that your name?" When she nodded, Phinnegan quickly added, "It's a very pretty name. I've never heard it before." The little creature shrugged.

"It's pretty common where I come from."

"My name is Phinnegan. Phinnegan Qwyk."

"Nice to meet you," the pixie said, her voice hollow and distant.

The two remained in silence for some time, the pixie swinging her legs over the ledge, her chin resting in her hand, while Phinnegan racked his brain for his memories of the previous night.

"I'm sorry," he said at last, shaking his head. " I don't remember much about last night. I remember the cold, the rain, the walk through the forest, and this cave." After a moment, he added, "And then there were those little fireflies."

"Little what?" she asked, her head rising.

"Fireflies. I saw several last night. Little bugs that light up at night. They were everywhere."

With a broad smile, the little woman jumped to her feet and unfolded her wings, which fluttered gracefully, lifting her so that her pointed toes were an inch off the ground.

"So you *did* see me!" She exclaimed, he lips parting in a grin.

"That was *you*?" Phinnegan gasped. "You mean you can light up like that in the dark?" Her head bobbed with enthusiasm.

"Yes of course, all pixies can. It's much easier for us to lead that way."

"Lead," Phinnegan said, a puzzled look on his face. "What do you mean?"

"Why, I led you here, of course." She put her hands on her hips. "How do you think you found this cave so easily in the dark, much less a horrible storm?"

"I hadn't thought about it, really. Everything was a bit hazy." The pixie nodded quickly.

"Yes, yes. That was just the enchantment."

"Enchantment," Phinnegan mumbled to himself.

"Yes, doesn't harm you of course."

Now Phinnegan had heard many stories in his twelve years, and a few had been about what the elders in his town called "the little people." More than once, he had heard a tale of some relative or another who had been led astray by a pixie into some bog or a briar patch. They called it being 'pixy-led' and said that the little people cast a spell on their quarry so that they would follow them, seemingly of their own accord.

Still others spoke of "the little people" as helpful, crediting them with a house that was magically cleaned while they slept or some other chore that was left undone the night before but miraculously finished in the morning.

There were also stories about a peculiar trait of the pixies. They were quite immodest and more often than not, went entirely naked, with exceptions being made for the odd scrap of ribbon or lace, or some other finery that had been given to them, as they were very keen on gifts. There were even reports of a pixie spotted wearing a shiny silver button as a hat. Unfortunately for all their fondness for pretty things, they possessed an uncanny lack of fashion sense.

Phinnegan was very grateful that this pixie had seen fit to lead him to safety instead of to trouble, and thought to give her a gift. But he had no ribbon nor lace, or anything so fine. But he did have a silken handkerchief. He plunged both hands into the pockets of his trousers, and after a moment was able to locate the handkerchief. He was confident that he had not had occasion to use it since his mother had last washed it.

"Umm...for you," he said, pulling it from his pocket and presenting it to the little woman with a flourish. "Thanks for bringing me here."

The little pixie's eyes widened and she took the handkerchief, which was more like a blanket for her, from Phinnegan.

"For...me?" She asked, her voice a small whisper.

"Yes...it's not much, but –"

"Why, it's beautiful!"

"Well, I'm glad you like it."

"Like it," she said, her eyes fixed on her gift. "I love it!" She held the handkerchief at arm's length and cocked her head to one side. "Now, how to wear it?" She stood for a moment, looking intently at the handkerchief, the tongue peeking from the corner of her mouth.

"Aha!" she exclaimed as she leapt from the ledge. She moved in a blur for more than a minute, and when she stopped the silken handkerchief was wrapped around her body much like a toga.

"Oh, it is so beautiful! And so soft! Thank you so very much," she said, looking down to admire her new outfit. "Just wait until the others see this," she muttered softly.

"You're welcome...and what others? Do you mean other pixies?" Phinnegan peered around the cave, presumably looking for other small people flying about.

"Well, they're not around here silly. We're quite far away from our little vale." She wrinkled her nose as she surveyed the barren rock walls of the cave. "This place has its charm, I suppose, but it is not a place a pixie would call home." Suddenly, as if she had just remembered something, she flew to the edge of the cave and looked outside.

"Oh my! It is getting quite late. I have been gone for far too long. I must get home." Without a glance back, she flew out of the cave.

"Wait!" Phinnegan managed to cry out as he pushed himself to his feet and raced to catch the pixie. He found her just outside the cage, hovering in line with his eyes.

"Yes?"

"M-may I come with you?"

"Come with me?!" she questioned shrilly. "Completely out of the question. No one is allowed in our vale!"

"But...I don't have anywhere to go. I have no one."

"Why don't you go home?"

"I can't...I don't know the way. The Faë were supposed to help me but-"

"What?" she asked sharply, fluttering closer to his face. "You're not Faë?" She hovered about him for a few moments, darting to check his ears, his hair and his eyes.

"No...I suppose you're not. You are far too dull. No offense," she added with a small smile. "So you're a human then?"

"Yes. Does that mean you will take me with you?"

The pixie was silent for a moment, but at last shook her head.

"I'm sorry, I cannot help you." She bowed quickly and then sped off.

"Mariella! Wait, please!" Phinnegan called out as he ran to follow her. But he did not get far before his foot caught on the root of a tree, and he was thrown forward. He fell flat on his face, inhaling a mouth full of crushed leaves.

When he lifted his head, sputtering the leaves from his mouth, the pixie had returned and hovered just above the ground in front of him.

"Where did you get that?" she asked quietly, her face ashen and her eyes transfixed on his chest.

"What?" Phinnegan managed, brushing the debris from his face. The pixie fluttered closer and landed lightly on the ground just beneath his head.

"That," she said, pointing to something just beneath him. Phinnegan followed her finger and saw that she pointed at his pocket, or rather, to something small and shiny that had been coughed up by said pocket when he had fallen. He pushed himself to his knees and picked up the small object.

He held his hand out in front of him and peered at the object. It was a small coin, smaller than a penny, tarnished silver, and with a strange character imprinted on the visible side.

"This?" he asked. The pixie sprang up from the ground and landed lightly in his hand. She bent down and traced the character on the coin with her hand.

"How..." she began in a whisper, but stopped, and then looked up into Phinnegan's eyes.

"You will need to be blinded, and you cannot ask any questions."

"What?" Phinnegan said in alarm.

"I said you must agree to be blinded. It is the only way I can bring you with me."

"But –", he began, but she raised a hand to silence him.

"You have displayed the Mark. You must not speak another word."

"I don't under-"

"Please. Will you consent? It is an enchantment, nothing more. The blindness will not be permanent. If you will not, I cannot take you with me."

Phinnegan sat on his knees, staring at this little pixie, who had returned her gaze to the silver coin in his palm. *Where did that come from?*

After a minute or more in silence, he finally nodded.

"All right, I agree." She fluttered up from his hand, hovering just in front of his face.

"Do not worry, I will lead you."

Phinnegan gasped when she blinded him, but before he could come to grips with this new sensation, the same haze of the night before settled itself upon his mind and he felt himself stand and begin to walk.

# 19

## An Ancient Token

They travelled for what seemed like hours, the sun warm upon his back, but it was hard for Phinnegan to guess time with his mind in such a fog. The daze he was in felt much stronger this time, perhaps it was because he was also blind. He could not keep his mind from replaying the events of the previous day. The castle, the stone, Howard. When he thought of Howard, he nearly fell, his feet stumbling over something in his path. But after that, the fog lifted slightly, and he felt much as he had the night before.

They stopped twice on their journey, for Phinnegan to rest and eat. The pixie guided him to some berries and nuts that grew from the surrounding bushes and to a cool stream for him to have a drink.

When he realized that the heat of the sun was no longer upon his back, he strained his ears for sounds of his surroundings. Mariella's charm still blinding him, his hearing served to orient him. First he heard the sound of his feet, echoing about him. Then there was the constant sound of dripping water seemingly coming from all directions. He guessed they were inside another cave, or some other type of passage.

"Almost there," Mariella muttered.

They walked awhile longer, together but each alone. Soon enough, he felt himself stop moving, and the haze began to lift from his mind.

"Wait here. I will ask permission to bring you in," she said, and then fluttered away before Phinnegan was able to ask any questions. Still blind, he stumbled around but eventually found his way to the ground awkwardly and sat down.

He listened intently in the darkness. At first, he heard only the dripping of the water, but then he heard the quiet echo of tiny voices. One was Mariella's, of that he was certain. The other was of similar pitch and smoothness, and he reasoned it must be another pixie.

He could not make out the words they spoke, for their voices were quiet and hushed, and they spoke quickly. But their voices became more rapid and their pitches rose until a sharp word from the second pixie brought silence to the cavern. A soft fluttering of wings announced Mariella's return.

"He has gone to fetch the Mother," she said, her voice quiet.

"Why?" Phinnegan ventured, but he was met with only silence. He felt quite vulnerable sitting there, with this small, fantastic creature in a cavern in an unknown world and with an enchantment upon him so that he could not see. Phinnegan shifted his position on the cavern's floor, drawing himself into a smaller presence.

"Here she comes," Mariella muttered. Within a moment or two, there could be heard quite the commotion coming from the same direction from which Mariella had just returned. Multiple voices chattered excitedly, with one louder and more discernable than the rest.

"The nerve of that girl! Bringing an outsider, *here*, to our home. Why, it borders on treason. A Faë would be bad enough. They are tricksters and crooks but they are magical and understand us...humans on the other hand, why...it *is* treason. I'll have her flogged with the whiskers of a rat! I'll..." the voice, which had been growing louder, stopped abruptly. There was a sudden chill in the air and the perspiration on Phinnegan's brow turned cool as it trickled down his cheek.

"MARIELLA!" the Mother's voice thundered.

"How DARE you bring an outsider to our home. And a human no less!" An angry flutter signaled the approach of the Mother, and then her voice came from just behind Phinnegan's right ear.

"Humans are dirty," her voice came in a hissing whisper. "They smell of smoke and fat, their greed floats around them like a pack of flies. Even now he plots to steal from us, to rob of us. Look! See how he fidgets so? A sign of treachery!"

"I don't –"

"SILENCE!" the Mother's voice screeched, cutting off Phinnegan as he tried to speak. "Do not speak to me! You will utter not a word unless I permit it, otherwise I will turn you into dust where you stand. Do you hear me?"

Phinnegan could only nod.

"Good. We have promised not to harm humans if at all possible, but your presence here strains my oath." There was a pause and then her voice began again, but not as near to him.

"And you, Daughter. What do you have to say for yourself?"

"Mother, he was lost –"

"Lost? More likely searching for this very passage to which you have brought him. At least you had the good sense to blind him. Yet what you have done is beyond some small error. It is criminal. High Treason against *my* throne. I'm afraid there is only one punishment that suits such a crime. Banishment."

The collective gasp from dozens of tiny lungs from all directions was the first clue for Phinnegan that a great number of pixies had gathered around him. Now, they muttered in hushed but excited voices.

"Banishment?" Mariella's voice said in a hoarse whisper. "Banishment? But I must explain myself, Mother. I led him here because-"

"We do not lead anyone, anywhere, save to keep them *away* from our vale. You have done the exact opposite!" the Mother cried. "It is terrible, this crime you have committed. Never in a thousand years or more has someone dared to do such a thing."

"Mother, please. He was in the Winding Wood."

"The Winding Wood," several voices exclaimed while others squeaked and piled their exclamations atop one another.

"The forest!"

"A human in the Winding Wood? Impossible."

"Only criminals are found there!"

"Then he must be a criminal! Thief!"

"Quiet, the lot of you," the Mother snapped sharply. Once again an angry flutter belied her presence just behind his ear.

"It is true what they say. The Winding Wood is unknown and unknowable to all save a few creatures. It is a place where Faë and human alike would wander until the end of time. It is a prison. There are only a few ways by which a person comes to be in the Winding Wood. Some are worse than others, and none are good. How did you come to the forest?"

"I...don't know," Phinnegan managed to speak from a throat that was dry and hoarse. "I was simply...there." None of the pixies around him uttered a sound, but the flutter of wings could be heard still, just behind his ears.

"Suddenly, was it? Did you touch a Will o' the Wisp?" the Mother's voice came in a stern whisper. He heard a hushed murmur flow like a waver through the pixies in the cavern.

"A what?" he asked.

"A Will o' the Wisp.

"No...no. I don't think so." A sigh of relief emanated from the crowd of pixies. Even the Mother seemed to have calmed when she spoke.

"Ah, that is good then. There is no more foul or sinister a deed than that which summons one to the Winding Wood by way of a Will o' the Wisp. Still, other ways can tell of –"

"Yes, you did," Phinnegan heard Mariella mumble softly from some short distance away. The pixies drew in a collective breath.

"What did you say?" the Mother asked, in a voice that was quiet but icy flat, a hint of fear barely detectable.

"He did touch a Will o' the Wisp," Mariella said more loudly, causing a commotion among the pixies.

"Quiet," the Mother snapped to the crowd before addressing Mariella.

"Are you sure, daughter? This is vitally important. How could you know such a thing?"

"I saw it," Mariella said after a lengthy silence. "When I was leading him, I...I probed his memories." Another gasp from the pixies within the cavern.

"Daughter," the Mother's voice was strained. "You go too far! You not only bring a human here, but you violate his mind as well? How could you–"

"He was trying to steal something that the Will o' the Wisp was guarding," Mariella interjected. He was caught. That is how he came to the Winding Wood."

*Howard.*

The cavern was quiet for a moment, but soon the walls echoed the tiny voices shouting accusations.

"Thief!"

"Liar!"

"What was he trying to steal?" The Mother's question cut them all off short. When Mariella did not answer, the Mother repeated her question.

"Mariella, what was he trying to steal?" There was still a pause before Mariella spoke.

"The Great Stone."

The cavern erupted in chaos. Small voices shouted and yelled around him, some in surprise, and many in anger.

"Silence! Silence, I say!" The tumult of voices lessened, but Phinnegan could sense the many pairs of small eyes that bore into him.

"The Great Stone," the Mother whispered, which began a fresh cascade of murmurs through the crowd of pixies, though it was not long lived.

"You seek such power?" the Mother asked sternly, though her voice quavered. "Why? Do you plan to dominate our world?"

The question was incredulous. *Dominate their world?*

"Power? Dominate?" Phinnegan sputtered in alarm. "There must be some mistake, I only wanted to go home..."

"Home?" the Mother asked.

"Yes, with the Great Stone...I was..."

"You have committed a serious crime, boy. It is no wonder you were sent to the Winding Wood. Mariella should have left you there, where you belonged!" The Mother's voice had risen in volume until she shouted. When she resumed, her voice had regained its earlier composure.

"The jurisdiction for this crime is beyond our means. Our duty is clear to me. As one of the esteemed races of this land, we must treat this attempted theft with the utmost seriousness. We must send for the guards of Féradoon."

At the mention of Phinnegan's one-time prison, a deathly stillness passed over those present in the cavern.

*To Féradoon. To trial. To prison.*

"But Mother," Mariella began, but she was cut off swiftly.

"There are no buts my child. We must follow the law in this. They will know that it was one of us who led him from the Winding Wood, for no other race knows its secrets."

"But, he has-"

"Mariella. Be still, now," the Mother said. "Zephyr!" The flutter of wings could be heard as another pixie joined the Mother just behind Phinnegan.

"Yes, Mother," came a second voice, small and soft.

"Fly to Féradoon at once. Inform them of everything you have just heard. Request that they send one of their gholems to take this...their prisoner."

"Yes, Mother."

"Fly fast."

"Yes, Mother." A rapid flutter of wings, and Phinnegan's hopes were slipping away.

"Mother," Mariella began once more, but the icy voice interjected again.

"Mariella! You have done enough for one day! Now, go to –
"

"Mother, you do *not* understand what you have just done!" Mariella said, her voice high pitched with alarm. Phinnegan felt a slight movement in his shirt pocket and then he heard Mariella's voice from just in front of him.

"Look," she said. "He has a Warber." The gasp that Phinnegan now heard was one not one of horror, but of genuine surprise and awe.

"A Warber," the Mother whispered. "How is this...possible?"

"I don't know," Mariella said. "This is why I brought him."

"I see," the Mother said.

And then suddenly, Phinnegan could see.

The light in the cave was dim and he was thankful for it, for even that dim light hurt his eyes. He blinked several times allowing his eyes to adjust to sight once again. As he blinked, he tried to take in his surroundings. The light in the cavern came from scatterings of mushrooms, some on rocks, some in holes, and others climbing the very walls. Each mushroom glowed with the brightness of a small candle, and together their luminescence filled the cavern with an eerie light.

As he had suspected, the cavern was indeed filled with pixies. More than he could have even imagined. There were hundreds of tiny people spread out in all directions, some with spiked hair, others with long, and nearly all were scantily clad, with only an arm or leg covered with a random piece of lace or ribbon. Only one was completely clothed. Covered in white lace from neck to ankles, her silvery hair was in long curls down to her waist, with two delicately pointed ears sneaked out beneath the waves. She was no smaller or bigger than Mariella, but she was clearly much older. She could only be the Mother.

"Zephyr?" she questioned, looking directly at Phinnegan, through she did not direct the question to him.

"Gone, Mother. None of us here could ever hope to catch him. He is the fastest, after all." The Mother nodded.

"Then there is not much time," she said, gesturing to Mariella. "He may not enter the vale. You must take him through the mountain pass to the other side."

Phinnegan's brow furrowed.

"Wait, I don't understand –"

"Leave this place," the Mother cut him off.

"But –"

"Go!"

Moments later, Phinnegan was jogging, trying to keep up with Mariella.

"What happened? Why did she let me go? What is a Warber?"

"You ask many questions, Phinnegan Qwyk," the pixie responded absently. The two moved swiftly through the passage for several more minutes, but then Phinnegan began to tire and slowed to a walk. Having no other choice, the pixie slowed to match his pace.

"A Warber is a token," Mariella said at length. Phinnegan took two large steps to bring himself nearly beside her.

"What sort of token?"

"An ancient one. I had never seen one, until spying yours. We are all taught about them, of course, but I never thought..." she stopped, glancing at Phinnegan. "You must be a rare person, Phinnegan Qwyk."

"What does it mean, this token?"

"Different Warbers mean different things. I don't recognize the Mark on yours."

How could he have come to possess this Warber? He did not remember it being given to him. Curious, Phinnegan reached into his pocket and removed the Warber, holding it between his thumb and forefinger.

As he surveyed the symbol imprinted thereon, a most curious thing happened. The Warber disintegrated. He rubbed the dust between his fingers, which gave off a slight warmth and had a faint metallic odor. When he pulled his fingers apart, he noticed a darker smudge on his index finger. He rubbed it on his pants, but when he looked at it again, the smudge was still there only now it was defined.

Now his fingertip bore the Mark.

*What just happened?*

He was so consumed with his thoughts that it was not for some time that he noticed they were no longer within the mountain pass, but had passed out onto a wider, gravely road between two grassy foothills. Two craggy tor perched high atop the hill to his right.

"Where are we?" he asked absently, forgetting about the Mark on his finger. He squinted as he checked the sun's position in the sky. *Mid-morning? How long was I with the pixies?*

"We are nearing the border of our land."

"The border to what?"

"The land of others, the land of the Unwanted." She noticed his glance to the sun and sought to explain.

"You have been passing through our lands for more than a day now. Though you have not slept, you will find that if you eat the berries from these bushes," she pointed to several bushes on either sides of the gravely road that bore bright orange berries, "you will feel well rested. You will have no need of sleep until nightfall, but as the sun sets, your weariness will return and you must rest. Do you understand?" When Phinnegan nodded that he did, she continued.

"Follow this path until you come to a fork. Go to the left. After an hour's walk you will come to a single cottage against the mountain. There you will find someone who may help you."

"Who?"

"We do not know his name. But he is old, and wise." She glanced down at Phinnegan's right hand.

"I see the Warber has Marked you. He will know this sign."

"So you are not coming with me, then?"

Mariella shook her head.

"This is where I leave you. We do not travel past this, our southern border. We are not welcome here."

Phinnegan nodded.

"Well, thank you. You've at least given me some hope."

The pixie smiled for the first time since she had seen the Warber fall from Phinnegan's pocket.

"You are most welcome," she said sweetly, but then her smile vanished and her face became stern.

"Now, do *exactly* as I say."

## 20

## Nightfall

Her instructions were brief but specific, and if she was to be believed, terribly important.

*Do not eat anything other than the orange berries.*

*Do not stop until you reach the cottage.*

*And above all else, do not stray from the path.*

This was the second time that Phinnegan had been admonished to stay on a path, the first being by Periwinkle Lark in Darkwater Forest.

*What is it with this place and paths?*

He had thanked her once more for her help, which he realized came only because he possessed the Warber. How he had come into possession of this ancient token still escaped him. Mariella had given him little information as to its meaning or purpose. Either way, he was grateful for it, as it had saved him a second, and likely much longer, visit to Féradoon. He shivered.

*Féradoon. Best not to think about it.*

But the final words of the pixie still weighed upon his mind.

*Remember, the Mother has already sent word to Féradoon. The gholem will come for you. Be careful, Phinnegan Qwyk. I sense that you are already followed by a shadow.*

He had seen a gholem once before, the great, ghost-like creature in the hall of Féradoon that was at the same time there, but not, appearing more as a disturbance than a physical being.

Phinnegan tried to push these thoughts from his mind. It was a futile effort. His eyes scanned the brush and the hillsides for any signs of disturbance, but he saw none. Of course not. It would take days for a gholem to reach him.

*Wouldn't it?*

He shook his head, clearing it of such jumbled thoughts.

The sun was beginning to descend now; it was early afternoon and he had left Mariella mid-morning. A few hours travelled already and he had not stopped once to eat or rest. He spied one of the bushes that bore the bright orange berries very close to the path not ten paces ahead, as good a place as any for a brief respite.

When he reached the bush, Phinnegan stopped and began plucking the ripened berries, careful to keep his feet on the path. He popped the berries one by one into his mouth, crushing them against the roof of his mouth with his tongue, feeling their sweet-sour juices rush forth in an explosion of flavor - the citrusy tang of an orange with the rich sweetness of a blueberry, a splendid combination.

As he had been told, the berries provided him with all the nourishment that he needed. He felt neither hungry nor thirsty after eating only a small handful, and his fatigue had vanished. When he had eaten his fill, he plucked a handful more and stuck them in his pocket. He had a few more hours of walking ahead of him and no assurances that any of these bushes would so opportunely present themselves.

His pockets and stomach full, Phinnegan set out again down the path, which had gone from gravel to dirt with a scattering of pebbles. He looked back over his shoulder to the distance he had already covered. Just visible in the haze of distance was the span between the two grassy hills that led to the exit from the mountain passage. Mariella had warned him not to try and return to the lair of the pixies for an enchantment to ward off intruders would lead him in circles for hours on end.

His only hope was to reach the old man and hope that he could help.

Phinnegan had not given much thought to the old man, but this suddenly seemed of great importance. Just who was this old man? A human? An Aged, one of the Faë that had given up on the vibrant and colorful life that Periwinkle and his kin so enjoyed?

*Perhaps they've turned their backs on the treachery as well.*

If he was an Aged, why would he help Phinnegan? The only Aged he had seen were those in the court of Féradoon. All but the clumsy witness, Sparrow, Periwinkle's old friend, had seemed a most serious and unkindly lot. Not the sort of people one went to when in need of help.

Perhaps this old man was different, more like Sparrow, too aloof to be serious and unkind. But if he was aloof, how would he be of any help?

But perhaps he was not an Aged at all, but a human, brought here like Phinnegan. Such a turn of events would be a boon, provided the old man remained in this world by choice, and not a lack of knowledge on how to get home.

So absorbed was he in his thoughts that Phinnegan did not see the large root that snaked out into the path. He tripped, falling hard onto his side.

Phinnegan pushed himself to his feet, dusting off his clothes, which were now quite dirty. He checked to see that he was still on the path, which he was, just standing at its edge. However, had he looked behind he would have seen that when he fell, his hands had landed in the grass just off the path. Two hand-prints remained in the green of the grass but they were slowly turning black.

But Phinnegan did not see these blackening hand prints that he had left behind. Instead he checked the height of the sun in the sky, frowning when he saw that it approached mid-afternoon. The mountain loomed in front of him as it always did, but there was no sign of the fork in the path that Mariella had foretold.

Little more than an hour later, Phinnegan had stopped in front of a massive tree. Here the path split into two: one to the left and one to the right. Phinnegan, as Mariella had instructed, took the path to the left.

The sun was still well above the horizon, but it was moving towards late afternoon. Phinnegan spied another small bush with orange berries just after the split and stopped to eat one handful and pocket another before continuing down the path.

The brush here was more overgrown, reaching intrusively into an already more narrow path. Twice a meddlesome tree branch scratched across Phinnegan's face as he pushed his way through ever more crowded vegetation. The ground, too, changed, becoming less sand and rock and more grass and moss. The path was less visible than it had been, but he was still able to follow it without too much effort.

He had seen little in the way of creatures on this path. A few rodents had crossed his path, but this was no different than he would have expected in his own world. Birds, too, chirped and sang all around him since the path had forked. Once a great black bird had lighted on the path in front of him, fixed him with a curious eye and then flown off in a rush of wings and feathers.

When the sun finally reached late afternoon, its light beginning to hide behind distant trees and horizon-hugging clouds, Phinnegan felt a chill run through him. He was not cold, and sweat even trickled down the back of his neck, but he still shivered. It was around this same time that he noticed the first aching joint, his right wrist. His left one soon followed, and then his fingers, elbows and knees. The lower the sun sank in the sky, the more the aches pained him and the more often he shivered.

A headache had assailed him at some point, and now his eyelids began to droop. He stumbled once, then twice. The third time, he sank to his knees. In the distance, he heard the faint clinking of metal. Like a wind-chime, but the clinks were heavier and of a deeper tone. The sound was peaceful, musical without being music and growing louder as the sun sank lower in the sky.

When a wailing moan pierced the evening quiet, Phinnegan tried to rouse himself but he could not. He fumbled clumsily in his pocket for his last handful of berries, smashing some in the process. From the crushed few he was able to remove from his pocket, he tossed two into his mouth.

But the berries made him gag, and he spat them out and saw that they were no longer bright-orange, but instead an oily black. Around him the clinking turned to clanking and the moans grew louder, and came from multiple directions.

A rustle in the bushes close-by sent his mind into a frenzied panic, but his body would not respond. He was so tired.

The last thing he saw was two heavy black boots stepping out of the brush in front of him.

# 21

# Elevenses

Phinnegan awakened in what could only be said to be an exceptionally comfortable bed, the blankets drawn up to his chin, and a terrible ache in his head. The smell of breakfast hung faintly in the air.

*Bacon.*

The crackling smell drew him from the bed. No matter how comfortable any bed, the smell of bacon is likely to pull one from it. How long had it been since he had last smelled that wonderful food?

*Certainly never in this world.*

But when he reached his feet, he found that he did not recognize the room or the bed. The walls were covered in strange drawings and figures, and bits of parchment with words written in a scrawled handwriting. There were two windows in the room and Phinnegan saw that it was a bright day outside.

The floor was a rustic wood, neither stained nor varnished, but darkened with age. The boards were wide and bowed on the edges and they creaked when Phinnegan took a ginger step forward. The sound was not that of the creak that shutters an uneasy silence, but rather the familiar creak of a weathered house, signaling that it has been well-lived.

A wooden door rested ajar in front of him, and through it the scrumptious smell wafted and the clanging sound of rustling pots and pans could be heard. Phinnegan moved closer to the door, listening for other sounds.

The clanging sound of pots soon gave way to the clink of glass or ceramic. To Phinnegan, these seemed to all be the sounds of breakfast.

He crept into the hallway beyond the door, and found that no way was to be had to his right. A short hall-way dead-ended there in a wall. Two other doorways dotted the hallway, one on the right, the same as the side from which Phinnegan had emerged, the other on the left.

No way to his right, he turned to the left and here the smell of bacon grew stronger, and the clink of glass louder. There was one door on his right, before the short hallway opened into a small space. To the left of his space a few soft chairs rested comfortably around an empty fire-place on the near wall. It was to his right where Phinnegan heard the clinking.

Here there was a wall with portraits adorning its face. The one in the middle was larger than the others and bore the bust of a rather distinguished looking gentleman, a black jacket high about his neck and a white ascot fluffing at his breast. His hair was short, curly and white, and his face was kind, yet wizened and serious. He held an open book firmly in his hands.

To the right of this kindly gentleman, a more sinister-looking face lurked. Close in upon his face, the top of the same-style black jacket could be seen, as well as the same ruffled ascot. But this face was not kind, instead being wrinkled and unmerciful, a hooked nose soaring out from a square and harsh face. White curls, too, adorned his head, though the locks were long and fell well past his ears and onto his shoulders. His visage was severe, and his blue eyes bored into Phinnegan until he looked away with a shiver.

The final picture hung to the left of the largest. The man therein appeared with the same jacket and ascot, as well as the same white hair, though he was clearly the elder of the three. The hair was straight and flowed long from a deep widow's peak on his forehead. His shoulders were hunched and he leaned heavily on the thick, gnarled head of an ornate staff. Where the other two had been clean shaven, he sported a long, flowing beard. His face was heavily wrinkled, further enhancing his age, while his nose was wide and long. He looked not at the admirer but down and towards the right, his eyes riveted on their quarry. The figure's gaze was so intent that Phinnegan looked to the spot where they gazed, but saw only a dusty floor.

Who these three men were was a mystery, for their portraits bore no titles or placards. Phinnegan spent only half a moment looking for some sort of identification before he remembered the bacon.

He had moved away from the hallway whence he had come and was now close to the end of the wall which bore the three portraits. Ahead the wall vanished and a great open space took its place. The sounds and smells of breakfast poured through.

No one was there.

Phinnegan saw a small table directly in front of this opening, which was paired with two chairs. Atop it rested a small, iron platter with a mound of bacon an inch deep. To the right of this was the kitchen, which consisted of a large bucket and an area of counter space, as well as a fireplace, which held a slowly burning fire with a black kettle dancing above it, a light steam slipping from its spout.

The clinking sound remained, but Phinnegan saw no one.

Hungry, he snatched two pieces of bacon from the platter before moving past the table and into the kitchen. The clinking came from his right, where he saw the wooden bucket seated atop the counter. The sound appeared to come from within it, and when Phinnegan peeked over its edge, he expected to see, perhaps, a mouse, scrounging amongst some soiled dishes. But he saw no mouse.

He did see several dishes. And they were cleaning themselves.

Or rather, a wooden-handled brush was cleaning them, though no hand could be seen to move the brush, or to hold the dish for that matter. But the brush did move and the dishes presented themselves for a scrubbing no differently than they would have had they been maneuvered by a hand.

"Aha! Found the bacon have you?"

The voice came from behind Phinnegan and its sudden appearance caused him to jump. He turned around quickly to find a portly man of middling height, grinning at him with a small basket of eggs in one hand and another full of berries in the opposite hand.

"Sit down, sit down," the man said, his weathered cheeks tight in the smile. "The eggs will be up shortly. Can't have elevenses without bacon and eggs!" The jovial man pushed past Phinnegan with a spring in his step, handing off the basket of berries before he continued towards the fire. "Go on, eat your fill. But do leave me some of the black ones."

Phinnegan stood frozen for a moment, but his hunger quickly won whatever battle raged in his mind. Heeding the old man's directions, he carried the basket of berries to the table and sat them beside the platter of bacon. Continuing to munch on the bacon he had already collected, Phinnegan seated himself and surveyed the man bustling about the kitchen.

His manner of dress would allow only to be described as unkempt, a bilious off-white shirt spotted with various dirty patches hung well past his waist, while his trousers were loose and a drab brown. His hair stood on end, in the places where it still grew, which was mainly the back and sides, the top being quite shiny. His face was weathered, but soft, and two bushy salt-and-pepper eyebrows stood above his eyes, matching the frazzled fluff of his thick beard.

All put together, he was quite a friendly looking chap, if a bit dirty.

"Sorry I didn't wake you for breakfast, but you looked to need your rest," the man called over his shoulder as he removed the kettle from the fire with a thick rag. In its place he hung an iron skillet. "Do you prefer your eggs broken or not?"

"Not, please," Phinnegan said between a piece of bacon and a mouthful of berries.

"Unbroken they shall be then." The familiar crack of eggs was followed by a loud sizzle as their insides fell on the skillet. The man proceeded to pour the contents of the kettle into two ceramic mugs before bringing them to the table where Phinnegan sat, placing one mug in front of him and the second in front of the empty chair opposite him.

"It's my own special blend," the old man said as he moved back to mind the eggs. "A strong tea made from the leaves of the vines growing on the outside of this cottage. It's mixed in with the normal, of course, black tea to be precise, but the vine's leaves give it a more earth quality. Does wonders for the mind!"

Phinnegan cupped the steaming mug in his hands and drew it to himself, inhaling a deep breath through his nose. It *did* smell earthy, like the mossy side of a rock. He swallowed the last bit of berries he had been chewing and took a tentative sip. It tasted earthy as well.

Like dirt.

"Isn't it pleasant?" the old man asked as he dropped a small plate with two eggs in front of Phinnegan before taking the seat across from him.

"Quite," Phinnegan said. "Thank you."

"Most welcome, most welcome," the man said with a bob of his head and a large toothy grin on his face. As Phinnegan watched, the man took a handful of berries and crushed them in his hands, letting their bits dribble atop the two eggs on his own plate, before wiping the soiled hand on his trousers.

"Sorry, but who are you? Where am I? The last thing I remember, I was on the path...and it was growing dark..." Phinnegan trailed off at the end, unable to suppress the shiver that came to him when he recalled the moaning wail that he had heard in the woods.

"Yes...lucky...dark...berries...wights." Speaking with his mouth stuffed full of eggs and berries alike rendered the man unintelligible. Phinnegan's brow wrinkled.

"What?"

"Pardon, pardon," the man said after swallowing his mouthful and wiping his lips on his sleeve. He clasped his hands atop one another as he leaned forward, his beady eyes as wide as they would go.

"I said that you were lucky I found you. In the dark as you were, the magic of the berries wearing off and the wights bearing down on you. Lucky you were indeed that old Asher was out hunting." He paused, drawing down one eyebrow and waving a finger at Phinnegan.

"You really should have stayed on the path at all times, you know. When the berries go bad at sunset, you'll pass out where you stand. Had you never strayed from the path, the wights never would have known you were there."

"I didn't stray from the path," Phinnegan said, defensively. "I was careful to be on it at all times."

"Bah," the old man barked, leaning back in his chair. "Whether you knew it or not, you stepped off. They'd never have found you otherwise. Lucky you were, very lucky."

Phinnegan frowned and looked away from the old man, trying to remember when he could have stepped off the path. But when he looked away, his eyes caught a glimpse of two heavy black boots caked with mud on the floor against the wall behind the old man.

"Those boots," Phinnegan mumbled before looking back to the old man. "So you...rescued me?"

"Aye, aye," the old man said with a wink and a nod before stuffing his mouth with a forkful of eggs and berries.

"Well, sir, thank you-"

"Asher," the old man interrupted. "Everyone with a right to call me anything at all calls me Asher."

"Thank you, Asher. My name is Phinnegan. Phinnegan Qwyk."

"Well, Phinnegan Qwyk, welcome to my humble home. It's not much, but has all the comforts a simpleton like I could every want." Asher beamed a broad smile, as he seemingly was apt to do, and then, having finished the last of his eggs and berries, set about munching strips of bacon while he sipped his tea.

"Sir, if I may ask – "

"Asher," the old man mumbled as he chewed.

"Yes, sorry. Asher. What is that?" Phinnegan asked, pointing in the direction of the wooden washtub in the kitchen where he knew the brush continued to clean judging by the sound of clinking.

"What," the old man said, turning to follow Phinnegan's pointed finger. Seeing the washing basin he slumped back in his chair with a grimace, the first unhappy gesture Phinnegan had seen from the man.

"Bah! *That* is some Faë's idea of ridding me of the most unpleasant of household chores. But the blasted thing is just as likely to create an even bigger mess as actually clean up worth a damn." The man raised one eyebrow and leaned toward Phinnegan. "You always must keep an eye on it lest it run amuck and soil the whole house with dirty dishwater." He turned for a moment to stare at the tub before slouching back in his chair.

"Should never have bought that bloody thing," he mumbled, tearing a large chunk from a strip of bacon.

"You bought it from a Faë?"

Phinnegan's question, however, fell on deaf ears, for the old man had leapt from his chair with surprising agility just as he finished speaking.

"Aha! To the devil with you!" Asher raced into the kitchen and was now wrestling with the washtub, which was putting up quite a fight. Just as he had said, it was running amuck. Water sloshed from the tub onto the kitchen's floor, as well as onto the old man, who held the tub in a bear hug just in front of his chest.

"Blasted fool of an enchantment," Asher yelled, assumedly at the tub. Phinnegan rose from his chair as if to come to the old man's aid, but just as he did, the tub and the man came crashing down to the floor, sending the contents of the tub, water, dishes, brush and all, across the floor and into the fire.

"Are you all right?" Phinnegan asked as he approached Asher, who was now sprawled on the floor in front of the fire, which had shrunk by half as the water put out some of the nearest wood. The handle of the brush was just beginning to be licked by the remaining flames. Phinnegan reached to salvage it, but Asher raised a hand in protest.

"Let it burn." The brush emitted a hiss at its master's words, the fires beginning to evaporate its moisture. "It has been a long time coming." Phinnegan offered him a hand and pulled the old man to his feet, though with a great deal of effort.

"Is...*was* that brush...*magic*?" Phinnegan asked as he watched the flames creep up the brush.

"On its own, no more than a pig's bum, but aye, it was enchanted. Lot of good it did me." Asher watched the brush awhile longer – until the flame around it flashed green and emitted a loud pop – before turning away with a nod, his smile returning.

"Ah, well then, have we finished with our elevenses?" He peered across the kitchen to the table, where a few strips of bacon remained, as well as two mugs of tea.

"Not quite," Phinnegan answered. "There's still a little left."

"Must finish, must finish," Asher said with a grin, striding back to his seat. "Waste not, want not, I always say."

He left wet footprints where he walked and his trousers and shirt were both well wetted from the tussle with the washtub. Phinnegan followed him over and again sat down across from Asher. They ate in silence for a few moments before Phinnegan posed a question.

"Do you have anything else here that is...ummm...enchanted?"

"The odd bit or two," Asher said between sips of tea. "There's a berry-picking basket which works quite well, though I find that I enjoy the task so much that I hardly ever use it. I did have an enchanted axe that would do to chop wood for the fire, but given how that blasted brush performed, I got rid of it."

"Probably a good idea," Phinnegan said, putting the finishing touches on the last strip of bacon.

"I thought so," Asher said with a wink. "I don't have much use for magical this or an enchanted that, to tell the truth. But," he said, dropping his voice and leaning forward as though sharing a secret, "I do have one item of which I am particularly fond. And it serves my...position very well."

"What is it?" Phinnegan asked, his curiosity causing him to lean forward as well, giving the appearance that the two plotted together.

"Ah, young master. Do I sense that you are intrigued by all things magical?" Asher asked with an upward nod of his head, before wrinkling his nose and frowning slightly. "But of course you are, the first thing you asked was not about me or *why* I helped you, but it was about that bedeviled brush."

Phinnegan looked embarrassed.

"I'm terribly sorry," Phinnegan said, his cheeks reddening. "You are quite right, you risked your life to help me – "

"Ah, it was nothing as grand as that!" Asher exclaimed with a chuckle. "And besides, don't let it trouble you. We all have eyes for the magic when we've only just come here."

Phinnegan's eyes widened.

"You mean you're human as well?"

"Human as well…" Asher said incredulously, before barking a loud, but pleasant laugh.

"Of course I am! You mean you can't tell the difference?"

Phinnegan looked abashed and shrunk himself down in his chair.

"Well, I thought I could…but then there are the Aged…"

"Ah, yes, yes. The Aged. But once you've met a handful, you'll see they're nothing like a human. Most are altogether grumpy as well."

"I'd noticed that…"

"Yes, well, it's one of their most obvious qualities." Asher leaned back in his chair, sipping his tea and eyeing Phinnegan over its lip.

"You are rather young to be here, aren't you?"

"What do you mean?"

"Well, just what I said. We're usually older when we're brought here, aren't we? I was just shy of thirty myself. Been here nearly thirty-five years now, more than half my life." When he finished speaking, Asher looked hard again at Phinnegan.

"Are you sure you are supposed to be here? You don't look a day more than thirteen."

"I'm twelve, actually."

"Twelve! Do tell! Did they have to ask your mum and dad's permission?"

"For what?" Phinnegan asked, startled by the question.

"Why, to bring you here! There are rules, you know, about age. In addition to all the other guidelines that must be followed.

"I don't know what you are talking about," Phinnegan said flatly. "But no, no one even asked *me* whether I should like to come to this place."

Asher's eyes-widened, but he quickly recovered himself, though his lips pursed slightly as he looked at Phinnegan.

"Truly? Brought you against your will did they?"

"Sort of. It was more of an accident, really."

Though his brow twitched in opposition, it ultimately furrowed and Asher brought his hand up to finger his beard absently.

"Hmmm. Quite strange." He continued to eye Phinnegan while he fingered his beard, leaning his chair back on its rear legs and rocking slowly. The man's gaze made Phinnegan feel quite uncomfortable, and he squirmed in his seat beneath it. The movement must have broken Asher's concentration for he slammed the forelegs of his chair down on the floor and placed his hands flat on the table, pushing himself to his feet.

"Well, would you like to see it?" Asher said.

"See what?"

"Have you forgotten?" Asher leaned forward, a sparkle in his eye. "My magic item."

"Oh, yes, of course," Phinnegan said, a little thrown by the change in topic.

"Follow me, follow me," Asher said, his grin returning once more. He left the table and went through the adjacent room, Phinnegan following him closely. They went into the hallway and past the door both to the right and left, before coming to a stop at the dead-end wall.

"Where are we going?" Phinnegan asked.

"Just up the stairs," Asher replied. Phinnegan turned about but he saw no sign of any stairs.

"What stairs?"

"Just through here," Asher said a moment before he stepped through the wall in front of him.

"It's only an illusion," Asher's voice came from just beyond the wall, though as loud and clear as if he were standing right next to Phinnegan, which, he was. "It's like a false wall in our world only, well, magical. It won't hurt, just walk right through."

Phinnegan did as he was bid, walking through the wall, though not without squeezing his eyes shut and bracing for what his mind told him would be a sharp impact.

But when he felt nothing, he opened his eyes to find that he stood in front of a large and ornate staircase. He also saw that the "cottage" was much larger than he had originally guessed, for there were more doors beyond the staircase on either side, as well as the second-story above. Looking back, he could see down the hallway and into the sitting room at the front of the cottage.

"Come on, come on," Asher encouraged, as he himself was already halfway up the stairs.

With one last glance back down the hall, Phinnegan hurried up the stairs after him.

# 22

# A Man and a Quill

The stairs ended at a large landing, three hallways leading off in three different directions: one to the left, one to the right, and one straight ahead. Asher led the way, heading for the hallway on the right. The light was dim and Phinnegan stayed right on the old man's heels until they ducked into the first doorway on the right.

The room they entered was full, from floor to ceiling in most cases, with books on top of books. Bookcases stood edge to edge along each wall, the books on their shelves having long ago ceased to have room to orderly arrange themselves. Some were stacked horizontally; others lined the edge of a shelf with their cover facing out instead of their spine.

But it did not end with the shelves: more books plagued the room, stacked several feet high from the floor and strewn across every table in the room except the center one.

Instead of mounds of books and papers, this table held only two books. One book was old and the pages had yellowed to a light brown. The other looked quite new. But it was the quill that truly caught Phinnegan's attention. For this quill, though it looked like any other quill, moved by itself, drawing a beautiful script across the empty pages of the newer book.

"What's it doing?" Phinnegan asked as he approached the center table.

"Why, it's copying of course. See, this one," the old man laid a finger on a darkened page of the older book, "has just about fallen apart. I can't even read it. And there's nothing I hate more than a book I can't read." He paused for a moment, squinting down at the faded print of the ancient book.

"Now," he said, pointing to the new book, crisp, cream pages in black leather, "this one is blank. The quill is copying the text, word for word, from this old book to the new. It can read nearly any language and translate as it copies." Asher took a moment to lean back and cross his arms over his chest, a smile on his lips.

"Wonderful, eh?" he said.

"Uncanny," Phinnegan whispered as he watched the quill continue to copy. "So you copy all of the old books and then throw them out?"

Asher threw his arms up with a cry of surprise.

"Throw them out?! Never!"

Phinnegan was taken aback when Asher snatched the old book from the table, clutching it to his chest covetously. The book was in such a state of disrepair that several pages fell from the binding onto the table.

"I would *never* throw out a book, even one I can't read. Books...why they have a life and a story of their own, beyond the pages which they carry. And even some are written in their master's own hand." Perhaps recognizing that he was hugging a book, Asher eased the book down onto the table.

"Asher, you old fool," he said, speaking to himself in a whisper. "Always in love with your books. But that's why they chose you, isn't it?"

"Chose you for what?" Phinnegan ventured.

"This," Asher said, opening his arms wide as a gesture to the room, the books, or perhaps the entire house.

"To be a Guide."

"A Guide? A Guide for what?"

"For whoever needs it."

"You mean for the Faë?" Phinnegan asked, still puzzled.

"Yes, mostly," Asher said, seating himself at the table and gesturing for Phinnegan to do the same.

"You see, there are many things the Faë can do, and there are others that they can't."

"Sounds like everyone in general," Phinnegan said, drawing a satisfied smile from Asher.

"Very true, very true, young master. But the Faë are unable, or possibly unwilling, to do things which you and I might consider quite simple and basic."

"Like what?"

"Ah, well let me see if I can explain. Faë are...well they're a cheeky bunch for one, but above all they are rather selfish and irresponsible."

"I'll say," Phinnegan mumbled.

"Had a few run-ins already, eh?" Asher asked.

"You could say that," Phinnegan said, but hurried to return to the subject. "Well what can't they do?"

"Well, for one they could never be trusted to care for such knowledge as this."

"What do you mean?" Phinnegan asked, a puzzled look on his face.

"These books around you," Asher said, gesturing to the room with a wave of his hand. "This is more than three millennia of history, law, art and magic."

"Three *millennia*? You mean three thousand years? How is that possible? There are a lot of books here, but not *that* many."

"True, true," Asher said, nodding his head and laying a finger beside his nose. "But there is more to these books than the eye can see. Take this one for example." With surprising quickness, Asher sprang from his chair and snatched a worn, red book from the shelf just behind Phinnegan.

"This is also why I don't throw away the original," he said as he began thumbing carefully through the worn pages. "There are some things even a magic quill cannot copy." He turned the book over and laid it in front of Phinnegan.

"Put your hand just there," the old man directed, motioning to a peculiar design in the bottom right-hand corner of the right page. Phinnegan reached out his hand and pressed two fingers gently against the design.

He gasped sharply, blinking once and then a second time.

"That was amazing..." Phinnegan breathed, leaving his hand on the book. "I saw a huge tower made of solid ivory, trimmed with gems and gold. And there were Faë, thousands of them, all milling about on the ground beneath the tower. There were two others, a man and a woman, standing on a balcony waving at the Faë below." Phinnegan looked at the old man.

"What was that?"

"The Lord and Lady Eagle," Asher said in a whisper, his mind seemingly occupied. "They were the first Faë to be given authority by their kin to rule this world."

"When was that?" Phinnegan asked. But Asher paid him no mind. Instead his gaze was fixed on the book between them, more precisely, on Phinnegan's hand, which rested atop the book.

"How long have you born this Mark?" Asher asked quietly as he lifted Phinnegan's hand from the book with one hand and placed a pair of spectacles atop his nose with the other.

"Only a day or two," Phinnegan said, squirming in his chair.

"Where did you get the Warber that made this Mark?" Asher asked as he peered at the Mark on Phinnegan's finger.

"I...I don't know. It fell out of my pocket."

Asher cast a skeptical glance at Phinnegan over his spectacles.

"Fine," he said with a small smile. "Keep your secrets."

"But I honestly do not know," Phinnegan insisted.

"Settle down, settle down," Asher mumbled under his breath.

"Do you know what it means?" Phinnegan asked, leaning forward in his own chair. "She said you would know what it meant."

"Who is she?"

"Mariella. A pixie."

"Mmmmm," Asher grunted as he took one last look at the Mark.

"I'm afraid I haven't a clue."

"Oh," Phinnegan managed, crestfallen.

"Now, now," Asher said rising from his seat. "I didn't say I couldn't figure it out. What kind of Guide would I be if I couldn't?"

Phinnegan straightened, his face taking on a look of hope.

"What do you do anyway? Besides keeping up with all these books, I mean."

"The same thing you would expect any ordinary guide to do. I help people who are lost to find their way."

"Do you think I am lost?" Phinnegan asked. Asher responded with a raised eyebrow.

"Do *you* think you are lost?"

*I suppose I am.*

Phinnegan shrugged his shoulders meekly, but otherwise ignored the question.

"But how do people find you?"

Asher looked down at Phinnegan, a wry smile touching his lips.

"How did you find me?"

Phinnegan pressed his lips firmly together.

*Good point.*

"What else can you show me in these books?"

Asher smiled at Phinnegan's quick change of subject.

"Ah, well, what sort of thing tickles your fancy?"

"I like stories," Phinnegan said.

"Stories, is it? And I bet you like the ones that relate the most to magic, don't you?" Phinnegan nodded that he did. "Well then, let's see."

Asher left his place beside the table and went to a corner of the room, where two stacks of books rested on the floor in front of a corner bookcase. He pushed the stacks out of the way and began to peruse the shelves. Before long he had gathered several books and had placed them on the table closest to him. Phinnegan amused himself by watching the quill, which again moved to draw a graceful script across the new pages in the black leather book. When Asher returned to the center table some minutes later, he had several small, thin books in his hand. Phinnegan saw that they all looked new, each thin and bound in dark leather of varying shades of brown and grey.

"Here we are, here we are," Asher said, sitting the books down on the table between them. "Many good stories in these two," he said as he passed two of the books, both covered in black leather, to Phinnegan, who opened each to the first page to read the title.

"'Seven Tales of the Silver Autumn'," Phinnegan read the title aloud from the first book before turning to the second. "And this one is 'The Five Lives of Prince Cadmium'."

"Aye, both contain quite a few good tales of magic and what not. Now this one," Asher said, handing Phinnegan a book bound in soft, grey leather, "is rather dry on the whole, but there is one story in particular that you should read. Page ninety-eight I believe it is." Phinnegan flipped carefully through the pages to the page Asher suggested.

"'Scourge of the Night Wolf'," Phinnegan read aloud. He grimaced slightly, looking across the table at Asher.

"It's about the Faolchú isn't it?" he asked, drawing a surprised look from Asher.

"You know of them?"

"Yes," Phinnegan said. "I was nearly killed by them."

"You've *seen* a Faolchú?" Asher asked, his eyes wide and his mouth agape. "And lived? My dear boy that is quite an accomplishment! How did you manage to escape?"

"I had a little help," Phinnegan said, and then proceeded to tell Asher an abbreviated version of his trip through the Darkwater Forest with Periwinkle and how Crimson saved them with arrows that released a poisonous gas. He left out the part where he nearly died.

"Remarkable," Asher said, with a wide grin. "That is truly remarkable. We should put it down."

"What do you mean?" Phinnegan asked.

"I mean put it down. I don't just read these books, you know. I add to them, when I can. Whenever I hear a particularly interesting tale, I put it down." Asher carefully closed the old book in front of him and grabbed a dark blue book from the shelf behind him. He turned roughly two-thirds through the book before laying it open on the table and moving the quill onto it.

"There we are. This quill also transcribes what you say, well, what *I* say. With some embellishments of course. Now go ahead, tell it again, from the beginning."


Phinnegan awakened from his nap on one of the sofas in the cottage's sitting room and rubbed the sleep from his eyes.

It had been a long day.

The two passed the entire afternoon in the library together, breaking only once when Asher insisted they have afternoon tea outside underneath several large apple trees behind the cottage. Phinnegan had again been astonished to see that from the outside the cottage looked quite small and quaint, altogether different than the size it appeared from the inside.

After tea they had returned to the library where Asher continued to coax the story of Phinnegan's trek through Darkwater Forest from him while at the same time repeating the words, with some embellishments of course, to the quill. By the time they finished it was getting into the evening and Phinnegan was growing very tired. Asher had insisted that Phinnegan take a nap while he prepared dinner.

Phinnegan had not asked what they were to share for dinner, but his groggy mind still retained enough sharpness to identify the savory smell of braised lamb on the air. With a yawn, he rose from the sofa and rounded the corner into the eating area and looked into the kitchen.

Asher was busy around the fire, his dirty clothing of earlier replaced by a slightly less dirty robe, which was cinched about his waist with a thick cord.

"Smells wonderful," Phinnegan said as he took a seat at the table, where a fresh baked loaf of bread rested on a tarnished silver platter.

"Who's that, who's that?" Asher asked, glancing over his shoulder. Upon seeing Phinnegan he quickly smiled.

"Ah, yes, young Phinnegan. I apologize; I was deep in my thoughts. Very deep." He turned back to the fire where he hovered for a few moments.

"Do sit down, it is almost ready. Just a minute or two longer."

Phinnegan seated himself at the table, in the same chair he had used earlier that day for elevenses. Asher came over soon thereafter, setting down two goblets, one in front of Phinnegan and the other in front of where he would sit. He poured a black liquid into both goblets from a small carafe, and then placed the carafe beside the loaf of bread.

"House wine," he said with a wink. "You've already eaten the berries that I used to make it. It is a very peculiar quality of those berries that they should be so edible during the day and so rancid at night, yet, they make a perfectly wondrous wine. Provided one drinks it after sunset, that is."

Phinnegan tilted the goblet towards him and surveyed the inky black liquid. He sniffed its contents and found them quite pleasant. He had rarely had any wine, it being a luxury in his own home, and he being young besides. He tilted his head back and sipped the wine. He had no expectations of what a good wine should taste like, but he decided that he did in fact like this one.

"Yes, it's quite good," he complemented. Asher nodded approvingly as he approached the table, a platter holding four braised lamb foreshanks before him. He sat the platter on the table beside the bread and wine and seated himself opposite Phinnegan.

"Ah! The potatoes!" Asher exclaimed, jumping quickly from his seat and trotting into the kitchen. He returned with a rough-hewn wooden bowl which was filled two-thirds full with creamed potatoes.

"Can't have supper without potatoes," he said, passing the bowl to Phinnegan, who used the provided spoon to shovel a heavy portion onto his own plate.

"It all smells delicious," Phinnegan said, his stomach growling in anticipation.

"Eat up, eat up," Asher said with a smile as he used a meaty hand to grab two of the lamb shanks from the platter between them.

Once the two had set upon the food, they uttered not another word. There were noises of course, the scraping of forks across the plate, the tearing of bread and the drinking of wine, but the two themselves, they were quiet.

When they had finished eating, Asher pushed himself back from the table, patting his rotund belly fondly.

"That hit the spot, indeed, indeed." He poured himself the last bit of wine and then gestured towards Phinnegan with his goblet.

"Tomorrow I shall be busy," he said. "I've got a lot of reading to do to find out about that Mark." He inclined his head in the direction of Phinnegan's right hand.

"All right. Can I help?" Phinnegan asked, but Asher shook his head.

"Nay, lad. The best thing you can do is just leave me to it. You've got a pile of stories to read besides." Standing up from the table he began to clear the plates. When Phinnegan tried to help, Asher stopped him.

"Ah, don't trouble yourself with these. You are looking tired already. Best you get some sleep." Asher piled the now empty platters, save for the bones of the shanks, atop one another and carried them to the kitchen.

"I'll leave breakfast out for you, but you shall not see me until dinner." Asher smiled and then shooed Phinnegan with a kindly gesture.

"Off to bed now. I'll see you tomorrow for supper."

Phinnegan smiled and turned to exit the room, but stopped, turning back to face Asher.

"Asher? May I ask a question?"

"Certainly, but make it quick," Asher said, already busying himself with pouring two buckets of water into a large washtub.

"Why do all the Faë have colors for names?"

Asher stopped and looked straight at Phinnegan.

"Don't be silly. How else would they do it?"

# 23

# A House of Many Secrets

Phinnegan spent his entire second day at the cottage outside, reading and walking in the gardens that surrounded it. He found the stories interesting, but, after the excitement of his own adventures these past several days, books had lost their intrigue. His exploration of the gardens yielded much more pleasure, seeing the strange plants and vines intermingled with the familiar.

All in all, however, the day was uneventful. Supper with Asher was much the same, for the man was quiet and distant, not at all his normal self. He had spoken only a few sentences to Phinnegan the entire meal.

"You will not see me tomorrow," he had said. "Much to read, much to read." The entire time they ate, Phinnegan would look up to find Asher staring at him, but the latter would quickly look away.

Now, on the morning of the third day in the cottage, Phinnegan sat at the table alone, breaking his fast on cold biscuits and fresh apples. Asher had given him no further direction on what to do this day, other than to leave him alone in the library.

When Phinnegan finished his breakfast, he placed the plates in the washtub and then, having already explored the grounds, set about exploring the house.

He had seen all there was to see of the downstairs, and so he passed through the invisible wall and up the stairs to the landing. There, he was confronted by the three hallways he had seen on the first day. The library lay to the right, but Phinnegan ignored that hallway and instead took the hallway straight ahead.

This hallway was short and ended abruptly in a heavy wooden door. The door had no knob, only a keyhole. Phinnegan gave the door a stiff push, but it barely shuddered, locked with no foreseeable way through.

Without a key, there was no chance to open it.

I w*onder what he keeps in there.*

Thwarted by the locked door, Phinnegan returned to the landing and started down the hallway that lay to the left of the stairs. Unlike the previous hallway and the hallway with the library, this hallway was long and riddled with doors on both sides, each a variation of brown.

The first door on his right opened easily, but was empty save for a few boxes scattered about. The room was dimly lit, having only one small porthole window on the far wall. Closing the door behind him, he took the first one on the left.

The door swung inward to reveal a room that was bright and well lit. Three windows encompassed nearly the entire far wall and several skylights overhead bathed the room in sunlight. The light, it appeared, was necessary for this room to function, for it was filled with all manner of plants. Some were in no need of light, dead and pinned to walls and boards, but others were growing from trays atop tables in the middle of the room. Several larger plants filled pots that were dotted at varying distances around the room's perimeter.

Phinnegan approached the nearest pot, which held a brightly colored plant with purple leaves and a white flower of spherical shape, like a ball. The flower looked smooth and doughy, like a ball of clay. He reached out and pressed a finger into the soft surface of the flower.

But just as he did, the plant began to move.

Not the whole plant, that is, but the spherical flower. Not side-to-side or back-and-forth, but like something was moving just beneath the surface. Phinnegan drew back and watched as the surface of the flower rippled and caved, puffed and swelled.

And when it finished, a perfect copy of Phinnegan's own head rested atop the flower's stalk, just where the spherical flower had been before.

Phinnegan stared forward, looking at what appeared to be a sort of three-dimensional mirror. He touched the nose on the flower and then his own, comparing the two.

"Amazing," he whispered.

He spied a small tag that was placed on the lip of the pot. He bent down to read it and saw scrawled there in rough print one word:

*MIMICER*

*Suits it.*

The discovery of this strange plant sent him around the room on a treasure hunt, checking the labels of each pot before checking the plant, trying to guess what it did from the name that had been given to it.

There was a dark green plant with spiked leaves that bore the name 'RUBBER-ROOT', which, when Phinnegan had tried to pull the plant from its pot to see these roots, found that the plant came right up, but the roots were still in the soil, having stretched when he pulled on it.

Another, with the name 'BANGER', took a swing at Phinnegan's hand when he came too close. A third, called 'TOOTHED-ROSE', bit Phinnegan on the arm when he reached for the flower. Several others dotted the room in pots of various shapes and sizes, but all were mundane, at least to him.

The final pot was near the door, as he had made a full circle of the room. The pot was enormous, wide in diameter and nearly as tall as Phinnegan, but it appeared to be empty. An empty pot was not that interesting at all, but there was a tag, and as the tag was at eye-level, he stared right at it.

'DEVIL'S MOUTH'

*What a funny name.*

Phinnegan ran his finger over the side of the pot, which was blood-red clay with a rough finish. He only looked up when the sun from the skylights no longer fell on his back. Perhaps a cloud had passed over the sun, blocking its light from entering this sort of green-room.

But what he saw was no cloud.

A massive mouth rose high on a winding vine from the center of the massive blood-red pot. It had no lips, but a large number of yellowed, fang-like teeth gnashed together as the mouth continued to rise.

Phinnegan wasted no time in reaching for the door. He fumbled the knob at first, and the mouth poised to strike. But he finally grasped it, and hurled himself through the door, slamming it shut behind him. The door shuddered violently several times, presumably as the plant struck it from the other side.

When at last it stopped, Phinnegan sat in silence in the hallway for several minutes.

*Perhaps I should be a bit more careful.*

His composure finally regained, he moved slowly down the hallway and cautiously opened a dark brown door on the right side of the hall. The door creaked loudly on its hinges, an eerie sound that caused the hair on Phinnegan's arms to stand on end.

But when he looked into the room, he found it completely empty. Neither a box nor a rag was to be found. Shutting the door, he moved on down the hall.

He opened several more doors on both sides of the hallway before finally finding a room with something of interest: an object in the far left corner covered with a great sheet.

He closed the door behind him and walked over to the sheet-covered object. He reached forward and pulled the sheet away, revealing a large rock, slightly taller than himself.

The rock was jagged and asymmetrical, and he cut his fingers when he ran them over its surface. He drew his hand away suddenly, sticking his bleeding finger in his mouth. Mixed with the irony taste of blood he tasted dirt as well. He was reminded of how dirty he was, how long it had been since he had had a proper bath. He looked down at his clothing and saw how ragged and torn they were from his days of trekking through this world. He closed his eyes and leaned back against the rock.

*I wish I had some clean clothes.*

A bit of movement at his feet drew his attention, and when he looked down he beheld a clean shirt, trousers and undergarments, all neatly folded and stacked as though just laundered. His eyes widened. Was he dreaming? He knelt down and touched the dark leg of the trousers with his hand. No, he wasn't dreaming, they were real.

His bleeding finger forgotten, he hurriedly stripped off his dirty and torn clothing, tossing them in a heap on the floor. But just before putting on the new clothes, he stopped. Where had these clothes come from?

He looked from the clothes to the rock and back again, a thought blossoming in his mind. He dropped the clothes and placed his uninjured hand carefully against the rock.

*I wish I had a hot bath.*

As soon as he had the thought, a tub of steaming water appeared a few feet away. This rock was much more than a rock.

Of all the things he could have wished for in that very moment, he thought of not a one. So anxious was he to be cleaned of several days of dirt and grime that he hopped into the tub, sucking in a sharp breath when the hot water met his skin.

The irony of him enjoying something that he had so often viewed as a chore was not lost to him, and he smiled at this fortunate turn of events. Once he finished his bath, he promised himself, he would get out and see what else the rock would give him.

But for now, he submerged himself to just below the nose, his back to the door.

Never had a bath felt so good.

"Found my Rock of Calabash, did you?"

Asher's voice jarred Phinnegan from his sleep, and he found himself sitting in the tub, the water now cool and his skin quite wrinkled.

"I'm sorry," Phinnegan began, but Asher interrupted.

"No, no. It is me who should be sorry. What sort of host does not offer his guest a hot bath?" he said with a slight chuckle. "But you should be careful what you find in this house for some things are not quite useful...or pleasant."

"Like the Devil's Mouth," Phinnegan offered.

"Ah. He didn't bite you did he?" Asher asked, pointing to Phinnegan's hand where the rock had cut his finger.

"No, this was from the rock," Phinnegan responded, taking a moment to scrub off the dried blood in the bathwater.

Asher nodded and then gestured towards the door.

"Well, get dressed and join me outside when you're done. There's something I need to show you."

When Asher closed the door behind him, Phinnegan got out of the tub and put his clothes on hurriedly. He took one last look at the rock before leaving and joining Asher in the hallway.

"Ah, there you are. All right then?" When Phinnegan nodded that he was, Asher led him back up the hallway to the landing and then headed straight for the center hallway.

When they reached the door with only a keyhole, Asher pulled a heavy-looking black key from his pocket. He patted his hand with it for a moment, a troubled look on his face. At length he sighed, thrusting the key into the lock. He twisted and there was a heavy clank, and then the door swung effortlessly inward. Asher stepped-aside, gesturing for Phinnegan to enter the room. When they were both inside, Asher shut the door behind him.

The room was dark except for a single beam of light which entered through a round skylight and fell on the center of the room, where, in an otherwise empty room, stood a small pedestal. Atop it, a large stone bowl stood, filled with an inky black liquid that looked not unlike the wine that Phinnegan had shared with Asher the prior evening.

"What is it?" Phinnegan whispered as the two stood before the bowl.

"It is a Looking Glass," Asher said quietly. When Asher stepped forward out of the darkness and towards the bowl, Phinnegan noticed that he now wore an impressively clean black jacket, which hung down to his knees. Beneath it, he wore a black vest and black trousers, with a white ascot fluffing from the neck.

"You look like the men in those pictures, the ones downstairs in the sitting room."

"It is the attire of a Guide," Asher said, his voice even and flat.

"I see," Phinnegan said quietly. "And this bowl, this Looking Glass? What does it do?"

Asher eyed the bowl apprehensively, as if he feared it may grow legs and jump at him.

"It shows you...things. Things that you would not otherwise be able to see." These cryptic words meant little to Phinnegan.

"What do you mean? What would I normally not be able to see?"

"Can you think of nothing?" Asher asked, leveling a penetrating gaze at Phinnegan. When he did not answer, Asher gestured to the Looking Glass.

"Take a look."

Phinnegan approached the bowl warily. When he reached its edge, he raised his head just enough to see into it.

"I don't see anything."

"Nor should you. It has no idea what to show you, nor if it can show you anything. But if I am right, it can. Try touching it."

Not before casting a wary glance in Asher's direction, Phinnegan reached towards the bowl with his left hand.

"No, not that hand. Your right hand. Use the finger that bears the Mark."

When Phinnegan touched the liquid with the finger that bore the Mark, the change was dramatic.

What had been the smooth, glassy surface of the inky black liquid rippled when his finger touched it. It bubbled and festered until it was frothy. Phinnegan drew his finger back and watched as the froth gelled into a thin, clear film, the inky black visible beneath.

A picture began to take shape in the center of the bowl. It was wavy at first and barely visible against the dark background, but then the vision took on a more substantial form. Phinnegan could just make out a column in what looked to be a dark room. Then another and another, until he could see an entire chamber filled with columns.

And then he saw it.

There was a shadow, a shadow that was not a shadow. A disturbance in the air. A mirage. Phinnegan's face went white. He recognized that disturbance, that creature. He recognized that place.

"What do you see?" Asher's voice inquired from behind.

"I see...Féradoon," Phinnegan whispered. "And a gholem." Phinnegan considered the old man's words, about what the Looking Glass would show him.

"Asher, I have been there before. Is this showing me my past?"

"No, not quite," Asher said quietly, stepping forward and stopping at Phinnegan's right elbow.

"It is your future."

Phinnegan's eyes widened.

"What? I can't go back there!"

"I am sorry, it is not debatable. You must go."

Phinnegan looked at Asher with horror on his face, but Asher only stared back, his face somber and grim.

"I am a Guide and this is my Looking Glass," he said, his voice rising. "It shows you what you must do, and nothing less."

"But...I can't go back. Vermillion...no, I will not go!"

"Phinnegan Qwyk," Asher intoned, the use of his full name breaking Phinnegan from his panic. "What is it that you want most?"

Phinnegan did not hesitate a moment.

"Home. I want to go home."

"Then you must go to Féradoon," Asher said, laying a hand on Phinnegan's shoulder. "You cannot return to your world if you do not."

"But why?" Phinnegan pleaded.

"I cannot say, nor can I tell you the meaning of the Mark which you bear, only that – "

"You don't know what it means? Then how do you know I must go to Féradoon? Why should I trust you?" Phinnegan waited for Asher to respond, but the old man spoke not a word, instead pulling a slim, black book from the pockets of his robe. The book was thin, but extravagant, with gold worked into the cover in superfluous designs.

In the center of these designs, in the center of the cover itself, lay a familiar design. A design that matched perfectly the Mark that Phinnegan bore on his finger.

"I cannot read it," Asher said, handing the book to Phinnegan, who took it carefully.

"And you think I can?" Phinnegan asked as he turned the book over in his hands. Asher shrugged.

"I do not know. In my reading I came across nothing like the Mark you now bear. There are many ancient Marks, Phinnegan Qwyk, and I thought I knew them all. But yours is beyond the knowledge which I am permitted."

"How do you mean?"

"I mean exactly that: I am not permitted to know. It is true that I found a few references to an ancient and mysterious Mark, but there was nothing more. Except that," he finished, pointing to the book in Phinnegan's hands.

Phinnegan stared at the small book in his hands. He ran his hand over the supple leather cover, pausing when his finger touched the embossed symbol on the cover that matched the Mark on his finger.

But when he opened the book, there was nothing. His brow furrowed and he flipped hurriedly through the book, but not a word, not a syllable, not even so much as a stray drop of ink graced the pages of the book. All blank.

"This book is empty," he said in frustration.

"I know. I told you. I cannot read it."

"But that's because there is nothing to read!" Phinnegan snapped.

"Just so."

When Phinnegan sought to hand the book back to Asher, the old man held up his hands and shook his head.

"It is yours. I have no use for it, and it is possible that you will."

Phinnegan looked at the book, plainly unsure that this book had any value at all. But in the end, he shoved it into his trouser pocket.

He returned to the bowl but the liquid had gone black again. He touched it with his finger again and again, but nothing happened.

"There must be some mistake," Phinnegan said, imploring the Looking Glass to show him another way.

"There is no mistake," Asher said. "And, it comes for you," he added quietly.

"What? Who is coming?" Phinnegan asked, turning sharply to stare at the old man.

"Why, the gholem, of course."

"What? But it cannot find me. I must hide!"

"You cannot hide," Asher said calmly, fixing Phinnegan with a steady gaze. "This is what must happen, and it will happen, no matter how you fight."

"No!" Phinnegan yelled, pushing past the old man and fleeing from the room.

"You cannot run, and you cannot hide, Phinnegan Qwyk," Asher's voice boomed through the house as Phinnegan hurried down the stairs.

"The gholem is coming. And it will find you."

But Phinnegan paid him no heed, for he had descended the stairs in a run and sped through the hallway and the sitting room, rounded the corner into the kitchen and fled out the door. He ran down the path, away from the cottage.

By the time he stopped running, the sun was low in the sky and the cottage was well behind him. But he could not rest.

The gholem was coming.

# 24

## A Visitor

Running without heed to where he was going, Phinnegan had long since left the path in his hurry to escape the cottage. Now, he was in the middle of the forest and the sun was barely visible through the branches of the trees, leaving perhaps two more hours before it would set completely and leave him in darkness. He shivered.

*The gholem is coming.*

Asher had told him that he *must* go to Féradoon, but how could he? Periwinkle had seemed genuinely afraid of that place, despite his arrogance towards the judge. Then again, Periwinkle had stolen from him, lied to him, used him, tricked him and left him behind when danger threatened.

*Some friend.*

Now, he was alone again, in the forest. He doubted a pixie would be there to rescue him this time.

*At least it isn't raining.*

He wandered in the forest for perhaps an hour, maybe more, the sun descending slowly in the sky until the branches about him more resembled boney ghouls than living extensions of a tree. His stomach rumbled in the stillness of the forest reminding him that he had not eaten since his late breakfast. He checked the lowest hanging branches as he passed them, hoping for the off chance that one would bear an edible nut or some type of fruit, but he found none.

The sky growing darker, he walked on as the sounds of evening in the forest emerged. He heard the hoot of an owl and then the lone howl of a wolf.

*Faolchú?*

But the howl was far away and he did not hear it a second time. Besides, Periwinkle had said that the Faolchú were only found in Darkwater Forest.

When the sharp sounds of frogs pierced the night, Phinnegan paid particular attention. Frogs meant water. The croaks and ribbits seemed to come from all sides, but perhaps just a little louder to his right than to his left. He followed his ears and indeed, the chorus of croaks was much louder here. Frogs could be heard from all directions, behind and in front, left and right, above and below.

But the darkness closed in around him and it was becoming very difficult for him to see more than a few feet in front of his face. When his feet splashed in thick mud instead of shallow water, it seemed more likely that the forest was home to a bog or marsh, and not clear, fresh water. Several more steps and the water covered the new boots he had received from the Rock of Calabash in Asher's cottage. The setting sun did not allow him to see far, but trees appeared to clog the area in front of him. When the buzzing of mosquitoes and gnats filled the air, his heart sank. A forest marsh.

He turned to follow the marsh's perimeter, hoping perhaps it led to a stream or creak, even a pond, though the latter's water would be as stagnant as the marsh.

The sharp crack of a branch underfoot off to his right startled him and he snapped his eyes toward the sound, not that he could see anything in this light. Could it be the gholem? A second snapping branch and the rustle of a bush belied a much smaller creature, however. Phinnegan remained still for several minutes until the sound passed some distance behind him and then splashed faintly as the creature, whatever it was, moved off into the marsh.

Moving again, he followed the marsh's edge to the right, but was forced to move even further right when the marsh became deeper. The further to the right he went, the closer the trees came to one another. Several times he felt his face assaulted by the sticky strands of a spider's web.

*I hate spiders.*

It was difficult to see at first in the darkness, but the trees began to thin. As they thinned, the slope of the ground beneath him inclined until he reached a small summit. Here, the tree line broke and he found himself standing above a small clearing. The sky overhead was dotted with the night's first stars, their light reflected in the ripples of a slow moving creek not twenty paces ahead.

The sight of the water rejuvenated him and he hurried forward, though nearly falling once as his foot caught a small depression. He fell to his knees beside the creek and cupped his hands, scooping the water to his lips and drinking his fill. He was on his third handful when he noticed the faint taste in the water.

*Apples.*

Standing, he followed the creek away from the trees whence he had come. And then he saw them, their branches arching thickly overhead. Three old apple trees, their roots running along the banks of the creek, through its bed and interrupting the flow of water. A multitude of glistening orbs lay at the feet of the trees and filled the creek-bed so that the water was forced to trickle between them and over top to continue its flow.

When he reached the trees, Phinnegan saw that these orbs were in fact apples, dozens of them. They must have fallen from the trees, their red skin so dark that they were nearly black in the starlight.

Phinnegan's stomach rumbled loudly at the sight of the apples. The branches were just out of his reach, so he grabbed several of the apples on the top of the pile in the creek. Their skin was cool and wet and he bit into the first ravenously, the satisfying crunch ringing in the night.

He sat down, his back against the nearest tree and devoured one apple after another. By the time he had finished his fifth, he was losing his taste for them. He tossed the cores one at a time into the creek, aiming for a large rock about fifteen paces from where he sat. Only once did he hear the thunk of his core striking the rock, the other four times hearing a splash.

The moon was just beginning to eclipse the top of the trees and now bathed the little clearing in a soft, white light. A rodent of some kind scurried along the opposite bank of the creek.

Phinnegan yawned, suddenly very sleepy from the combination of running through the woods and now a pleasantly full stomach. The ground beneath the tree, at least the area not covered by apples, was soft and comfortable, blanketed by a layer of lush, damp moss. A perfect spot to bed down for the night.

Making a pillow from old leaves and fallen apples, Phinnegan stretched out beneath the aged apple trees, the moon, and the stars.

Within a mere few minutes, he was fast asleep.

Phinnegan awakened with a start to the acrid smell of smoke, and the orange-red brightness of a small campfire. Just on the other side, gazing at him through the tips of the flames, were two intense green eyes in a pale face. The face was immediately recognizable. It was that of the Faë with whom he had danced at Castle Heronhawk. He pushed himself to his elbow and met her gaze.

"You are quite brave," she said, a smirk just touching the corner of her lips.

"I'm sorry?" Phinnegan questioned.

"The gholem. You must be quite brave to sleep as soundly as you do, out here alone, in the dead of night." The smirk broadened into small smile. "Quite brave indeed. Or quite foolish."

"I...I was tired," Phinnegan mumbled.

"Of course you were. And quite full of apples too, I would wager. Come," she said, grabbing a small bowl and gesturing with it in his direction. "I've made a stew."

"You made that while I slept?"

The Faë smirked.

"I told you that you slept soundly."

"How did you find me?" Phinnegan asked. He couldn't put his finger on it, but the Faë was somehow different from when the first time they had met.

"Does it matter?" she said, her voice sweet and comforting. "Come, it will warm you up."

No sooner had she mentioned that the stew would warm him up than a chill was apparent on the breeze, a chill that had not been there before, at least Phinnegan did not think it had. He rubbed his arms reflexively. The stew did smell delicious, and a handful of apples were hardly a fitting dinner.

He pushed himself to his feet and walked over to the Faë, taking the bowl she offered as well as sitting on the small log to which she gestured.

"Thank you," he said, before bringing a spoonful of the still steaming stew to his lips. The flavor was rich and the stew was hearty. The apples had satiated him less than he had imagined, and he devoured the stew within minutes.

When he sat the bowl down, he saw that the Faë was smiling at him.

"Feel better?" she asked.

"Much," he replied with a small smile. Just as she had in the courtyard at Heronhawk, her presence cheered and calmed him. "Thank you, again. It was delicious."

"You are most welcome...you know, you never told me your name. Awfully rude for a dancing partner not to share a name, you know."

"Sorry. I am called Phinnegan. Phinnegan Qwyk."

"Very nice to meet you," she said with a light, airy laugh. "Or meet you again, I guess it is. I'm Emerald, by the way, in case you have forgotten.

"Yes," Phinnegan said, his cheeks blushing slightly. "I remember. You are hard to forget."

"Very sweet," she said, rising from her own log and moving to sit beside Phinnegan on his own log. "I remember you as well, very clearly."

Phinnegan was suddenly aware that his hands were quite moist, and he wiped them hurriedly on his trousers. He was glad that he did, for within a moment, she had taken his hand in her own.

"Where is your friend?

"Who?"

"You know, the flashy, purple-haired one."

"Oh, him," Phinnegan said, his shoulders sagging slightly. "He's gone."

"Ah," she said quietly, her hand squeezing his gently. "That's just as well."

Phinnegan turned to face her, but saw that she was not looking at him. At least not his eyes. Instead, she studied his hand closely, a quizzical tilt to her head. Phinnegan suddenly felt uneasy. How *had* she found him?

"Thank you, again," Phinnegan said, "for the stew. But I still don't understand how you possibly could have found me.

The Faë only smiled and scooted closer to him on the log.

"Are you afraid of the gholem?" she asked, her gaze remaining on his finger.

"Of course," Phinnegan said sharply. "It's a gholem."

"To fear something because it is that which it is seems silly to me," she said with a shrug.

"Well," Phinnegan began, his voice defiant. "It wants to take me back to Féradoon. *That* is a good reason to fear it."

"Perhaps."

"Perhaps?" Phinnegan said, eyes wide. "Do you know what that place is like?"

"Oh yes. But do you?"

"They lock you in dungeons so dark you cannot see your own hand!" Phinnegan snapped. "And they put you on trial only to declare you guilty and sentence you to torture and death!"

The Faë wrinkled her brow.

"Perhaps. Who told you these things?"

"Well, it..." Phinnegan began, but he trailed off. He had been warned of Féradoon, certainly, but the visions of death and torture had been just that, visions, brought on by the poisonous gas Crimson had released to free them from the Faolchú.

"Well...they threatened to force Periwinkle to Age!"

She shrugged.

"Perhaps. But you are not a Faë."

"No...but...but," Phinnegan sputtered. "But Vermillion!"

"What about him?"

"He's evil!"

"Yes, but would you live your life always running from evil?" Emerald gazed steadily into his eyes and he shifted uncomfortably. "Did it hurt when the Warber fused with your skin?" she asked, nodding to his hand which bore the Mark.

Phinnegan felt the hair on his arms rise as a shiver ran up his spine.

"How do you know about the Warber?"

"Simple," she said. "Because I was the one that gave it to you."

"What are you – " Phinnegan began, but stopped.

*When she kissed me...she touched me on the chest, just there. Right above my pocket. The pocket where Mariella saw the Warber when I fell.*

"You...you gave it to me?" Phinnegan whispered. "Why? I don't understand."

"Because," she said, leaning closer to him. "You needed it."

"Needed it?" Phinnegan exclaimed. "How could you know I would need it?" He pushed himself from the log and backed away from the Faë toward the apple trees.

"Who are you? How did you find me?"

"Phinnegan," she said, her voice caressing his name as she spoke it. "It's me, Emerald. I am a friend."

"Are you? If you are a friend, how did you find me?"

"I followed you," she said, rising from the log and following him towards the apple trees.

"Followed? From where? Heronhawk? How could you have followed me from there? *I* don't even know how I came to be here from that place."

"I have followed you for much longer than that. Ever since you came into this world I have followed you, helping you, though you do not see it."

"Helping me? Helping me with what?"

"You will see," she cooed, drawing nearer to him, stopping a mere foot or two in front of where he now stood, his back against the tree. "You will understand more than you ever imagined, in time." She stepped closer, her face inches from his.

"You are a very special person, Phinnegan Qwyk."

The sound of her voice speaking his name in that soft tone made his knees quiver.

*She is so very pretty. But...*

Phinnegan shook his head, trying to clear away her effect upon him.

"You say you are helping me, yet you question me about Féradoon? Why?"

"Because I would have you go there."

"What?" Phinnegan asked in alarm. "I won't!"

She pulled back from him, her brow furrowed.

"Did the Guide not tell you as much?" she snapped, her eyes flashing.

"How do you know what he told me?" Phinnegan asked, his wariness of the Faë increasing. "And why should I trust either of you?"

"I do not know what he told you, but I can only assume that he did. His role is to guide. It is to Féradoon that you must go, therefore he must have told you this. I have come to ask you to go." She approached him again. "Trust me."

"Why? I hardly know you." He said, his shoulders sagging. "I cannot go back."

"Yes, you can," she said, creeping close to him again so that her face was inches from his own.

"Close your eyes," she commanded softly.

"Why?"

"Just do it," she said, her tone firm but soothing. "I will not hurt you." She placed her hand on his cheek. Phinnegan shifted slightly beneath her touch, but he obeyed. Her fingers were warm and they caressed his cheek tenderly.

"Good," she said. "Very good."

The chill that had appeared so suddenly before now began to deepen, and a rising breeze ruffled Phinnegan's hair and lifted his shirt-tails. But her hand remained warm and his cheek relaxed against it.

"Relax. Let your mind wander."

"But," he protested.

"Shhh," she murmured, her breath hot against his ear. "Do you miss your family, Phinnegan Qwyk?"

"Y...yes," he muttered, caught off-guard by the question.

"I can take you to them."

"You can," he said, his back straightening and his eyelids threatening to open.

"Keep your eyes closed," she said quietly but with firmness. "And yes, I can." As she spoke, the breeze continued to rise, becoming a light wind. Phinnegan shivered.

"Will you let me take you? Take you home?"

*Back to my family...*

"Yes," he mumbled.

*Back home...*

"Good," she said, and Phinnegan felt her breath moist and warm upon his lips. When her other hand came to rest upon his other cheek, he welcomed the warmth, for the wind continued to grow around him and he was becoming quite cold.

"Come with me," she murmured, her lips now lightly touching his.

And then she kissed him.

Phinnegan had never kissed a girl before – he had never really wanted to. Her mouth was warm and wet, something he had expected to be unpleasant, but he in fact found it just the opposite. Still, he fought her at first, not sure how to respond. But she pressed her lips more firmly to his, and as the wind began to howl more loudly, he found her warmth most comforting. He kissed her back.

This surrender broke the spell.

Phinnegan opened his eyes with a start and saw that all was black around him. The forest, the creek, the apples - all gone. With the icy wind raging about him, his eyes met Emerald's, just as she pulled away from him. She wavered, she flickered, and then melted into shadow.

A shadow that was not a shadow.

*She* was the gholem.

And she had him.

# 25

## A Dinner Party

*Where am I?*

Emerald – that is to say, the gholem – had enveloped him in a translucent bubble, and whisked him from the blackness of a starless night to the whiteness belying a thousand suns. Scenes of forests and rivers and things in between had flashed around him, and then, nothingness.

A dizzying moment had passed, somewhere between being and not being at all, before he felt whole again. When his feet touched solid ground, he blinked the shock from his eyes.

The gholem was nowhere to be seen. Phinnegan was alone.

It couldn't be Féradoon; at least it wasn't any part he had ever seen. There were no columns, no high court. He was in a bedroom and one full of pomp and decoration at that.

The walls were composed of large stones, squarely cut, and rose high above him to a dark wooden ceiling with monstrous beams spanning the room's length. A gigantic bed took up nearly an entire wall, easily big enough for several of him to sleep upon. Floor to ceiling large-paned windows spanned another wall. Beneath his feet, a lush, patterned rug spread across much of the room's stone floor.

There were other objects in the room as well: a writing desk with intricate carvings crafted into its dark wood; a sitting area with chairs; a wash basin and chamber pot; and a roaring fireplace, which spewed forth a striking heat from massive jaws taller than Phinnegan plus a hand. Chambers fit for a king, or at least, a prince.

Phinnegan had never seen such wealth. This could *not* be Féradoon.

*Could it?*

A sharp rap at the door brought Phinnegan from his thoughts, just in time to see a slim, white-haired man dressed impeccably in a black suit with a black vest slip through the door. A starched white shirt was visible from the chest up, with a white tie at the neck. His slender fingers were sheathed in white gloves.

"Forgive me, sir," he said in a nasal voice, bowing stiffly at the waist. "My master wished you be informed that dinner shall be served shortly. He asks that you dress and make your way to the dining hall. I, of course, shall accompany you."

The man had spoken his entire piece without so much as looking in Phinnegan's direction, instead keeping his eyes focused on the floor in front of him.

"I'm sorry," Phinnegan said, "but who are you? What dinner are you talking about? And who is your master?" Before the man could answer, Phinnegan hastily added, "and dress myself in what? I'm dressed already."

The man raised his eyes then, regarding Phinnegan with a gaze that was cold and filled with annoyance.

"Forgive me, sir, but perhaps something a bit more...sophisticated...is in order." He pointed to a large wooden wardrobe near the gigantic bed. "There you will find clothes more fitting for a guest of honor."

"Guest of honor? Me?"

"So my master tells me. Sir," the man added, drawling the word so that Phinnegan ears reddened from the mockery.

"And who is your master?"

The man raised an eyebrow, casting a cutting glance at Phinnegan before he spoke.

"My master is the lord of this castle, this mountain, even this land. And he is your host. He is the Lord of Féradoon."

Phinnegan's knees buckled when the word was spoken, yet he stood his ground.

"Tell him I am not coming."

"I am afraid, *sir*," the man said, as his lips curled back in a ghoulish smile, "that refusal is not an option. I shall return for you."

The man bowed stiffly before turning and leaving the room. The door closed behind him with a heavy thud, leaving Phinnegan alone, dumbfounded.

He stood motionless for a moment, unsure of what to do. But it seemed he had little choice. Moving to the wardrobe, he mechanically removed his own clothes and replaced them with the much more fancy attire that had been left for him. They fit him perfectly, the velvety fabric of the black shirt fitting snuggly against his skin. The outfit reminded him of something that Periwinkle might have worn. The black leather shoes with shiny silver buckles that completed the outfit made the comparison even more fitting.

Scarcely had he had time to complete his transformation when the rap at the door came again, followed by the appearance of the white-haired man.

"Very good, sir," the man sneered, opening the door wide and gesturing for Phinnegan to exit the room. "This way please."

He followed the white-haired man through several winding hallways, past open doors leading into a massive library, multiple sitting rooms and a large room with an ornate piano. He could hear voices and laughter in the distance, which became clearer and more boisterous as they walked.

When the two stepped through a large archway, the voices slowly trailed off until only silence reigned. Phinnegan and his guide stood in the entrance to a large hall where dozens of people stood, most with a glass of wine in one hand. All were older, with gray or white hair, man and woman alike. Phinnegan guessed that they were all Aged. And all of them were staring at him.

A flash of color and movement just visible through the throng caught his attention. He strained to see the source, but there was no need. The color and movement were coming towards hm. The sea of Aged in their blacks and grays parted, and then Phinnegan saw him.

*Vermillion.*

His hair was a deep, lush red mixed with tendrils of gray. His face was a similar combination of the bright, colorful youth of the Young and the stern coldness of the Aged. The nose was sharp and hooked, but the mouth beneath was full and a wistful smile played across his lips. Fine wrinkles touched the corners of eyes that sparkled with excitement and power. His clothes, too, blended these two sides, a lush black shirt and trousers encased by a dark red jacket with flowing sleeves and tails down to his knees.

When his reddish-brown eyes beheld Phinnegan fully, his smile broadened revealing white teeth.

"Aha! Here he is. My Lords and Ladies, may I present to you our honored guest for this evening." With three long strides he had covered the distance and now stood just beside Phinnegan, a heavy hand resting on his shoulder.

"It is my honor to present Phinnegan Qwyk, human of Ireland, and," he paused, well-aware of the attentive silence around him, "a Bearer of the Mark."

A murmur rolled through the crowd like a wave, and was swiftly followed by a quiet applause. A polite but firm pull on Phinnegan's shoulder alerted him that Vermillion wished him to join in a walk through the crowd. The flock of Aged remained parted, providing a clear path for Vermillion and Phinnegan to make their way through. Several of the Aged dipped a head or offered a hand as he passed.

"Good to meet you, young master Qwyk."

"'Tis a pleasure, young master."

"Welcome to Féradoon, master Qwyk."

This strange show of deference by these Aged left Phinnegan quite perplexed. The firm grip of Vermillion's hand upon his shoulder, firm but not painful, further confused him. As they passed certain Aged, Vermillion would lean close and whisper a secret.

"Lucius there killed a Young once, but then haven't we all? But he went so far as to bury him beneath the floor of his own house."

"And there, Brutus. He's addicted to dragon brandy, though you will never see him take a drink in public."

"Ah, and you must stay wary of Septus," he said, nodding in the direction of a particularly creepy Aged. "He has a fondness for humans that goes beyond that which is deemed proper." Sure enough, as Phinnegan kept an eye on Septus as they emerged from the crowd, the disturbing Aged kept an eye on Phinnegan as well.

Vermillion led him towards a large dining room with a heavy, dark wooden table that stretched for perhaps a hundred feet. Both sides were lined with ornately carved chairs. At the head of the table, its back to a roaring fire in an enormous fireplace stood a chair much larger and more ornate than the rest. Its wood was lacquered in a shiny black and anointed with two red cushions, one on its seat and the other on its back.

"You may sit here, Phinnegan," Vermillion said, leading Phinnegan to the chair on the right of the large, ornate chair. "At my right hand." The smile and eyes that looked down on Phinnegan were not unfriendly, but neither were they altogether friendly.

Phinnegan stood behind the chair that Vermillion had indicated, mimicking his own stance. As they waited, the throng of Aged filed into the large dining room. Many, if not most, cast an interested glance in Phinnegan's direction. Those who caught his eyes dipped their heads slightly, their faces remaining emotionless.

When the last of the Aged had found his seat, each chair had been claimed. That is, all but one: the chair directly across from Phinnegan.

But its master, or rather, its mistress, soon arrived.

Emerald strode to her chair, her eyes fixed on Phinnegan as she walked. She continued to stare at Phinnegan while servants bustled to provide each patron of this large dinner party a crystal goblet filled with a draught of golden liquid. When Vermillion raised his glass, every one quickly followed suit, including Emerald, who continued to stare at Phinnegan.

"It is with great pleasure that I welcome you all to my home. Tonight shall be a wondrous feast, an early celebration of the coming events. For tomorrow at dawn, with the help of our honored guest," here he paused, and everyone inclined their glasses slightly in Phinnegan's direction, "we shall bring a new hope and a long-wanted change to our world. Tomorrow we open the long lost gate into the Circle, a source of power long-forsaken by our fore-fathers. Tomorrow, together, we will change our world. Forever."

"Here, here!" the assembled Aged intoned in unison. The clinking of glasses could be heard all around and then everyone began to take their seats, waiting, of course, for Vermillion to seat himself first.

Once everyone had been seated, Phinnegan still felt Emerald's eyes upon him, but his own attention was now on the bustling servants, who quickly began placing silver-domed plates in front of each patron.

With one exception, all were alike. But Vermillion's plate bore a golden dome, with five large rubies encrusted into its circumference.

All at once, in a perfectly choreographed move, the servants removed the domes with a flourish, revealing bowls of steaming soup.

"Enjoy, my friends," Vermillion said, picking up his golden spoon and gesturing for others to do the same.

Murmured sounds of approval meandered down the length of the table. Phinnegan eyed the orange soup before him, its aroma wafting enticingly to his nose. Despite being at the table of one he feared greatly, he was in fact quite hungry. The first spoonful of soup released an explosion of flavor on his tongue. The soup's texture was smooth although slightly grainy, much like applesauce. A hint of cinnamon and nutmeg was detectable, but otherwise he had never tasted anything quite like it. He was continuing to savor the soup when Vermillion's voice caught his ear.

"Tell me, daughter, did you have any trouble escorting our honored guest here this evening. I do hope you were not rough with him."

"Daughter?" Phinnegan blurted, a full spoon perched just in front of his mouth. But the two ignored his comment, though Emerald kept her gaze on Phinnegan as she spoke. Phinnegan remembered everything that Periwinkle had told him, the stone stating its mistress as Emerald Wren.

*Vermillion Wren. Of course.*

"It was no problem at all, father," she said, her eyes shifting from green to gray. "He came along quite willingly."

"Bollocks," Phinnegan muttered into his soup, his eyes averting Emerald's.

"Splendid," Vermillion responded, with a bit too much cheer in his voice. "How is the soup?" he asked, directing the question to Phinnegan.

"Actually...it is fantastic," Phinnegan answered truthfully.

"Respect, young lad," a gruff Aged seated beside Emerald chastised, waving his spoon at Phinnegan. "Address him as My King."

"We mustn't be so formal, Secondus. He is not of our world; he cannot be expected to know our customs. And besides, I am not his king for that very same reason." He turned and the wolfish grin returned as he looked at Phinnegan.

"You may address me as Your Highness. That should please all, yes?" Vermillion looked to the gruff Aged, who nodded curtly and then rejoined his soup. Phinnegan swallowed his last spoonful slowly and then re-addressed Vermillion.

"The soup is fantastic, Your Highness."

"Excellent, I am glad to hear it," Vermillion responded, his teeth still bared in that harsh smile.

Phinnegan suppressed a shiver. For all his hospitality thus far, something did not feel right about this Aged. If he was indeed an Aged. He was the first Aged Phinnegan had seen who smiled thus, who wore flashy garments and had colored hair, even if it was only partly so. He wondered if the Faë went through some type of process when they went through their Aging as Periwinkle had called it. Perhaps this was why Vermillion was something that seemed in between the two extremes.

After perhaps a quarter of an hour, when everyone seemed to have finished their soup, the servants returned to whisk away the empty bowls. When they were gone, Vermillion clapped twice, startling Phinnegan.

"Time for a little entertainment, I think," he said. Just as he finished speaking, a trio of tall, lithe women appeared in the doorway. Phinnegan caught only one word in the hushed whispers that rose up around him.

*Sirens.*

Phinnegan had read about such creatures, women with the wings of a bird or birds with the heads of women, depending on who was telling the tale. These most certainly the former. But in either case, their voices were said to lead men to their deaths in one manner or another. Phinnegan was at once eager to see, and hear, such renowned creatures, as well as terrified by what the outcome might be. But he needn't have worried. Vermilion leaned close to his ear just as all sound seemingly disappeared from the room.

"I've placed a charm around you," he said, his voice piercing through the silence. "Only my voice can breach it. I am afraid you would not survive the song we are about to hear. It is likely others might not as well, but that is what makes it such a fascinating game."

Vermillion leaned back, a sly smirk playing across his lips. Phinnegan heard not a sound, and sat wide-eyed and fearful. What sort of person would play such a wicked game with his guests?

"Fear not, ladies," Vermillion said, standing up at his position at the head of the table. "I am certain all of your men are strong enough to withstand the Sirens' song."

Phinnegan saw, but did not hear, Vermillion clap again. Within moments the eyes of every man were wide with their necks craning their heads to get the best view of the Sirens, now gliding from their place at the entrance of the dining hall to move down the line of guests.

The song went on for several minutes, all the while Phinnegan watching as the men around the table struggled to maintain their composure. All save Vermillion, who watched quite comfortably from his gilded chair, his fingers tapping its arms as his eyes darted from one potential victim to the next. Phinnegan also noticed that the ladies in the room appeared completely unaffected by the Sirens song. Most were instead completely absorbed in keeping the male Aged from leaping from their chairs.

Upon completing their circuit of the room, the Sirens made their way back to the entrance, where they hovered, swaying with their song.

A sudden movement to his right caught Phinnegan's attention. Jumping from his seat with a spryness that did not match his shriveled appearance, one of the Aged now ran towards the Sirens. When he reached them, they each patted and caressed his arms and back, drawing him away from the dining hall and into a growing darkness.

When they vanished from his sight, Phinnegan felt a slight release of pressure and suddenly he could hear again. There was a mumbling occurring in the room around him but all was silenced when Vermillion spoke.

"Apparently dear Aulus has grown weak in his age." A thin smile haunted his lips and his eyes bore into one Aged and then another. "I am glad to see that the rest of you were able to maintain yourselves." The smile vanished and the hint of a snarl curled the right side of his mouth.

"If there is anything I loathe more than all else, it is weakness."

A sharp clap brought the servants once again, this time setting multiple dishes of various sizes in the middle of the table in one long line from end to end. The domes hiding the contents were again all silver, as were the plates being placed in front of each patron. Vermillion's plate was, of course, golden, edged in a dusting of crushed garnet.

When the domes were lifted, the Patrons were assailed by a variety of sensuous smells. There were two different kinds of fish, roasted rabbit, and a leg of lamb, one of each dish for every four or five guests. More food than anyone could hope to eat.

The smells drew Phinnegan to the edge of his seat. He had been just about to ask Vermillion a question, but the thought was now gone from his mind as he took in the dishes before him. Besides, Vermillion's mood seemed to have soured since the departure of the sirens, whether because they were able to lure away one Aged or because they were *only* able to lure one Aged.

Phinnegan looked from the food to the other patrons, but no one made a move. They all seemed to be looking at him, as did Vermillion. When his eyes found Emerald's, she smiled softly and gestured to the table's bounty.

"They are waiting for you. It is our custom. The host eats the first bite of the first service, while an esteemed guest is given the honor for the second."

Phinnegan regarded the four options before him, his tongue peeking from the corner of his mouth. He glanced to Vermillion, who nodded, a bored, distant look upon his face. Wasting no more time, Phinnegan removed a thick slice of the lamb and placed it on his plate. When he took his knife to cut his first bite, it passed with ease through the tender meat.

The juices flowed freely over his tongue when he bit into this first morsel. He had never tasted anything so delicious. As he chewed, he became aware of the clinking of knives and forks on plates and a renewed chatter as the other patrons chose their own second service. Murmured satisfaction could be heard all around as the others sampled the four offered fares.

Even Vermillion's mood seemed to return to his sly contentment of earlier, and as Phinnegan ate, his courage to ask his host the questions that burned in his mind grew, until he cleared his throat and ventured to speak.

"Excuse me, sir, I mean, Your Highness. May I ask you a question?"

"Yes, of course. You *are* our honored guest, after all. Go on." His tone was receptive, even kind, and he went so far as to place his own fork and knife on the table to devote his full attention to Phinnegan.

"Why are you being so nice to me?"

"Whatever do you mean?" Vermillion said, a broad smile spreading across his face, which was surely meant to comfort Phinnegan, yet it had the opposite effect.

"Well, what I mean is- I mean, Your Highness," Phinnegan said, correcting his slip. "What I mean is, well, when I was here before, I was put into a dungeon and then put on trial. Well, truthfully Periwinkle was put on-"

"Do NOT," Vermillion thundered, interrupting Phinnegan and causing him to cower in his seat, "speak that name in my presence. Ever! Am I clear?" Vermillion's reddish-brown eyes shifted more toward the red and they bored into Phinnegan, who managed to nod quickly.

"Y-yes, Your Highness." Phinnegan was so frightened by this outburst that he put aside all thought of asking his question. But Vermillion, relaxing a bit in his seat, seemed to recognize where Phinnegan had been headed.

"As for you, it is unfortunate that you were caught up with that...criminal. We had no choice but to assume that you were with him. But, my daughter," he paused nodding in Emerald's direction, who sat with her back straight, calmly chewing her food while her gray-green eyes stared at

Phinnegan, "she could...sense...something about you. When Periwinkle...escaped...she trailed you both. And it turns out she was right. You are very special." The smile Vermillion bestowed upon Phinnegan at that moment was anything but warm, and Phinnegan could only think of one word: greed.

He was also reminded of Periwinkle, and the story that the purple-haired Faë had told him during their time in the darkness of Féradoon. He had mentioned Vermillion's daughter and the love he had borne her, and how Vermillion had taken her away from him. As he regarded the Faë across from him, her eyes flashed from green to gray and back again, and he was reminded that she was more than a Faë, if she was still a Faë at all. She was a gholem.

Perhaps this explained why Periwinkle had not recognized her that day in Castle Heronhawk.

He puzzled over these questions, but he could hardly ask them now. Instead he returned to the discussion at hand, for he still did not understand his own predicament.

"But I still don't understand. Why am I special? Why have you brought me here? What is this Mark?" He finished by thrusting his finger forward for all around him to see. A hush fell upon those closest and it spread until Vermillion needed to speak with a voice only just above a whisper.

"You ask many questions," he said, his eyes fixed on the Mark on Phinnegan's finger. Those other Aged within earshot had set down their forks and listened intently. "I will say only this: It has been foretold that a human would come to our world, and that he would be able, with the proper guidance, of course, to open the First Gate. This gate has been closed and locked for millennia. We believe that you, Phinnegan Qwyk, are that human."

"But...why me?" Phinnegan asked after a short pause.

"The Warber was a test. When we learned that it had marked you, we knew that there was a very good possibility that it was you. And now we have brought you here for the final test."

"What is the final test?"

"Why, to open the Gate, of course," Vermillion said with a slight shrug.

"But...what if I cannot open this Gate? What if I fail?"

Vermillion smiled coldly, his reddish-brown eyes sparkling slightly.

"The Gate does not tolerate failure. If you fail, you will die."

Phinnegan swallowed the lump in his throat. He met Vermillion's gaze for a moment before letting his eyes fall to the table.

"And if I refuse to help you?"

"Refuse?" Vermillion questioned with a raised eyebrow. "If you refused, then you would be of no further use to us." The threat was veiled but only slightly. Phinnegan had little doubt what this type of person would do with him if he was of no further use.

"But," Vermillion continued, wiping his hands on a golden napkin trimmed in dark red ribbing. "Once you have helped me to open the Gate, I will of course be in your debt. I would be more than willing to grant you whatever you wish. To send you home, perhaps? That is what you want, isn't it?"

Phinnegan raised his head, his eyes widened with hope.

"You can send me home?"

"Of course. And I will, if you agree to help."

Phinnegan looked around and noticed that all of the Aged within earshot had their eyes upon him. Across the table, Emerald's now green eyes burrowed into him. Vermillion was the only one who appeared relaxed, leaning back in his chair.

Phinnegan thought of everything he had experienced during these several days of adventure. He remembered Periwinkle's hatred of this powerful Aged who sat only an arm's reach away. There was no denying that Vermillion left Phinnegan ill at ease. However, one thought more than any other loomed large in his mind.

*Home.*

"All right," Phinnegan said quietly. "I'll do it."

Emerald's eyes flashed dangerously, and he thought perhaps she would speak. But she held her tongue, and regained her composure.

Vermillion only smiled.

"I knew you were a smart boy."

# 26

# A Book of Secrets

Phinnegan sat alone in the large chambers that had been given to him for his time in Féradoon, his stomach full from the seven-service dinner he had endured. After he had agreed to help Vermillion open the First Gate, the services continued as did the in-between service entertainments. Thankfully, no one else seemingly had met their end, as the latter entertainment had been much more benign and even enjoyable at times.

Now, with the sights and sounds behind him, it was refreshing to be alone. These Aged made him feel uncomfortable, none more so than their leader, Vermillion, who Phinnegan still was not sure whether he was actually an Aged, a Young, or something in between.

Save for the crackling fire, the room was quiet and dark. Though, as the fire was large, it cast a bright glow over half the room. Phinnegan sat now in one of the two heavily carved chairs arranged before the fire. On the other chair lay the sleeping clothes that a servant had left for him.

With a yawn, he stood and stretched. He had not slept in what he guessed was at least twenty-four hours, for it was well into the night when the dinner party had ended, and the previous night he had spent in the clutches of the gholem, being brought to Féradoon from the forests outside Asher's cottage. The large bed beckoned behind him and he removed his clothes and tossed them on the floor, throwing his travelling clothes on top of them.

When his shirt fell, the unexpected thump caught his attention. He stared confusedly at the small black object which had fallen from his pocket before he recognized it as the book that Asher had given him.

He donned the sleeping clothes and neatly folded the fine garments he had been provided for dinner before sitting on the floor in front of the roaring fire, the small black leather book at his feet. When he grasped it, he found the supple leather to already be quite warm from the fire's heat. Phinnegan sat several feet from the fire himself but felt the warmth keenly upon his face. The crackling logs were calming and he fingered the gold-etched design on the front of the book absently as he was soothed by this sound.

Flipping the book over, he scrutinized the back cover for any other discernable symbols, but the intricate scrollwork meant nothing to him. The spine of the book, which was only perhaps half an inch thick, revealed nothing further, save a smaller version of the symbol on the front cover.

When he opened the book, Phinnegan found it just as he had before, blank and empty. The book held no more than a hundred pages, and each was completely devoid of any writing. He traced over their surfaces with his Marked finger, hoping to coax the pages to reveal their secrets, but to no avail. The pages remained as blank as ever.

Somewhere in the castle, a bell intoned the hour. Twelve long notes signaled the advent of a new day. Phinnegan sighed heavily and moved to close the book, as he was anxious for sleep. But just as the last peal of the bell vanished into the night's embrace, a flicker of something caught his eye.

And then it was gone.

But he had seen *something*. A word? A letter? He flipped quickly through the pages of the book, searching for the flash he had seen. He was nearly to the end of the book before he found it. There, on the third to the last page, at the very top in the center, a small symbol in rich black ink. A symbol that matched the one on the cover, and the Mark on his finger.

His spine tingled and he dared not to breathe lest the symbol disappear as quickly and mysteriously as it had come. He wondered why it would appear now, but suddenly remembered a remark made by Vermillion near the end of the dinner. He had said that Phinnegan's arrival was just in time; that tomorrow was a special day. A coincidence perhaps, but Phinnegan thought it more likely that all of these things were linked. The book, the Gate, the Mark on his finger. And now, when the bell had tolled the new day, this special day, the book had spoken its first word to him.

It could *not* be coincidence.

He sat quietly before the fire, pensive, with the book open in his hands. With a shaky hand, he touched the Mark on his finger to the symbol on the page. Though nothing else appeared on the page at first, a *tingle* in his finger told him that something had happened, that somehow his touch had made an impact.

Then the words began to appear. Finally he would have some answers.

But his heart sank just as quickly as it had risen. Though several lines had appeared on the page, they were all gibberish to him, written in a language he could neither read nor recognize. The letters were familiar, though many had been written in a manner he had never before seen. Yet even with this familiarity, he could make out not one word in the entire piece.

ABE AR EROFT HEMA RKM AY

ATT HEAPP OINT EDIT MEAN DATTH EA PPO INTE DPL
ACE

CO MEUPO NANEN TRAN CETOT HEP ATH

EMBA RKIN GUPO NTHI SPAT HMUS TNO TBET AKE
NLIG HTL Y

FO RTHEG UAR DIA NWITH INW ILLPUR GETH OSED
EE MEDU NOW RTH Y

THEB EAR ERMUS TEN TERW ILLIN GLY

TH EBE ARERM USTEN TERA LON E

"I can't read it," he whispered.

He stared at these words for several minutes, vainly trying to sound out phrases that resembled no tongue he had ever heard. In the end he slammed the book closed squeezing it tightly in his fingers.

"What good is a book if you can't even read it?" he grumbled to himself, frustrated that once again he would need to find his own way when it just appeared he had found help. In anger, he raised his arm, preparing to hurl the book into the fire.

"Would you make a second foolish mistake in one evening," a voice said quietly from behind, causing Phinnegan to nearly fall over backwards in alarm.

He turned to see Emerald appearing from the shadows on the other side of the room.

"How-how did you get in here? The door was locked."

"Do you think that the keepers of this castle would allow you to lock a door to which they do not have a key?" she said, a small smile on her lips as she made her way across the room to where Phinnegan sat in front of the fire.

"Besides, I have little need of keys. I have my own," she paused, a sardonic smile upon her lips, "talents."

"You mean because you are a gholem," Phinnegan said flatly.

"Yes."

"But yet, you are his daughter? How can you be a Faë and a gholem?"

Emerald looked away, staring into the fire for several moments, her eyes flashing from green to gray and back again. Phinnegan thought that perhaps her eyes stayed gray for a bit longer this time.

"It is a long story," she said at length, a resigned tone in her voice. "Perhaps I will have a chance to tell you it some time."

"Why not now?" Phinnegan questioned.

"Because there are more important things to discuss. For one, why you are about to make a fool of yourself twice? Is it not enough to agree to help my father? Now you are about to throw a book more valuable than you could ever imagine, into the fire?"

"He promised to send me home," Phinnegan said sheepishly, his eyes falling to the floor.

"We shall come to that in a moment," Emerald said dryly. "What of the book?"

Phinnegan eyed the supple-bound book in his hand.

*Valuable? How could it be valuable to me? Perhaps if I could read it.*

"It's useless, I can't read it."

Emerald appeared disturbed.

"You mean no writing appeared in the book at midnight?"

"How could you-" Phinnegan began to question, but the Faë-gholem gave him a dangerous look.

"No, I mean, writing *did* appear, just at the last strike of the bell." Phinnegan saw her visibly relax, but he felt no such relief. "But it's of no use. The writing is all gibberish. I can't read it."

"Let me see," she commanded, and Phinnegan obeyed immediately, tossing her the book. She flipped through its pages, searching for the writing.

"Third page from the last," he offered, but she shook her head and closed the book.

"I am afraid you can do more than I, for I cannot see it at all." She tossed the book back to him and he flipped feverishly to the page where he had previously seen the writing. It was still there. Even as he had been about to throw the book into the fire, the sight of the words, words he could not even read, brought him comfort. But the frustration soon returned.

"I can see it, but what good is seeing it if I don't know what it means. It's in another language."

Emerald raised an eyebrow.

"Another language? I doubt that." Returning her gaze, Phinnegan was reminded how much her demeanor had changed from the first time he had met her in the courtyard of Castle Heronhawk. Only a few days it seemed had passed since then, yet what had been a sweet-smiling, laughing Faë now seemed a shadow of herself. As her eyes passed again from green to gray and back again, Phinnegan wondered if whatever had happened to her, whatever made her the gholem, was progressing. Would she one day be only a gholem? He pushed the thought from his mind.

"Why do you doubt that it could be in another language?"

"It's possible, of course, but being that it was written for a human, as no Faë could bear such a Mark, I would guess it is in a tongue you would know. Although it is old. It could be Latin or Greek even."

"No," Phinnegan said, shaking his head. "I would recognize both of those languages. I can't read them, but I would recognize them. This is something different."

"Perhaps it is hidden."

"Hidden? What do you mean?" Phinnegan turned the book over in his hands but Emerald shook her head.

"Not like that. The words, they could be encoded somehow, intended to make someone ignore them, to make someone think they could not read it. That book contains *many* secrets - powerful secrets. And they are hidden in ways most will never find them. But..."

"But what?" Phinnegan interrupted, impatient for some way to read the text that had appeared.

"But, given the timing of this text, appearing just as it has on this day, just as the bell pealed the hour, I think it is only a simple message and would guess it appears every year on this day. Though, as we have seen, few still could see it, let alone read it."

"What is so special about today, anyway?"

"It's the equinox."

"The equinox?" Phinnegan said, wrinkling his brow. "That's not possible. It'll be only a month 'til Christmas now. The next equinox isn't for four months yet."

"Not so," Emerald said, smiling softly. "Although our worlds are connected, time passes differently between them. They are not at all in sync. Here, today is the equinox, and it is the only day of the year when legend says the Gate can be opened." She nodded toward the book in Phinnegan's hands. "And as you are one of the only ways that the Gate can be opened, I'd guess that book has some instruction for you." She paused and her eyes passed between colors. "Or a warning."

Phinnegan swallowed and looked down at the book.

"Well, how are we going to figure out what it says?" he asked quietly, enlisting the Faë's help with the question.

"We shall just have to try some common ciphers. I can't believe it would be too hard to get through."

"What's a common cipher?"

"One is a simple substitution pattern where each letter is replaced with another letter. The easiest is by reversing the alphabet. But these are usually obvious as there will be numerous Zs replacing As."

"There aren't any Zs."

"Here, why don't you copy it out so that I can see it? There should be paper and ink in the writing desk."

Phinnegan got up from his place by the fire and followed the Faë to the writing desk. Here they found paper, a quill and a nearly empty bottle of ink. Still, there was enough ink for Phinnegan to scribble out the coded message for Emerald to see.

Abe ar eroft hema rkm ay
Att heapp oint edit mean datth ea ppo inte dpl ace
Co meupo nanen tran cetot hep ath
Emba rkin gupo nthi spat hmus tno tbet ake nlig htl y
Fo rtheg uar dia nwith inw illpur geth osed ee medu now
    rth y
Theb ear ermus ten terw illin gly
Th ebe arerm usten tera lon e

After only a moment, a wry smile began to curl her lips.

"It truly is quite simple."

"Simple?" Phinnegan said, with a frown, upset that she could see through this code so quickly. "How? What do you see?"

"Look here," she said, pointing to the first line of the script. "What if you shifted things about?"

"You mean shuffle the letters about like a puzzle?"

"No, not quite. Not shuffle, shift. Write the first line again, this time with no spaces. He did as she asked, now looking at something even more unusual.

Abearerofthemarkmay

"Now, give me the quill."

Phinnegan passed the quill to the Faë and watched as she drew several quick lines between the letters of the first line. When she handed the paper back to him, Phinnegan sucked in a breath.

"Brilliant," he whispered. Even with the letter's jumbled together, the lines that Emerald had drawn made it perfectly legible.

A | bearer | of | the | mark | may

"Here, you finish the rest," Emerald said, offering him the quill. Phinnegan hesitated a few moments over the first line, but soon he grew accustomed to the simple cipher and divided the letters in each line into intelligible words. He then wrote each line correctly spaced, revealing the cipher's secret.

A bearer of the mark may
At the appointed time and at the appointed place
Come upon an entrance to the path
Embarking upon this path must not be taken lightly
For the guardian within will purge those deemed
    unworthy
The bearer must enter willingly
The bearer must enter alone

Sentences constructed of familiar words brought a smile to Phinnegan's lips.

"Don't get arrogant," the Faë scolded. "This is an incredibly simple cipher. The hidden nature of the text itself protects it more than the cipher."

Phinnegan frowned as he read the words twice more.

"I'm still not sure what it means."

"Aren't you?" Emerald asked. "Hear, follow along." She drew close to him.

"It seems simple enough. The first line is talking about you, a 'bearer of the mark'. The next two lines describe the present - it is the appointed time and this is the appointed place. The First Gate is the entrance. The rest...a warning to you, with the last line being very clear."

"Yes," Phinnegan said quietly. "I suppose it isn't all that difficult after all. But...how could I enter alone? I've already said I would help him, you know, your father."

Emerald snapped an icy glance in his direction.

"Yes, and as I said, a fool's mistake. You have no idea the power that lies beyond the Gate. Nor do you understand the rules that govern our world. Bargains that are made at certain times cannot be broken. A bargain made at a feast is one of the most sacred."

"So...if I opened the Gate for him, he would have to send me home?"

"Yes," she said slowly. "Perhaps. Although as much as bargains are considered sacrosanct, so is the art of not fulfilling one's own end but without breaking the bargain."

"How do you mean?"

"Well, think back to dinner. Did you actually promise to let Vermillion enter the Gate?" Phinnegan thought back to the dinner and replayed the words that Vermillion had spoken to him.

"No, I didn't," Phinnegan said at last. "But I did agree to help him open it. How am I supposed to stop him from entering?"

"I am afraid I have no answer to that. It is something you must discover for yourself. I may have helped you too much already."

"What do you mean?"

"I must go," she said quietly, stepping toward the door. Phinnegan remained at the writing desk, the paper clutched in his fingers.

"Oh, and Phinnegan," the Faë spoke just as she reached the door, turning back to regard him over her shoulder.

"Yes," he responded, a hopeful tone in his voice.

"Be careful once you have passed through the Gate. The book mentions a guardian. You never know what you may find – or what may find you."

# 27

# The First Gate

Phinnegan was awakened from a restless sleep by the shrill cries of birds outside the window of his chambers. He listened to their early morning banter for several minutes, drawing more calm and energy from that brief span than he had during the entire night. Although he had tried to sleep, he had met with little success. Vermillion haunted his mind the entire night, first in one form and then another.

He counted the peals when the castle's bells rang the hour.

*Seven.*

Vermillion had told him the night before at dinner that the ceremony to open the Gate would begin promptly at eight.

*Only one more hour.*

A sharp rap at the door startled him. Escaping from beneath the ivory silk sheets, he called out for the person to enter. The same servant from the night before entered, an elegant silver tray held in his right hand.

"Breakfast, little master," the servant said, his tone mocking the honorific that many of the Aged had bestowed upon him the previous night.

"Put it over there," Phinnegan directed, pointing towards the small table between the chairs that sat in front of the fire.

"Of course," the servant sneered, striding with his nose in the air to the appointed spot.

"Will you require anything else?"

When Phinnegan shook his head no, the servant presented a stiff bending of the neck before striding from the room, closing the door behind him.

Despite feelings swirling within him about the day's coming events, Phinnegan was quite hungry. Even with the domed cover, also made of silver, covering the tray, a hint of the aroma of fresh bread wafted from it. When he lifted the cover, the smells assailed his nose, causing his hunger to grow.

The breakfast was simple, but elegant. A still-steaming small bread loaf filled one side of the platter, while the other contained a smattering of brightly colored berries, still fresh on the vine. In the center, a half moon clod of deep yellow butter rested on a square stone plate.

He tore ravenously into the bread, using the provided knife to spread the butter liberally over each chunk of bread he ripped from the loaf. Before long, the loaf was nearly gone. Taking the vines of berries into his hands, he took them to the window ledge of his room. Looking out he saw that his room faced the castle's gardens. Lush greenery and flowers in all shapes, sizes and colors greeted the morning with vigor.

A single peal of the bell broke the silence, and Phinnegan paused with a ripe purple berry paused just in front of his lips.

*That'll be the quarter-hour bell, I'd guess.*

Fifteen-minutes had already passed while he had eaten breakfast. Now, only forty-five minutes stood between Phinnegan and the Gate. The Gate and Vermillion.

He stomached the remaining berries before stripping and washing up in the provided basin. The water was cold and goose bumps peppered out on his skin as he washed.

He donned his travelling clothes, just as the bell sounded again.

*Half-past.*

Phinnegan hurriedly recovered the leather-bound book given to him by Asher. The paper that he and Emerald had deciphered the riddle on marked the page where he had seen the writing the night before. He quickly scanned the paper, revisiting each line and the warnings contained therein.

But when he glanced at the page in the book, he saw that the words had vanished. Fumbling, he flipped through the pages nearest the end of the book, searching for the passage.

Yet they were nowhere to be found.

Emerald had been right. The words had appeared at midnight providing the book's bearer a warning before vanishing into the stark pages once again.

Laying the book aside, he returned his attention to the paper with his writing and Emerald's lines. The final line stood out to him. *Alone.* But to enter alone would surely destroy any chance of going home. Whether he had ever actually promised to allow Vermillion to enter, the mad tyrant surely wouldn't help him if he felt cheated.

*Allow.* He snorted to himself at the ridiculousness of the thought. Allow Vermillion to enter? How could he possible stop him?

The gears of his mind turning, he tossed the paper into the remaining embers of the fire and watched to be sure that the paper took light.

Reaching for the book, Phinnegan started where he sat. There, on the page that had been blank only moments before, one line of scribbled text had appeared.

TH EYA RECO MING.

It took Phinnegan only a moment to decipher the thinly veiled message - just in enough time for his hackles to rise before the bell pealed loudly a third time an instant before an insistent knock struck the door.

Phinnegan was led on a winding path through the castle's corridors. The journey was made darkly eerie by the complete absence of any signs of life, besides the guards that led Phinnegan, one just off each shoulder. At least he guessed they were guards. They wore snugly fitting dark-grey tunics and trousers. Their hair was an inky black, straight and falling to their shoulders. Their skin was pale and their eyes a flat grey, staring straight ahead the entire time that they led him through the castle. He wondered if perhaps they too were some type of gholem. It saddened him to think that Emerald could meet this same fate, pale and lifeless with an emotionless stare.

Just as he thought of her, the green-haired Faë appeared, leaning causally against a thick marble column on one side of two large wooden doors. Phinnegan saw through the large windows on either side that the doors led outside.

"Father is ready for him," she said coolly. "I will take him the rest of the way." The two black-haired guards nodded stiffly and spun on their heels, striding off in the direction they had come.

"Come," she said softly. "It is nearly time and my father loathes tardiness. Almost as much as weakness."

"The book spoke to me again," Phinnegan whispered as he moved to stand beside her.

"What did it say?"

"*They are coming.*"

The Faë-gholem regarded him with a raised eyebrow.

"Truly," she began, interrupting herself to ram the large knocker on the door twice, sending a low reverberation into the air around them. "That book holds many secrets. I've never known anything of magic to speak so directly, so presently."

When the large doors in front of them began to open, she turned for a moment, locking her now bright green eyes on his.

"My father must not pass through the Gate."

Phinnegan never had a chance to respond, for the doors swung outward on their great hinges, revealing a large stone terrace. Hundreds of Aged stopped and stared at the Faë-gholem and the human boy. In silence, they moved to the sides of the terrace, leaving a large opening through the center. Beyond, large steps led down from the terrace into the gardens. A path led from the stairs, splitting in two to go around a large fountain. Beyond the fountain, the path led to a second, perpendicular path, which ran off in each direction. To the far right and far left, the path split into numerous smaller paths, which weaved in and out amongst statues, flowering trees, fountains and other displays of wealth and luxury.

But in the center, where the path leading from the terrace met the perpendicular path, a massive hedge stood. The hedge was easily three or four times the height of a man, and its walls spread in each direction two-hundred feet or more. From his height at the top of the terrace, Phinnegan could not quite see over the top of the hedge to judge its depth.

On the wall of this hedge running parallel to the path, stood a large black gate. The gate spanned the entire distance from the ground to the very top of the hedge. It was constructed of thick iron bars running both vertically and horizontally, forming small squares like a great metal lattice. Even from this distance, the evidence of age was heavy. Rust marked the hinges and thick gnarled vines had long ago spread from the hedge to worm their way through the bars and cover the entire façade. No leaves grew on the vines, only their thick, gnarled and knobby limbs remained.

Standing just before it was Vermillion, bedecked in resplendent red robes, his grey-flecked red hair rippling in the morning breeze.

It was a foreboding sight and Phinnegan swallowed hard as he took the first steps across the terrace, following the Faë-gholem as she led him toward her father. As they descended the steps from the terrace, the Gate loomed larger and larger. From this reduced height, the true size of the Gate and the hedge was more readily apparent. It was truly enormous.

When the pair finally reached the bottom of the stairs and navigated around the large fountain, they approached Vermillion, who stood some twenty feet from the Gate, his hands clasped behind his back and a broad smile on his face.

"Thank you, daughter. You have brought him just in time."

As if on command, the castle's bells promptly tolled the hour. Eight long peals broke the still morning before fading into the breeze.

Vermillion, with an uncharacteristic lack of pomp and circumstance, turned to face the Gate. Emerald backed away, but not before sharing one final look with Phinnegan. Drawing a steady breath, Phinnegan approached the Gate to stand beside the red-garbed figure.

"Your Highness, what-" Phinnegan, began but a raised hand silenced him.

"Patience. Even now the moment arrives."

Phinnegan followed Vermillion's gaze to the very top of the gate. A circle of light had just appeared there and he turned to see the sun peeking through a hole in one of the tallest parts of the castle. Turning back, he saw the circle move slowly down the front of the Gate as the sun rose in the sky, the changing angle causing the circular light to move downward.

Approximately a quarter of the way down the height of the Gate, the light reached a golden square set into one of the squares formed by the criss-crossing iron bars. It appeared to have writing or some structured design upon it but it was illegible from where they stood.

Like a muffled crack of thunder, a sharp thud of metal-on-metal came from the Gate, piercing the quiet. Phinnegan saw no change in the Gate at first, but then only four feet from the ground an intricate disc presented itself. Even at a distance of twenty-feet, Phinnegan's stomach flipped as he discerned the pattern presented on the disc's center. He recognized it immediately as the same pattern now etched into his fingertip.

"The Gate has shown us the Mark," Vermillion thundered, causing Phinnegan to cringe. When the reddish-brown eyes turned toward him, Phinnegan shivered.

"Go on then," Vermillion urged him in a low tone. "The Mark will remain visible for a short time only. We have an accord, do we not?" The eyes narrowed and the intended whisper came out in a snarl.

"Now!"

Phinnegan leapt forward at Vermillion's command, but soon slowed to a walk as he approached the Gate. Its iron bars now loomed before him, high overhead. When he stood just before it, the disc only a few feet away, he turned back to see Vermillion's heated gaze still upon him, willing him forward. Just behind him, Emerald stood. A slight nod was the only form of encouragement she dared.

Turning back, Phinnegan stepped forward until the disc was just in front of him. The pattern was an exact replica of the one on his finger, as well as the one on the cover of the leather-bound book resting in his pocket. The disc itself was perhaps as large as a dinner plate, a convex surface which was thicker in the center than along the edges. The design was worked from the same material, a bronzy metal, and was raised above the remaining surface of the disc. He had wondered whether he would have need to search the book for instructions, and how in doing so he would keep its existence secret from Vermillion and the other Aged.

But his next step could not have been more apparent.

There in the center of the disc, too small to see from where Vermillion and Phinnegan had stood, was a slight indention. Just the size of a finger-tip, it bore a smaller version of the Mark.

Looking up, he could see the circle of sunlight beginning to move off the bottom edge of the golden square. The creaking of metal in front of him signaled the disc's reverse movement, sinking back into the waiting arms of the Gate's iron bars.

Not a moment too late, Phinnegan pressed the indention with his finger, pushing firmly until the indention would give no more. The disc's regressive movement halted and all was quiet for several moments while Phinnegan took a step back from the Gate.

Then, it began to move. Slightly at first, the doors just inching inward on their ancient, rusted hinges, each emitting a grating shriek. Phinnegan slammed his hands against his ears, as did many of the Aged. Vermillion, however, stood his ground, his lips parting as he beheld a sight he had so longed to see.

The Gate was opening.

After the doors had swung inward several feet, they stopped, clanging heavily against their hinges. The path between them was narrow, only several inches separating the two halves of the Gate; a space wide enough for the slim boy of twelve to slip through, but not for the Aged.

Without sparing another moment, Phinnegan pushed his way through the opening. Heavy footsteps on the ground behind told of Vermillion and the Aged hurrying down to the Gate.

Phinnegan found himself in a long, high-walled path into the hedge. Very little light penetrated the hedge at this hour, leaving the air damp and cool. But it was not the air that caused Phinnegan to shiver.

There, not thirty paces from him stood a white stag.

The stag's eyes were large and a bright blue, and as he gazed into them, its antlered head tilted to the right to regard Phinnegan with a feigned disinterest.

The sudden grating of metal behind him reminded Phinnegan of the task at hand. He could not let Vermillion, or any others, enter. Turning back to the Gate, he could see the tyrant's scarlet garments through the crack between the doors and could hear him ordering his followers to pry the doors further apart. He watched in horror as first one door and then the other inched inward slightly, widening the opening between the two doors. He guessed that they could not use magic for the same reason that they had never been able to open the Gate in the past: The Gate was impervious to their magic.  Having no magic of his own to call upon, Phinnegan did the only thing he could. He ran forward and pushed with all his might against one of the doors.

The effort was one in futility. Even as he struggled mightily, the Gate's rusted hinges working in his favor, he felt the door move slightly towards him. He pushed harder, his feet sliding on the moss-covered ground. Again the door slid inward another half-inch.

He took a step back, aware that he could not hope to hold so many. One door creaked again. The crack was becoming wider, almost wide enough for Vermillion to attempt to squeeze himself through. He could see the tyrant's reddish-brown eyes flashing as he yelled for his followers to push harder still.

Phinnegan turned in a panic, catching sight of the white stag once again. The creature had clearly not forgotten him. It still regarded him with a casual gaze, showing little interest. The stag had not moved at all since he had first seen it, and he wondered if it was truly a living stag or some kind of statute.

*Close the Gate.*

The thought had come to him so quickly and abruptly that Phinnegan was not sure whether it was his own.

*You must close the Gate.*

The thought came again, this time as a command.

*Close the Gate.*

"How?" Phinnegan blurted aloud.

The tone of the thought was more urgent now and Phinnegan could hear the sound of the Gate's two iron halves grating ever wider. He looked and saw that the Gate was only a few inches from being wide enough for Vermillion to squeeze through.

*Close. Close.*

The thoughts were his own now as he focused his mind on closing the door.

*Close! Close!*

His mind pounded the thoughts strongly toward the Gate.

"Close!" he yelled finally, thrusting a hand forcefully towards the Gate.

To his astonishment, it did just that.

Not slowly or with a labored creaking, but swiftly with a thunderous clang as the two halves slammed forward on their great rusted hinges. A rush of air washed over him and then all was quiet. He could no longer see or hear Vermillion and the Aged

Turning, he found himself completely alone. The stag was gone, and with no way back, only the narrow path into the hedge remained.

## 28

# Labyrinth

Despite the early morning glow that had shone upon the Gate from the outside, there was little in the way of light now that he was on the inside. The hedge rose high about him, higher still than it appeared from the outside. A thin mist stretched from the ground to high above Phinnegan's head, cool and damp where it touched his skin.

In the dim light, he could not fully make out the ground beneath his feet through the translucent mist. Yet its springy-softness led him to the conclusion it must be moss.

His first steps forward were nearly silent, cushioned as they were by the mossy ground covering. He paused briefly, listening for any sound of life in the hedge, but he heard none. Starting again, he took several steps forward before a flicker of movement and the sound of rustling bushes caught his eye from the right.

When he turned, he saw the hedge parting, as if pushed apart by unseen hands. A narrow path had opened before him, just wide enough that he could have lifted both of his arms and grazed each side with his fingertips.

Down this path, the white stag stood. When Phinnegan stepped forward onto the path, the stag turned and moved on, quickly becoming obscured in the mists.

No sooner had Phinnegan completely crossed through the hedge onto this side path than the hedge closed abruptly behind him. The rustling startled him, but not quite as much as the fact that he was now once again cut-off from retreat.

Again, the only way was forward.

Following this new path, it was not long before the white stag appeared. It stood still, just as before, a dozen or so paces ahead at the edge of visibility just beyond the curtain of mist. Not much further along, a rustling of bushes to his right again signaled the opening of a new path. Again the stag awaited him.

This pattern continued several more times, and each time Phinnegan followed the new path. On the sixth or seventh time, a path opened to his right, just as before, but when he went through, the stag was nowhere to be seen. Instead, he saw a scene that made his blood run cold.

There, in a small clearing twenty paces down the path, stood Vermillion, his red hair unmistakable even in the dim lit mist. But even worse, there were others with him. Periwinkle and Crimson stood to one side, strangely rigid, as if held there by some unseen force.

And in Vermillion's right hand, he held an orb of iridescent white. How he could have come into possession of the Great Stone, Phinnegan could only guess. How he had gotten past the Gate, he could not fathom.

"You foolish rebels," Vermillion said. "Did you think you could wield the power of this stone?" Even at this distance, Phinnegan could see the tyrant's condescending smile.

"No matter," Vermilion snapped, raising his voice as Periwinkle had been about to speak. "It is within competent hands now."

"You're as foul as they come," Periwinkle spat, breathing quickly with the effort.

"Foul?" Vermillion asked, feigning shock. "Such a mouth on you, Lark. I will teach you to *respect* your superiors. Remaining among the Young well past your time. You should have joined the Aged long ago. But," Vermillion paused, a wicked grin spreading across his face, "this is not uncorrectable."

"You would dare to force an Aging?" Crimson exclaimed, speaking for the first time.

"Let it rest, Crim," Periwinkle said, glaring at the tyrant. "Not even *he* has the power to do that by himself."

The tyrant raised an eyebrow.

"My dear, dear Lark," he said quietly. "Aren't you forgetting something?"

The purple-haired Faë's eyes slid to the Great Stone held triumphantly in his adversary's hand. What little color there was in his pale face quickly faded.

"You wouldn't..."

"No? It is time you and the rest of your insolent ilk learn the new law of the land. Me."

In a flourish, Vermillion raised his hand to cast the horrible spell that would transform Periwinkle from Young to Aged. Phinnegan had no idea what he could do, but he lunged forward anyway from where he stood in the shadows of the hedge.

"No! Stop!"

In the blink of an eye, the entire scene vanished.

Phinnegan froze. In front of him, all was but quiet and mist again. There was no sign of Vermillion or Periwinkle, Crimson or the stone. They had all simply vanished. Peering ahead into the mist, he could just make out a glimpse of white.

The stag he presumed. A few steps forward confirmed his guess.

His mind churning over what he had just seen, he resumed the previous chase of following the white stage from old path to new, down one path then another. Each time he was cut-off from retreat by the closing branches of the hedge.

He knew not how many paths he had crossed when a second scene appeared before his eyes. Whereas the previous vision had stopped his breath with fear, this new vision caught his air in a different way.

Resplendent in silken dress, green as spring's moss, she stood with her back to him. Her long, vibrant hair fell down her back to her waist, shifting slightly in the breeze. As always, she mesmerized him.

"Emerald," he called out. Unlike before, she did not disappear. Her back stiffened. She had heard him. Phinnegan took a few steps forward, drawing to within a dozen paces of her.

"Emerald, how did you get here? What's going on? I saw your father..." Phinnegan's voice trailed off as she turned to face him. Her face was ashen and her once-green eyes were now a lifeless grey.

"Wh-what happened," Phinnegan managed to stutter. "Your eyes..."

He saw her mouth move in response, but no sound reached his ears. He moved closer, suppressing a shiver as he regarded Emerald's frozen features, her hollow eyes fixed upon the distance, staring right past him.

"What did you say? I couldn't...I couldn't hear you." Phinnegan was closer now, only a few feet away, but still he heard no sound when her lips moved again.

Moving closer still, he stopped just in front of her, his face as close as it had been on the night she kissed him, the night she brought him to Vermillion's castle.

"Emerald," he said quietly, but started when her eyes flicked to his own, burning into him.

"Help me," she breathed.

Phinnegan's heart leapt to his throat, but he was never able to speak. Just as with the others, Emerald vanished.

He stood for a moment, unmoving while his heart pounded in his chest.

"Help her," he whispered.

The impatient stamping of hooves drew him from his thoughts. Looking up, he saw the white stag some several yards ahead, shifting its weight between its fore and hind legs.

"Coming," Phinnegan said quietly to himself.

His feet carried him along the path, following behind the white stag with subconscious determination, for his mind was unable to direct them. He stumbled once as his foot caught a root that was raised above the mossy carpet of the path. Still, he followed on, absorbed in his thoughts.

Although Phinnegan paid little heed, the path he now followed curved to the right. It had been some time since he had been led down a side path by the white stage; the last had been prior to his vision of Emerald. When the path widened, he again paid little attention. Not until the sounds of his footfalls changed from soft thuds to a more hollow, yet sharper sound, did he break from his thoughts.

Looking down, he no longer saw the green moss but instead saw wood. His eyes roamed the area around him and he saw that he was in a room. But not just any room.

He was in *his* room.

To the right was the window that Periwinkle had used to enter those many nights past. To his left, the dresser that held his clothes. And straight ahead lay his bed, his mother resting atop it, his pillow clutched in her hands. Above the bed, his older brother stood, a tray holding a stone mug brimming with tea.

"Here, mother," Quinn said, gesturing with the tray. "Have some tea. It will help." Phinnegan's mother only shook her head.

"Will it? Will it bring him back?" Her tone was sharp and scathing, and Phinnegan saw his brother shrink back slightly, obviously stung.

"I'm sorry," his mother said, rubbing her temples with the tips of her fingers. "It was sweet of you to make it for me. I will have it, of course." Quinn smiled briefly as he handed his mother the tea.

"Thank you," she said softly. Closing her eyes, she inhaled the aromatic steam wafting from the mug.

"Black tea with clove," she whispered. "That was his favorite. He always loved it so when I would make it for him around Christmas." Quinn nodded.

"I remember."

"And now," she began, her bottom-lip quivering an inch from the mug's lip. "And now I'll never make it for him again."

The tears she had fought to keep within her burst forth and Quinn quickly drew his mother into his arms as she wept. Phinnegan, too, felt his eyes burn and he moved forward toward the bed.

"Mother-"

But she was gone, as he knew she would be. His feet fell on the softening ground, the wood of his room gone in a moment as with his other visions.

He knew the visions were not real, at least not real in the sense that they were not really there. He could not interact with them, could not touch them or speak to them. But whether they showed events that happened elsewhere...he did not know.

In front of him, the widened path remained. In fact the entire hedge spread greatly apart, revealing a large clearing covered with the same moss. The sound of slowly moving water just reached his ears. Moving towards it, a great tree appeared before him, separating itself from the mist as he drew closer.

The tree was immense and when he reached it, he saw that it was easily three or four times his height in circumference. A thicker patch of moss grew between two large roots, giving the appearance of some type of cushion or seat. The water that Phinnegan had heard was a small and shallow stream which came and left in a similar direction, forming a loop of water a few feet from the tufted moss.

Phinnegan began to realize a nagging thirst as he stared at the water. He had been wandering within the hedge for some time without as much as a drop of something to drink. Going down to his knees in front of the loop of water, Phinnegan leaned forward, smelling the crystal clear water that flowed quietly from its unseen source.

"The water is quite safe," a strong, earthy voice said from behind him, causing Phinnegan to nearly topple forward into the stream. He recovered, sprawling back to look in the direction of the voice.

Perched atop the tuft of thick moss, a man leaned back against the thick tree, a leg thrown casually over each exposed root. At least, he was part man.

His torso was bare and well muscled, slightly hairy but not overly so. Long lean arms led to hands resting upon each thigh. Had Phinnegan looked only at his chest, his arms, or his stomach, he would have said that yes, he was a man. But beyond this, things began to change.

For one, the thighs where his hands rested were covered in a tan-colored fur, as were his lower legs. The knee, Phinnegan realized, appeared to hinge in the wrong direction. Where he expected to see feet, he instead saw hooves.

Above the neck, a similar change from the human torso took place. His chin and jaw too, were human, but above them, the face began to change. A fur akin to that which covered his thighs spread across his cheeks, as well as his forehead. It even crept down his nose, which was somewhere between the nose of a man and the nose of a stag. Green-eyes flecked with brown looked out from beneath heavy, arched brows.

The crown of his head shared little in the way of similarity with that of a man. A stag's ears stretched out from the sides of his head, twitching slightly as he regarded Phinnegan. Jutting from the space just above his forehead were two large antlers. Just behind, two bony arcs like the horns of a ram completed the visage.

"Wha...who are you?" Phinnegan asked.

"You have found me, do you not know?" the half-man said, his brow drawing down in a look that Phinnegan thought altogether dark.

"I...I've only just followed the stag. The white one."

The man jumped to his feet so suddenly that Phinnegan flinched back, fearful that he would be struck. But the man only rumbled a deep laugh.

"The white one, he says! As if any other could have brought him to me."

"Brought me to you?"

"Yes, of course," the half-man said, drawing himself to his full height. A cloak of woven moss hung about his shoulders, clasped in front by braided vines.

"I am Cernon," he said, his cloak swishing gracefully as he flourished a bow. "Fear not, for you are welcome here, Phinnegan Qwyk. Welcome to the Grove.

# 29

## Cernon

"You...you know me?" Phinnegan asked with some trepidation.

"I have always known you. Even before you knew yourself, before your mother brought you into your world, I knew you. You are the Balance."

"Balance? Balance to what?"

"So many questions," Cernon chided, stepping surely over the roots at the base of the large, ancient tree. "All will be made clear to you in time. Come."

Phinnegan grasped the hand that was thrust down to him, pulling himself to his feet. Dusting himself off, his hand brushed against the small book in his pocket. He had nearly forgotten about it. He thought to pull it out, but while Cernon seemed to mean him no harm, he sensed an otherworldly power in the half-man that made him uneasy.

"What is this place...the Grove? They called it the Circle."

"It goes by many names. But to be true, it is the Center," Cernon replied cryptically.

"Center? Center of what?" Phinnegan asked.

"It is *the* Center," Cernon replied. His eyes stayed steady on Phinnegan, who broke first and looked at his feet.

"The things I saw..." Phinnegan began, but he was cut-off brusquely.

"Visions."

"Visions, then…why did I see them? I couldn't do anything. I tried, but they all vanished."

Cernon snorted, throwing his head back in something between anger and humor.

"You were not supposed to do anything. You saw them because you were *supposed* to see them. There was no answer to what you saw, no response. You humans are always so concerned with the answer, with what you must do. But it is rare indeed that the answer is ever as important as the question, let alone more so. It is the struggle, the awareness of it, which is paramount. This too you will learn in time." Cernon frowned, tilting his head so that he looked skyward into the fog.

"But now, time is your enemy."

"My enemy? Why?"

"You have a task. You must be the Balance."

"The Balance," Phinnegan echoed. "You said that before. What do you mean, I am the Balance?"

Cernon turned away from Phinnegan, striding a short distance from the great tree.

"In nature, there is always a balance," he began, his back still towards Phinnegan.

"There is Fire!" he cried, whirling and throwing an arm towards Phinnegan. A white-hot flame shot past him, incinerating the tuft of moss at the base of the tree, further spreading a trail of fire into the surrounding moss.

"And then, there is Water," Cernon said more softly flicking a hand in the direction of the creek so that an arc of water flowed toward the fire, dousing it with a hiss.

"There is Light," Cernon cried again, his strong voice ringing in the grove. Around them the fog dissipated as a bright sun appeared high above, bathing the clearing in a brilliant light.

"And there is Dark," Cernon intoned. The sun vanished as quickly as it had come, the fog returning in a heavy rush, thicker than before. A blackness settled over them for several moments before returning them to the dimly-lit fog.

"There is Order and Chaos," he said, turning back to face Phinnegan. "Predator and Prey, Earth and Air, as well as many others. Each is deadly, and each is life-giving. There are two sides to every coin."

"I understand," Phinnegan said. "But what does this have to do with me?"

"Let us have an understanding," the half-man said as he approached Phinnegan. Towering above, some seven feet tall, his brown-flecked green eyes stared down at Phinnegan.

"I care not what happens to this world, or any other, in the end. Time will go on. But," he said, pausing to raise a slender finger. "But, there must be Balance."

"I still don't understand..." Phinnegan said quietly.

"Can you think of no one in this world who seeks to destroy that Balance? Who seeks a power for himself that is beyond what any one mortal should wield?"

"Vermillion," Phinnegan whispered.

"That is the one."

"But, what can he do? Destroy this world?"

"Destroy the world? Bah! He is like the many waves of the ocean crashing against the shore. Try as he might, he will never succeed fully. He aims too high. However," Cernon paused, his eyes narrowing, "just as a storm swells the power of the sea, rendering it capable of destruction normally beyond its means, there are things that he may attain that would swell his power to unfathomable levels." Cernon stopped and arched an eyebrow.

"I believe you know of such a source of power."

Phinnegan swallowed, thinking back to his vision.

"The Great Stone."

"Indeed. Such a thing would give Vermillion power to alter this world significantly. In the end, he will fail, as do all who seek such power. But for the inhabitants of this world...his failure may well come too late."

"The Faë?" Phinnegan asked. Cernon nodded.

"I must admit, I am fond of their kind, particularly the Young. In the end, I will not save them, though it is within my power to do so - to so directly interfere is, regrettably...forbidden. But, I have brought them you."

"You are a very special person, Phinnegan Qwyk," Cernon, said, the thin lips turning up in a smirk.

"You're not the first to tell me that," Phinnegan said quietly. "But what can I do to help the Faë? How could I possibly stop him?"

"My vision does not show me how, or if you even will. It is," his lips curled in contempt, "limited. However, it does show me that you can."

"But-"

"Do you not bear the Mark? Few humans enter this world," Cernon said before leaning down suddenly, his face inches from Phinnegan's.

"Fewer still can do magic."

"Magic?!" Phinnegan exclaimed. "I can't do magic."

"Can't you?" Cernon said with a smirk. "The Mark says that you can. You could not bear it otherwise. That was a test."

Phinnegan's eyes narrowed.

"Test? What kind of test?"

"When I learned of your passing into this world," Cernon began, stooping down to allow a small, red snake to entwine itself around his arm, "I believed you to be the one who could be a Balance. The one who could find a way to stop him. But it is perilous for me to interfere as I sought, and now have, and so I had to be sure. It was a tricky thing. How to test you?" His lips curled into a smile as he raised himself to his full height.

"But then Vermillion made his first mistake. When he cast the enchantment over his daughter, seeking to further broaden his power, he opened the door for me. A gholem is a creature of the earth, and I am the Keeper of this earth."

"You mean," Phinnegan whispered, "Emerald?"

"Yes, that one. He opened her to me. She resisted at first, but soon, she listened. Though in the guise of her father's work, it is *my* bidding she does now."

"It was you, then," Phinnegan said, anger creeping into his voice. "You had me brought to this castle - to *him*."

"I had you brought to *me*!" Cernon said sharply in correction.

"When I learned of your escape from Féradoon, I sent her to follow you. Her father, too, learned of your value, but only after you had vanished. His orders coincided with mine, leaving him unaware of her new allegiance. She was there when the Faolchú attacked you; there to slip the Warber into your pocket in the courtyard of Heronhawk; there in the Winding Wood to see your Marking. She thought to take you then...but there was still one piece missing. A piece without which you could never hope to accomplish what you must."

"The book," Phinnegan mumbled, his hand moving absently to rest on the leather-bound book in his pocket.

"Yes, the book. You have it with you, yes? Show it to me."

Phinnegan moved to take the book from his pocket, but hesitated. This man, half-man, *creature*, had done him no harm, it was true. But the uneasiness Phinnegan felt in his presence remained.

"Do you fear me, human?" Cernon said, barking a laugh. "As well you should, for I could destroy you in a moment. I have no need of that book. No, it is for you, and only you. Still, I am curious as to its properties. Show it to me."

Phinnegan pulled the book from his pocket, hesitating only briefly before passing it to Cernon. The half-man surveyed the cover for a moment before opening the book, flipping casually through its pages. With a grunt, he slammed the book shut and tossed it back to Phinnegan who only just saved it from splashing in the stream.

"Do you know the purpose of this book?" Cernon asked with a wave of his hand, slender fingers twirling.

"I think so," Phinnegan replied, staring down at the symbol etched into the cover of the book. "It tells me what to do, like it told me to enter the Gate, but to enter alone. Emerald said it meant I must not let her father pass."

"Partly," Cernon said, pacing slowly in front of the ancient tree. "One of its secrets is to show you a path, but not necessarily the only path. You always have a choice in whether to follow it. For there to truly be Balance, there must always be Free Will."

"But...what if I had let him enter behind me? Would he have found...found the power you said he seeks?"

"Possibly," Cernon said. "But the peculiar thing about a labyrinth is that you never truly know what you might find in the end. It is a journey to the Center, to your center. The visions you see tell you much about yourself, your loyalties, your fears. With a wretch like Vermillion, the visions may have driven him to madness - or worse. I trust the book said as much."

Phinnegan thought back to the book's warning to him. It *had* spoken of purging the unworthy.

"So...if he had followed me...he may have found the power he seeks, or he may have gone mad?"

"More or less," Cernon said with a sideways tilt of his head. "The book showed you a path, the path with the least risk for the wrong person to enter the labyrinth."

"Emerald said the book always gave that message..."

"And she is likely right. Any person who had yet to understand the book's full power would not know the dangers of one such as Vermillion being allowed to enter this labyrinth. Four millennia it has been sealed, and for good reason."

Phinnegan sat in silence for a moment, turning the book over in his hands. At length he spoke, opening the book to stare at its blank pages as he did.

"You said someone who had to understand the book's full power. What else can it do?"

"The uses and secrets of this book are many, but perhaps most pertinent to you," Cernon paused, arcing his hand above his head, creating a slight disturbance in the air, just visible to the eye, "it will show you how to use your powers."

"My powers?" Phinnegan said with a small laugh. "What can I do?"

"Tell me," Cernon began, locking his eyes on Phinnegan. "How did you stop Vermillion from following you through the Gate? It is old, yes, and I imagine nearly rusted shut. Still, he would have opened it eventually. What did you do?"

Phinnegan thought back to the moment in front of the Gate, the moment when the inexplicable happened.

"I closed the Gate."

"And how did you accomplish such a task? How could you, a mere weakling of a human boy, stop the might of the most dangerous creature ever to tread upon the soil of this world?" Cernon's eyes bored into Phinnegan. "How did you close the Gate?"

Phinnegan broke his eyes away from the brown-flecked green of Cernon, instead casting them upon the book.

"I...I told it to."

"You told it to," Cernon echoed softly. "Do you not think this is *power*? When Vermillion and a hundred Aged sought to open the Gate," Cernon's voice thundered, before he continued in a whisper. "You closed it with a word. A single word."

"But...but I've never been able to do anything like that before. How did I do it?"

"You are too young to feel the magic within you. It has only begun to awaken since you came to this world. But here, in the Grove, your powers are stronger. Though you cannot feel them, they come to you in your moment of need, just as they did at the Gate."

"But *how* did I do it?"

The great half-man shrugged.

"Magic is different for all races of mortals, particularly for one of the Chosen."

"Chosen...I've heard that word before," Phinnegan whispered, recalling the word as spoken by Mariella.

"This book is meant only for your kind, only for the Chosen."

"What does it mean, *Chosen*?"

"The book will show you," Cernon said, nodding in the direction of the book in Phinnegan's hands. "It can show you many things...how to harness your gifts outside the Gate...what you need to know to be the Balance."

Phinnegan flipped quietly through the book's pages.

"How? The book is completely blank."

"Is it?" Cernon asked, an edge of surprise perceivable in his tone.

"Yes," Phinnegan said, closing the book. "Completely."

"Ah, I did not foresee this," Cernon mumbled to himself. "Of course, the wretch has pushed events...they move too quickly...there is not much time..."

Suddenly, Cernon leapt forward, startling Phinnegan when the half-man's bulk landed just in front of him.

"Vermillion has pushed events ahead of their natural course. But the book cannot be persuaded. It will not reveal itself to you until you are ready."

"But you said-"

"I know what I said," Cernon snapped. "I also said that you are too *young*. But what is, is. The book is of no help to you, yet, and Vermillion closes in on his goal too quickly." Cernon paused, tilting his head back, gazing into the sky. When he turned his eyes back to Phinnegan, they smoldered in a green fire.

"You are young, and weak. But perhaps..."

"What? What?" Phinnegan insisted when the half-man's voice trailed off.

"Perhaps you can serve as a conduit for one spell. You will not understand it, but I can embed it within you. When the time is right, you can release it outside the labyrinth to stop him."

"Embed?" Phinnegan recoiled in horror. "How? Will it...hurt?"

Cernon shrugged impatiently, a scowl darkening his face.

"Time runs short. Even now your friends are being brought to him. Yes, those two," Cernon said with a nod, his lips upturning into a snarl. "Captured and bringing the very object that he seeks right into his waiting hands."

"Then the vision I saw was true," Phinnegan whispered, his eyes widening.

*If one vision was true...*

"Wait," Phinnegan blurted. "Can you send me home?"

"Home?" Cernon said with surprise. "Impossible! You have been brought here for a purpose. You cannot leave until you have served that purpose."

"How do you know what purpose-" Phinnegan began defiantly, but he was cut off by the half-man's thundering voice.

"Because it is I who have brought you here! Do NOT presume to lecture me, human."

Phinnegan's shoulders sagged and he thought for a moment before speaking up quietly.

"What about Emerald? Can you reverse what has been done to her? Can you stop it?"

"Stop it? Why would I want to stop it? The closer she comes to being fully a creature of the earth, the better for us all. Then she would be completely under my control."

"But...can you?"

Cernon's eyes narrowed and he regarded Phinnegan warily.

"Yes...I *could* stop what is being done."

"So you can make her fully Faë again? Make her eyes only green and no longer gray?"

"I said I can stop it, but not reverse it. What's done is done. I cannot change what has happened, but yes, I could stop the transformation. But I won't."

Phinnegan shuffled his feet nervously before peering up at the giant half-man.

"What if I asked you to?"

Cernon threw his head back, guffawing a great laugh.

"If you asked? Do you take me for some genie of the lamp that your race has concocted as a slave to the wishes of their human masters? Some carnival magician to do your bidding for a penny?"

"You said I had a choice," Phinnegan mumbled, sheepishly.

"What did you say, *boy*?"

"I said," Phinnegan began weakly, but cleared his throat before continuing more strongly, "you said everything is about balance. Balance and free will, choices." Phinnegan raised his head, his brown eyes steady.

"I choose to help her."

"You do not have the knowledge to make such a choice," Cernon growled, his hooves scuffing the ground in anger.

"Who are you to say?" Phinnegan retorted, growing bolder.

"Who am I?" Cernon sputtered, his eyes ablaze with an angry green flame. "He challenges me!" Cernon cried, throwing his arms wide, as if speaking to a throng of listeners. "He challenges *me*! Here!"

"He challenges me," he finished, his voice falling to a whisper.

"I am not challenging you. But if you will not let me go home and say that I am here for a purpose, let me choose."

"Your choice is a mistake," Cernon said sharply, his eyes smoldering. "You are the only one who can stop him from gaining the power that he seeks."

"How do you know that what I want to do is wrong? That I cannot stop him some other way?"

"What other way? You have no idea how to use your powers. He will turn you to dust."

"Cernon," Phinnegan said curiously. "Why do you care so much? You said you didn't care what happened to this world, yet you want me to destroy Vermillion to save it, even when I choose to do something else."

The half-man's face twisted in a suppressed rage. Phinnegan sensed some deep division within this creature. The slender fingers of Cernon's hands curled into a tight fist that shook by his sides.

"Fah!" he barked, casting a hand towards the ancient tree that had served as his perch when he first appeared. Before Phinnegan's eyes, a roughly hewn wooden cup began to form on the side of the tree, growing directly from the trunk like an oddly formed branch. When the cup was finished, Cernon pointed at its coarse form and spoke in a commanding voice.

"Take it."

Phinnegan grasped the bark-formed cup and tugged gently, but the cup did not move. Setting his feet against the ancient tree's large roots he placed both hands around the cup and pulled hard. Nothing happened at first, but eventually the running sound of wood-splitting arced through the grove. And then the cup was free.

"Fill it with water," Cernon commanded.

Phinnegan obeyed silently, crouching down to fill the cup with water from the horseshoe shaped stream. The water was quite cool as it slid across Phinnegan's fingers. The cup full nearly to the rim, he arose and held the cup before him. When his fingers touched the water, they now tingled.

"As you believe yourself wise enough to make the choice you desire,' Cernon began, walking stiffly towards Phinnegan until he towered above, staring directly down at him, "then I shall allow it. But," he paused again waving his slender fingers over the brimming cup, "I shall require something in return."

Phinnegan eyed the water in the cup, which had begun to swirl slowly in rhythm with the movement of Cernon's fingers. The transparent liquid now began to thicken, its surface darkening until it resembled a mirror, swirling like oil against the sides of the cup.

"What?" Phinnegan managed with a gulp, his eyes transfixed on the swirling liquid.

"A debt."

"What sort of debt?" Phinnegan asked sharply, his eyes flicking to the fur-covered face of the tall half-man.

"A *personal* debt. This Faë you seek to help, she is by all right's *mine*. With your choice, you take her from me." Cernon's eyes flashed violently and he leaned over until his face was very near to Phinnegan's.

"It displeases me."

"How...how can I pay this...debt?"

"That is to be determined. Not now," Cernon said as Phinnegan opened his mouth to question the half-man. "Not now. But one day I will require you to pay this debt."

Phinnegan's eyes fell away from the fierce green of Cernon's and he stared down into the mirrored liquid in the cup. His own brown eyes stared back, full of the fear and confusion that he knew swam beneath them.

"Do you accept?" Cernon prodded, the fingertips of each hand pressed together so that his hands formed a sort of pyramid. "Your time is dwindling. Soon, no matter what your choice, your efforts will be futile. Even now that which he seeks draws near-"

"Stop it!" Phinnegan yelled, his chest heaving with quickened breath.

Cernon straightened at the cry and stood now with one arm crossed over his chest and the other bent so that his chin rested in its hand.

"So," he said as his thin lips curled in a smile. "You realize the ignorance of your request? You yield your choice?"

Phinnegan's eyes glistened when he raised his head towards Cernon.

"I choose her."

Cernon's face twisted in anger and he quickly pointed a finger at the cup in Phinnegan's hands.

"Then you agree to assume this debt," he yelled.

"I do," Phinnegan replied, his tone defiant.

"Then drink," Cernon commanded. "A shared cup of this grove's water will bind you to this course. Drink."

Before his will could falter, Phinnegan lifted the cup to his lips, drinking deeply. The liquid was thick and syrupy, but harbored little taste. When he removed the cup from his lips and passed it into the waiting hands of Cernon, its contents were nearly half gone.

"Hah," the half-man barked as he tilted his head back to receive the remaining contents of the cup.

When the liquid from the cup touched Cernon's tongue, Phinnegan fell to his knees. Grunting in pain, he held both hands to his stomach.

"What's....happening?" he managed through clenched teeth.

Cernon tossed the cup aside and chuckled quietly. He crouched down over Phinnegan, grabbing his right-hand harshly, turning the index finger towards him.

"This," he hissed, his eyes on the Mark on Phinnegan's fingertip. "Marked you as special." He paused, now placing a hand over Phinnegan's stomach.

"This Mark's you as mine."

Phinnegan's breath quickened as he threw the half-man's hand from his belly. Pulling up his shirt, he gasped when he saw a second Mark forming on the center of his torso, just beneath the bottom of his sternum, arising between the two arms of his ribcage as they separated. He touched the Mark, but withdrew his hand quickly. The Mark seared like a burn and its lines rose above the surrounding flesh as though swollen and injured from a branding.

"What..." Phinnegan began, but he was met with a melancholic laughter.

"Go now, little one," Cernon said as he backed away. "The bargain is struck. You have made a fool's choice. Let it be known I tried to sway you from this path. Go, and test your might against that of the scarlet tyrant."

"But," Phinnegan cried as he scrambled to his feet in a panic, his hand still clutching at his stomach. "What about Emerald? What about the spell to save her?"

"It has been done," Cernon's voice came faintly from the distance, for the half-man had backed away until his form had become shrouded by the quickly thickening mist.

"The power lies within you."

"Wait! How do I use it?" Phinnegan scrambled over the roots of the ancient tree, which were not hidden from his view in the mist.

"How do I save her?"

Only silence answered him.

Phinnegan ran in the direction in which Cernon vanished.

"Cernon! How do I get out? How do I get back to the Gate?"

Again, silence greeted him. But just when despair threatened to overwhelm him, the half-man's voice came to his ears as a whisper upon the breeze.

"Silly boy, you still do not understand."

"What?" Phinnegan shouted into the invisible depths of the grove.

"You never left."

"Wha-" Phinnegan began, blinking away the mist. But at the second blink, he stopped.

He stood, just as he had before, on the path at the entrance to Cernon's labyrinth. Behind him stood the white stag; in front the Gate creaked awkwardly on its hinges, the eyes of Vermillion and the Aged glaring through the gap.

# 30

# Escape

"Wha-" Phinnegan began, blinking away the mist. But at the second blink, he stopped.

*How is this possible?*

Phinnegan stood where he had earlier, before his words inexplicably closed the Gate, before he released a magic he neither felt nor knew how to control. To his left, the white stag stamped impatiently at the ground before dipping its head and backing away into the darkness of the hedge.

To his right, the Gate creaked awkwardly on its hinges, the eyes of Vermillion and the Aged glaring through the gap. Phinnegan wondered for a moment why Cernon had sent him back to this moment before the Gate, but then he remembered the half-man's words.

*"You never left."*

Had it all happened so fast? The journey through the labyrinthine hedge, the visions, Cernon in the Grove? Had it all been in his mind? He shook his head to rid it of these thoughts. Whatever had happened, he stood here now, with Vermillion forcing the Gate.

Phinnegan thought of closing the Gate as he had before, but that was not an option now.

He had to get to Emerald.

"Wait!" he shouted as he ran towards the Gate and pushed himself through the gap. This seemed to surprise both Vermillion and the Aged for they all stopped their jostling and pushing at the Gate. But Vermillion's eyes still burned hotly.

"What devilry is this?" Vermillion said sharply, pushing the other Aged aside to stand before Phinnegan. "Why won't the Gate *open*?!" he snarled. "And you-" he began, but Phinnegan cut him off.

"There's something wrong with the Gate. It won't open. I went through to check but -"

"Fah, wrong? How?"

"I don't know, it just seems-" Phinnegan whirled suddenly to face the Gate.

"Close!" he yelled, just as he had before.

And, just as before, the Gate slammed shut with a thunderous clang, knocking several Aged from their feet.

"No!" Vermillion bellowed as he leapt toward the Gate. He grasped its bars through the thick vegetation. "Hurry, you wretched fools," he screamed at the Aged standing beside him. "We must open it! Already we are losing time. The sun..." His voice trailed off as he caught sight of the sun's morning-yellow glow ascending above the castle. Looking up, he saw the beam of light slip away from the golden square.

"No," he hissed. As the metallic sound of the Gate's bronzed disc sliding back into its depths reached his ears, Vermillion's voice became more frantic.

"No, no, no!" he yelled, grasping at the disc as it retracted into the Gate. But his efforts were futile. Despite his grasping, the disc descended into the viney growth that encapsulated the Gate.

Vermillion's shoulders sagged as he stood before the Gate.

"Gone," he said hoarsely. "The planning, the investment. Everything was perfect. The boy..." he paused, his head snapping up.

"The boy," he repeated, his hoarse voice rising into a snarl.

"What have you DONE!"

Phinnegan turned to run, but he had nowhere to go. Perhaps a dozen Aged stood before him, forming a semi-circle to stop his retreat. Behind him, Vermillion's voice uttered a string of unrecognizable words, his voice strong and guttural. Phinnegan felt himself collapse as pain lanced through him.

"Father!" he heard Emerald cry, but then Phinnegan could make out nothing further. The pain that racked his body prevented him from focusing on the words being said around him.

The pain coursed through him for what felt like an eternity, but then, just as suddenly as it had begun, the pain stopped. Phinnegan continued to breathe heavily. His body felt weak and unusable. He tried to roll over, for he was flat on his stomach, but his body would not cooperate. His skin crawled. Above him, he heard Vermillion shout several orders, only one of which he could make out.

"Bring the rebels."

Phinnegan forgot these words as soon as he heard them, focusing all of his attention and strength on rolling onto his side. When he finally succeeded, he saw Emerald hurrying toward him. She crouched beside him, putting a hand on his chest when she saw that he continued to struggle toward a sitting position.

"Rest now," she said quietly. "You have done all you can. You stopped him from going into the Gate. But..."

"But what," Phinnegan mumbled. His body trembled slightly with the remembrance of the pain.

"He has found another way," she said, nodding her head off to the right. With her help, Phinnegan was able to push himself to his elbow. The scene he saw was one he had already seen.

Though he could not hear their voices, Phinnegan knew the words spoken between Vermillion and the two captive Faë.

"Emerald," Phinnegan whispered. "I've seen this before."

"What? Seen what before?" she asked, never taking her eyes off the scene unfolding some several yards away.

"In the hedge. I saw them, Vermillion, Periwinkle and Crimson. He takes the Great Stone from them. He's going to Age them."

Phinnegan watched in horror as the scene continued to unfold before them. They were only moments away from Vermillion unleashing his power on Periwinkle.

"Quickly!" Phinnegan said, summoning enough strength to push himself to his knees. "Can't you do something?"

Emerald turned her head to face him. Grey, flat eyes stared out at him.

"No, there is nothing. He has too much power over me."

Phinnegan's eyes widened at the words.

"Emerald, I had almost forgotten. I can help you."

"Help me?" she said before laughing softly. "I appreciate the gesture, but I am beyond any means you have to help me."

Phinnegan looked to Vermillion and the two Faë. Time was nearly up.

"Quickly," he said. "You must stop him."

"Phinnegan, I am sorry, but I can't-," she began but stopped when Phinnegan grabbed her by the wrist.

"I can help you," he said firmly.

The moment his hand touched hers, he felt the power within him, the spell that Cernon had placed there. Emerald felt it to, for her eyes widened and she locked them on his own.

"Wha-"

Emerald's voice froze in her throat as the spell's full force hit her. Phinnegan had no idea how he had released the spell. He had wanted to release it, but he could not force the magic out of him. Yet, somehow the spell knew on its own that its moment had come. It sprang forth from him, weakening him as it left. He no longer had the strength to hold himself up, falling back to the earth, but holding fast to Emerald's wrist.

Phinnegan watched her face as the transformation took place. He had felt her stiffen as soon as the spell had begun to release. And now he watched as her face twitched and her eyes slid rapidly between gray and green. When they stopped, their color lay somewhere between the two.

"Phinnegan," she said in a whisper. "How..."

"Hurry," he said hoarsely.

With one last look to Phinnegan, she arose to her feet, her hands clenched into fists at her side. Beyond her Phinnegan could see Vermillion's arm raise, the stone held high in his other hand.

"STOP!"

Emerald's voice rang out across the garden and Phinnegan could just make out Vermillion's head snapping in their direction as his raised arm fell.

"Daughter, you meddle in events beyond your reach. Go. Now." When she did not move, Vermillion pointed at her and raised his voice.

"I said GO!"

"You command me no longer, father," she said.

"Emerald!" Phinnegan heard a familiar voice cry. He struggled to incline his head and saw Periwinkle struggling against the force that bound him.

"You bastard!" the purple-haired Faë spat at Vermillion. "What did you do to her?"

With an angry snarl, Vermillion back-handed Periwinkle.

"Shut up!"

What happened next appeared to Phinnegan to happen in slow motion. He saw the scarlet-haired tyrant thrust an arm towards Emerald. From his finger-tips, Phinnegan could detect some sort of distortion. The air appeared to thicken and swarm upon itself, a translucent weave of air.

Phinnegan did not know how he knew, but he recognized the disturbance to be magic.

And this magic was moving away from Vermillion's fingertips and directly towards Emerald, who stood just to the right of Phinnegan.

He tried to scream out a warning, but like everyone else, he seemed to be moving in slow motion. Everyone that is, except for Emerald. Her movement appeared normal as she closed her eyes and brought her hands before her, the palms facing up.

Phinnegan expected her to do something, to perform some sort of counter-magic, not that he knew what she could do. But she only stood, her eyes closed, appearing oblivious to the magical distortion that had now covered half the distance between the two.

Again Phinnegan struggled to warn her, but though his mind raced, his body would not respond. He watched as the distortion moved closer and closer to her. Yet still, she did not move.

The distortion passed between her hands, moving directly towards her chest. As if awakened, her eyes opened. When she spoke, her lips parted in a slight smile.

"Éalaigh," she breathed, her eyes fixated on her father.

The air around them quivered and shook, and a familiar tug pulled at Phinnegan's navel. He felt himself falling...falling...falling...

And then it ended. There was no impact, no painful collision with the ground. Instead, the ground was soft and lush; the air filled with a sweet aroma.

Weariness descended upon him like a storm cloud. He was so very tired. His mind slowed as he inhaled the sugary smell around him.

So tired.

Another deep breath.

So weak.

A third deep breath.

Sleep...

He heard them calling his name, but his mind had already begun to slip into itself. The voices were so far away, and he, so very tired.

So very, very tired.


Phinnegan's eyes opened slowly, but then took only a few moments to adjust to the light around him, dim as it was. The only sound that reached his ears was the methodic ticking of a clock on the table beside the bed.

"You're awake," a voice said softly to his left. Turning, he saw Emerald sitting in a small chair, her legs crossed and an open book in her lap. She smiled warmly at him as she unfurled herself from the chair and moved to his bedside.

"How do you feel?"

"Tired," he answered truthfully. "What happened?"

"You saved us all," she said, her voice barely above a whisper as she placed a hand upon his brow. Leaning over, she kissed him delicately upon the cheek as she came to her knees beside his bed, her face now even with his.

"You saved me."

Phinnegan grinned.

"Then...it worked? The spell worked?"

"Yes," Emerald said. "I am not...normal. But whatever..." she paused her smile faltering. "Whatever he did to me...it's quiet. It's still there, looking out at me. But it's quiet."

"You'll be all right then?" Phinnegan asked.

"Yes, I will," she said, taking his hand and squeezing it firmly. "I will."

"But...what happened?"

"We escaped. I brought us to a place where neither my father nor any of his people could follow. You've been here before, if I recall."

Phinnegan's mind traced back to some of the earliest hours after his arrival in this world. He recalled the escape from Féradoon and their flight through Darkwater Forest, and from the Faolchú.

"Then we are in Crimson's house. Where is he?"

"Yes," she said, her face growing dark. "I didn't want to bring you here, not after what they did to you. But you were weak, and the flowers had put you to sleep very quickly. In the end, I decided I had little choice."

"They're all right then, too? Crimson and Periwinkle?

"Yes, they're fine, though they don't deserve it. Not after everything that they have done."

"What about the stone?" Phinnegan asked, ignoring the comment about the two Faë.

"Unfortunately," she said quietly, "my father has it."

Phinnegan's eyes began to fill with tears.

"Don't cry," she said soothingly. "It will take time for him to grasp the stone's powers completely."

"No, it's not that," Phinnegan said, wiping his eyes. "I mean, it's terrible, but..."

"But what?"

"But now I shall never get home. The stone was my only way home...I knew at least one of the visions would come true."

"What visions?" Emerald asked softly, but Phinnegan only shook his head as he fought back the tears.

"Phinnegan," she said, pulling his head so that he faced her. "I can send you home."

"You can?" Phinnegan exclaimed, bolting upright so quickly that his head swam with dizziness.

"Yes, I can," she said as she guided him back onto the bed. "But tomorrow. You need to rest."

"But I want to go now."

"I understand that, but you are already weak. This journey will tire you further. Tomorrow morning, I promise." Her warm smile and gentle demeanor quieted Phinnegan's insistence.

"All right..."

"Here," she said, passing him a glass of milky liquid that smelled faintly of ginger. "Drink this. It will help you sleep and regain your strength."

Phinnegan took the glass and drank its contents without complaint, though the taste was bitter and not at all sweet like he had imagined.

"Very good. Sleep now and tomorrow we will send you home."

"Promise?" Phinnegan said sleepily, the draught's effects already taking hold.

"Promise."

# 31

## Home

When he stepped outside the following morning, Phinnegan found the three Faë, their green, red and purple hair dancing in a warm breeze. He had slept soundly, Emerald's draught helping to clear his mind and ensure a deep sleep. He had awakened refreshed, and now the breeze and the warmth of the sun further energized him.

Today was a big day. Today he was going home.

But all did not appear to sit well with the three Faë. Phinnegan could see from Emerald's body language that she was still angry with Periwinkle and Crimson for their abandonment of him - their use of him. As he thought about it, his face warmed at the memory of the disinterested shrug Periwinkle had shown him before disappearing with the Great Stone.

And now, Vermillion had the stone.

Phinnegan shook his head to push the thoughts from his mind.

He took a moment to take in the world around him, the last time he thought he would ever see it. The trees were tall and strong, not unlike any tree he would see at home. Nor was the sky or ground truly different from what he had seen his entire life. And yet, everything here possessed some air of surrealism - a color here was not quite right, or this one seemed too vibrant. The air, Phinnegan felt, had an energy to it that he did not remember from his own world.

"Feeling better?" Emerald questioned, pulling Phinnegan from his musings. Though she was now clearly different than when she was fading into a gholem, Phinnegan still detected a grayness to her eyes, and her hair, while still a bright green, had a less vibrant quality than the first time he had seen her.

"Yes, much," Phinnegan said as he stood to greet her. "I never said thank you, for saving me." Emerald waved a hand dismissively.

"Thank me? You did more for me than I could ever hope to repay. But I shall try," she said, presenting a sly wink as she took his hand. "Are you ready?"

"You mean to go home?" Phinnegan asked, a tinge of excitement creeping into his voice.

"Yes. But first," she paused, her smile fading, "they want to speak to you." She jerked her head in the direction of Periwinkle and Crimson, who stood some several yards away.

"Why?"

"To apologize, I believe. You don't have to listen, of course. If I had my way, they wouldn't even be here."

Phinnegan's face hardened momentarily as he flicked his gaze to the two Faë.

"No, it's okay. I'll talk to them."

The pair walked the several yards separating them from Periwinkle and Crimson. The two Faë could be seen to end their conversation as he and Emerald approached.

"Hallo, mate," Periwinkle said with a short bow. Crimson cleared his throat, directing a sharp look at the purple-haired Faë.

"Well, I mean, I am sorry, you know. Hated leaving you like that, I did. Terrible thing. But, well, the giants were roaming and," the Faë trailed off, his voice withering under a menacing glare from Emerald.

"Look, no excuses," Periwinkle began, pulling Phinnegan aside and speaking quietly. "What I did...I understand if you can't forgive me. Terrible friend, I was, but –"

"But what?" Phinnegan whispered sharply, the memory of Heronhawk blazing in his mind.

Periwinkle glanced quickly in Emerald's direction before leaning even closer to Phinnegan."

"I did it for her."

"What?" Phinnegan blurted, confused by this confession.

"The Great Stone. I thought with its power I could find her, that I could save her."

Phinnegan's face softened as he heard the sincerity in Periwinkle's voice. He remembered their conversation in the dark, the love that Periwinkle had confessed.

"Did you ever plan to send me home? Was it all a ruse?"

Periwinkle shrugged apologetically.

"I admit I wanted the stone first for her...but I always planned to send you home, mate. Honest, I did. But when you couldn't pass through the doorway and I already had the stone, I...." The Faë's eyes fell and he was silent for several moments, his eyes searching the ground for words his mind could not find.

"Here," he said, handing Phinnegan a small purple gem he took from his vest pocket.

"What is it?" Phinnegan asked, accepting the gem.

"A symbol of the debt I owe you. You saved her when I could not..." Periwinkle's eyes met Phinnegan's, fierce and gleaming.

"One day, mate," he said, nodding to the gem in Phinnegan's hand. Without another word, Periwinkle turned and walked back to the other two Faë. Phinnegan stood alone with his thoughts, rolling the gem between his fingers.

"Phinnegan," Emerald called. "We should get started."

"All right," he said, stuffing his hand, and the gem, into his trouser pocket. But as he moved to join them, Phinnegan's knees buckled as pain lanced through him.

"Phinnegan, what's wrong?"

The other Faë had noticed as well, and the three rushed to his side as he clutched his stomach.

"It's nothing," Phinnegan said through clenched teeth. "I'll be fine."

"Doesn't seem like nothing, mate. Here, let's have a look." Before Phinnegan could stop him, Periwinkle had lifted his shirt, exposing his stomach and the Mark now branded there.

The collective gasp from the Faë was followed by an extended silence. Phinnegan shifted his feet, embarrassed and awkward feeling now that the Faë had seen the symbol he bore.

Emerald was first to break the silence. She moved to Phinnegan and pulled his shirt down. When she looked at him, Phinnegan saw multiple emotions swimming beneath her eyes.

"I fear that though you may not wish it, you will return to us one day." She took each of his hands in one of hers and leaned closer to him. "I will not forget what you have done," she continued in a whisper.

"Come on," she said, speaking normally with a weak cheer in her voice. "Let's get you home."

Periwinkle and Crimson moved to join them, but both avoided looking directly at Phinnegan.

"How will you get me home?" Phinnegan said, trying to deter everyone's minds from his Mark. "I thought Periwinkle said it was impossible."

"Well, we have a bit of an advantage now, haven't we?" Periwinkle reached into his pocket and pulled out a small object, which he proceeded to toss to Emerald. Phinnegan recognized it once it was in her hands.

"That's like the stone that brought me here."

"Not just like, mate. It is the stone."

Phinnegan thought back to Féradoon when the juror had questioned the stone.

"It said its owner was Emerald Wren." He looked at the green-haired Faë beside him. "You? But how did Periwinkle..." He stopped when she raised a hand.

"That is a story worth telling, but not now. Time is short. The effects of the Great Stone will not last too much longer."

"How do you mean? Did it sort of...strengthen it?"

"Yes, something like that. Any ordinary stone would soak up some of the Great Stone's energy if placed near it. Periwinkle had both for quite awhile. More than enough time for this task."

"What do we need to do?"

"Just hold my hand," Emerald said. When Phinnegan placed his hand in hers, she squeezed it reassuringly.

"Should I close my eyes?" he asked.

"You can if you like."

Phinnegan closed his eyes, just as a gentle breeze began to playfully tousle his hair. The breeze became cooler, prickling his flesh with hundreds of tiny bumps. He expected the characteristic tug at his middle that he had come to expect from travelling in this world. The breeze became cooler still, and when the first drop of rain dotted his cheek, he opened his eyes to check the sky for he could not remember seeing even one cloud.

But he opened his eyes not to a sky aglow with the morning sun, but instead to darkness. Not a total darkness like the belly of Féradoon, but a more familiar, comforting darkness, one dimly lit by a full moon whose light only just penetrated the rain clouds.

When his eyes adjusted to the reduced light, they quickly settled on that most longed for sight. His heart seemed to skip a beat and a sense of relief coursed through him.

"Home," he whispered.

"Yes," Emerald said, squeezing his hand. "Home."

Sitting alone in his room the following morning, the window shut fast against cold and relentless rain, Phinnegan sipped cautiously from the cup of black tea his mother had just brought him. The spicy scent of clove drifted from the cup to his nose. It was her way of showing that she was no longer angry, despite sending him to bed the previous night without supper.

After Emerald had said her goodbyes and disappeared in a faint distortion, but not before once again expressing her gratitude, Phinnegan had run all the way to the front door of his home. When he burst through the door, his mother had scolded him both for being gone the entire evening and missing supper, as well as tracking a bucket's worth of water in with him and onto the floor.

One afternoon. It all happened in one afternoon.

The thought was so unfathomable that he nearly wondered if he had imagined it all. When he had awakened earlier that morning, the Mark on his stomach had almost faded completely. So faint were its lines that he thought perhaps those, too, were something he had dreamed.

But what about the book?

Setting his tea on the bedside table, he rushed to the pile of dirty clothes he had tossed into a corner. Finding the pants he had worn the previous night, he searched the pockets until his fingers touched the supple leather of the book's binding.

Withdrawing the book, he stared at its cover for several moments, tracing the now familiar symbol emblazoned upon its cover.

"What secrets do you hold?" he whispered, turning the book over in his hands before opening its cover.

There, on the first page, the answer awaited him.

# About the Author

When not working at his day job, Thews divides his time between his family, books and the outdoors. He is a lover of stories, gardening, fine pipe tobaccos and making stuffed animals talk. A native of North Carolina, he lives in a small neighborhood nestled in the woods of Orange County with his wife, daughter and their four cats. Yes, that's right, FOUR.

Keep up with the latest news about Thews and sign-up to receive e-mails announcing new books by visiting www.samuelthews.com

42335280R00211

Made in the USA
Lexington, KY
17 June 2015